KILLSWITCH PROTOCOL

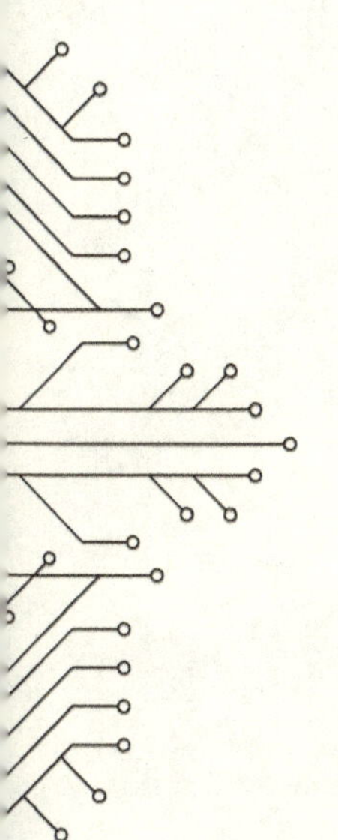

A NOVEL BY

M.J. KUHN

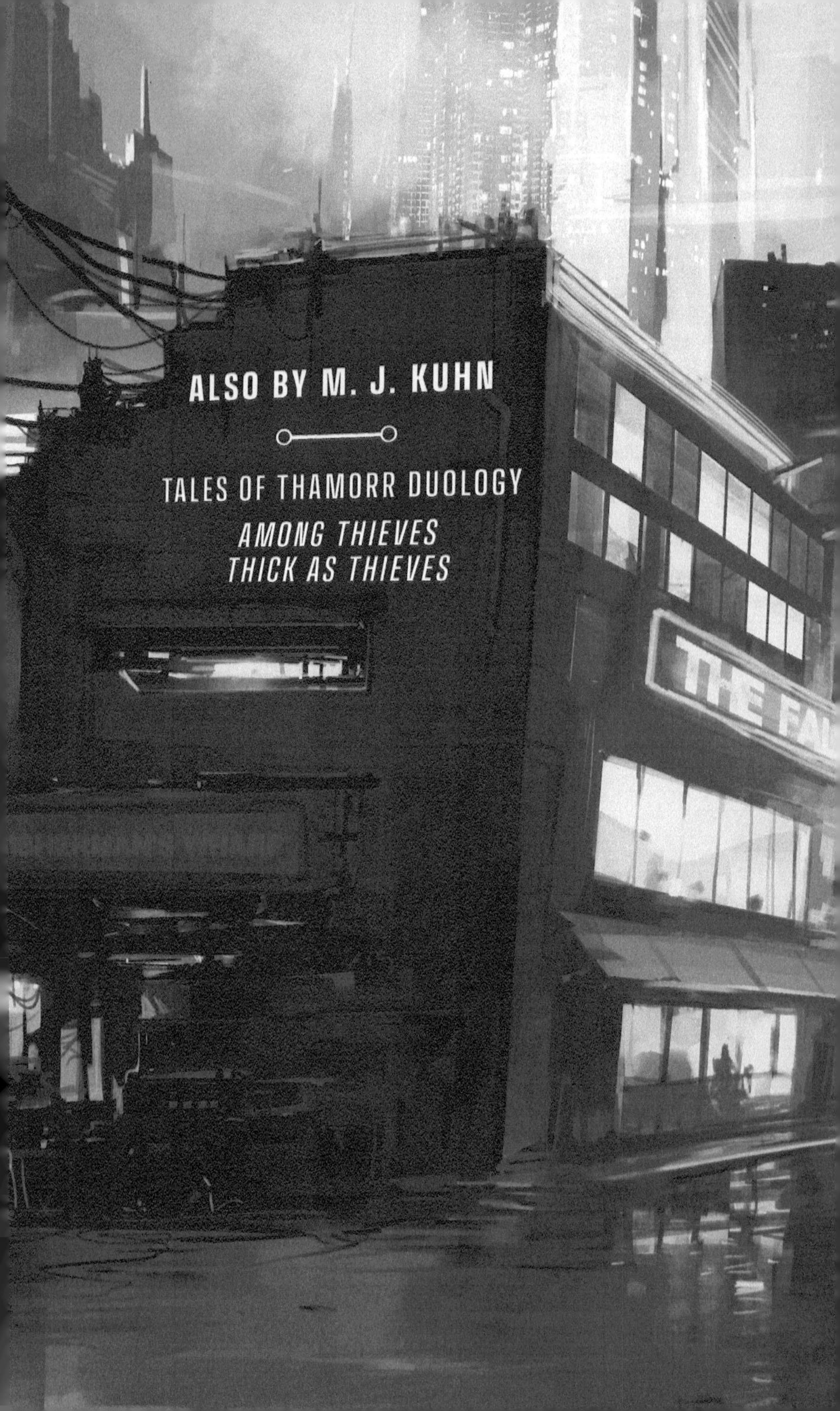

ALSO BY M. J. KUHN

TALES OF THAMORR DUOLOGY

AMONG THIEVES
THICK AS THIEVES

KILLSWITCH PROTOCOL

M.J. KUHN

KILLSWITCH PROTOCOL

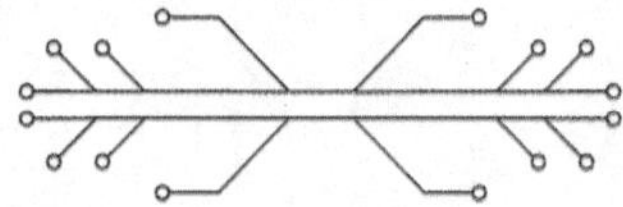

This book is a work of fiction. Any references to historical events, real people, businesses, or real places are used fictitiously. Other names, characters, places, and events are products of the author's imagination, and any resemblance to actual events or places or persons, living or dead, is entirely coincidental.

This book—its content, cover, and graphical elements—were written and created entirely using the real human brains of the author, cover artist, designer, and editor. Artificial intelligence was *not* used in any capacity.

All interior graphics created using licensed materials from elements.envato.com

First Edition: July 2026

Cover Art: Katerina Belikova
Cover Design: Adrian M. Gibson
Interior Design & Typesetting:
Adrian M. Gibson
Editor: Kat Howard

ISBN: 979-8-9936620-0-8 (Paperback)
ISBN: 979-8-9936620-1-5 (Hardcover)
ASIN: B0GRY15N2M (eBook)

Published by Cade & Camda Press

For Haley and Mike,
my eternal first-round beta readers.

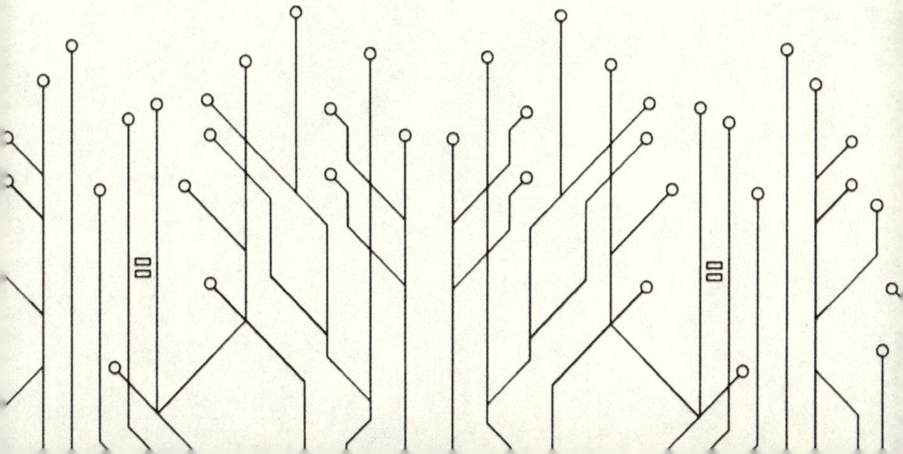

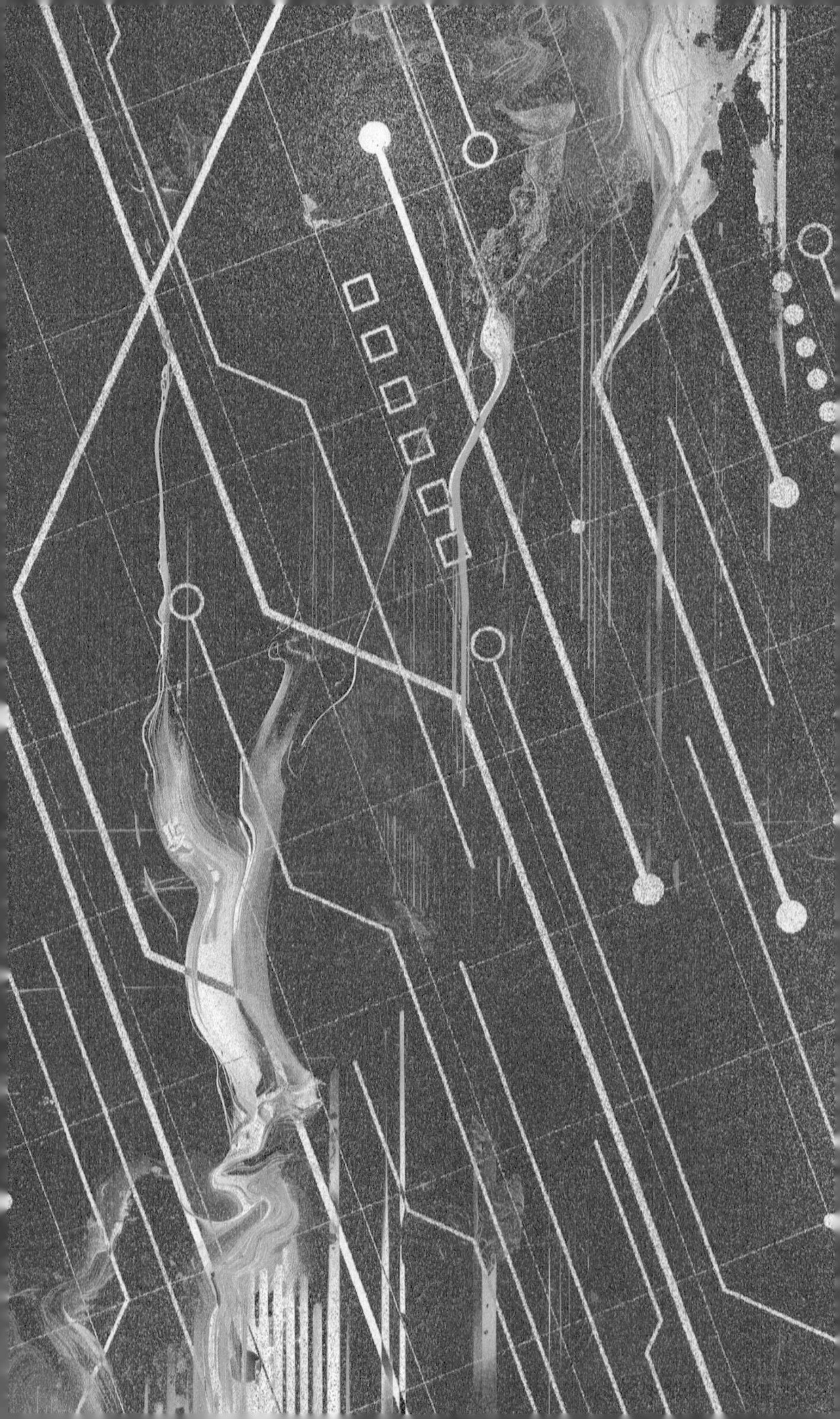

01

LIV

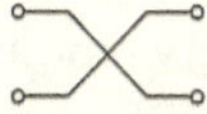

A citizen of New Avarita can pursue any number of aims, but all must remember to keep the ultimate goal on the horizon. Any goal that doesn't bring a citizen closer to becoming worthy of being selected for Ascent is a goal not worth chasing.

—THE HANDBOOK OF LUCRE, *CHAPTER 1*

LIV SPENCER WAS running late.

She rushed through the Berger Security office hallways as quickly as her impractical footwear would allow, anxiously checking her unicomm as she walked. The interface winked awake, projecting the time over the inside of her wrist.

17:26

The original plan had been to catch the 17:15 train, but obviously that was out of the question now.

"There you are, Spencer," said a voice behind her, accompanied by rushing footsteps. She turned to see her colleague, Grant, speed-walking down the hall, jacket draped over his forearm. "Not used to seeing you out of your chair before 18:00."

It was true, usually she was one of the last ones in the office, anchored to her chair, poring over security schematics in her windowless cubicle, trying to figure out how to cover the most space with the fewest cameras and sensors possible. Boring work to some, but to Liv every day was a new puzzle where, if she cracked it just right, there'd be a bonus waiting for her in her next paycheck.

"Yeah, today I'm heading to—" she started, but Grant had already started a new sentence, so she cut herself off.

"A few of us are heading to The Dandelion Room for a drink—you in?" He referenced a few messages on his unicomm. "Sarian, Trevor, and Byrnie are already there, they've got the corner table. We're going to try to guilt Byrnie into using company credits to pick up the tab. Celebrating the end of the Huldra job and all."

On any other night, Liv would have gladly accepted the invite. Their team had been stretched thin for weeks. Huldra Industries was one of the biggest—and richest—companies in all of New Avarita. It had been Berger's biggest job since the massive overhaul of the Principal Chairman's offices last year. And, somehow, it had felt even more stressful.

Three team members had breakdowns over routers. Byrnie just about shorted out his chip every time anyone mentioned the Huldra CEO, Reina Arthur, by name. The man had flitted over the rest of the team so much and so uselessly they had taken to calling him "The Mosquito" behind his back (a nickname that may or may not have been Liv's invention).

Liv had seen how many vodka sodas their boss could put away at a regular Happy Hour meetup, so she could only imagine how many he'd pound down tonight. Post-project celebrations like tonight might be singlehandedly keeping The Dandelion Room in business, honestly.

Grant was still babbling about their plans for the night as they crossed into the entry hall of the Berger Security building. Liv held up a hand, "I'm sorry, Grant, I'm not going to be able to make it tonight. I've got other plans."

Plans she was almost certainly going to be late for.

She ran a few mental calculations as she hoofed it across the lobby, Grant struggling to keep up.

Three hundred and sixty-four steps from her desk to Berger's front doors. Eighty-four steps from the door to the train platform. At her usual walking pace, that took three minutes. What time was it now?

Liv checked her unicomm again. 17:28. She picked up her pace. If she could catch the 17:30 train, she could still make it. If she missed that train, she'd have to wait for the 17:45 one, and at that point, she might as well just go straight home. For an event like this, showing up late was worse than not showing up at all. And going straight home would mean waiting all night for Liam to get home so she could share the news she'd gotten this morning.

The message was bookmarked in her unicomm interface, the little notification symbol flashing in the corner of her field of vision at all times. If she had to wait another six hours to share that news, she was pretty sure she might explode.

One might think that a person with Liv Spencer's ridiculous attention to detail would have an easier time keeping herself on schedule. Unfortunately, her mind was more likely to cling to details like how many ceiling tiles there were in her floor of Berger's offices—*two thousand and twenty-four*—than useful information like what time it was or where she was supposed to be.

"Do those 'plans' involve sitting on your ass plugged into your VR enhancements until Liam gets home, by any chance?" Grant asked. He stepped sideways to allow a runner mech to speed by, zipping past on slightly squeaking wheels.

"For once, they do not," Liv said. "You've heard me talk about Liam's coworker Charles before?" When Grant just stared at her blankly, she motioned to her face and clarified, "The one with the little beard that looks like he painted it on?"

"Ah, the Marionette Man, yes."

"He was selected for Ascent yesterday," Liv smiled over her shoulder at him, gesturing down at her outfit—tall heels and her nicest black dress. "The ceremony is tonight."

"Ascent?" Grant whistled. "How old?"

"Just turned sixty-two last week."

Not that Liv generally knew the ages of all her husband's colleagues, but she and Liam had a lengthy chat about Charles and his career, and the projects Liam was sure to inherit from his old workload, now that he'd ascended beyond those tasks.

"Damn, that's impressive." Grant leaned back, hands in his pockets. "Senior executive for Vinco's transcription division, too, right? Should be a kickass party."

Liv nodded, walking out the towering main doors of the security firm and onto the streets of Upper Lucara. "Charles has been a direct report to Eliza Vinco for over two decades." She pulled her jacket around her, warding off the early spring chill.

"All right, don't rub it in," Grant joked. "I see you've outgrown The Dandelion Room—you might be rubbing shoulders with the Principal Chairman himself tonight, eh?"

Liv snorted. The people she'd be making small talk with in the next hour were impressive, there was no doubt, but the Principal Chairman's list of public appearances outside of formal addresses were so rare she seriously doubted the Ascent ceremony of a journalist would make the list, regardless of the journalist's track record.

The 17:30 train arrived then, whizzing silently into the station, its side stamped with the massive blue-and-yellow Lobos Transport logo. The rest of the car was plastered with advertisements for the latest holovid in the blockbuster *Doctor Gamling* franchise. A trickle of relief ran through her veins like a morphine drip as it slid to a stop. She hadn't missed the train. She was going to make it on time. Thank Lucre.

The train doors hissed open, bisecting an image of the actor who played the titular Doctor Gamling in the vids as they did. Liv stepped onto the train, turning to shoot Grant a grin as the scanner processed her train fare through her chip. "See you tomorrow?"

"You better tell me *all* the details," Grant agreed. "These upper-level execs always have the best Ascent ceremonies. I'll be lucky if Mary has a potluck for me when I earn mine."

"Yeah, this is definitely *not* going to be a potluck." Liv would be eating like a holovid star or a Core executive tonight, she was sure.

Grant mimed stealing a piece of food off a tray and stowing it in his pocket, then winked. Liv just laughed and waved him off as the train doors hissed shut.

Liv checked the train schedules on her unicomm. No delays or slowdowns on the railways. The ride from the south station of Upper Lucara to the Central Core station would be forty-three minutes exactly. That would give her seventeen minutes to speed-walk three blocks to the Central Museum, find Liam, and get inside.

All in the least walkable pair of shoes she owned.

She stared absently at the screen on the opposite wall of the train car across from her and drummed her fingers on her kneecaps to the beat. It was the latest pop tune from Sparkle Noir, if Liv wasn't mistaken. It was the type of music her mother would have called *"bubblegum for the eardrums."* And the type of music Liv called *"annoying."*

On screen, a newscaster in a trendy, gold-trimmed suit jacket introduced a clip from the Principal Chairman's latest public address. Liv hadn't connected her in-ear enhancements to the train car's network, so she couldn't hear what the man was saying, but she remembered watching the address live last week. An inspirational address discussing the meaning of the word 'effort,' how it had come from an old-world term that meant 'strength.'

"It is through your efforts that you create strength in yourself.
It is through our joint efforts that we make New Avarita strong.
Without effort, without work, there is only weakness
and withering."

The screen jumped back to the well-dressed newscaster and Liv let her eyes slip from the screen down to the train car's window. The train streaked through the pin-neat streets of Upper Lucara and toward the shining bastion of life that was the Core. It was busier than Liv's usual train home to the northern station in Upper Lucara, with nearly every seat filled. The closeness and press of other bodies made her anxiety prickle, almost like an itch forming inside her skull. Plus, someone was wearing far too strong a perfume. The scent of rosewater and white lilies coated the insides of Liv's nostrils, making her nauseated. She checked her unicomm again. 17:36. She was stuck in this tube for the next thirty-six minutes and checking her unicomm over and over again wasn't going to make it go any faster.

And so, Liv tapped her temples, exhaling the stress from her lungs as the crowded train car faded away, replaced with the cool darkness of her VR enhancements. She navigated through a few menus, and within seconds a new world populated before her eyes: the vast desert plains of *Wasteland Warriors*.

The game was simple enough; a story of survival, encompassing both the beauty and the darkness in humanity at the tail end of the Last War right after the Fall. Players teamed up with other gamers across the sprawling digital realm of the rinth to build camps, societies, and gangs in the Dead Zone—the uninhabitable dust bowl to the west of New Avarita. Groups could then fight off the elements, wild animals, and invading clans of survivors.

As the CyberNexus Studios logo faded into the background of the game, Liv opened the in-game messaging app, fingers twitching as she tapped out a message.

<Liv_Struck99: Up for a quick campaign?>

The username was stupid, she knew. But she had created it when she was barely fifteen years old. She hadn't fully realized then that the gaming tag would follow her for the rest of her natural-born life.

Liv sent her avatar stalking across the settlement, gathering virtual tumbleweeds to pass the time as she waited for a response. Then,

<RinthRat12: When am I not?>

Liv grinned. She had no idea who RinthRat12 was, where in New Avarita they lived, what their life was like outside of the rinth, but the pair of them had been playing *Wasteland Warriors* together for over a year. They had carved out a decent corner of Old Texas for their base. RinthRat12 might not have a name Liv knew outside of their gaming tag or a face she knew outside of their avatar, but they had become one of her closest friends.

<RinthRat12: You finally finish that big project you've been pissing your pants over?>

Liv typed out her reply with one hand, using the other to guide her avatar through the bullet-crafting process.

<Liv_Struck99: You'd be pissing yourself too if you had a CEO like Reina-fucking-Arthur breathing down your neck for two months.>

<RinthRat12: How do you know I'm not Reina Arthur?>

<Liv_Struck99: Oh, fuck off.>

Liv chuckled. She might not know who RinthRat12 was, but she sure as hell knew they weren't the surly Hulda CEO she'd seen on all those vid calls.

Conversation shifted to gameplay after that as they plotted an ambush on the colony that had formed a few miles west of their own in-game settlement. RinthRat12's avatar, clad in a bright purple shirt and a ridiculous hat, slunk along the wall as Liv's character, sensibly dressed in attire that actually matched but had slightly worse stats, tiptoed along behind him.

The pair of them clung tight to the wall, edging forward while the frustrated players on top of the wall shot down toward them. The game's guns could only angle about seventy-five degrees downward, meaning if they sidled directly along the wall beneath the shooters, there was no way they could get hit. Sure enough, they made it to the door unscathed.

<RinthRat12: Gotta wake up earlier than that to snare the RinthRat!>

Liv shook her head in amusement, using one hand to control

her avatar, raiding cloth and water canteens from the enemy players' shelter while she typed out a reply with the other hand.

<Liv_Struck99: You need a new line.>

<RinthRat12: I'll workshop it.>

Liv felt a shift in the movement of the train in the outside world and her eyes flicked to the top right of her display. 18:12. The train must be pulling into the central Core station.

<Liv_Struck99: Nice raiding, gotta go.>

<RinthRat12: Not back to work, I hope…>

<Liv_Struck99: Nope! Going to a party in the Core. Ascent ceremony.>

She included a few images from the in-game emoji library. A party streamer. A tiny moving image of a famous holovid star dancing that had become a meme in recent years. A grinning face.

RinthRat12 was typing for a long moment. Then, finally,

<RinthRat12: Hmm. Enjoy.>

Liv wasn't quite sure what to make of that answer, but she didn't have much time to consider it—the train was already gliding to a silent stop. She tapped her temples to re-enter the real world and gathered her things. The instant the train's doors hissed open, she was up and waiting, tapping her left foot impatiently as she waited for the passengers ahead of her to exit. *One, two, three, four, five taps.* Then the line finally started to move forward.

She started running the second her heels hit the platform. Well-dressed people scoffed and drew back as she burst past them, but Liv's anxiety at the idea of being late was too high to care all that much about looking like a lunatic on the streets of the Core.

The Core's energy was radically different from Upper Lucara's. Upper Lucara ran like a metronome—smooth, steady, and reliable, filled with the same people doing the same things in the same order, day after day. The Core was the section of New Avarita where the rich and powerful worked and the *obscenely* rich and powerful lived. Every person was dressed head-to-toe in the latest fashions. Street carts sold foods that wouldn't be out of place in a five-star restaurant in any of the other districts of the city-state. Liv's stomach growled as she surged past a tidy cart serving sushi handrolls.

In Upper Lucara, every office building looked like all the other office buildings around it. Every townhome in her neighborhood had the same layout. Even the playgrounds were boxy, gray things built to blend in with the surrounding buildings. It was a place built for efficiency, churning out consistent products—and people—day after day.

The Core was a tangle of silvery, towering buildings in all kinds of shapes and sizes. StarBuilt, one of the most famous architecture firms in the city-state, specialized in tall, needle-like structures, where the competing firm, Palladium, was known for interesting window patterns, making their buildings look like honeycombs, stretching up toward the electric dome that crackled high above, shielding New Avarita from the nuclear wasteland that stretched for thousands of miles in every direction.

In short, if Upper Lucara was a metronome, the Core was a Rube Goldberg machine. Every person, transport train, and activity seemed to be doing its own thing, but ultimately, they all fit together to keep New Avarita's heart humming. As much as she knew Liam loved the Core, she hoped he'd never want to move them here. She didn't mind it for a visit, but she couldn't imagine living somewhere this chaotic, especially considering the notice she'd gotten this morning.

Her eyes flicked to the little notification symbol hovering in the air in front of her. Distracted, Liv jumped halfway out of her skin as a holographic advertisement stepped out onto the sidewalk in front of her.

"DO YOU LOVE YOUR CAT, BUT HATE THE SMELL OF THE CAT BOX? TRY AUTOSCOOP PLUS!"

Liv snorted as she regained her footing. A cat? Only in the Core would there be enough people who could afford a pet permit for an advertisement like this to be worth the pixels it was made of. She waved the hologram away, quickly adjusting the ad blockers on her unicomm to prevent any more jump scares.

She stripped off her jacket, fanning herself as she started to sweat as she rounded the final corner. Liam was there. The second she saw him, her stress melted like an ice cube dropped in hot coffee. They'd been married for six years now, but every time she saw him, he still took her breath away just a little bit. He was everything she could have dreamed of in a partner: charming, handsome, driven. All the Lucre-blessed traits and then some. It was a combination that had already carried him to a senior position in the news division of Vinco Telecom at just thirty-two years of age. He already had an office in the corporate headquarters—just a few floors below Eliza Vinco herself.

Liv existed in a constant state of mild amazement about her husband. That was doubly true tonight as he stood, leaning casually against one of the dagger-like pillars outside the museum, bathed in the glow of the setting sun, casually adjusting his sleeves as she sprinted up, out of breath and shining with sweat.

He held up his wrist as she approached. His unicomm glowed under his sleeve, projecting the time onto his forearm.

18:58

"Cutting it a little close, aren't you, love?" he asked.

His brows were set in a stern expression, but his hazel eyes twinkled playfully. He knew her tendency to get absorbed in her work to the point that it could take the equivalent of an air raid siren from the days before the Fall to pull her out of her trance. Liv limped the last few steps, tottering on her sore feet and too-high heels before half-falling into her husband's arms.

"I have no idea what you mean, I've got plenty of time to spare," she said, her voice muffled by the fabric of his suit. She grabbed his lapels, pulling herself back and steadying herself. "Is this new?" She rubbed the fabric between her fingers. "It feels almost like real cotton."

Real cotton was beyond expensive. It wasn't something that any of the grow domes inside New Avarita had space for. Companies had to trade for it with a place called the Federation of South Brasilia. Every stitch of cotton clothing was taxed to hell and back.

"Yeah, I just picked it up on my lunch break today." Liam

scrubbed the back of his neck with one hand, then gave a sheepish smile. "What do you think?"

Liv stepped back, giving him an exaggerated look up and down. "I think you look like a damn knockout." She cocked her head to one side. "What happened to your old suit though? You spill something on it?"

"I ah, I just wasn't sure it was... nice enough for a celebration like this," he said, clearing his throat awkwardly.

Liv raised an eyebrow. "Ah, so Reid said something about it, then?"

Reid Allen was Liam's boss, and he was a Grade A prick. Not that they could say anything of the sort here tonight. In the privacy of their townhome, however...

Liam gave his usual lopsided grin—the one that had first caught Liv's eye across the university courtyard all those years ago. "Maybe." The display on his wrist ticked to read 18:59. "All right, let's get inside."

"Wait!" Liv said, fiddling with her unicomm. She pulled up that beautiful, perfect notification that had been winking in the corner of her vision since 09:43 this morning when she first received it, then adjusted the settings to project it to Liam's interface.

He blinked as the message transferred, then stood still for a second, eyes darting back and forth, reading. Then, he let out a loud *WHOOP!* and grabbed her around the waist, picking her up and spinning her in a circle, not caring about the stares he was drawing from the other well-dressed people streaming into the museum beside them.

After another full rotation, he set Liv back down and pulled back, holding her at arm's length. His eyes twinkled, his grin so wide it looked liable to split his face in two. "We're going to have a *baby*, Liv."

"Not yet, not yet," Liv said, laughing. "I still have to schedule an appointment to get my blockers shut off. And there's still some paperwork and details and—"

"And then copious amounts of sex, oh no, how will we ever cope?"

"We'll manage, somehow, I think."

They had submitted their childbearing application over a year ago. They had been denied the first time, though Liv didn't know why—no one did. The Algorithm and the Algorithm alone made those decisions. And now, finally, it had decided that Liv and Liam were cleared for procreation. After all these years of waiting, it was finally their time.

"Should we go inside, now?" Liv asked, smoothing out her dress and catching her breath.

Liam nodded, still glowing from the inside out, and took her arm, escorting her off the bustling sidewalk and into the most lavish room she had ever been inside. Top-of-the-line security mechs scanned them as they entered, verifying their chips and linking them to their invites before parting to let them inside.

The main hall of the Central Core Museum was one of the largest rooms Liv Spencer had ever been in. The only other one that came to mind was the sports arena at North Genstra U, but she wasn't sure even that had been quite this cavernous. Not that she was surprised by the size—she'd done hours of research on the museum the previous night.

It held the largest collection of non-rinth-generated paintings in New Avarita, including a few pieces from the Russo-Europa Empire—*second floor hallway above the entry hall*—and even one painting from before the Fall: a work from a man called Jackson Pollock that was over three hundred years old and preserved in a temperature- and moisture-controlled electric frame—*fourth floor, third room from the right.*

She'd done her homework. If any of Liam's colleagues engaged her in conversation, she would be ready with more than a smile and a nod. She might not really belong in the Core the way he seemed to, but she could fake it with the best of them.

The museum was decked out for the celebration. Every inch of the place was dripping with flowers, both natural and synthetic, from the mix of scents. There were also motifs of growth and expansion everywhere, twisted into the floral arrangements and worked into the rest of the décor. The far wall displayed a looping hologram of a series of stylized creatures breaking free of too-small skin, shedding it and stretching their limbs in imagined sunlight.

The floor between Liv and the projection was crawling with

people dressed in clothes so fine it made Liv want to slink off into the bathrooms—*first floor, behind the information desk*—and not emerge until the celebration was over. Even the few children dotting the place, looking bored and miserable as they fidgeted at their parents' sides, were dressed in pricier clothes than Liv's dress.

A glowing glass stage hung suspended from the ceiling, bearing four musicians picking at the holographic strings of their LuminaCellos, sending an uplifting and ethereal soundscape sweeping through the hall. Liv recognized a refrain of "Ode to Lucre" as it began.

A plaque hung by the door, listing Reina Arthur as the founding contributor of the museum. She snorted to herself, snapping a quick pic with her eye enhancements and messaging it to Grant and the rest of the team with the message,

<I can't even escape her on my night off!>

Within a few seconds, she had a message back from Byrnie. The manager had simply added a string of emoticons: mostly skulls and tiny depictions of characters fainting. She huffed a small laugh before closing out of her unicomm interface. Liv wondered dimly how much coin the Huldra Industries exec would have had to shell out to fund a building this massive in the Central Core. Although maybe it had been more of a trade deal. Three of Arthur's own paintings graced the halls of the museum, after all, the most famous of which being *Essence of Life*, a painting of an organic cell with the towers and streets of New Avarita's Core in place of the nucleus.

Assistance mechs flitted through the crowd, carrying trays of appetizers and drinks. Liv spotted bites of steak crostini on one tray, and something that looked like brie with dots of jam on the next. Real meat and cheese were rare in New Avarita. Even with the money Liam brought in since his promotion last year, the two of them only treated themselves to real, hab-grown pork or chicken instead of the cheaper synthetics on special occasions.

She wished she was bold enough to reach out and snag a taste of every dish as it passed. Instead, she just stood uncomfortably to the side, smiling gently as Liam fell into a conversation with a group of other Vinco executives who each probably earned ten times the coin Liv did in a year.

Reid Allen was there, his pinched face locked in its usual expression of false friendliness. Liv didn't recognize the rest of the group, but she listened carefully for their names to drop in conversation. She never forgot a name once she heard it—a rather fortunate side effect of her tendency to hyperfixate on details.

"What was Charles's most recent project, again?" Reid asked the group.

"Why, are you looking for tips you can follow to ensure you're chosen for Ascent next?" asked a woman with a severe face and a vivid red jumpsuit.

Reid gave her a simpering smile. "Let's not be foolish, Karoline. I'm a bit young for that yet, I think."

And, for the high-achieving people of New Avarita, he was right. Liv had heard rumors that some people in places like Lower Baranthrum would be selected for Ascent during their younger years—it was easier to achieve your life's purpose when expectations were low, perhaps—but the earliest Ascent ceremony she'd ever attended had been for her own mother, who had reached it at the age of 54 after nearly three decades as a holovid actress. A slimy worm like Reid would be lucky if Lucre's Algorithm saw a spark of value in him before he was seventy.

Liam grabbed a pair of wine flutes from the nearest assistance mech as it rumbled by, passing one to Liv and holding onto the second himself. It took almost all of Liv's self-control not to just down the entire flute in a single gulp to calm her nerves. Instead, she kept herself to a small sip, savoring the way the dry bubbles fizzed on her tongue. The flavor was fresher and crisper than the wine she picked up when grocery shopping back in Upper Lucara. It must be made from real grapes—the ones in the grow-domes down in Lower Baranthrum, by the coast.

She took another sip. If Liam kept climbing like he was, someday soon they could have an entire fridge stocked with fine food and drink.

She could deal with that. Just as long as he didn't turn into an insufferable ass like Reid in the process.

Karoline tapped her left temple, querying the automated rinth chat and reading its answer out verbatim.

"Charles Branston, famed news transcriber for Vinco Telecom, was selected for Ascent on April third of 2347 after completing his masterwork; a full transcription of the histories of Principal Chairman Geast."

"Well, that would do it," Liam said, acting as though he hadn't recited that exact rinth-generated snippet to Liv over dinner the night before.

Liv let her eyes roam over the crowd as Reid piped up with something else inane to add to the conversation. After a few seconds, she caught sight of a familiar face among the well-dressed masses. She ran a hand along Liam's shoulders to signal to him that she was leaving, uttered a soft "excuse me" to the rest of the group, then made her way across the room.

"Ayla!"

The other woman turned to face Liv, her face breaking into a smile as she caught sight of her. "Liv, I knew you had to be somewhere in this mess!"

Liv pulled her into a one-armed hug, then leaned back, holding her at arm's length. "Holy shit, you've gotten huge! No offense."

Ayla snorted. "Thanks, you jerk."

"'*Jerk*'?" Liv mocked, taking a sip of her drink with a raised brow. "That's the best insult you have for me?"

Ayla pointed down at her pregnant belly, swelling under the shimmering fabric of her dress. "Trying to get my language under control before this little monster gets here."

"Yeah, okay, good luck with that."

Liv had met Ayla Voland back in their primary school years. They had remained friends throughout those early years and had shared an apartment during university. Five years ago, Ayla married her husband Kiran and the pair moved into the townhome next door to Liv and Liam. In all that time, Liv wasn't sure she'd ever heard the woman go longer than twenty minutes without cussing.

Even though they lived next door to one another, work had been so busy that Liv hadn't seen Ayla in almost two months—since Kiran's Ascent ceremony. In that time, Ayla had gone from vaguely pregnant to looking like she might just give birth right here on the museum floor.

"So, how are you feeling?"

Liv ran a hand over her own stomach, imagining what it would feel like to have life growing in there. To feel the press of tiny hands and feet and knees. The thought had always been exciting, but now that her permit had been approved, now that all she needed to do was schedule an appointment to her hormone blocker temporarily removed, there was a tinge of fear to the thought, too. Within a year's time she could be just as pregnant as Ayla was now.

Were they really ready?

A silly question. Lucre's Algorithm knew more about them than they knew about themselves. If their permit was approved, they were ready.

"I'm feeling alright," Ayla said. "Bladder is always fu-freaking full, though." The other woman gave a wan smile, acknowledging her near slip-up.

"Well, you do have a small human dancing on it all the time," Liv said, taking another sip of her wine. She debated telling Ayla about her and Liam's permit approval, but held her tongue at the last second. The news was still too new—it felt too precious to share. Instead, she asked, "Where are you going for Care?"

After a birth, new parents could either enter their child into full-time Care in a local facility or apply for a full-time parenting permit. The FTP permit was something of a death-sentence to a person's career, but for some parents it was worth it to stay home with their little one. Liv still hadn't decided what she wanted to do when her time came, but Ayla was a surgeon for the head Medla House facility in the Core. If anyone was going to opt for Care without another thought, it was Ayla.

"Not sure yet," Ayla said, running a hand absently over her stomach again. "I need to get that sorted out soon though. It's just been so busy at the facility lately. Lots of double shifts."

Liv peered closer at her friend's face. There were dark circles under the woman's eyes, almost like she'd darkened them with deep purple eyeshadow. Ayla had always had a slightly frazzled, drawn look about her, but it was stronger than ever. Altogether not surprising, she guessed. She had read that pregnancy could drain the energy from the mother. It was hard work on the body, after all, growing a whole human.

Ayla had always been a lot fitter than Liv. If it was hitting her this hard, Liv hated to think what the process was going to do to her.

"Lots of mech-enhancements?" Liv asked, swallowing her worries.

"Lots of chip installs," Ayla corrected. She rubbed the back of her neck subconsciously: the place where her own chip lay, nestled against her spine, wired into her central nervous system.

Liv didn't fully understand the science, but she knew enough. New Avaritan life was centered around these tiny pieces of metal and circuitry. Without the chips, there would be no unicomms, no mech-enhancements, nothing. They'd have to operate like the people of the Old World, carrying keys to unlock things and fragile plastic cards to access their coin. With every chip install Ayla performed, she was basically welcoming that infant into New Avaritan society: giving them the tools they needed to survive and thrive in this world.

"Hey, you think they'll let you install the chip on this little one yourself?" Liv asked, gesturing down to Ayla's belly.

There was an overlong silence, then Ayla let out a huff of laughter. It sounded oddly forced. "Maybe," she said. Then, she gestured toward the presentation room where some of the guests were already starting to gather. "We should probably find a seat, shouldn't we?"

"Oh, right!" Liv glanced at her wrist. Her unicomm now displayed 19:28. Two minutes until the speeches began, then the ceremony itself at 20:00 sharp.

After that, the celebration would really get underway. Wine and liquor would flow freely, people would sing Charles's praises and toast until well after midnight. Even now, twenty-five years later, Liv remembered the party to celebrate her mother's Ascent. They had reviewed all her best hits, her awards, her accolades. They'd danced to all her favorite songs, eaten her favorite food—*strawberries dipped in synthetic yogurt*—by the bucketful. Liv had been barely six years old, and she'd sung that night until her little voice gave out. It was a beautiful memory of a beautiful day—memories just as sweet as the ones Charles's own kids would be making tonight, she was sure.

She perched herself on the edge of a chair, sandwiched between Ayla and Liam, as the remarks began. Everyone from Reid to Mrs. Branston to Eliza Vinco herself said a few words about how deserving Charles Branston was of Ascent and how everyone in New Avarita should strive to reach his level of dedication and achievement. Liam took the microphone for only a few moments, stuttering through some comments with uncharacteristic unsteadiness. Somehow, the nervousness only made him more charming. At least, Liv thought so.

When the remarks were complete, a pair of men in the dark blue suits of the Principal Chairman's office took the stage. Between them, they wheeled a long, ornate metal box. The gathered guests all rose to stand, craning their necks to see as the men unlatched the lid.

There, inside, lay the guest of honor himself. Charles Branston. His too-neat beard was even neater than normal, his suit pressed, his hands folded gently over his chest. His eyes were closed, his form motionless.

A hologram sparked to life just beside the box: the figure of Principal Chairman Waldgrim. A few people in the crowd touched the space behind their left ear, then their heart, in the customary salute, even though this was clearly a pre-recorded hologram of New Avarita's leader.

"It is the rightful goal of every worthy citizen in this great city-state to live, strive, and grow. The creatures of the old world sometimes shed the skin that held them back from growing and achieving. The people of New Avarita are no different. Ascent is the ultimate promotion, and today, we celebrate the achievements of this citizen."

The hologram bowed its head, then flickered out of existence.

Charles's wife took his place on the stage beside her husband a moment later, eyes shining with adoration and verve as she spoke the traditional final rite of the ceremony:

"And so, now, we send my Charles to the next tier, where his accomplishments and riches await him a hundredfold."

Liv raised her voice to sing with the rest of the crowd as the men in blue suits wheeled Charles Branston's body toward the piping in the center of the stage. When the box had been moved behind the plexiglass surface, the gathered group sang louder still, the song almost becoming a chant or a battle cry. The body that had once housed the mind of Charles Branston was then engulfed in flames. The crowd continued singing as they watched the ashes spiral up the piping and out into the sky, as Charles shed his mortal flesh and moved onto the next plane of existence.

She turned to share a smile with Ayla only to find the other woman's eyes shining with tears. Tears of joy, surely. Because everyone in New Avarita knew, Ascent was the most beautiful thing a person could witness.

02

SIGNE

Of all the nations and city-states of the world, only New Avarita is pure, and that purity is what allows us to achieve Ascent. To protect our home from the spread of the diseases and failings of the outside world, all trade with foreign nations and states will be strictly governed by the Principal Chairman and his advisory board.

—THE HANDBOOK OF LUCRE, ***CHAPTER 13***

WHAT A FUCKING dump.”

“What were you expecting, the Medial Complex?”

Signe Remy snorted. As though anyone in their right mind would let Emerson within spitting distance of the Principal Chairman’s seat of supposed power.

She wrinkled her nose against the smells of the docks. Toxic waste, rotten fish, and Lucre only knew what else mixed together into a vile cocktail she wouldn't have drunk even in the depths of her drinking days. There wasn't a soul in sight as she peered down the next alleyway. She twisted her wrist, waiting until her unicomm blinked green through the skin of her forearm. No cameras either. *Clear to proceed.*

"Not exactly," she muttered, picking up the conversation as she skirted a pile of what looked like human shit. "But I was expecting it to be better than the fishing docks up by Switch'r's Alley, at least. You'd think they would at least *try* to maintain this place. It's their stuff coming through here."

She didn't bother elaborating who 'they' were.

"Ah, but that's just it, my gun-toting friend," Emerson said, his voice piping in through her ear implants. He wasn't there on the docks with her but tucked away at his cozy terminal back at the Penthouse. Lucky for him—if he was that much of a know-it-all to her face, she might just be inclined to introduce him to the backside of her mech-hand. "Their *stuff* comes through those docks, but none of their *people* actually do. You're in Mech Country now."

"Mech Country, eh?" Signe asked. "Sounds like your kind of people."

Emerson's obsession with his terminal was infamous back at the Penthouse. The crew liked to joke that it was his girlfriend; his one and only true love. At least she hoped they were joking. In Signe's nine years with Torrin Calix's crew, she wasn't sure she'd ever seen the kid without the glow of that terminal bathing his gaunt, too-pale face.

"Sounds more like *your* kind of people," he shot back.

Signe looked down at her left arm, clenching and unclenching the mechanical fingers extending from the titanium wrist. The HULDRA INDUSTRIES logo was faded and scratched after all these years, but still visible, stamped into the bolt holding her elbow joint together.

The symbol matched the logo stenciled onto several of the massive shipping crates making a maze of Lower Baranthrum's main docks. Huldra wasn't the only brand represented here. There were also crates from Lobos Transport, Propagn Advanced Systems, and the rest. The ghosts of all nine shadowy conglomerates who owned

New Avarita. The docks were New Avarita's only link to the outside world: the world beyond the sea. No self-respecting CEO would want to miss out on the profits they could make from the expensive shit that filtered through this port every day.

"This your way of telling me you have a crush on me, Em?" Signe asked, running her mech-hand over a blood-red graffiti tag as she rounded another container. "Hate to break it to you, but you're not really my type."

The light on Signe's unicomm flashed to red and an alarm beeped a quick warning through her ear enhancements. She ducked into an empty shipping container, pulling her rifle, Sally—short for 'Salvation'—around on its strap. She held the weapon at the ready against her chest as a mechanical clanking sound registered, then grew steadily louder. After a few seconds, a maintenance mech clomped by, its metal feet crashing against the metal docks, sounding like the world's loudest and rustiest cymbal.

"I know," Emerson said. "Too brainy for you."

Signe snorted, checking that her path was clear before moving forward again. "No, I just tend to like partners who don't look like starved, basement-dwelling children."

"Explain Natalie, then," Emerson said, naming a partner Signe hadn't seen in years.

The kid was right, though. Now that she thought on it, Natalie *had* looked a little basement-dwellerish.

"Fuck off."

Emerson had never had much of a filter on that mouth of his. If literally every member of Torrin's crew didn't owe him their lives, comments like that made to the wrong person at the wrong time would have gotten him strangled to prem-death a long time ago.

Signe cut the chatter, focusing on slipping between shadows, scanning for cameras and sensors, and listening for the clang of mechanized footsteps. The guidance beacon Emerson had programmed into her unicomm grew brighter with every step, but even without that guidance, Signe would have known she was getting close to her target. Each step brought more sensors, more bots, and trickier maneuvering and sidestepping to avoid it all.

By the time the sound of sloshing waves drowned out the distant pulsing of bass from Lower Baranthrum's nightclubs, she hit a point where she couldn't move forward at all.

"Little help, Em?"

"What, you don't just want to shoot your way in?"

Signe rolled her eyes. The twerp had saved her ass when she'd tried to do just that in her first month with Torrin's crew. "You're never going to let that go, are you?"

"Someone's gotta keep you humble, Sig. Otherwise, that head of yours will get too big to fit in the Penthouse elevator."

"Why don't you humble me *after* you clear my path to that building?"

"Already done."

Signe could hear the smirk in Emerson's voice even through the buzzing interference in her outdated enhancements.

"Care to explain how I need to—ow." Signe cut herself off as a jab of pain shot through each of her eyeballs.

A map of the docks stretched across her entire field of vision, superimposed over the real world. The filthy ground beneath her boots began to glow with light only she could see, indicating the path forward through the tangle of shipping containers, cameras, and sensors.

Impressive.

"A little warning would have been nice," she quipped, carefully disguising any appreciation she had for the hacker's skill with a heaping tablespoon of sarcasm.

"A warning would have ruined the reveal."

"It's a job, not a magic trick."

She could picture Emerson lounging back in his chair, one loafered foot resting on his opposite knee as he shrugged and said, "Why can't it be a little bit of both?"

Keeping her ears pricked for mechs and alarms, Signe followed

Emerson's glowing map forward. In her decade of service in Reina Arthur's private security force, she had seen her share of imported goods. Fruits and vegetables that didn't grow well in New Avarita's grow-domes, real meat that hadn't been cooked up in a Koegen Corp lab, resources, machine parts, and more. But this was the first time she had seen the place it all came from.

It was half-past two in the morning and the docks were quiet except for the slight sizzling sound of the nearly-invisible electronic barrier stretching from the sky and down toward the water like a massive bubble. The dome covered all of New Avarita—for their "protection," of course. Convenient for the powers-that-be that the barrier was also basically a giant prison cell. No one with a chip could pass through the barrier without getting fried to a crisp.

Three massive, automated freighters bobbed silently in the dark water, silhouetted against the purplish-black sky. Unfamiliar flags hung from poles on their sterns, flapping pathetically in the chilly spring breeze, like tethered birds eager to escape their captivity. They featured colored bars and symbols that were undecipherable in the darkness. The foreign flags were more than just scraps of fabric, they were tangible evidence that the city-state of New Avarita wasn't alone in this world.

Not that the Board didn't do their damnedest to make the people forget.

Signe was so distracted by the ships, wondering if the world was as fucked up where they came from as it was here, that she almost made the rookiest of mistakes. Almost stood there, staring off into the middle-distance, letting herself be caught unawares.

Almost.

Her intuition spiked at the exact right moment. Someone was coming. And not a mech, this time: a human.

She ducked behind the nearest cover—a large, rusted gear used to haul freighters close enough to the dock to unload—and dropped to one knee, crouching, listening, waiting.

There.

A pair of shadows emerged from the direction of Shipyard Control. They moved in near-perfect unison, their all-black outfits and matching matte-black helmets making them nearly invisible in the night.

"Find cover," Emerson's voice chirped in her ear. "Two tubheads incoming. Just showed up on the cameras to the southeast."

"No shit," she whispered back.

The guards were close enough now that their standard-issue night vision enhancements would have been able to spot her if she wasn't already hidden. Emerson's tech skills had saved her skin more times than she could count, it was true. Still, some situations called for a soldier's instincts.

She peered between the spokes of the gear at the officers. Anyone in New Avarita was allowed to get a mech-enhancement in place of an arm or a leg, but Correxion officers were required to. They were also the only people in New Avarita who were legally permitted to have weaponized mech-enhancements. Plenty of people had armguns anyways, but they were bootleg, which meant they were out of date at best and defective at worst. Whatever weaponry and sensors these assholes were packing would be the real deal.

Everyone knew Correxion Group was the corporation in charge of all law enforcement in New Avarita. What most people *didn't* know was that Correxion Group was actually just one arm of a larger corporation, Grimme-Folson United, which also owned GenstraCo, New Avarita's education conglomerate.

A strange combination? Perhaps, on the surface. But upon second glance, it was all too easy to see what the fuckers at Grimme-Folson—and the rest of the Board—were up to. GenstraCo indoctrinated the masses in whatever bullshit best served the status quo. Then Correxion Group came in to sweep up the remnants of anyone who dared step out of line. Even better, Correxion Group could then loan those offenders out to factories run by other massive corporations for free labor.

And on and on the tangled-up web of New Avaritan politics and greed was spun.

Hundreds—maybe thousands—of companies with their own logos and corporate structures and marketing departments and all of it an illusion. Every credit that went into StarBuilt or Palladium actually ended up padding the ledgers for Cora Calvin and Teras Systems, who, through a series of shells and ghost corporations, owned both. People could choose to buy Glaze eye enhancements instead of the more common BetaCaro model Signe herself had, but it didn't matter because both companies ultimately filtered up to Huldra Industries in the end.

Thousands of companies that, in the end, resulted in nine corporations. Nine CEOs, nine titans of industry, nine greedy motherfuckers. The Board. According to the vids and the newsfeeds, Principal Chairman Waldgrim was the leader of New Avarita. The truth was, even the Principal Chairman bowed to the power of the Board.

And if that Board found out what Signe and the rest of Torrin's crew were up to, they'd have much worse things than a cell waiting for them.

If it weren't for the work of Emerson Quinn, Signe would have found herself switch'd the day she left Reina's security team. And if anyone on the Board got wise to the fact that she was still alive, it would be all over for her. A quick vote and a few taps on a keyboard, and before she knew it, she'd be "selected for Ascent." Her chip would zap the life from her, and she'd slump to the ground, limp and useless as a spilled bowl of noodles.

A fact Torrin wielded like a nuclear detonation code whenever someone got sick of his violent moods and threatened to leave his crew. It was awfully hard to abandon a group holding the pin on the grenade strapped to your chest.

Signe held her breath, watching the officers approach. She held Sally cradled across her chest, one hand on the fore-end, the other flicking between trigger settings. *LETHAL… NONLETHAL… LETHAL…* Then, the officers clomped right past her hiding spot, blind as fucking bats, and disappeared into the maze of shipping crates further up the docks. Signe snapped her gun's safety back into place an instant before Emerson's voice sounded in her ear again.

"All clear."

"Is it *actually* all clear, or am I about to walk into a damn hornet's nest again?" Signe griped.

"Forgive me for thinking a seasoned soldier like you could manage yourself against a pair of tubheads," Emerson said slyly.

The kid was trying to play on her ego. It wasn't going to work.

Even now, past her prime, Signe was more than capable of laying out half a dozen Correxion officers before they could even prime their armguns, but that wasn't the point. Torrin might not even blink at the idea of taking out small-time guards and officers, but that was never Signe's goal. After all, low-level dock guards weren't the problem here. Her eyes were locked on a bigger prize. A much bigger prize.

Taking down the Board itself.

A mission that, on its face, was as impossible as trying to lasso the moon. And if it came to a fight, Torrin's crew would be more outmatched than an ant against a boot. But that didn't mean it was hopeless. It just meant they had to be subtle, patient. They needed to chip away at the Board's power like a group of termites chipped away at the foundations of an old, wooden house.

Which was exactly why Signe was here on these docks. To take one more termite-sized bite out of the load-bearing beams of the Board's metaphorical house.

Or something like that.

Signe followed Emerson's path, sticking to the glowing lines beaming into her eye enhancements. She kept one finger on Sally's trigger as she stole across the last stretch of the shipyard, keeping her knees loose and her steps light. And there it was: her quarry. A lone building standing on the edge of the dock, its first-floor windows getting slapped by the choppy waves. The dock's control building.

While other structures this far south had been crushed by waves and battered by winds during the last hundred years of brutal hurricanes, the control center still stood proud. It was made of cinderblock and iron, its doors too heavy to be battered in and unlocked only by biometrics—measures too complex and, in some cases, too old-school for even Emerson to hack.

But the control center's greatest strength—the thing that had kept it standing all these years—was about to become its greatest weakness. The drainage system.

Every time a hurricane blasted through Lower Baranthrum, the building would flood. Then, the drainage system would allow the water to flow back out to sea when the storm waters receded. That drainage system was a series of pipes that led to a final grate; all large enough to accommodate a massive volume of flood water.

Torrin had bribed the building's schematics off of some StarBuilt architect in return for a few bootleg enhancements, so Signe knew exactly where to find that grate.

It was smaller than she'd expected. She grunted, then knelt down, using her mech arm to pull the grate free. It came loose with a wrenching squeal that was mercifully drowned out by the slosh of waves slapping against the docks and the sleeping freighters all around her. She wrinkled her nose in displeasure at the slime that coated her arms as she pulled herself into the mouth of the pipe. Never a dull moment in this damn life. Or a clean one.

"Blech," she said choking on the smell of it. It was like the ocean had eaten and then vomited up spoiled mushrooms.

"Can I interest you in hurrying it up a bit?" Emerson said.

"I'm sorry, Em. Why don't we trade next time?" Signe sniped, wriggling forward another few feet. "I'll sit in the nice comfy chair back at the Penthouse and you can crawl through a moldy pipe dodging gunfire. Sound good?"

"You're awfully dramatic sometimes, did you know that?" Emerson chuckled. "I'm just trying to get your ass out of there before those guards finish their rounds and come back to finish their coffees."

Signe winced as Emerson hacked her eye enhancements again, projecting a ghostly image over her vision. It was a scene from one of the cameras inside the control center. A small table stood beside the terminal with two half-drunk coffees on it. She could see the steam rising from the cups in slow-motion through the shitty camera footage.

Fuck. Coffee wasn't cheap in New Avarita—especially not for someone on a tubhead's salary. No bottom-tier Correxion officer would abandon a cup long enough to let it go cold. Wherever those guards had gone, they would be back within a few minutes.

Signe gritted her teeth, crawling forward on her elbows with twice the vigor. When light started to filter into the pipe from the grate above her, she knew she was close. Emerson gave her the all-clear, but still, she checked her unicomm, scanning the room for sensors, cameras, mechs, anything that might give her away and sound an alarm.

Three dots winked into life, hovering over her wrist. Cameras. The three Emerson had already hacked.

"I'm feeding them loops," Emerson said, his voice impatient in her ear. "Let's go."

Signe pushed up on the grate until it popped out of the floor like a kernel of popcorn on a cook plate. Then she heaved herself out of the hole. She pulled off her boots, leaving them inside the pipe, surrounded by the greenish-brown sludge that now covered Signe's entire front, and padding into the room in her socks.

"Wow, you look disgusting," Emerson said. "Don't drip any of that sludge on the floor."

Signe flipped off one of the cameras before turning her attention back to the terminal at hand. She held her unicomm up, hovering the holographic menu over the interface. "All right, kid. Work your magic."

"I'm twenty-four," Emerson griped.

"And I'm forty-three," Signe said. "That makes you a kid. Shit, you could be *my* kid, actually."

"Well, thank Lucre that's not the case."

"For both our sakes."

The terminal winked on as Emerson hacked in using Signe's unicomm. Menus and screens flashed by so fast Signe was sure she missed half of them just by blinking. The plan was simple enough: re-route a pricey shipment of copper wiring that had just come in from the Federation of South Brasilia. Cora Calvin of Teras Systems had made the purchase, but Emerson was making it look as though Huldra Industries had swooped in to poach their shipment.

Cora and Huldra's CEO, Reina Arthur, already hated each other—always had, as far as Signe knew. Something like this could start a feud that forced all nine of the powerful bastards to take sides.

Would it be enough to bring the Board crashing down? Of course not. Would it bring an end to Lucre's Algorithm and all the cultlike bullshit that went along with it? Also no. But it would weaken the legs upon which the Board stood, ever so slightly. Then, someday, when they were ready to strike their final blow, hopefully the Board would be too weak to recover.

That was the idea, anyway.

"All right, that's it," Emerson said. The terminal blinked back to its home screen. "Now, get the hell out of there."

"Sir, yes sir," Signe said, giving one of the cameras a mocking salute. She slipped back into the pipe, sliding right into her boots and pulling the grate back into place over her head. She ducked out of the light the second the door banged open. The tubheads were back to finish their coffees.

And now, we wait, she thought as she crawled arm over arm back the way she had come. Wait for the Board's infighting to make them splinter. Wait for their perfect opportunity—the one that would finally let them deal a blow the powers of New Avarita couldn't recover from.

It would be worth it in the end… but Signe had to admit she was getting sick of waiting.

03

LIV

New Avarita alone has the vision and guidance necessary to build a balanced, thriving population. Through strategic hormone regulation, the Algorithm ensures every child born in our great city-state will serve our society and workforce, creating opportunities for all to strive toward their ultimate goal.

—THE HANDBOOK OF LUCRE, *CHAPTER 9*

LIV HAD NEVER had never been much of a partier—more of an *early to bed, early to rise* kind of person—and as she dragged herself through the motions the day following Charles Branston's Ascent ceremony, she was reminded why. She and Liam had stayed in the Core until well after ten o'clock, dancing and drinking and wandering the halls of the museum, listening to important people make absolutely insane interpretations of the artwork.

Then, they'd limped to the train station and taken the hour-long ride home. Liv had nodded off, using Liam's shoulder as a bony pillow. Somehow, he'd managed to get up the first time his alarm went off and left the townhome before Liv even managed to peel her eyelids open. He'd left her a surprise on the counter, though—an apple-and-cheese pastry drizzled with honey. An appetizer he must have swiped from the celebration the night before and saved for her breakfast.

Between the lack of sleep, the tedium of today's project, and being pestered by Grant for every last detail about the party, she was utterly wiped. Liv checked the time on her unicomm as she reached for her fifth cup of synthetic coffee.

16:47

She paused before grabbing the cup. *Caffeine took thirty minutes to take effect.* Her day would be over by the time this sip started jolting her blood awake. Then, with her luck, she'd be wide awake until the wee hours of the morning. She pushed the cup aside. She could power through the next thirteen minutes sans-stimulant.

If she timed things right, she might even have time to take a nap before Liam got home. Even in slow times, the man worked at least sixty hours a week. Now that Charles had been selected for Ascent, there was an executive position open for the taking. He'd be putting in extra hours for the next quarter if he thought he had a shot at a gig like that. Liv couldn't imagine where he found the energy. These days, she barely had the energy to work and make food.

Life after thirty was a bit of a bitch.

After the longest thirteen minutes of her life. Liv's unicomm finally blinked 17:00. She pushed in her chair, powered off her terminal, and kept her head down, avoiding eye contact with any colleagues who might be tempted to stop her for small-talk as she made her way to the train station.

The train ride from Berger Security to Liv and Liam's neighborhood was less than twenty minutes long. In better weather, Liv could walk the distance in under an hour. She spent the train ride immersed in her VR eye enhancements, scrolling through the feeds on the rinth and trying to block out the smell of body odor emanating from her seatmate. Before five-thirty rolled around, she was off the train and booking it across the platform toward the tangle of townhomes in the distance.

Eighty-eight identical units in one point six acres. Seven hundred square feet per townhome. Three hundred and fifty-two windows. She knew this complex so well she could outfit the entire thing with cameras and sensors within a week without even checking a single schematic.

When she arrived home, Liv's eyes flicked to the door beside hers. Ayla's unit was quiet, but the upstairs light was on. Her friend was home—awfully early for her, too. She chewed her lip, thinking about how Ayla had acted the day before. How she'd skirted questions about her baby and the way her eyes had filled with tears during the ceremony. She'd left the celebration before dinner was even served—also uncharacteristic for her friend.

Liv had never been a partier, but Ayla was usually first in line for the buffet and the last one to leave the dance floor.

She hesitated at the stoop, glancing between her porch and Ayla's. Liv had always been better with numbers than with people, but she had a strong feeling that something was wrong with her friend. It was like the prickles that rose on the back of her neck when she could sense that a creep was staring on the bus. A primal sense that whispered *caution.*

But between worry and exhaustion, exhaustion had the stronger grip today. She could check on her friend tomorrow. Tonight, Liv's comfiest chair was calling out to her. She could practically hear it through the door.

Liv, come play some video games and maybe take a nap!

The prox reader registered Liv's chip and the door lock clicked open as she reached for the handle. The townhome was exactly the way she had left it: quiet and dark. The lighting system kicked on as Liv eased the door shut behind her, bathing the space in honey-gold.

There wasn't much on the walls, even though they'd lived in this unit for five years, now. Décor had never been Liv's forte, and Liam wasn't home often enough to care, so they hadn't gotten around to more than the basics.

A few digital frames hung on the walls, populating with an ever-rotating collage of images and videos from Liv and Liam's time together. Liv smiled tiredly at the photo currently winking out at her—a snap from their wedding day. Liam dipped Liv low to the ground, both of them were laughing, clad head-to-toe in silver, and surrounded by synthetic flowers.

Liv kissed her fingertips, then pressed the hand to the holographic image of her husband's smiling face. "Thanks for breakfast. It was fucking delicious."

Speaking of delicious, Liv hadn't eaten anything since that pastry. *Nine hours and twenty-seven minutes without food.* She was surprised she wasn't getting shaky yet.

Right on schedule, her unicomm *pinged* on her wrist. A message populated above her wrist in angry red text.

BLOOD SUGAR: 63 MG/DL

"Yeah, yeah, alright, I hear you," she said.

She hung her coat on the retractable rack beside the door, then crossed to the kitchen to grab a pack of dried noodles. Liv tapped the wall as she passed through the doorway, activating the sound system. The soothing rhythms of Orange Ocean pulsed gently through every room in the townhome. The band was an old one, popular in the mid-2200s, but they'd been one of her mom's favorites. Liv hummed along to the melody as she cracked the noodle packet open, crunching into the hard brick inside and settling into her gaming chair.

How long would she last before she inevitably nodded off upright and Liam woke her up with a mock-disapproving look on his face and his hands on his hips? Only time would tell. She curled her legs up under her and tapped her temples, taking another bite as she sank into her VR environment.

RinthRat12 was online. Not surprising—they were *always* online.

Liv wondered what kind of job they had where that was possible. Maybe they were a developer at CyberNexus Studios, the company that developed *Wasteland Warriors*. Or maybe they worked for the competing game company, ShadowForge. That would explain why they never wanted to talk about work—they wouldn't want to admit to playing a competitor's game with as much gusto as RinthRat12 played *Wasteland Warriors*.

Liv invited RinthRat12 to play and within seconds the pair of them were adventuring through the desert wastes, rebuffing an ambush by another colony. As Liv scrolled through her in-game arsenal, looking for something that could shore up the defenses on their south gate, her thoughts flicked back to Ayla.

Now that she thought back on it, Ayla had been acting off for months. She'd been locking herself away since Kiran's Ascent. The way she was retreating from the world, it almost felt like she was *grieving*. But that couldn't be it. Kiran hadn't met prem-death, he'd been selected for Ascent.

Still, maybe Ayla was afraid of raising their little one alone now that her husband had moved on. Especially since she and Kiran hadn't applied for a childbearing application like Liv had; they'd just gotten a notice one day that the Algorithm had selected them for reproduction. And so now, she was facing the idea of raising the kid she hadn't volunteered to have, and she was completely on her own.

Liv supposed she could understand that. Still, if Ayla wasn't careful, she was going to be deemed unstable. She might lose her position at the hospital, or worse, get placed in a Medla facility and lose custody of her little one the second she gave birth.

She needed to get Ayla to sit down and tell her what was really going on inside that brilliant skull of hers.

<RinthRat12: Whoa, whoa, where's your head at?>

Liv returned her attention to the game just in time to see her avatar slump over, her VR environment surging with red light as a villager from the opposing colony pulled an energy sword from her avatar's chest.

"Ah, shit," Liv said out loud.

<Liv_Struck99: Sorry. Just a little distracted.>

<RinthRat12: You mean there's something more pressing in your life than defending our virtual colony? Rude.>

Liv snorted.

<RinthRat12: What's going on?>

The townhome's sound system thudded on in the background, starting up another Orange Ocean tune. *"Nectarine Reverie," released in 2303, third track of their* Marigold *album.* Liv drummed her fingers on the arm of her chair for a moment.

<Liv_Struck99: Just my friend. She's acting off.>

<RinthRat12: The pregnant one? The one whose husband got switch'd?>

Liv winced at the offensive term for Ascent. It wasn't the first time RinthRat had used it casually in their conversations, and it made her uncomfortable every single time. The best course of action, she'd learned, was simply to ignore it.

<Liv_Struck99: How did you know?>

<RinthRat12: You don't have that many friends.>

Liv huffed out a laugh. They weren't wrong.

<RinthRat12: What's she doing? Is she okay?>

"I don't know," Liv said out loud.

But before she had the chance to tap out a reply RinthRat12 could actually receive, the door to the townhome clicked open. Liv frowned, checking her unicomm. It was barely a quarter past six. What was Liam doing home already?

He must have been just as exhausted as she was.

<Liv_Struck99: Sorry, buddy. I've got to go.>

RinthRat12 was still typing when Liv tapped her temples, re-entering the real world.

"What have I done to deserve this treat?" Liv asked, un-pretzeling her legs and pushing herself to her feet. "Is it our anniversary or something? This is the earliest you've been home in—"

The words rotted on Liv's tongue as she caught sight of her husband.

He looked flat, like someone had taken the Liam Spencer she knew and deflated him like an old birthday balloon. He stood, silhouetted in the still-open door to their home, shoulders hunched and eyes haunted.

"What's wrong?"

For a moment, Liam just stared into space. Then, he turned his head, almost mechanically, meeting her eye at last. "I just got fired."

Fear and disbelief chased the blood from Liv's face. *Fired.*

The calculations started flitting through her skull.

Townhome: 8,600 per month. Train fares: 1,200 per month. Groceries: 5,500 per month, give or take. Utilities and insurance and enhancement upkeep. Altogether, their monthly expenses came to more than 20,000 credits—and that was *now*. What would happen when they had a child to worry about, too?

Liv felt like someone had vacuumed the air from her lungs.

She hadn't gotten her hormone blockers shut off yet. The application had gone through, but the Algorithm could surely rescind it. Without Liam's salary, the pair of them would be hard-pressed to support themselves, never mind supporting a child.

"Fired? What for?" she asked. Her voice sounded far away to her ears, like something spoken inside of a dream. Somehow, she had the wherewithal to pull Liam inside and shut the door behind him.

"I'm not sure," Liam shook his head, allowing her to usher him through the entry hall and into the kitchen. "I'd been working on a project Reid kicked over to me last week—a deep dive into the grow domes. I wrote up the whole piece, got it to Reid ahead of schedule, even. But I think I..." He looked at her with a strange spark in his eye. Fear? Then he scrubbed a hand over his face and slumped into his usual seat at the dining table.

"You think you..." Liv prompted.

Liam shook his head. "It doesn't matter. What matters is that Reid put the kibosh on the piece as soon as I started asking about..." He trailed off again. "Anyway, by the time I got back to my desk from his office, I was locked out of the system, and the termination message was waiting for me in my unicomm."

Reid. Liv flushed with rage. She should have known it was that weasel. That brown-nosing, selfish, scapegoating bastard. She could forgive the asshole for wheedling his way up to a position he was woefully unqualified for. She could even forgive him for his backhanded compliments and general assholery. But this?

"Mhm," Liam said dimly, as though he was reading her mind.

"All right, all right," Liv started.

The logical side of her brain kicked into high gear, pushing her panicked self into the back corner of her skull. She envisioned Emotional Liv sitting back there, rocking back and forth in the darkness. But now wasn't the time to fall apart. Now was the time to put her skills to good use and logic their way out of this mess.

"We can figure this out," she said, drumming her fingers silently on her hips as she talked. She envisioned all her anxiety pouring out of her fingertips with the motion, like she was siphoning the fear from her body. "You have over a decade of experience with Vinco! You can find something else. Maybe over at Brinnings Media? It's a little smaller, but you could carve out a spot for yourself, there. I bet they'd be dying to snap up someone who worked for Vinco!"

"Brinnings is owned by Vinco," Liam said dimly.

"What?" Liv frowned. Everyone knew Brinnings was one of Vinco's biggest competitors. Liam must not be thinking straight.

"It's just like the grow domes," Liam said dimly, staring into space, looking hopeless. "It's all rigged. It's all fake."

He wasn't making any sense. Stress was one hell of a drug.

She lay a hand on his forearm before pushing herself up. "We'll figure everything out tomorrow, babe. Everything is going to be okay." She crossed to the fridge, pulling out a slim metal can of KoegenMalt beer. She popped the tab, then set it on the table in front of him.

Liam stared at the can for a few seconds, then picked it up and drained it in one go. He then ran both hands back through his hair, the carefully gelled look dissolving into a series of odd angles that made him look more than a little deranged. "I don't know, Liv. I just…"

Liv took the seat across from him, reaching over the table to grab both his hands in hers. "Everyone knows Reid Allen is a slimy motherfucker, Liam. Don't let him get in your head like this."

"Yeah..." Liam said, staring at their intertwined fingers for a few seconds. Slowly, he started nodding to himself. He looked up at Liv, giving her a wan smile. "What would I do without you?"

"It'll be a long time before you have to find out, if I have my way about it," Liv chuckled. She gave his hands a squeeze, then pushed herself to her feet, turning back toward the fridge. "What do you say we treat ourselves a bit for dinner? No fish tonight—let's defrost the last of the pork from summer holidays and—"

She cut off mid-sentence at the sound of a vague *thud* behind her.

Liv turned to find Liam face-down on the table, his hands still outstretched, resting where they had clasped her own hands just seconds before. Her heart beat a steady path up her throat. His eyes were wide open, his body completely still.

"No, no, no," Liv muttered, rushing over to feel his neck, hunting for a pulse. Had the stress given him a heart attack? His chip would trigger a call to the nearest Medla facility in the event of a medical emergency. Techs would already be on their way. His unicomm would have the details—a full log of the call his chip had placed.

"Liam? Liam!" she heard herself speaking but it sounded distant, like words spoken by someone else from the far end of a long, long hallway. She grabbed onto his shoulders, pulling him upright and shaking him. "Babe? Can you hear me? It's going to be alright, Medla's on the way. They're on the way. They're going to help you."

His body was limp, but his eyes were still open. Was he awake? If he was awake, why wasn't he moving? Why wasn't he responding to the sound of her voice? He was going to be all right. He had to be.

Liv reached for his arm, pulling up his unicomm's health log with shaking hands.

Her mind turned to static as her eyes scrolled over the readout, reading the words without really processing them.

HEART RATE: 0 BPM

RESPIRATORY ACTIVITY: NONE

BRAIN ACTIVITY: NONE

There had to be some kind of mistake. His log was glitching. His eyes were still open; he was still here. He had to be.

Liam couldn't be gone. Not now. Not yet. Even if his career *was* over, he still had so much to do, so much to be, so much to accomplish. He was going to be a *father*. They had barely gotten a chance to start building their lives together. This was some kind of technical error. The Medla techs would sort it out when they got here.

"Liam, babe, it's alright. It's going to be okay." Her voice was breaking. "You're going to be fine, but you need to stay awake. Stay with me. We can explain it all to the Medla staff when they get here."

Liam's eyes were still open, but they were blank. Nausea crept up the back of Liv's throat like a spider scaling its thread, slowly, slowly. "Stay with me," she intoned, "stay with me, stay with me." The words bled together in her skull as she repeated them over and over again like a prayer.

Liv didn't even hear the townhome door open. She only knew the medical staff were there when one of them pulled her off of Liam with firm hands.

"Please, please, you need to help him," she said, babbling, turning to face the man closest to her. "He's just collapsed, I think it's stress. And his unicomm is glitching. But I think he may have had a heart attack or..."

She trailed off as her eyes took in the figures in her kitchen. They weren't Medla House techs in their pale green scrubs. They were well-groomed men and women in neat, blue suits. Representatives from the Principal Chairman's office.

"It's not a heart attack, Mrs. Spencer," said the man next to her. His face swam in front of Liv's unsteady gaze as he took her hands in his. He was smiling gently, reverently. "Your husband has been selected for Ascent. Congratulations! We will transport him to the nearest facility to remove his chip and prepare him for the ceremony." Her unicomm *dinged* with a notification. "Our office has just sent you all the details so you can start planning the celebration!"

The blood drained from Liv's face, leaving her feeling cold and hollow. She couldn't even summon the will or the ability to reply.

"Congratulations!" the man said again. He patted her hand amiably. "We'll leave you to your planning."

Liv backed up, her feet moving of their own volition as the men and women in their neat blue suits lifted the shell of what had once been Liam Spencer onto a stretcher. She stood numbly, pressing her back against the refrigerator. The Principal Chairman's workers smiled and offered her their congratulations. Then they carted the stretcher out the door and into the night.

Alone, Liv stood in silence for a minute, an hour, a lifetime, staring at her hands. Hands that had just been holding her husband's. Hands that would never hold Liam Spencer ever again.

Finally, the panicked side of her brain overrode the logical and she crumbled, sobbing, to the floor.

04
REINA

Healthy citizens create a healthy society. The Algorithm plans the optimal blend of crops and livestock to keep our population healthy and thriving until it is their time to transcend this plane. To receive a grow dome permit from the Principal Chairman's office, each grower must be willing to comply with these measures.

—THE HANDBOOK OF LUCRE, *CHAPTER 5*

REINA ARTHUR MOVED through the hallways of InsertiaTech like a ship's prow cutting through seawater. Humans, doors, mechs, all of them slid neatly out of her way as she passed, her pristine shoes clicking on equally pristine floors. Her chip automatically unlocked and opened every door in this building, and the mechs ran on programming that kept them out of her way. She couldn't program the humans, unfortunately, but her reputation was enough to get them moving.

She lifted her chin another quarter inch, setting her jaw and narrowing her eyes. Once she got her current experiment to work, her reputation would be secure for centuries to come.

The Dev Lab was on the fifteenth floor of InsertiaTech's main building, behind more than half a dozen different security doors. Reina strode through the two on the first floor, then made her way to the secure elevator at the far end of the hall. She waited for the doors to *whoosh* open. All the technology in this damned building and she still had to wait for the elevator? Ridiculous.

Reina stared at the painting on the wall across from her as she waited. *Dome of Poppies*, it was called. A stylized representation of a sea of red flowers contained within a perfect bubble. It had originally been produced in 2143, painted by a man named Samuel Rostlin and later used by the first-ever Advisory Board in rinth advertisements and campaigns to promote the implementation of grow domes and the subsequent emancipation of New Avarita from the territories surrounding it.

Fine and rare artwork such as this covered nearly every hall of every Huldra Industries subsidiary in the city-state. Was it an odd choice, mixing classical artwork and bleeding edge technology? Some may have thought so. Reina, on the other hand, knew that speaking to the pains of humanity's past was the only way to sell solutions for its future.

The elevator ride from the first floor to the fifteenth took less than twelve seconds. A few scant moments after that, Reina was shrugging into her lab coat and striding through the last two security doors into the Dev Lab.

"Report," she said to no one in particular, activating her eyeshield enhancements with a tap. Electronic fields projected down from her eyebrows, covering her eyes with a thin, bluish glow that would deflect anything smaller than a standard-issue lethal round.

"We are preparing for test A-43, Madam Arthur," said one of the engineers. Reina didn't even pretend to know his name.

"The implant surgery was successful this time?" Reina folded her arms behind her back, pacing toward the electronic barrier separating her team of engineers from their test subject.

"Yes, Madam Arthur," the same engineer said. Was he the new Head Engineer in Dev? He certainly knew the proper way to show deference to a superior of her caliber. Perhaps she would learn his name after all. "Dr. Pilet came in from Medla's headquarters to perform the installation."

Reina's eyes turned hard, her metaphorical hackles rising. "And what did you tell Dr. Pilet the enhancement was for?"

Of all the other Board members, Reina hated Louis Gideon, Medla's CEO, the least. But that didn't mean she wanted him to know what she was on the precipice of creating. She envisioned her creation as a slab of meat and herself as a coyote out in the Waste, teeth bared as she snapped at anyone who dared stray too close. More people involved in a project watered down her innovation. More people wanting credit—and coin—for playing their small part in enabling her genius.

"We told him it was an improved measure to counteract the effects of alcohol and poison, Madam," the nameless engineer said.

Reina nodded, her defensiveness subsiding. It was a good cover. Useful enough to be believable, boring enough to be utterly forgettable. Dr. Pilet probably hadn't even told his wife about the procedure that night over dinner.

In reality, the test subject before them would have a greater impact on the future of New Avarita than allowing a few overindulgent fools to drink as much as they liked without losing their heads or their livers. If today's test was successful, it would solidify Reina Arthur's place in the history books of New Avarita, and solidify the security of her bank balance, to boot.

Her test subject milled around its enclosure, its snuffles and snorts muted by the buzz of the barrier. The creature was a pig. A hab-grown pig created in a tube and grown in a Koegen lab on the far side of the Core. Their digestive systems were quite different from a human's it was true, but they were about the right size and relatively easy to procure, if you had a few million coin to throw around.

This particular pig was the seventh test subject Reina had gone through in the past year. The first four had died during the implantation process. The fifth had succumbed not long after a seemingly successful implantation from internal swelling and complications. The last had gone through surgery just fine but had died during testing.

It remained to be seen whether this seventh subject would survive the day. If it did, Reina was one step closer to securing not only her legacy but her future with the Board. If not… She stroked her hair, surreptitiously rubbing the place behind her left ear where her chip sat, nestled under her skin against her brainstem. Her unicomm buzzed gently, alerting her that her stress hormones were spiking, her blood pressure rising to 136/80.

She cleared the notification before anyone else in the lab could see. Perhaps it was best not to think about the consequences of repeated failure just now.

She would not fail. She could not. Her mother had always said if there was a way to bend the laws of nature with nothing but pure will, Reina would be the one to do it.

Perhaps today would be the day she managed it.

"Commence test one," she said, straightening her spine and expunging any hint of nerves from her voice.

Six project engineers lined up against the electric barrier, standing so close that, had it been made of glass, they would have fogged it with their breath. Reina schooled her expression, keeping herself as flat and unreadable as an unprogrammed chip as she watched the robotic arm descend from the ceiling. It deposited a dish filled with thick, viscous liquid. It was a synthetic fuel made by Xirloc, a lesser-known brand in the Huldra portfolio, mixed with base organic material and a paste made of vitamins Reina purchased from a corporation across the sea in the Russo-Europa Empire.

Not incredibly appetizing to look at, but if the new product worked as designed, it technically contained everything the pig needed to survive.

The creature snorted and grunted, making its way toward the dish.

"No signs of impaired movement," said the head engineer, his voice tinged with a hope Reina didn't dare let swell inside her own chest. Not yet.

"Chip readings stable," reported another engineer, eyes flicking rapidly between the display hovering above her forearm and the scene taking place behind the plexiglass.

Reina dimly wondered if there had ever before been a time in human history when a group of highly educated people had watched a pig eat slop with such intensity. But the results of this particular pig eating this particular slop could change the future for everyone living in New Avarita. And, most importantly, for every person with a stake in Huldra Industries.

She had never wanted to be a software engineer, not really. No, Reina Arthur had wanted to be a painter. But her father wouldn't stand for any of that *wishy-washy nonsense,* as he put it. And so, at the age of fourteen, Reina had packed up her paintbrushes and delved into coding.

In the time since, she had helped code some of the most well-known and revolutionary chip enhancements in all of New Avarita. When working at Zen Labs, she'd created enhancements that released chemicals and waves to encourage dreamless sleep. She'd taken a promotion over to Berger Security and worked on eye enhancements that automatically recorded any time a wearer's heart rate went above a certain level (an invention that was seeing far more action in the adult film industry than its intended use, interestingly enough).

In another role with Berger, she'd helped to develop the program within the trigger chip that went into the armgun enhancements now installed on every Correxion officer in the city-state.

All told, Reina Arthur's name was on hundreds of patents—six hundred and thirty-seven, to be exact. But this? This would be her crowning glory.

For hundreds of years, the land where New Avarita now stood was wracked by famine. Millions died of starvation, and millions more died in the riots that came after the Fall. It was then, in 2183, that the company that had now become Huldra Industries invented the chip. Or, more specifically, they perfected it.

Instead of embedding a chip into a wearer's skull for communication or entertainment or any of the other dozens of reasons humans had used wearable technology for centuries, Huldra's predecessor created this chip as a solution to a very specific problem.

Overpopulation.

Most of the world disagreed with the invention, calling it inhumane. Much of the world still felt that way—it was why New Avarita's trade arrangements always felt like they were treading on half-cracked eggs—but one man saw its value. A man by the name of Herman Lucre.

Most of history had forgotten that Lucre had not actually created the Algorithm that took on his name. He'd done something more important, though.

He'd given it a brand. Where much of the world saw a crime against humanity, Lucre saw an opportunity. And, with his silver tongue, he'd helped the rest of New Avarita see it as a blessing.

With the urging Lucre's writings and under the guidance of the first—and only actual—Principal Chairman of New Avarita, each infant was implanted with their chip within a month of their birth, and within a generation, the chips had gone from a scary new method of control to an integral part of everyday life.

While those people used their chips to access their coin, unlock their homes, and identify themselves, the Algorithm was gathering data. Biometric data, rinth access patterns, and more. The Algorithm then used that data to run calculations, determining ideal food production schedules, identifying the citizens most suited to childbearing, and, most importantly, deducing who was still a valuable, contributing member of New Avaritan society… and who was not.

Thanks to the chips, overpopulation was no longer a problem in New Avarita.

And, thanks to Arnaud Lucre, the people of New Avarita no longer stubbornly clung to life long after their usefulness had passed. Instead, the people of New Avarita celebrated their deaths—their Ascents. After all, Ascent meant a person had accomplished all they could on this earth. It was the ultimate sign of a life well lived.

Reina had believed that, once.

Before she was selected to join the Principal Chairman's Board. Before she learned that this Principal Chairman—and the three who had come before him—were not real men but rinth-generated holograms created by the board of advisors he had supposedly selected. Before she saw for herself the ways the nine people who had essentially bought their way into the highest power in New Avarita could hurry along Ascent for a particularly troublesome member of society. How they could override the system and fry any citizen's chip, even if the Algorithm hadn't decided it was their time to go.

Reina fiddled with the bracelet circling her left wrist, toying with one glittering sapphire as she studied her test subject with enough focus to set the pig ablaze. Huldra Industries had not come out with a truly game-changing enhancement in nearly five years. If that didn't change soon, she could find herself ousted from the Board.

If that happened, she knew her fellows would cast a vote, and she'd be "selected" for Ascent before her shoes hit the concrete outside the Medial Complex. She'd seen it happen before. She'd been one of the ones casting that very vote when Paul Viesto, the previous representative for Huldra Industries, had been demoted some ten years before.

She hadn't been handed the reins of Huldra Industries. She had taken them through force and cunning, and she wasn't the only one. The members of the Board had not gotten to their lofty seats through teamwork and hugs.

But this enhancement could change the face of New Avarita nearly as much as the original chip had changed the world that came before. Food shortages were one of the constants in New Avaritan life. But if the enhancement inside that pig's digestive system worked as designed, all that could change.

A picture of a glorious future flashed before Reina's eyes as she watched the beast nose through the dish of slop. A future where no one needed grow domes or lab-grown meats. A future where every single soul in New Avarita got an implant from InsertiaTech, then survived purely on the fuel-based paste sold by Xirloc. A future where every citizen depended on Huldra brands to survive, not just because of their chip, but because of their entire bodily structure.

Forget her fears of early Ascent; once she perfected this invention, she'd be the richest and most powerful person New Avarita had ever seen.

Those daydreams dissolved like sugar in hot coffee when the subject's breathing grew labored. Over the next thirty minutes, the pig showed more and more signs of discomfort. Its heart rate readings spiked. Eventually, it began to squeal—a sound of anguish and rage that Reina wished she could make herself at the moment.

"Pull it," the head engineer finally said.

Reina was tempted to override the order. Maybe if they held on *just a bit longer* the experiment would succeed. But he was right; there was no chance of a full recovery at this point. It was becoming difficult to watch, even in the pursuit of progress. One of the lab technicians tapped a sequence on his unicomm and the pig's labored breathing cut off abruptly. The animal slumped to the floor. It took all of Reina's self-control not to mirror the beast and collapse in despair herself.

Another failure.

"Madam Arthur, there you are."

Reina knew that voice. It was the one that haunted her dreams just as her own voice had surely haunted the dreams of Paul Viesto before her. She plastered an unconcerned, haughty expression onto her face before turning to face the woman who had just entered the lab.

Jaya Ravenna.

The woman was a snake in human form. She was also the VP of Engineering for Huldra's main office. It was the same position Reina herself had held twenty years ago. Jaya was young, only thirty-seven years old, and just as ambitious as Reina had been at that age. Reina's chip seemed to tingle against her skull, like it was threatening to zap the life from her right then and there.

"Jaya." Reina tapped her temples, turning off her eye shields. "To what do I owe the pleasure of this visit?"

"I had hoped to witness something incredible, what with a person of your immense experience in the lab," Jaya said. She glanced at the dead pig, now being pulled from the testing room by a pair of assistant mechs. "Perhaps another time."

"Perhaps," Reina said, speaking through her teeth. Jaya was practically slavering over her position on the Board these days. She was probably already conspiring with the other Board members, gathering the votes to have Reina ousted. Cora Calvin would agree immediately, if she hadn't already, Reina was sure.

"But no, I am here on far more interesting business than dead pigs, fortunately," Jaya said smoothly. Her thin, freckled face broke into what was clearly meant to be a rueful smile. She looked like a wolf baring her teeth. "Madam Calvin has called an emergency meeting in the Medial Complex."

"Is that so?" Reina said cocking her head to one side to disguise the rush of anxious nausea that rushed up her throat. "Why am I hearing this from you instead of dear Cora herself? She has my unicomm code, I assure you."

As did Jaya. There was no reason for her to communicate this in person. No reason aside from making Reina appear out of touch and incompetent in front of the entirety of the Dev Lab staff.

"She has elected to exclude you from the invitation, apparently," Jaya said. "Something about poached imports?"

"Poached imports?" Reina's cold mask almost slipped. She secured the expression with a flick of her eyebrow.

She and Teras System's CEO, Cora, had been enemies since the moment Reina had joined the Board. The rat had apparently had some kind of off-the-record arrangement with Paul Viesto—something to do with discounts and noncompete agreements and all other kinds of things that would cost Huldra profits just for the sake of keeping Cora Calvin happy. Reina had put a stop to that the moment she took over Paul's seat. And Cora had never forgotten.

Unlike Cora, Reina was not an insufferable hothead. She had not ordered any imports to be poached from Teras. Still, she knew Cora wouldn't let something as insignificant as the truth get in the way of her quest for retribution against the only Board member who refused to put up with her tantrums.

The fact that she was sending Jaya Ravenna as her little messenger pigeon made it all too clear what she intended to accomplish at this meeting. She was to be taken down a peg, both now and in person. Jaya knew it too, from the smirk on her worthless face.

Her VP of Engineering was a shark. Any sign of fear or weakness from Reina would be blood in the water. And so, Reina just nodded smartly, pulling off her lab coat and handing it to the nearest lab tech. "Call a private transport, would you?" she asked, keeping her tone as flat and disinterested as possible.

She didn't wait for a reply, marching out of the Dev Lab and through headquarters. Whether Jaya had called the transport herself or made someone else do it, she didn't know, but the vehicle was waiting for her as she walked out the front doors and into the mid-afternoon sun. That was a small victory, at least; Jaya was not willing to openly disobey and disrespect Reina. Yet.

The streets were bustling with afternoon traffic. Businessmen and women wearing a thousand different logos that, ultimately, represented nine total corporations power-walked past. Holographic advertisements popped up every few feet, startling the less-seasoned professionals while those who had lived in the Core a long time simply walked through them like they weren't there.

Huldra Industries was the tallest building on this block, but the lesser towers were no less impressive, built of gleaming glass and reinforced steel, built in the craziest (and often least practical) shapes the architects of StarBuilt and a dozen other Teras subsidiaries could dream up.

In the distance, she could see the sparkling surfaces of the grow domes: Koegen Corp's massive, half-sphere greenhouses that grew the crops that fed New Avarita's population. Trains and transports whizzed past on their neat tracks, carrying people through the Core from the other, lesser districts of New Avarita.

The door to Reina's private transport sprang open as soon as she reached for the handle. She slid inside, setting her desired location and leaning back as the vehicle hummed and began to glide forward.

She checked the time. 16:47. Even the most routine meetings in the Medial Complex were never shorter than two hours. She'd be home late tonight. Again. Braxton would be livid. Not that he would ever say so.

"Might as well get ahead of it," she muttered to herself, tapping a code into her unicomm. Within seconds, a holographic view of a man hovered over her wrist. Braxton Grant, her husband of twenty-two years. His scrubs were dotted with an unidentifiable fluid. As an experimental surgeon, it could be almost anything. Reina had stopped asking after pointless details like that many years ago.

"Reina?" he asked, "What's wrong?"

"Nothing," Reina lied. "I just wanted to let you know I'll be home late."

"How late?" Braxton asked. The exhaustion at her inability to make time for their family was palpable in his tone. "You know this is the only night this week both of the kids will be home, right?"

"I do," Reina responded coldly. Zane and Alayna were both studying in universities outside the Core. It was rare to see either one of them outside of a holo display; she hadn't seen them both in a room together since late last Fall.

Her chip seemed to tingle again, as if in warning. If this meeting went poorly, she might never see her children again.

Perhaps Braxton could sense her unwillingness to discuss the matter, or perhaps he simply didn't care. Either way, he didn't press the issue. Her holo-display faded as she ended the call, leaving her alone in the muted darkness of the transport. She allowed herself to dissociate for a while, staring into space as deeply average and inoffensive transport music played gently on the speakers.

Far too soon, the transport buzzed onto the Medial Complex. It was a sprawling campus that ate up the center of New Avarita's Core. The transport took a left, then a right, then another left, finally slowing to a stop in front of the tower that rose up from the center of the complex like a dagger sticking out of a heart.

Reina took a deep breath. "Alright, Cora. I'm ready for you, you bitch," she muttered to herself. She took a second to adjust herself, straightening her blazer and twisting her bracelet so it lay just so on her wrist. Then, she opened the transport door to greet her fate.

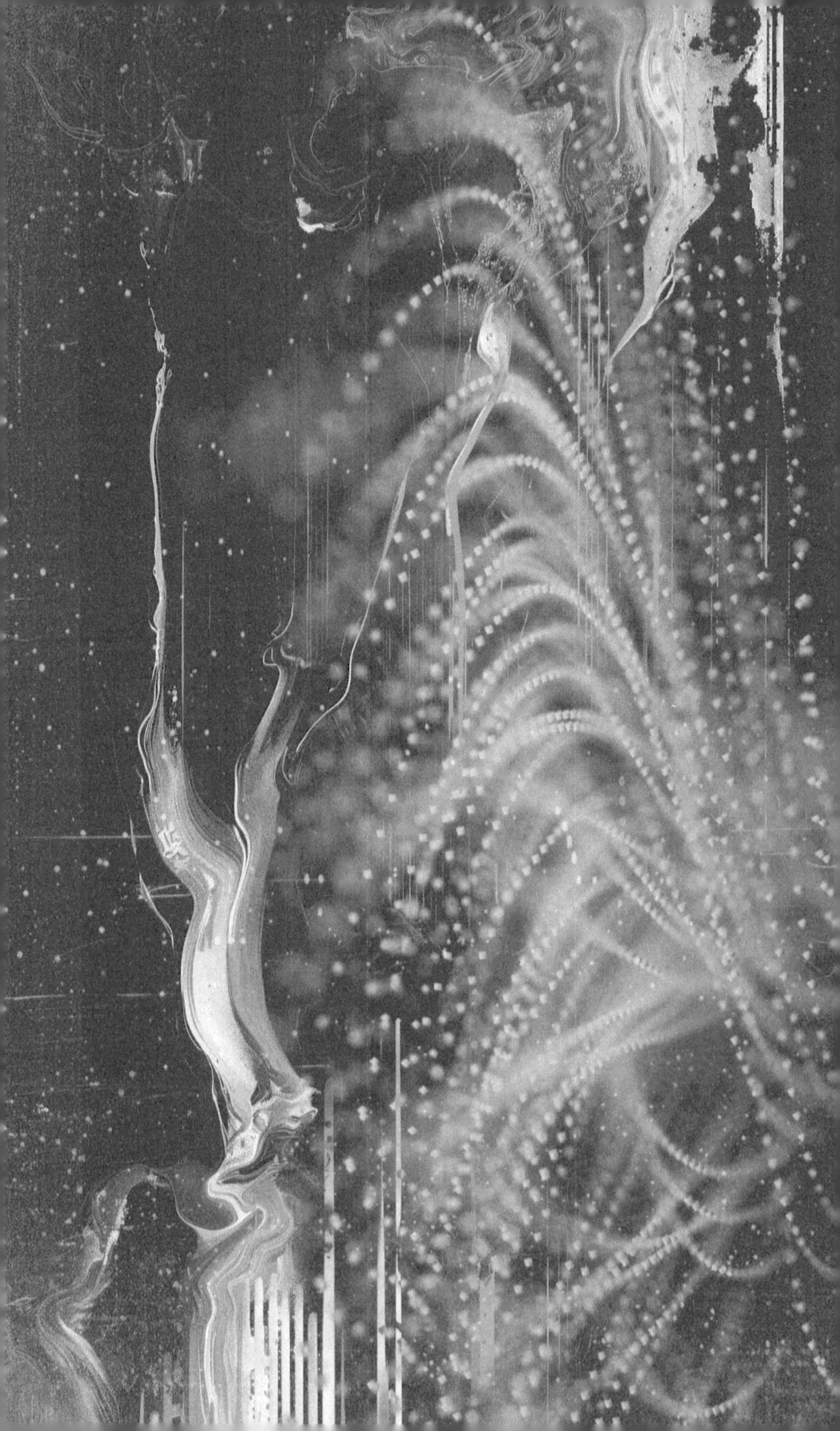

05

LIV

Our great society can only maintain its purity and greatness when all our citizens work together, building toward the same glorious future. The Algorithm is designed to identify those attempting to deviate from the optimal path so they might be removed until such a time that they can be reintegrated to resume their work toward the common good.

—THE HANDBOOK OF LUCRE, *CHAPTER 2*

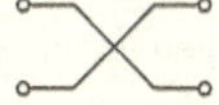

IF ONE MORE person congratulated Liv on Liam getting selected for Ascent, she might snap and throttle them straight to their own early incineration.

Planning Liam's ceremony had been hard enough, but sitting through the damn thing had been next to impossible. She'd forced herself to smile, sing, dance. She'd gracefully accepted comments about how exceptional her husband must have been to get selected so young. But the tiny Liv in the back corner of her brain hadn't stopped shaking, crying, and screaming since that night in the kitchen.

What was wrong with her?

She missed Liam's company, of course—surely that much was normal—but it wasn't like he'd died of sickness or been struck by a transport. He had reached the finish line. Selected for Ascent. At only thirty-two years of age, it was true, but maybe that was just a sign of how exceptional he'd truly been. Maybe it was like that one woman had said, patting her arm in congratulations after they all watched Liam get turned into a flurry of ashes. Maybe he'd had a short life because the Algorithm knew he was meant to live as a firework instead of a candle—touching the lives of many for a short time instead of a few for longer.

Had Liam lived his life as a firework, serving so many people in his first thirty-two years that he met his lifetime quota, or had he been more like that boy Icarus from the old story? Maybe Liam had just gotten too ambitious too soon, rising higher and higher until he finally flew too close to the sun.

A sun named Reid Allen, in this case.

She thought she deserved some sort of achievement award for refraining from decking the slimy motherfucker in his slimy face the second she'd seen him in Liam's ceremony hall, sipping a finger of synthetic whisky and sharing stories about her husband's achievements as though he wasn't to blame for the mockery of Ascent that had taken place that awful night.

Or maybe it wasn't a mockery of Ascent, at all.

Maybe this is what Ascent had always truly been.

A dangerous thought that made her pulse quicken and her stomach churn. She pushed it away.

Liv kept her DO NOT DISTURB PROTOCOL engaged for her entire commute home from work. Music blasted her eardrums—*60 BPM to synchronize with her heart rate and produce alpha brainwaves—*

as her unicomm broadcasted signals to anyone nearby indicating that she was not to be bothered. She only lifted the protocol when she reached the door to her townhome. Liv paused there, taking a shuddering breath as a wave of memories washed over her, clear as a holovid.

October 22nd, 2342:

Liam stood in the doorway of the townhome, knocking on the door frame. "Solid construction."

Liv huffed a laugh. "Oh, that's right, I forgot you were a foreman."

Liam raised a hand to his chest in mock offense. "Are you saying I can't be a foreman?"

Liv ducked under his arm, standing on her tiptoes to press a peck to his lips. She still remembered how his stubble had poked, just a little. "You can be whatever you want, oh genius husband of many skills."

"That's more like it."

Liv's eyes welled with tears. They had put the offer in on the townhome that day. Almost six years ago. It felt like yesterday. Her perfect memory had never felt more like a curse. It was like Liam was still here with her, only he lived purely inside her head now. It felt like a punch to her stomach every time she remembered she would never again see him walk through the door or feel his arms wrap around her or feel how his lips smiled against hers when they kissed.

When she remembered she would never hold their child in her arms. How could the Algorithm do this so soon after promising them their greatest wish?

"Liv."

The sound of her name startled Liv out of her miserable reverie. Ayla stood in the doorway of the neighboring townhome, both hands resting on top of her swollen belly.

"You're getting home late," her friend observed.

She was right. It was now well past nightfall—several hours after Liv would normally arrive home from work. Funny how there was no reason to leave work when there was nothing to come home to.

"Oh, you know," she said, forcing her tone to stay light. It sounded faker than synthetic honey. "Just a busy week at the office."

"Right…" Ayla said. There was a pause nearly as pregnant as she was. Then, "I'm sorry about Liam."

Sorry?

Liv blinked. It was the first time anyone had ever expressed anything but joy over Liam's Ascent. It felt wrong—alien and uncomfortable.

Or perhaps she was just telling herself that it did.

She pushed the feeling down.

"It's all right—he achieved everything he was meant to achieve. New Avarita will remember him as a successful contributor." Her voice sounded as hollow as she felt.

"I'm sure they will," Ayla said slowly. "If you ever need someone to, ahm… reminisce with…"

She left the sentence unfinished. Liv nodded. "I'll keep it in mind."

What was Ayla playing at? She had been acting off ever since her own husband was selected for Ascent a few months ago. Had she somehow infected Liv with whatever unnatural thoughts were plaguing her? Either way, there was no way she was going to talk to Ayla about this. Not here, not now. It was impossible to know what digital ears might be listening, and the things on the tip of Liv's tongue, threatening to burst from her like vomit, were not things she should say to anyone—not even Ayla.

They were the kind of treasonous thoughts that could get someone chucked in a madhouse at best. Or shackled to some machinery in one of those rehabilitation facilities.

Muttering a quick "goodbye," Liv slipped through her door, turning around to slam it shut and engage the locks as fast as possible, just in case Ayla tried to pursue the conversation further. She pressed her back to the door, eyes squeezed shut, waiting for the *knock, knock…* but it didn't come.

Relief and disappointment flooded Liv's veins in equal measure and she slid down the door, coming to rest on the cold, tile floor. The townhome was far too dark. Liv had turned off all the holographic frames the day after Liam's ceremony. She didn't need the pictures to remember her husband, and every time she found herself face-to-face with his broad grin and twinkling eyes she started crying so hard she threw up. But the photos weren't the only issue. The whole townhome was filled with more memories than Liv could bear. She hadn't been able to bring herself to set foot in the kitchen since that night.

Luckily, she didn't feel much like eating, anyway. She felt like there was too much grief clogging her throat, like mucus, making it impossible to swallow, to breathe. *She wasn't supposed to feel this way.* He had made it to the end goal. He'd been selected for Ascent. It was the ideal ending for every person in New Avaritan society.

But the longer Liv thought about it, the more certain she was that Liam's "Ascent" was bullshit.

Liam hadn't reached his potential—he had just been getting started. He could have revolutionized the transport system in New Avarita, if he'd had the chance. More than that, he could have spent the next thirty years being a kickass husband—a kickass *father,* raising a little genius that could have changed the course of New Avarita's future.

Liv brought her feet up, crossing her legs and tucking her toes tightly underneath her, the way she used to sit as a child. What happened to Liam hadn't been Ascent. Not the Ascent she'd spent her entire life learning about. The more she thought about it, the more she thought something shady was going on. She remembered how Liam had gotten nervous telling her about what had resulted in his firing. About the "fake" grow domes. About Brinnings Media being owned by Vinco. About how so many of the corporations in New Avarita were actually the same company, just hiding under different names and identities. He hadn't wanted to share all the details with her, at the time. She remembered the fear in his eyes. Could he have been scratching at the surface of some inevitable truth? Something he wasn't supposed to know? And then, he'd been...eliminated.

Switch'd.

A shiver ran through Liv at the word. She looked over her shoulder, like she was worried someone had heard the word, even though she hadn't said it out loud.

It was a word that people didn't use in polite company—a word people didn't use in *any* company, really. A slang term for Ascent she'd heard people once used, back in New Avarita's infancy. A term used by people who didn't have faith in Lucre's Algorithm or the rule of the first Principal Chairman. A slang term Liv wasn't sure she'd ever heard used outside of a history lesson or a news report. She paused, then straightened. No, that wasn't exactly right. There was one other person she'd seen drop that term before. And they had dropped it so casually, she was certain they had used it a thousand times in their life.

Without bothering to get up from her position, slumped against the front door, Liv tapped her temples. The cold, lonely entry hall of her home disappeared, replaced by the barren deserts of *Wasteland Warriors*. Her avatar barely had time to stretch out her animated arms before a message blinked on the screen.

<RinthRat12: Hey, stranger. I was starting to think the WasteBeasts got you.>

Liv huffed a mirthless laugh. Her entire world might have shattered with Liam's Ascent, but the world of *Wasteland Warriors* was the same as always. Maybe she should just live here—stay inside the game, living in the illusion, pretending nothing had happened. Maybe, if she stayed here long enough, she would close out of her VR to find herself curled up in her gaming chair with Liam napping in his own chair beside her.

But she hadn't come here to live in a fantasy. Not even one as appealing as that one. She took a deep breath, stretching out her fingers and hesitating, just for a moment. *Penalty for treason: three years of manual labor for reconditioning at best. Prem-death by Correxion Group firing squad at worst.*

Fuck it.

<LivStruck_99: My partner got switch'd.>

Four simple words. Four words that could destroy her life if RinthRat12 wasn't as open-minded as she thought they were. But her life was already destroyed. Putting that pain and doubt into words felt good the same way muscle soreness felt good—pain that felt more like progress than defeat.

For several long moments, RinthRat12 said nothing. Liv's heart thudded in her chest, drowning all thought with the steady thrum of blood rushing over her eardrums. Had she misread her anonymous friend? *The townhome was four point six miles from the closest Correxion facility. The emergency line traveled at seventy miles per hour. It would take officers three minutes and fifty-six seconds minimum to arrive.*

The in-game messaging history suddenly wiped the last message, then closed out altogether. Liv's stomach curdled, but before she had the chance to panic in earnest, she had a new invite from an application she'd never heard of: R0D3NT.

She accepted it dimly, entering a skeletal application with only two options; message and call. There was a message from RinthRat12 waiting for her.

Liv swallowed. Then, she opened the message.

<RinthRat12: Do you want to do something about it?>

She scoffed. There was nothing to *do* about it. Not even the richest bastard in the Core could bring back the dead. RinthRat12 seemed to guess her thoughts, because another message followed within seconds.

<RinthRat12: I didn't ask if you wanted to reverse it. I asked if you wanted to do something about it.>

<User29: Like what?>

Another pause. Then:

<RinthRat12: Revenge.>

For a moment, Liv stared at the screen, listening to the surge of blood pounding through her veins. Revenge. Revenge against whom?

But she already knew the answer: Reid.

That slimy bastard had cost Liam his job. He had cost Liam his *life*. He had stolen her husband, her future, her *child*, from her. And he was still strutting around the Core, walking the halls of Vinco Telecom like he owned the damned place, kissing his wife and kids goodnight every evening.

Her heart rate slowed as cold fury replaced her panic and grief. She *did* want revenge. She wanted to make Reid Allen pay for his crimes if it was the last thing she did on this earth.

<User29: How?>

All RinthRat12 sent back was an address and a name:

4287 GLEN RD. SIGNE REMY.

<User29: When?>

<RinthRat12: How fast can you get there?>

Liv didn't even say 'goodbye,' just numbly closed out of her VR environment and leaning her head back against the door. She stared up at the ceiling of her entry hall for several long minutes.

She had never heard of Glen Road before. A quick rinth search showed her the location was in Lower Baranthrum. She'd never been there before, but she knew of it. The people in the other districts of New Avarita often said the name of the southeastern district softly, like it was a curse. She could have queried the rinth for more info on the district, but her near-perfect memory had snagged onto a few snippets from news broadcasts and articles Liam had talked about over the years.

86% of all crime in New Avarita happened in Lower Baranthrum. The violent crime rates were 643% higher there than in Upper Lucara. 79% of violent crime victims in Lower Baranthrum were women.

Lower Baranthrum was a different world. Drugs, bootleg mech-enhancements, and illegal weapons were nearly as common as water down there, according to the news feeds. It would be foolish for a lone woman to meet a stranger there any time of day. After dark? She was practically asking for prem-death.

So why was she standing up and shrugging into a dark, hooded sweatshirt? Why was she kicking off her loafers and lacing up a pair of old, beat-up running shoes? She didn't know what she should wear to look like she "belonged" in Lower Baranthrum, but at least the outfit she picked was comfortable and easy to run in.

Though, if she found herself needing to run, she was probably already as good as dead.

The Lobos station was quiet when Liv stepped onto the platform. She checked the board. The next train heading south would arrive in seven minutes. A group of youngsters, about university age, were already on the platform, no doubt waiting to take the train into the Core for a night of partying. A pair of them were clearly a couple, teasing each other as they waited for the train, much to the annoyance of the rest of their group.

A pang shot through Liv as her imagination superimposed hers and Liam's faces over the couple. They had been just as young and obnoxiously in love when they were at university together.

She shook the thought from her head, looking away from the group of college kids and out over the rest of the empty platform instead. On a weekend, there would be far more people here, heading into the Core for a night out. On a Tuesday, however, the only people over the age of thirty were the guards running security.

Liv wasn't the only one who noticed that.

One of the Correxion officers had her eye on Liv. The fingers of the guard's left hand twitched. Was she looking Liv up in the system? Referencing her facial scan against her records to try to ID her without scanning her chip? Liv resisted the urge to pull her hood up. *Relax.* There was nothing illegal about her boarding a train at any hour. New Avarita had no curfews.

Still, she was glad there was no train straight from Upper Lucara to Lower Baranthrum. If the guard was suspicious now, imagine how she'd feel if Liv boarded a train making a straight shot to the criminal hub of New Avarita? But no, it would just look like she was heading to the Core. She could be meeting a friend for drinks. Even going on a date—it wouldn't be the fastest she'd seen someone move on after their partner reached Ascent.

She regretted that thought the moment she had it. Her chest seemed to compress as the crushing weight of the idea of spending the rest of her life alone—or, worse, with someone *else*—joined the acute pain of Liam's absence.

The train ride to the Core took forty minutes. They stopped at three other stations in Upper Lucara, picking up a dozen more university students. The youngsters spent the ride singing along to music someone was playing through their unicomm's external speakers and taking what they probably thought were clandestine sips from the bottles tucked in their sleeves. Liv spent the ride with her forehead pressed against the train window, wondering if she was actually unafraid of what she was about to do, or just *so* afraid her brain had short-circuited.

She had longer than that forty-minute ride to consider the question. At the station in the Core, she switched trains, taking the 362 to the central transport station in Old Altum, the district southwest of the Core. From Old Altum, it was another two train switches before her transport finally hummed to a stop at the station in the northeast quadrant of Lower Baranthrum.

The later it got and the farther south she went, the more Liv's nerve began to waver. The further she got from the Core, the older and more unkempt the trains were. Where the ones in the Core and Upper Lucara were gleaming, silent, and new, the transports here were rusted and creaky. Irresponsible university students and harried, overworked businesspeople were traded out for technicians and Medla workers, then for a scruffier sort of clientele whose roles in the New Avaritan economy were harder to discern.

Liv exited the train, glancing up at the flickering lights struggling far too hard to keep the transport station from plunging into utter blackness. The Correxion officers on duty here weren't polished or pressed like the ones back in Upper Lucara. If the Upper Lucaran guards were security dogs, these ones were more like wolves. They wore the same uniform, but their eyes were sharper and they held their armguns more readily, like they had already used them tonight and wouldn't hesitate to do it again.

It could be true, for all Liv knew.

The streets of Lower Baranthrum couldn't be more different from the ones Liv was used to walking. Neon signs buzzed on nearly every building, screaming names like CIRCUITS UNLEASHED and CYBERNETIC SANCTUARY. Dark, pulsing music pounded through the alleys, coming from a dozen different nightclubs and filthy bars.

"Where are you sending me, RinthRat?" Liv muttered to herself, shrinking further back into her hood as a man who desperately needed alcohol filters catcalled her from the doorway of an establishment called *SoundSonick* (though the sign actually read SO---S--ICK, with the burned-out letters). She'd memorized her route on the trip here, so she didn't even need to tap into her unicomm for directions as she wound through the grimy streets.

Two lefts, one right, one more left. There's Glen Road.

When Liv caught sight of her destination, she let out a soft huff of incredulous laughter. It was nearly midnight now, and she was in one of the darkest corners of all of New Avarita, sent on a mission by a stranger from the rinth for the purpose of exacting revenge on the people responsible for her husband's death. With all the things she'd seen up to this point, she had been half-expecting some sort of drug den or illicit mech-enhancement shop to be the end point of her journey.

Instead, she found herself faced with a quaint-looking tea shop.

The shop was sandwiched between a monolith of neon light and pulsing music called *The Fall* and the kind of pawn shop where Liv would expect to find at least a dozen weapons that had been used in unsolved prem-deaths for sale. She caught a glimpse of the sign hanging above the pawn shop's door and choked, somewhere between a sob and a laugh. It was called *The Prawn Shop,* and the logo featured a shrimp in sunglasses.

Liam would have loved that pun.

Liv pushed the thought away, avoiding eye contact with the pawn shop clerk through the grimy window as she stepped forward and pushed the door to the tea shop open.

It was surprisingly well-insulated, the sounds of gentle lo-fi piping through the tea shop's speakers somehow drowning out the pulsing beats and shouting drunks from the club next door. A soft jingle sounded as Liv closed the door behind her and, for a moment, she wondered if maybe she had fallen asleep slumped over on her entry way floor and this was all some kind of strange, stress-induced fever-dream.

This shop wouldn't have been out of place in Upper Lucara—maybe even the Core. The sounds of steaming milk and boiling kettles mingled with the soft music. The air smelled like chai with a hint of vanilla. A dozen small tables dotted the room surrounded by overstuffed chairs.

Despite the fact that it was after midnight, the shop bustled with energy. The man behind the counter was in constant motion, his mech-enhanced left arm seemingly moving of its own accord, selecting scoops of loose tea leaves from various jars and preparing kettles while his organic right hand tapped out prices and scanned for payments.

"You looking for someone?"

Liv jerked herself out of her trance. She spun on a heel, looking for the speaker. A woman lounged on one of the overstuffed chairs, a steaming cup of what looked like green tea held in one hand.

The woman could have starred in just about any holofilm about the thugs of Lower Baranthrum. She was tall and lanky and dressed in an ill-fitting jumpsuit, one arm mech-enhanced, one organic, both equally scarred and scuffed. Her dark, curly hair was pulled back into a careless ponytail, leaving some gray-streaked ringlets to frame her severe-looking face. Liv gulped as she caught sight of what looked like a rifle barrel poking out from behind her right shoulder.

"N-no," Liv lied.

"No point lying about it," the woman said. Her eyes flicked up and down Liv, examining her from head to toe. "Even if Emerson hadn't told me you'd be coming, I'd have known from first glance that you weren't Lower Baranthrum stock. You stick out worse than a malfunctioning mech finger." The woman wiggled one of her own mechanical fingers to illustrate.

Liv thought that, of the two of them, the battle-scarred woman before her stuck out a hell of a lot worse than she did in this posh-looking tea joint, but she wasn't about to say so—especially not to a woman openly carrying an illegal weapon in the most dangerous part of New Avarita.

The fear Liv had been surprised not to feel all night since leaving her townhome finally crashed over her all at once. What was she doing here?

"I-I don't know anyone named Emerson," she said. "Sorry, I—"

"Yeah, you do," the woman interrupted. "You and our little rinth rat go way back."

Liv swallowed. So, RinthRat12's real name was Emerson. Shooting a glance over each shoulder, she took a tentative step toward the woman's table. "You're Signe Remy?"

"I am," the woman cocked her head and drained her teacup. "And you're Liv Spencer. Now, are we going to play the Name Game all fucking night, or are you ready to get down to business?"

Liv's eyes grew wide and she lunged forward, perching anxiously on the edge of the overstuffed chair across from Signe. "How do you know my name?"

The woman appeared amused. "You knew mine."

"RinthRa—Emerson told me yours."

"We have that in common, then." Signe waved her mech-arm at the man behind the counter, flashing two titanium-plated fingers. He nodded, grabbing two delicate porcelain cups and filling them with tea before sending them over on the tray of one of the assistant mechs buzzing through the shop, clearing mugs and delivering fresh tea.

"How did Emerson know my name?" Liv wondered aloud. But it was a stupid question, really. The *Wasteland Warriors* accounts were anonymous, but her account was still linked to her chip. A hacker who knew what he was doing could probably strip her identity from her game profile.

She just would never have thought RinthRat12—Emerson—would have done that to her.

Signe pushed herself upright, grabbing the teas and depositing one in front of Liv. She leaned forward, resting her elbows on her knees. "He knows a lot more than that, Liv."

"Like what?"

"Like the fact that you work for Berger Security. You take the 214-transport home every day. Your partner was a senior news brief writer for Vinco Telecom."

Liv's stomach dropped into a pit of bubbling acid. Betrayal and terror warred for control of her mind. She'd been so stupid. She had talked to this Emerson person on the rinth for years, but she didn't *really* know him. Then, when he told her to go to a mysterious address in the most dangerous part of the city-state in the middle of the damn night, she had just trusted him?

You're smarter than this, Liv.

"What do you want?" she asked, lowering her voice. "I don't have much coin, but I can transfer you—"

Signe Remy laughed. It was a surprisingly pleasant sound, low and melodic. She gestured around the tea shop. "Do we look like we need your coin?"

"You… run this shop?" Liv asked, perplexed.

"I don't, but my boss does," Signe answered simply. "And the club next door. And about a dozen other places in this part of the city. We're doing just fine." She cocked her head to one side, tapping her right wrist to indicate her unicomm. "From Emerson's message, it sounded like you were the one who needed something."

"No, I…" Liv started, then cut herself off. She had lost all her nerve in the past few minutes, but that was stupid. This Emerson person already knew who she was, and he knew the treasonous, anti-Algorithm thoughts spinning through her head. Or, at least he could surmise them based on what she'd told him. She had already trekked the entire length of New Avarita, put herself in harm's way at least a dozen times.

There was no point in backing out now.

She gathered every ounce of courage she had in her exhausted body, then looked back up at Signe. She felt a fire ignite behind her eyes as she pictured Liam's limp form, lifeless in their home. "Emerson said you could help me get revenge."

Signe's face split into a crooked grin. Unlike her warm laugh a few moments ago, this smile looked dangerous: icy as a walkway in wintertime, sharp enough to cut glass. "Revenge is something of a specialty of mine." She took a sip of her tea, leaning back in her chair and crossing one ankle over the opposite knee. "What did you have in mind?"

"I want to hire a hit."

Liv didn't know that was her intention in coming here until the words were out, but once she said them she knew with complete certainty that this was the reason she had left her townhome and boarded that first train. Liam was dead, not because he'd reached his full potential, or even in retribution for something he'd done. He was dead because of one man.

"A hit," Signe repeated, stroking the side of her neck. "That's a bold thing to ask for in a crowded tea shop."

Liv blanched, looking around nervously, but no one there appeared to notice or care about her conversation.

Signe was evidently not all that concerned either, because all she said next was, "Who's the target?"

"Reid Allen." He was the one who had fucked up, if anyone should have paid the price for that it was him.

She couldn't change what had happened to Liam, but if she could make Reid pay that price now, she would.

Across the table, Signe Remy started laughing. It wasn't the same infectious, genuine laugh from before. This one was mirthless and mocking.

"What?" Liv demanded, forcing herself to sit upright, spine stiff, chin high.

Signe pointed at her with the hand holding her teacup. "You just said you don't have much coin a few minutes ago. Now you want to hire out a hit on Eliza Vinco's fuckbuddy?" She shook her head. "No way."

Eliza Vinco's fuckbuddy. That wasn't a rumor Liv had heard before. Reid was married, after all, had a whole troupe of kids, from what she knew. Of course, if he was scum enough to do what she suspected he'd done to Liam, he was probably scum enough to cheat on his wife, too. Especially if it would get him ahead… and sleeping with someone as powerful as Eliza Vinco would definitely help him get ahead. Liv wondered briefly how this thug from Lower Baranthrum knew more Core gossip than she did.

"How much coin would I need?"

"There isn't an amount of coin in the entire rinth that would convince me to do a hit in the Core right now."

Liv clenched her jaw, frustrated. "Emerson told me to come find you. He told me you could help me get revenge for what happened to—"

Signe held up a hand, stopping her mid-sentence. "See, revenge I can still help you with."

"I'm not interested in revenge that doesn't result in Reid Allen's prem-death," Liv said. The coldness in her tone surprised her, but she really meant what she said.

"Is Reid Allen *really* the cause of all your pain, girl?"

Girl. This woman couldn't be more than five or ten years older than Liv was. "Who else would—"

"Tell me," Signe leaned forward, setting her half-empty teacup on the table between them and resting her elbows on her knees, "do you think a simple firing was worthy of a death sentence before the Fall?"

"That's not really relev—"

"But it is relevant," Signe interrupted her yet again. Her olive-green eyes flashed in the warm light of the tea shop. "Reid Allen is probably an asshole, but he's not the cause of your problem here. He's just a symptom of the real problem." Signe tapped the base of her skull—the place where every New Avaritan's chip lay, embedded in their flesh.

Liv paused. She opened her mouth to answer, then closed it again. Just a few days ago, she would have dismissed this woman as one of those crazy revolutionaries, the ones that were always labeled "terrorists" and imprisoned or put to prem-death as soon as they were sussed out. And while there was no doubt in Liv's mind that the woman *was* a crazy revolutionary, she wasn't sure she was ready to dismiss her ideas just yet.

"There's a man with a plan to change the future of New Avarita. A plan to oust the Board, destroy Lucre's stupid fucking killswitch for good, and build a new system of government from the ground up." Signe leaned back. "A plan we're hoping you'll help us with."

Liv let out a huff of laughter that was more perplexed than amused. She'd only understood half of what the other woman said, and the parts she did understand made little to no sense to her. "Signe… Ms. Remy… I've never even held a gun before, I don't think you need—"

"We've got plenty of people who can hold a gun just fine," Signe said, waving her comment away with her mechanical hand. "You've got something our boss finds way more valuable," Signe said. "The blueprints to Huldra Industries' headquarters, half the Medla House facilities in the upper districts, Koegen Corp production lines, the fucking Medial Complex."

Liv's stomach dropped, the blood draining from her face. "I'm not—"

Signe plowed on, "What's more, from what I hear, you have a photographic memory, which means that all the information we need to stop spinning our wheels and actually get our plan in motion," she leaned forward tapping Liv's temple, "is right in here."

Liv jerked away from Signe's hand. "How… how do you know all of that?"

The revolutionary picked her tea back up, smirking. "Do you think it's a coincidence you happened to meet our little rinth rat in *Wasteland Warriors,* Liv?" She took a sip. "We've been targeting you for months. Years, really."

We've been targeting you. Liv's head spun. When had she met RinthRat12? It had been over a year ago… Her stomach sank. *One year, three months, and twenty-two days ago.* Two days after her team had finished the Medial Complex job.

How had she not seen it?

Betrayal and embarrassment warred for control of her thoughts. Emerson had only kept in contact with her to keep tabs on her. To watch for a moment of weakness, then lure her into some dark and horrible underworld plot. And she'd fallen for it, hook, line, and sinker.

"If..." Liv's voice came out small and squeaky. She cleared her throat, straightening in her chair, then tried again. "And if I decide I don't want to join your little terrorist organization, what then? I suppose you'll send someone to kill me?"

They knew where she lived, where she worked, nearly everything about her, from the sounds of it. She wasn't particularly important—even less so now, without Liam's influence. She had no security aside from the standard protocols programmed into every citizen's chip. Whoever the leader of this shadowy organization was, if he wanted her dead, she had no doubt that he could make it happen.

"You're the one who came here for a hit," Signe reminded her. "But no. We tend to leave the pointless killing to the Board and their cronies. If you're out, the door's there."

There it was again—the mention of this 'Board.' But Liv didn't want to ask a single unnecessary question. She just wanted to get the hell out of this tea shop. This had been a waste of time. A pointless risk. A risk Liam would have hated her for taking on his behalf. She needed to get out of here. Now.

She pushed herself to her feet, setting her undrunk tea back on the table. "I'm not interested in dying for your doomed revolution," she said.

"Dying for the profits of the Board more suitable to you, then?" Signe asked. She took another sip of her tea, then shrugged. "That's fine. If you change your mind, come back here and say you're a friend of Torrin's looking for Signe."

"I'll do that," Liv said tersely.

She left the tea shop without another word.

06

REINA

The Algorithm always knows what is best for New Avarita and its people, but for our great city-state to remain pure, its outputs need to be implemented with care and consideration. It is up to the Principal Chairman and any board of advisors that surround them to make well-considered interpretations of the Algorithm's outputs, then implement them in a fashion that creates the best path forward for all.

—THE HANDBOOK OF LUCRE, *CHAPTER* 33

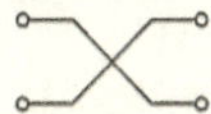

THE ADVISORY BOARD is called to order for an emergency meeting on this, the twenty-first of March, 2348—"

"Let's leave the theatrics to the holovid actors, Cora," Reina said drily, cutting off the Teras exec mid-monologue. "Can we get to the reason why you have dragged us away from our vital work and into these stifling chambers?"

In truth, the Board Room wasn't stifling at all. It was a beautiful space in the heart of the Medial Complex. The room was furnished with an imported mahogany table, lush carpeting, and stained-glass windows in the style of the late 2200s. It was kept at a comfortable temperature year-round, spotless, and filled with the scent of fresh flowers, but every moment spent in this room was more dangerous than walking the darkest alley in Lower Baranthrum.

Together, the Board was strong. They were the rulers of New Avarita—the creators of the Principal Chairman and the authors of the scripts the fictional figurehead recited in all his public addresses. But if any person in this room threatened the strength—or, more importantly, coin—of the others, the rest of the advisors would turn on them faster than a shark turned on a bleeding diver.

Baiting Cora was a risky play, but Reina had done her calculations. Cora Calvin was infamous for being emotional and over-dramatic. She had no place on this Board, honestly, and many of their colleagues surely agreed, whether or not they would say so aloud. Goading her into a show of emotion would send Cora farther down the path of wishing Reina dead, it was true. But alone, she wouldn't have the votes to make that wish a reality.

The gambit paid off almost instantly.

"What have I *dragged* you all here for?" Cora asked. Her white-blonde hair quivered in its bun, like it was embarrassed to be seen with her and was trying to pull itself free of her scalp. Blue-grey eyes bulged from their surgically wrinkleless sockets as the woman slammed a manicured hand on the table. "Theft and *justice,* that's what!"

"Theft and justice," Audrey Lobos repeated flatly. She rubbed the bridge of her nose beneath her glasses. "You're going to have to be a bit more specific, Madam Calvin."

The Teras exec fumed like a schoolgirl for a few seconds. Then, she collected herself and said, "There are two executives in this room capable of answering all your most pressing questions." She shot Reina a meaningful glare.

Reina drummed her nails on the table, the perfectly squared tips producing a satisfying *thunk* as they hit the lacquered wooden surface. "There is one executive in this room who insists upon treating a Board meeting like a homepage piece on a gossip site."

"Yes, out with it, Cora," said Soren Otis. "We have other business to attend to."

He was the head of Propagn Advanced, the energy conglomerate that owned every fuel and electric company in New Avarita. Apart from her own brand, that was. Right now, Xirloc was small enough that Soren largely ignored it. But once Reina got those new enhancements up and running, she would need to either cut Soren in or box him out entirely. If she attempted to initiate true competition with another advisor on the Board, she'd find herself in even more dire straits than the ones she was currently mired in. But that was a crisis for another day.

Cora lifted her chin another fraction of an inch, like she was physically encouraging the man's disdain to roll off her back. "I spent a good amount of coin on a shipment of copper wiring from the Federation of South Brasilia," she started. "A shipment that was diverted upon arrival. Instead of arriving as scheduled at the central Teras plant, it was sent to a subsidiary of Huldra Industries. Reina has undermined me. I believe she seeks to sour my relationship with the Federation."

The rest of the advisors pivoted to face Reina. Trade with the outside world had been fraught even in the days before the Fall. But now? Interfering with another advisor's trade relations with a foreign federation was tantamount to high treason.

Ever since Reina had taken her seat on the Board and made it clear she had no interest in playing Cora Calvin's stupid little games, the Teras exec had been waiting for an opportunity to vote Reina out of her seat. And now, seventeen years later, she had finally found it. From the smirk on her face, she knew it, too.

Still, Reina remained calm. The facts were on her side. She had not interfered with Cora's shipments. If she had, she would have been smarter about it than simply diverting an entire order straight to her front door. Besides, she had her own relationship with the Federation of South Brasilia—if she set her mind to it, she could blackball the Teras executive altogether. The idea that she would stoop to petty theft instead of any number of more intelligent tactics she might have deployed was so insulting she could almost forget the danger of the situation she was in.

"Madam Calvin," said Eliza Vinco, "this is a serious accusation to leverage against a fellow advisor of the Board." The head of Vinco Telecom had almost as much of a penchant for the dramatic as Cora. All those holovids she produced must have bled right into her skull, bad acting and all.

"Yes," said Jasper Koegen of KoegenCorp, owner of every major food production company in New Avarita. "Our relations are already tenuous with the Russo-Europa Empire, and we've lost the Western Confederation altogether. We don't need the Federation to the south to turn on us, as well."

"It would be grounds for a vote to see if the Principal Chairman would like to select a new advisor for the tech sector," Lobos said, as though the Principal Chairman existed outside of a rinth program and the peoples' imagination. But the insinuation was clear.

"It might be, were it true," Reina said. She leaned back in her chair, leveling a stare at Cora Calvin. Her severe, auburn-colored hair framed her face, just skimming her shoulders as she tapped her fingernails on the table again. "Where is your proof of wrongdoing?"

Cora blinked those aging doe-eyes of hers. "Proof? Reina, the proof is the cargo crate of copper wiring that is currently sitting in your warehouse instead of mine."

"I don't mean proof of a logistical mix-up, Cora," Reina said tightly. "I mean proof of my meddling with the Federation." She cocked her head to one side. "Do you have unicomm logs indicating my intent to steal your crates of scraps? What about written orders from me indicating the re-routing of the shipment? Or communications between myself and Master Amos regarding the defense of the shipment while in transit?"

"Now, hold on just a moment—" Winston Amos of Grimme-Folson United started.

Reina held up a hand. "Relax, Winston. No one is suggesting you did anything of the sort. I'm simply making a point. For me to truly go over Cora's head in this manner, it would require cooperation from multiple parties in this room." She gestured across the table toward Socie-Corp's CEO. "Clement would need to convert my New Avaritan coin into Federation dollars. Audrey, your people would need to assist in transporting the shipment to the Core rather than Austrum… you see my point."

She turned to face Cora again. "Do you truly believe that I have somehow organized half the Board in defiance of you for the purpose of stealing a shipment worth what, two million coin? Or does it seem more reasonable that there was a simple mix-up at the docks?"

The Board Room was silent for several long heartbeats. Fear coiled around Reina's chest like a python, squeezing tighter and tighter until she felt like she couldn't breathe. Still, she kept her face flat, one eyebrow raised just a hair in a mask of calm incredulity. After another long moment, Cora final relented.

"I expect to be repaid in full," was all she said, her jaw so tight the tendons in her neck looked at risk of snapping like overtaxed rubber bands.

"Yes, yes, of course, Reina said, waving her hand. "I think I have two million coin in my petty account."

Several other Board members laughed at that. Cora, unsurprisingly, was not one of them. She still had her lips pursed in a petulant frown.

"I also expect that we will take appropriate action against the person who caused this headache in the first place," Cora said.

"And who might that be?" asked Soren Otis.

Cora considered for a moment, then turned to face Audrey Lobos.

"Madam Lobos, who is in charge of dock management at ShipRight these days?"

Audrey sighed, as though this whole conversation was beneath her. Then she twitched the fingers on her right hand. Holographic records for the Lobos subsidiary responsible for the docks flashed in front of her eyes, projecting from her eye enhancements as she scrolled through them. "Someone called Catherine Pierson," she finally said. "Forty-four years old, been with ShipRight for... twenty-three of them."

"All in favor of termination for Miss Catherine Pierson?" Cora asked.

"Mrs. Catherine Pierson," Audrey corrected.

A wife, then. Maybe a mother, too. Reina's stomach twisted. She pushed the feeling away. It was only business.

Audrey made a case for the woman—for how expensive it would be for her to train a replacement now, right before the chaos of the impending hurricane season—but Cora wouldn't budge. Of course she wouldn't. She had already lost one battle today. If she couldn't have Reina Arthur's head on a platter, she would settle for Catherine Pierson's, but she wouldn't settle for anything less. She wouldn't settle for anything short of blood.

"Let's just put it to a vote so we can move on, shall we?" Winston said tiredly. "All in favor of early termination for Mrs. Catherine Pierson?"

Cora's hand shot up faster than a teacher's pet in primary school. One by one, the rest of the Board member's hands followed suit. Reina's hand was among them the moment she saw five others up. The majority had spoken, and it never paid to be a dissenting voice on the Board.

"All opposed?" Winston asked. There were no hands left to raise. Winston nodded. "Alright, it's settled then." He tapped the table in front of him, bringing up a holographic interface and navigating to pull up Lucre's Algorithm.

Lines and lines of code scrolled past. The Ascent Program. A listing of every living person in New Avarita, their health, their professional achievements, their personal lives and connections.

The Algorithm sorted through all this information, continually assessing and adjusting, predicting which society members were contributing and which were not. Which members of society had peaked and which were still rising. Who was still profitable and who was simply a drain on resources. No one was safe from Lucre's Algorithm, technically not even the Board members themselves. The only people who did not appear in the calculations were those who were already dead.

The Board Room was the only location in all of New Avarita where the program could be accessed or altered, and even so, it was done only rarely.

Though less and less rarely, of late, Reina noted bleakly.

Winston Amos tapped through the system, navigating until he located the record of one Catherine Pierson. All it took was a few taps of the holographic keyboard in front of him, after that. He selected her record, then hit "override," then "execute."

And just like that, somewhere in New Avarita, Catherine Pierson would have slumped over where she stood.

"Alright, *now* can we get to more important business?" Winston said, closing the program and cocking his head at Cora impatiently.

Sated by the blood she'd managed to spill, Cora Calvin nodded primly, settling back in her chair.

"Thank you," Winston said mockingly. "I've received word that the President of Atlantica is amassing forces."

He was referencing the nation-state northeast of New Avarita—their closest neighbor and most aggressive enemy.

"We've intercepted no less than four attempts to breach the rinth this month alone," Eliza added.

The rinth was accessible only within New Avarita, and it was the only network New Avaritan people could access. There were wider networks available, enabling connection to the outside world, but like the Ascent Program, they could only be accessed by the people sitting in this room.

If Atlantica managed to breach the rinth and spread their propaganda within New Avarita, the Board could have an uprising on their hands. It was easy enough to arrest a noisy rebel, send a detractor or two off with an early Ascent like they had just done to Mrs. Catherine Pierson, but they could hardly kill their entire population.

Imagine the profits lost from lost labor alone.

"What if we retrain the H-17 to focus on Baltimore?" asked Clement, naming the capitol of Atlantica. "As a warning?"

"Then what would focus on the central cities of the Russo-Europa Empire?" Cora asked.

"We have a trade relationship with them, we have no relationship with Atlantica," Reina cut in. It might be worth the risk.

New Avarita was small, but when it came to international relations, they had a distinct advantage: their arsenal. Before the Fall, the country that sat on this land had the largest nuclear arsenal in the world—an arsenal now controlled, ostensibly, by the Principal Chairman. An arsenal controlled, in reality, by the people in this very room.

Many of the other nations in the world did not approve of Lucre's Algorithm; of the way New Avarita operated in general. But the missiles trained on city centers around the world kept them at bay. An attempt to poison the minds of the New Avaritan people or interfere with the operations inside their electrically fortified borders would ensure the saboteur's destruction, should the Board prove unstable enough to retaliate. The fact that the rest of the world didn't know what they were capable of meant that most of the foreign nations were smart enough to leave well enough alone.

The idiots in Atlantica seemed to be a different breed.

After several more hours of deliberation, the Board voted eight-to-one (Cora the only dissenting voice—shocking, disagreeing simply to disagree) to retrain the H-17 missile onto Atlantica, sending word to their leadership that future attempts to breach the rinth would not be tolerated.

"It's settled, then," said Otis, leaning back in his chair. "Now, we just need to take care of follow-through."

Follow-through, of course, meant drafting the order and generating the approvals that would, supposedly, come from the Principal Chairman. Within the next hour, the script was written. They watched the rinth-generated holovid of Principal Chairman Waldgrim as he recited the script in the compelling, direct tone they'd programmed him to use. When they were satisfied with the results, they sent the file to the powers that ruled Atlantica and reprogrammed the weaponry accordingly.

And then, the group dismissed themselves. By then, the sun had long sunk beneath the horizon, leaving the Board Room to be lit by the neon glow of the floor tile lights alone. Suppressing a yawn, Reina gathered her jacket from the back of her chair, then stalked out of the Board Room, taking a waiting elevator down to her transport just outside the tower doors.

It was already half-past nine when her transport slid to a stop on its track just outside her building. She would have long missed dinner by now, but perhaps the children hadn't left to return to their own districts just yet. But as her private elevator doors opened into the entryway of the Arthur family penthouse, she knew her meager hopes had been foolish at best.

The penthouse was quiet, the lights dimmed, bathing the carefully curated art collection in elegant shadows. The only sounds were the quiet bubbling of the saltwater fish tank separating the kitchen from the living quarters, and the muted sound of running water coming from the kitchen.

Reina entered the kitchen to find her husband elbows-deep in a sink full of sudsy dishes.

"What are you doing?" she asked. "You know we have mechs for that?" she gestured toward the dormant home-assistance mech, tucked in the corner beside the pantry.

Braxton turned to face her, cocking his head and holding up a particularly sticky-looking pan. "It's like surgery: there are some jobs a mech just can't do as well as a human."

"Right," Reina said. She hung her coat up by the now-sealed

elevator door. She tended to disagree with that assertion. After all, Huldra Industries designed the most advanced robots this world had ever seen. But now was not the time to start a purposeless argument. "How long did I miss the children by?"

"Not long," Braxton said. He glanced at his wrist, checking the time projected there by his unicomm. "Missed Zane by an hour, Alayna by maybe half that long." He resumed his scrubbing and a silence fell between them. "Was it worth it?"

Reina pursed her lips, forming a flat, thin line. *Was it worth it.* As though she'd had a choice in the matter. As though she could have refused Cora Calvin's summons, neglected to defend herself, and lived to tell the tale. If she had not attended that Board meeting, she would have been voted out in absentia. Then, it would have been her slumping onto the dinner table instead of Catherine Pierson.

Her family would have celebrated her Ascent, never knowing the truth. Never fully understanding just how contorted the program had become—how enslaved they all were to it. How they could never escape it. After all, if Reina Arthur couldn't escape the power of the killswitch, no one could.

But Reina said none of this. She simply gave her husband a guarded half-smile and a shrug and said, "Yes, it was."

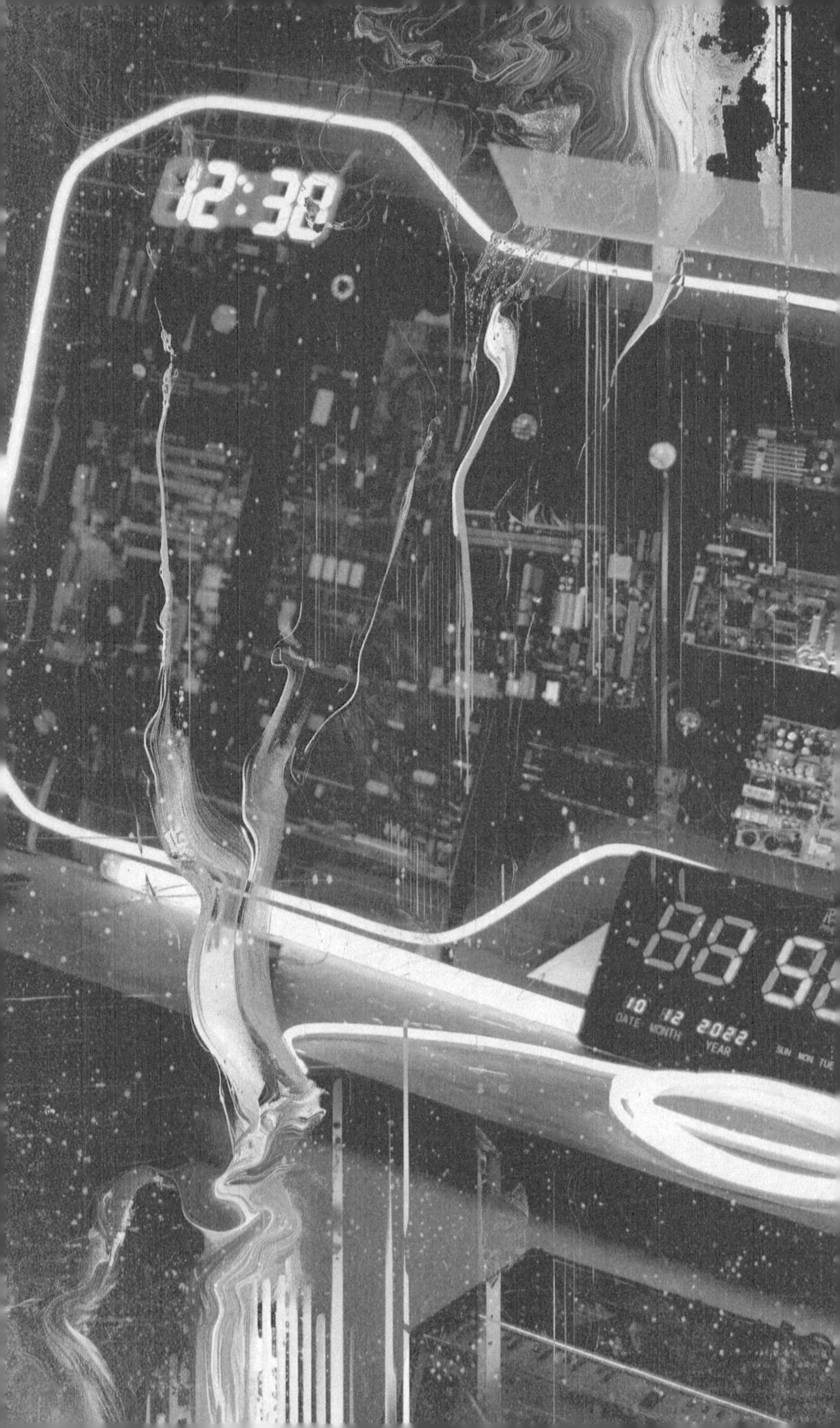
12:38
10 12 2022
DATE MONTH YEAR
SUN MON TUE

07

SIGNE

Community and work ethic are the twin pillars that hold up our great society. The Algorithm will work tirelessly to ensure that the citizens who produce the most value for our society reap the largest rewards until they are worthy of Ascent.

—THE HANDBOOK OF LUCRE, *CHAPTER 7*

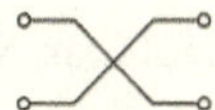

SIGNE WASN'T EXACTLY a fan of any part of Lower Baranthrum, but if she had to pick a least favorite spot, it had to be Romy the Wolf's territory.

It wasn't any dirtier or smellier than any other part of the district, but it had a taint no amount of soap or fresh sea air could ever wash away: traces of sour memories and endless regret. Teen afternoons spent tucked away, high out of her goddamn mind on whatever concoction her friend Dezria had been able to buy off one of Romy's sellers with the coin the pair of them had scraped together.

She hadn't touched the stuff in years, but just being in these dark, run-down alleys again brought it all screaming back. The overwhelming spins and crippling anxiety of a bad trip. The sickness of a come down. And, bizarrely, the aching desire to try it just one more time.

Even people who didn't have memories and regrets like Signe's tended to avoid Romy's territory at all costs. It was a bit of a running joke that Romy was the closest thing Lower Baranthrum had to active government. In reality, the woman was a low life who had boosted herself up onto a pedestal, then held herself there with a tangled web of threats, coercion, and bribery.

Honestly, if it wasn't for her personal history, Signe might have respected the bitch. The kind of grudging, fearful respect mankind had always had for its most dangerous predators.

"Are you sure about this?"

Torrin Calix shot her a sidelong look as they walked down the alley, side by side. He was a good-looking enough man. His light brown hair was cropped close on the sides and long on top in a style that was at least ten years out of fashion, but the neatly kept beard on his face somehow balanced it out. His right arm was covered in tattoos from shoulder to wrist, and, like Signe, his left arm was missing, replaced by a shining mech-enhanced arm. Unlike Signe, his mech-arm was bootleg—and seriously illegal. The forearm held an automatic weapon that might be even more powerful than Signe's beloved gun, Sally.

Not that she'd ever admit that out loud.

"Are you sure Spencer's not coming around?" he asked instead of answering her question.

Signe chewed the inside of her cheek, revisiting her interaction with Emerson's pet project back in the tea shop. She'd seen a hint of steel in the woman... but nowhere near enough. If her husband's death wasn't enough to shock her out of the brainwashing she'd received courtesy of her GenstraCo education, nothing would be.

"Hard to turn a tame beast feral," she said.

"I'd thought with enough motivation, with just a little push, perhaps..." Torrin said, gnashing his teeth.

Signe's stomach turned. *A little push.* The thing that had brought Liv Spencer to Lower Baranthrum was her husband getting switch'd. Torrin couldn't have had anything to do with that, could he?

Spencer had seemed so sure that Reid Allen was to blame. She knew that rat was *not* on Torrin's payroll. But still...

Torrin cocked his head, studying her with his greenish-blue gaze, changing the subject. "I'd hoped Spencer would be more like someone else I know, I guess."

Signe raised a brow. "Are you suggesting that I was tame before I came down here?"

"I'd call a decade of service to the Queen Bitch of the Board 'tame,' wouldn't you?"

"First off, if anyone is Queen Bitch on the Board, it's Cora Calvin." Signe wrinkled her nose. "The most annoying woman in New Avarita, I'd bet my life on it." They took a right at a familiar corner—a burlesque club where Signe had met her last ex. "Secondly, the 'service' you're referring to involved me walking around, armed to the teeth, ready to shoot anyone who looked at Madam Arthur wrong, right?"

Torrin sneered, slipping his hands into his jacket pocket as they rounded another corner, winding deeper and deeper into the heart of Romy's territory. "Doesn't matter how hard she bites, a guard dog still wears her collar and sits on command."

Signe scowled. As usual, the man was right. But if she was a dog, she was a dog who had been kicked one too many times and finally bit back.

She still remembered the final kick like it was yesterday. The one that finally made her wake up from the fever dream she was stuck in and give the middle finger to the Board, the farce that was the 'Principal Chairman,' Lucre's Algorithm, all of it.

She'd spent a decade with Reina Arthur's private security squad, coming on the force just a few months after Reina took over as tech advisor on the Board. During that time, she had learned a great many things the people of New Avarita weren't supposed to know. Chief among them was the fact that the Principal Chairman wasn't real; that New Avarita wasn't run by a charismatic man in a dark blue suit, but by his supposed "advisory board" of powerful executives.

That discovery had shaken her, for sure, but it hadn't been the final push. That had been Marxus.

During her entire time on Reina's security team, she had only one person she would consider a friend. Marxus. The man was an asshole, but that was exactly why she'd liked him—no bullshit.

Marxus wasn't one for fake smiles or sugarcoating. While everyone else listened to Signe stumble through the morning shift announcements every day, trying to bully her rampant dyslexia into submission, Marxus had gone out and bought her an install code for a ReadRight enhancement.

He didn't present the code like a gift, though. Instead, he tossed it to her, saying it was a gift to himself—the gift of *"not waiting ten hours to hear the shift assignments every goddamn morning."*

Signe had considered him a friend from that moment until his last. Until Reina Arthur decided to terminate him. She didn't want him on her squad anymore, and instead of giving him the opportunity to take another gig—sign on with the tubheads over in Correxion Group or offer private security to some rich bastard in Upper Lucara, she'd switch'd him. He was dead on the ground, eyes blank and chip fried before he even got halfway down the front steps of Huldra Industries' headquarters.

That day, Signe had realized two things: first, that everything she'd been raised to believe was a lie she couldn't bear to be responsible for enforcing. And second, that if she tried to leave, she too would be switch'd before she made it to the closest train station.

She liked to think that Marxus would appreciate how she'd used his snarky-ass gift after that. With the help of her ReadRight enhancement, she plowed through half the content on the illegal side of the rinth known as the 'veilrinth.' Eventually, she'd found her way to a man named Emerson Quinn. Once that overgrown string bean found out who she was and the intel she had on the security procedures for the Medial Complex and the advisors on the Board, he'd made his offer. It was the same offer Signe had extended to Liv Spencer the night before. But unlike the prissy upper district woman, Signe had jumped at the chance to escape Reina Arthur and fuck over the Board, bringing the killswitch protocol crashing down around their pride-swollen heads.

"Well, if you're sure Spencer's out, we don't really have another choice," Torrin said. Signe jerked her attention back to the present noting that Torrin had stopped at a street cart. Judging from the smell, they were serving fish katsu—deep-fried fish battered in panko and served on a stick. The man had never been able to resist the chance to stop for a snack at the most inopportune moments.

"Fair enough," she said, sticking her hands in her pockets to wait as Torrin paid the vendor, then moved on, crunching into the fried fish with all the gusto of a starving child. When they were out of the vendor's earshot, she continued. "How much do you trust this contact of yours? Given the neighborhood..." she trailed off meaningfully.

Torrin scoffed, licking the metal stick that had held fish five seconds ago clean and tossing it onto the litter-strewn streets. "I'm not afraid of Romy the Wolf."

There was the trademark cockiness the man was well-known (and hated) for.

"In a hand-to-hand? Neither am I," Signe agreed. "But even you have to admit—the bitch has connections. Connections that could make things... problematic for us."

Romy's drugs had trickled through the streets of Lower Baranthrum for almost three decades now. In all that time, she had never gotten so much as a slap on the wrist from the Board. Rumor had it there was only one of two reasons why: one, a drugged population was a docile population, and the Board wanted to keep the people of Lower Baranthrum as docile as possible, or two, Romy had one of the Board members on the take.

Having worked in the Medial Complex for a decade, Signe knew the truth was actually a mix of both. The Board loved control. People hooked on synthetic drugs were easier to steer like the cattle Lucre's Algorithm and the people who ran it saw them as. Also, Louis Gideon of Medla House made a mint developing addiction therapy treatments to counter Romy's concoctions. The treatments were always batshit expensive and only became available some six months after Romy's newest drug took over New Avarita's streets.

In short, Romy the Wolf had the ear of some very important people. People who believed Signe and Torrin and the rest of the crew at the Penthouse were dead. People who needed to keep believing they were all dead if Torrin's plans were to succeed. If the Board ever discovered they were alive, they would know they'd found a temporary fix to the killswitch system. As soon as someone discovered that, it was all over—for all of them.

Even walking these streets was a risk, not just to their lives, but to their whole operation. It was the kind of reckless thing the Torrin Calix of the past would never have even considered, but the kind of thing today's Torrin Calix was doing more and more frequently.

"True," Signe allowed. She shot a dirty look at a man who stared at the pair of them just a hint too long for her liking. He scowled and looked away. Signe lowered her voice. "But given what we're here for…"'

"We aren't here for shit-poor street drugs," Torrin said flatly.

"No, but we're here for custom-synthed poison. At the end of the day, it's all chemistry, isn't it?"

Everyone on the Board had enhancements to immunize them against common poisons like arsenic and dioxin. That meant if Torrin wanted to assassinate them (and Signe doubted the man wanted anything more in his life, honestly), they'd need to use a new poison—one no one in the Core could defend against, because it was one they didn't know existed.

Signe had tried to draw his attention to the fact that even if this Board died, another one would surely just spring up to take its place.

Just like a new advisor took over one of the nine existing seats when one of the current Board members got switch'd. But that kind of logic wasn't the sort of thing Torrin had the patience for when he got into one of his moods.

"Romy isn't the only chemist in Lower Baranthrum," Torrin said. He didn't elaborate, but that wasn't unusual. After a few more minutes in silence, he came to a stop beside a particularly run-down doorway.

There was no way in Hell Romy would tolerate anything resembling competition on her own turf. However, this building looked more like an abandoned factory than a functioning business. Somehow, the fact that the place looked like it had been chewed up and shat out again made her feel a bit better. Maybe this contact was small-time enough to stay under Romy's radar.

Just as long as they weren't so small-time that their poisons didn't actually *work*. A failed attempt would be worse than ten steps backward, something that would result in increased security at best and their own discovery at worst.

But Torrin Calix thought it was worth a shot. So here they were.

Signe's soldier reflexes kicked in and she took a defensive posture just behind Torrin as he reached for the rusted door and swung it open, entering the warehouse. The inside of the building looked even shittier than the outside. Every piece of machinery worth salvaging had been scrapped from the factory long ago, leaving the space looking like a rotting carcass on the shore, picked clean by the seagulls.

The shelves and the few pieces of machinery left behind were so old and unclean that Signe felt like she would get tetanus just from breathing the air in this place. She resisted the temptation to hold her breath, instead just curling her lip and keeping pace one step behind Torrin, one hand on the rifle slung over her back.

Torrin showed no sign of discomfort. Then again, he'd grown up on Lower Baranthrum's docks, spent his formative years in grimy halfway houses and children's shelters. He'd seen much rougher places than this in his day. He picked his way through the maze of overturned oil drums and splintered pallets until he reached a long, flat counter against the back wall. There was no one behind the counter, nothing there but a stretch of rusted iron plating. But Torrin wasn't deterred.

He rested his right arm on the countertop, reaching over to rap three times on the wall. Almost immediately, a section of the rusted steel wall pulled aside, revealing the face of a woman who could have been anywhere from thirty to sixty years old, depending on how many of Romy's drugs she'd injected in her time on this earth.

"Order?"

"Pick-up," Torrin replied. He pulled up a document on his unicomm, showing it to the woman. Signe craned her neck to read the doc over his shoulder. A communication log—the conversation he'd had with this woman over the veilrinth to place the order. The log was real. The name on the order—HARLAN VIRON—was fake.

The woman examined the log, then gave a grunt of assent. The pull-away panel snapped back into place, leaving her and Torrin ostensibly alone in the factory again. Rustling sounds emerged from the hidden chamber where the woman apparently ran her operation.

Just then, Signe's intuition prickled. She readjusted her grip on Sally, flicking the safety off and toggling to prep her nonlethal rounds. It was her protocol for when she was on alert, but not alarmed just yet. Torrin noticed the shift and raised an eyebrow.

"Everything all right?"

Signe shook her head, frowning. "I don't know."

At that moment, her enforcer-issued hearing enhancements picked up the tell-tale zap of a silenced round on the far side of the panel. The thud that followed confirmed Signe's suspicions. Relying on her muscle memory, Signe whipped Sally up, resting the butt of the gun against her shoulder. She shoved Torrin down just as the panel whipped open again, this time revealing a man with an armgun.

Her pectoral absorbed the kick of her rifle as she fired three shots through the narrow opening. The shots were nonlethal—warning rounds. One found its mark. The man slumped forward, his mech-arm hitting the pitted concrete of the warehouse floor with a heavy *clack*.

"Was that—" Torrin started, but before he could finish his sentence, the back door to the factory burst open again. Signe heard three priming clicks—the sound of three separate armguns or rifles chambering their rounds. Lethals, from the tenor of it; they always had more weight to them than a nonlethal shot.

Three figures stalked toward them through the graveyard of rusted barrels and crates. Two wielded bootleg armguns and the third held a rifle similar to Signe's. The gun was painted—a vibrant yellow mark standing out against the black of the gun. The mark of a howling wolf. Romy's people had tracked down this woman's little operation, it seemed.

Their timing was impeccable.

Signe's eyes flicked back and forth, searching for an escape route. Finally, she found it—a shattered window, some six feet off the ground. She glanced over the crates beside the window. If they'd hold their weight, she and Torrin could climb them to get out the window. As long as they shoulder-rolled on impact, the fall shouldn't fuck them up too much.

Either way, they'd be less fucked up than if they tried to stick it out in the middle of a shoot-out between a poisoner and Romy's gang.

Signe spoke low, aiming the words directly into her wrist, speaking to Torrin through unicomm rather than just aloud so only he could hear. He needed to get out of this building, and he needed to do it right now. She nodded toward the crates and saw in his eyes that he understood.

Torrin Calix was no coward. He didn't like to run when things went to shit, but even he knew that without him, the revolution he was forming would die. So, he primed his armgun and shot two quick rounds at Romy's men. Lethals: Torrin never bothered with nonlethals. He didn't tend to concern himself with shit as trivial as human life unless it was his own. He sprinted across the room and up the crates.

"You coming?" he shouted from the windowsill.

"Let me just clean up first," Signe said. From her tone, she might be talking about clearing the table after dinner. The truth was a bit grimmer than that.

These men needed to be eliminated. Not from life, fortunately, but from the current equation. If she and Torrin just tried to outrun them, they'd be chased down within a few blocks. Romy's people knew these streets better than Signe and Torrin did. They'd know all the side streets and shortcuts, all the sneaky paths that would end up with her facing the business end of a gun barrel again way sooner than she preferred.

Armguns and rifles flashed in the dark as Romy's fighters began to fire. Torrin didn't even look back as he leapt out the window, shattering what was left of the filthy pane and dropping out of sight just as a lethal round embedded itself in the sill.

With Torrin safely out of the way, Signe was free to do what she did best. She ducked in and out of cover, avoiding the near-silent blasts of enemy fire. She needed to get to higher ground for better visibility. The oil drum nearest her would do. She climbed up its side, rolling sideways and adjusting her grip hand-over-hand as Mr. Ugly Gun tried to take her head off with a well-placed shot.

Signe returned fire one-handed, hanging off the lip of the drum with her mech-arm and firing on Mr. Ugly Gun with the other. Her nonlethal round caught him square between the eyes and he dropped like a stone.

She made similarly quick work of the next armgun-wielding man, flipping off the drum to land a few paces in front of him and knocking him out from point-blank range. Thirty seconds into the fight and already Signe was already down to a single opponent? Romy needed to invest in some better talent.

Maybe the three she'd already shot would be suddenly inspired to become less shitty guards when they woke up in a few hours.

Signe whipped around a tower of pallets, gun up and pointed directly into the face of Romy's last soldier. Before Signe could pull the trigger, she saw the spark of recognition in the other woman's eyes.

"Signe?" she asked.

Signe's heart dropped as she realized she recognized the other woman, too. It was Maye—a woman Signe hadn't seen in years. Someone she'd grown up with just a few blocks north of this very warehouse.

"Signe Poulson, it is you," Maye said. Her armgun dropped a quarter of an inch.

It wasn't the first time Signe had run into someone from her old life. Nor was it the first time she'd been recognized. That recognition always put Signe in her least favorite position. After all, no one was supposed to know she was still alive. If anyone found out, it would put her at risk of getting found out and switch'd... which would, in turn, put Torrin's entire operation at risk.

"I thought you were dead," Maye said. "Your father told us—"

Setting her jaw, Signe flicked her thumb along Sally's stock. A reading flashed on the stock of the gun: LETHAL.

Before she had the chance to second-guess herself, she pulled the trigger.

The recognition in Maye's eyes was replaced momentarily with shock. Then with blank nothingness.

"Sorry," Signe muttered. She truly meant it. But there was nothing else she could have done. Just like there was nothing else she could have done the last three times someone had the misfortune to recognize her. When New Avarita was finally free, all the prices she'd paid in blood would be worth it.

She flicked Sally's safety back on, slinging the gun over her shoulder and darting up the crates and out the window.

Torrin was still there, waiting for her in the shadows.

"Threats?"

"Neutralized."

"The poison?"

Signe shook her head. "Negative."

Torrin's jaw clenched. He turned woodenly, standing utterly still for a moment. Then, he reared back without warning, unleashing his fury on the brick wall beside him with a stone-crumbling punch from his mech-arm.

"FUCK!" His feral scream echoed through the night.

"Fuck," Signe agreed.

They turned down the nearest street, putting some distance between themselves and the warehouse. "We need a new idea," Torrin finally said tightly, breaking the silence between them.

Signe nodded, but she knew that wasn't really the case. They already had the perfect idea, they just needed to be able to execute it.

They needed Liv Spencer.

08

LIV

To keep our society healthy and thriving, the Algorithm must protect New Avarita's citizens from all threats, foreign and domestic. The security protocols surrounding the rinth are designed to shield it from outside actors with harmful intent. These features are what will keep our people safe and striving toward their ultimate goal of earning Ascent.

—THE HANDBOOK OF LUCRE, *CHAPTER 29*

LIV WOKE UP barely two hours after her head hit her pillow, feeling like she'd been run over by an industrial tram. She dragged herself heavily from her bed, already running twenty minutes late for work, and went through her day in a sleep-hazed blur.

Grant delivered her an extra-strength energy supplement to her desk, which she accepted.

RinthRat12—Emerson—delivered her several messages to her unicomm, which she declined.

First, he attempted to contact her through the strange application he'd remotely installed on her unicomm. Once she force-deleted that application for the third time in a row, he reverted to other channels; traditional message apps, emails, and messages through the *Wasteland Warriors* server.

Every time his gaming tag popped up on her display, she heard Signe Remy's words echoing inside her skull, stabbing at her brain like a thousand tiny needles. She'd been singled out—recruited. But why?

What about the past year or so of their interactions over the rinth would make Emerson believe Liv would ever want to join a revolution?

First off, joining a revolution was suicidal. The powers of New Avarita and their Algorithm had digital eyes and ears in every corner of the city state: she should know, she'd mapped the installation of most of those eyes and ears herself. Secondly, she knew better than to upset the delicate balance of New Avaritan society. This city state only functioned because of the stability and security provided by the Algorithm and the Principal Chairman. Without them at the helm, society would crumble into chaos.

Not stability, said a little voice inside her. *Not security. Obedience. Control.*

She glanced hurriedly over both shoulders at the thought, as though someone would have heard it. Not only could her colleagues not read minds, but they were all already gone for the day. The terminals around her lay dormant and silent, the only beacon of bluish light in the whole room coming from the series of screens hovering in front of her.

Scrubbing her hands over her face, Liv began to pack her things. These rebellious thoughts of hers were pointless. A fight against a power like the one the Principal Chairman wielded would be like trying to attack a reinforced tank with a three-inch pocketknife.

Whoever this Torrin Calix was, he would be dead within the month. Then, he'd have nothing to show for all his efforts in this life.

Just like Liam.

The thought punched Liv in the stomach and she waved her hand over her terminal, rather more aggressively than was necessary to shut it off, stalking out of the office and into the twilit streets. The 214-transport back to northern Upper Lucara pulled in a few seconds later. She took her seat and leaned her head back against the window. A good night's sleep would clear up these thoughts. She'd wake up tomorrow without these dangerous ideas swarming her brain like gnats.

She'd also wake up alone.

A new pang of loneliness and grief shot through her and she turned up the music in her ear enhancements, letting the sounds of Fisherman's Curse pulse through her soul. The band was one of Liam's favorites. He always liked the upbeat rhythms and pulsing bass, even though the lyrics were always rather dark. Liv wrapped herself in memories like they were cozy blankets, sinking into a half-sleep as the transport rumbled toward home.

It was a Saturday morning—the day after the installation in the Medial Complex was completed. Liv had been working seventy-hour weeks for the past two months. A Fisherman's Curse song played on the sound system, rhythms pulsing through the floorboards as Liv padded across them in her pajamas, rubbing her eyes and checking her unicomm. 10:34. She'd slept late, but she felt more invigorated than she had in weeks.

She rounded the corner into the kitchen, then stopped in the doorway, biting back a laugh. Liam stood in front of the stove, stirring something in a pan and singing along to the song in a whisper—trying not to wake her, she was sure—using his spoon as a microphone. When the string interlude hit, he resumed his stirring, doing a little dance with his hips. Liv cleared her throat and leaned against the door frame, eyebrow raised.

Liam turned to face her with a wink. "Like what you see?" he turned back, wiggling his hips again. "I made breakfast—your favorite."

Liv could smell it now, the buttery warmth of grits mixing with the salty, sea-like aroma of cooking shrimp...

The dreamlike memory evaporated as her unicomm chimed urgently, breaking through the music and jerking Liv out of her stupor. For a second, her stomach sank, thinking that Emerson had finally gotten bold enough to harass her by video call. But when she peered down at her unicomm, she saw who it really was.

Ayla.

She sighed with relief, then accepted the call, holding up her wrist to capture her own likeness as Ayla's holographic form jumped into her field of vision. In an instant, her relief crumbled into confusion.

Ayla looked awful.

Her teeth were gritted in apparent agony, and the first words out of her mouth were more a bestial scream than they were actual words.

"Shit, Ayla," Liv said, scrambling to sit up straighter, as though somehow that would help. "What's going on? Are you okay?"

"I'm fine," Ayla said. Sweat beaded on her brow and she grunted, clearly suppressing another scream. "I just.... I need...." She trailed off, breathing heavily. "Are you home, by chance?"

"Not yet," Liv said. "I will be in..." She tapped one temple with a shaking hand, emerging from her VR environment with her left eye to check the status meter on the transport. "Three minutes and forty-six seconds."

Ayla huffed a laugh. "Always so fucking exact." She let out a hissing breath, her pale face crumpling in on itself. "Can you... can you come straight here? I'll reprogram the locks to let you in."

"Of course," Liv said. All the tiredness she'd felt a few seconds ago was long gone now, replaced with pure, unfiltered adrenaline. "Do you want me to call the nearest Medla facility? Or are they already on their way?"

Ayla shook her head, letting out another scream. "No, no don't call anyone. Just get here."

Liv chewed her lip. "Are you sure you don't want me to call—" she started. But Ayla broke off the connection before she could finish her sentence. Ayla worked at a Medla facility—she had obviously already contacted someone. But she knew Liv was closer than they were.

She probably just needed someone to squeeze her hand and tell her everything was okay until they got there.

That was a role Liv could fill.

The second the transport came to a stop, Liv shoved her way to the doors. "Sorry, medical emergency, I'm sorry, family emergency," she muttered in an effort to explain her rudeness. She doubted any of the other passengers gave a shit about her emergencies, but at least no one could say she hadn't tried to be polite.

Liv sprinted through the maze of townhomes, darting out of the way of pedestrians and private transports as she went. Thank God she had decided to wear flats today—she was sure she would have broken her ankle trying to run this distance in heels. By the time she skidded to a stop at Ayla's doorway it had been only three minutes and twelve seconds since the woman had ended their call.

Liv could hear screams coming from inside. They were muffled, but still audible. Even if Ayla hadn't managed to reach her Medla House colleagues, no doubt someone already knew what was going on—if the neighbors hadn't called in the emergency from the sound, hopefully her chip would have sent the alert directly to Medla on her behalf. One way or another, help was on the way. Thank Lucre.

The door unlocked with a satisfying *click* as Liv reached for the handle. She slammed the door open, running inside. The smell of honeysuckle and lavender washed over her; Ayla's favorite scents since she first discovered candles back at university. Some things never changed.

"Ayla? I'm here!"

"Upstairs!" Ayla shouted back.

Liv didn't really need the direction—the constant stream of grunts and cussing was enough to guide her. She took the stairs two at a time, finding Ayla on the floor of her bedroom, propped up against the edge of the bed, breathing heavily and soaked in sweat. Liv took her hand.

"I'm here," she said, giving her friend's hand a squeeze. "And it looks like someone else is ready to be here too, huh?"

Ayla nodded wearily. "Almost two weeks early."

"Well, they get their sense of timing from Kiran, then," Liv said. Ayla huffed out a laugh—her husband had always been early to everything. Liv craned her neck, peering out the window above the bed. "How long until the transport arrives?"

"No one's. Coming," Ayla said, speaking between panting breaths.

Liv's eyes widened. "What do you mean they're not coming? They didn't have any available transports? That's bullshit, you *work* there, for Lucre's sake." She raised her arm, pulling up her unicomm. "We can call one of the other facilities, let me try—" But she trailed off as Ayla's hand latched, vicelike, around her wrist.

"No. I didn't call them. And you're not. Going to call them either."

Liv felt like her brain was buffering; loading more slowly than a VR game on a public network. Ayla must be having a nervous breakdown. She had heard about cases like this before, where expecting mothers got so scared of giving birth that they tried to pretend they weren't in labor. She placed her right hand over Ayla's talon-like grip.

"Ayla. You have to give birth today. The baby is ready to come. But it's going to be okay—we'll get you to the nearest facility, and I'm going to stay right by your side the whole time, okay?"

"I'm giving birth," Ayla started. "You're staying by my side." She cut off, grunting out a half-scream, then fixed Liv with the most piercing stare she'd ever seen in her life. "But I'm not going to a fucking facility."

"I—I don't understand," Liv said. She was starting to panic now. She wasn't strong enough to lift Ayla and carry her down the stairs, and with her old friend crushing her forearm in her freakishly strong grip, she couldn't use her unicomm to call for help.

"If I go to a facility, they're going to tag him so they know to install the chip," Ayla said, her voice coming out as an urgent whisper. "I don't want my baby to have a chip, do you understand?"

"Ayla, your baby has to have a chip," Liv said, trying to stay calm. "Are you worried about the surgery? It's a perfectly safe procedure."

Ayla should know that better than anyone, she did ten a week. "I'm sure you can get approval to wait until you're healed enough to do it yourself if that's what you're—"

"No." Ayla eyes screwed up as another wave of pain seemed to wash over her. She collected herself again a few breaths later. "I'm not worried about the surgery. I just want. My baby. To be free."

"What do you mean, to be free? We're all free, Ayla. New Avarita is a free city-state."

Ayla's voice dropped to a low whisper. "If it were a free city-state, you'd still have a husband. And so would I."

Liv felt like the entire world dropped away in that moment. This wasn't the kind of thing people said—not outside of the dark corners of the veilrinth or, apparently, unsettlingly posh tea shops in Lower Baranthrum. Through her fear and panic, another feeling started to build inside of Liv: vindication.

She wasn't alone.

If she felt this way, and Emerson felt this way, and Signe Remy felt this way, and now, Ayla Voland, prominent surgeon, felt this way... maybe a lot of New Avaritans did. How many people silently grieved their loved ones after an unexpectedly early Ascent, pretending to celebrate while crying alone in the solitude of their lonely beds each night?

Maybe this Torrin Calix and his revolution had a fighting chance after all.

But there wasn't time to think about that now. First, Liv had to figure out how to deliver a baby inside a townhome bedroom.

"Okay," she said. Then repeated, "Okay," this time stronger. She squeezed the back of Ayla's hand. "You're not going to a facility. We're gonna do this right here." She was talking to herself as much as she was to Ayla. "What happens after you give birth?"

"Fake the baby's death. Report stillbirth," Ayla panted, evidently in too much pain to speak in full sentences. "Raise in secret."

Liv bit her lip, thinking. That plan was optimistic at best. The walls of these townhomes were nowhere near thick enough to disguise a crying infant. And who would care for this hidden, secret baby when

Ayla returned to work? Clearly, her friend had not fully thought this through. But Liv was here now, and she'd help however she could.

Would Torrin Calix take in a new mother and her unchipped baby? It might seem like one hell of a burden… but there was a chance. A highly trained doctor *had* to be a useful recruit for any revolution.

Once Ayla gave birth she could reach out to Emerson and arrange a meeting.

Liv had no idea how to deliver a baby, but thank God, Ayla did. She walked Liv through the basics, telling her how to position herself, what to look for, and how to help guide the baby out into the world. The process was long, slow, stressful, and messy. But still, within the hour Liv was laying on her back on the floor, hands filthy with fluids she didn't even want to think about, and Ayla was leaning back against the bed, her new baby cradled in her arms.

"What's his name?" Liv asked, flopping her head sideways to meet Ayla's eye.

Ayla looked down at the tiny infant, his skin still pinkish red, his tiny eyes fluttering open and closed. "Kiran."

Liv smiled. "Perfect."

"Whatever happens, Liv, we can't let them chip him." Fear and determination swam in Ayla's copper-colored eyes in equal measure.

"Don't worry," Liv said. "I've got a plan."

'Plan' was a bit of a stretch. But she had something.

She tapped on her left temple, opening up a window to *Wasteland Warriors*. The comm messages from RinthRat12 sat there, unread. As she opened them, she saw he had sent her a series of links—links to articles on the veilrinth, based on the sketchy looking domains. Ignoring these messages, she began to tap out a new message, asking to arrange a meeting with Torrin Calix himself.

Before she managed to send the message she heard a series of loud thuds coming from downstairs.

"Did you call someone?" Ayla asked sharply.

"You know I didn't," Liv hissed back, pushing herself upright and positioning herself between Ayla and the door to the bedroom.

"Correxion Group detail," came a gruff voice from the far side of the door. Without waiting for an answer, the officer booted the bedroom door open and three uniformed, helmeted officers rushed inside.

"Doctor, we're here to escort you to the nearest Medla House facility for treatment," the first said.

"There's no need," Liv tried to interject. "The baby was—"

"Doctor," the lead officer interrupted, speaking as though Liv was not there. "The nearest Medla House facility. Now. We have a private transport waiting."

"I'm not going to a facility," Ayla said, her voice barely more than a whisper.

"What was that, Doctor?"

Ayla looked at Liv, then down at baby Kiran. Her spine stiffened and when she spoke again, her voice was far stronger than it had been the first time. "I said I'm not going to a facility. I'm not in any need of medical attention."

"That's not really your call, Doc," said one of the other officers. He was starting to lose his patience; Liv could tell from his tone. "Besides, it's not you that needs medical attention." He indicated the infant with his chin. "You still need to go through newborn processing. You of all people should know that."

Liv stared at Ayla, trying to communicate a dissertation-length thought process with just her eyes. The game was up. There was no way these officers were leaving without Kiran. Once the officers left, she'd tell Ayla everything she'd learned from Signe Remy the night before. All about the revolution. See if she wanted to join with her—rebel against Lucre's Algorithm. Find a way to guarantee Kiran never needed to fear Ascent, even with a chip.

But either Ayla misread the pleading message in Liv's eyes or she chose to ignore it, because she didn't back down. She didn't shrink and acquiesce, passing her child into the officers' outstretched hands. Instead, she seemed to inflate. She pulled herself shakily to her feet, steadying herself against the wrought-iron bedpost with one hand and cradling Kiran in the other.

"He's not going through newborn processing."

"Processing and chip installation is mandatory per New Avaritan law and the Handbook of Lucre, Doctor," said the lead officer. As he spoke, Liv saw one of the other officers speaking softly into his unicomm. She thought she saw his lips form the words, *Code Alpha*.

"Then *fuck* New Avaritan law!" Ayla said, shouting now. "Fuck the Handbook! Fuck Lucre Himself!" Little Kiran sensed his mother's distress. He started wailing in her arms.

"Ayla, stop, there's another—" Liv started, but she cut herself off, biting her lip. There was no way she could tell Ayla about her plans in front of these Correxion officers. She settled on, "Trust me, Ayla. Let's go with the officers for now and—"

"And what?" Ayla spat back, rounding on Liv. "And let Kiran end up like Liam?"

Liv jerked back as though she'd been slapped.

"I won't allow it. Not while I'm breathing," Ayla continued.

The head officer looked back at the one who had spoken on the unicomm. The men shared a nod and the head officer turned back to Ayla. "You'll be receiving a communication any moment, now, Doctor. You've been relieved of your duties for Medla House. You've been found mentally unstable and unfit for work of that level of importance."

"I've what?" Ayla asked. Her arms began to shake like unsecured luggage on a rattling transport car. Liv leapt forward, grabbing Kiran from her grip just as it slackened and Ayla fell to her knees on the floor, landing in a puddle of cooling placenta.

"You'll also be receiving a communication from the GenstraCo Children's Care Division," the head officer plowed on. "You've been found to be unfit for parental duties as well."

Liv's entire being went numb. They were going to take Kiran away—not just for processing, but forever. "Officer, please, she's just emotional and exhausted from the birth. Can't you—"

"Every decision of the GCCC is final," he said coldly, plucking baby Kiran from Liv's shellshocked grasp. "Doctor—er, *Ms*. Voland, you can file an appeal with your local Correxion Group headquarters. In the meantime, you're welcome to apply for any job positions below Level C."

Job positions below Level C wouldn't pay enough to afford the rent on a spare bedroom in a place like Upper Lucara. That was okay, Liv would let Ayla move into her townhome with her. It would be nice to have the company, anyway.

"Good day," the lead officer said flatly, turning to leave with Kiran bundled in the crook of his remaining biological arm.

"No!" Ayla tried to claw her way back to her feet, but her physical exhaustion won out and she collapsed again, fingers outstretched, barely scraping the back of the head officer's flak jacket as he and his fellows marched out of the room and down the stairs. "No," she said again, this time weakly. Her shoulders wracked with sobs.

Liv moved toward her, not caring how much disgusting fluid she got on her pants as she sank to the ground at her friend's side, cradling her. The smell of honeysuckle and lavender flooded over her as she buried her face in Ayla's tangled hair. "It's going to be okay. We'll file that appeal. Get your job back. Then, we'll get Kiran back. This isn't over."

"I just wanted to keep him safe," Ayla muttered. "I just wanted to keep him safe."

"I know, I know," Liv said. "We'll keep him safe. We'll figure something out. I promise." She truly meant it.

Ayla stopped shaking abruptly. At first, Liv thought she'd succeeded in calming her friend down.

Then, she noticed Ayla had stopped breathing.

"Ayla?" Liv asked. "Ayla?" she tilted the woman's head up until their eyes met. But her friend's eyes weren't full of grief. There was no twinkle of hope, no spark of rage. There was nothing at all.

Ayla Voland was dead.

09

SIGNE

Sowing confusion is the easiest way to divide a society and throw it into chaos and disorder. Our great society must avoid that confusion at all costs if its citizens are to reach their ultimate goal. All citizens should look to the Office of the Principal Chairman as their sole source of direction and truth in uncertain times.

—THE HANDBOOK OF LUCRE, *CHAPTER 2*

SIGNE SWIRLED HER tea listlessly in its cup, reclining back in her seat and staring up at the glowing tiles of the tea shop ceiling. The air in her lungs felt heavy, making it hard to breathe and weighing her down, down, down. If she was still the drinking type, tonight would be the sort of night she'd turn off her alcohol filters and let herself get completely shitfaced. Even that probably wouldn't be enough to peel the image of Maye's face from the inside of her eyelids, though.

Signe believed in this revolution as much as anyone, and she was tired of waiting for their chance, too. Still, she hadn't signed up to hurt innocent people—she'd had her fill of that shit working for Reina Arthur. Like the others Signe had been forced to kill to keep her secret safe, she knew Maye might not have been completely innocent (she did work for Romy the Wolf, after all) but still, if Torrin had just waited and thought things through instead of charging out to meet the first poisoner he found on the veilrinth, the woman would probably be alive today.

Or, at least Signe wouldn't have had to be the one to kill her.

She wasn't the only one in a shit mood over their failed mission into the Wolf's territory. Torrin had been a whirling dervish of broken dishes and bleeding knuckles when they arrived back at the Penthouse earlier that night. Not that she couldn't see why.

He'd spent the past twenty years of his life rising from a lowly dockworker to a powerful crime lord—the top supplier of bootleg mech-enhancements in New Avarita—and still, Romy's people had sent him running for the hills in ten seconds flat.

For a man like Torrin, wounded pride was worse than broken bones.

He'd bounce back, but if experience was any sort of teacher, when he did, he'd be twice as violent and half as patient.

God, she wished she was still a drinker.

The shop's door chimed. Signe glanced up out of habit. When she saw the figure standing there, she blinked twice.

No fucking way.

There, silhouetted against the neon billboard across the street from the tea shop, was Liv Spencer. Unlike the last time she'd come, Spencer had made no attempt to blend in with the people of Lower Baranthrum. Today, instead of a hooded sweatshirt and dirty trainers, the woman wore a dark green blouse and gray slacks with shiny, businesslike loafers. It was a miracle she hadn't been mugged fifteen times on the walk from the train station.

Though, as Signe looked closer, she realized that all the clothes were covered in what looked like blood. That might have been enough to keep the muggers at bay.

It wasn't even just the blood that made Liv look a little unhinged, either. The way she moved was off... almost like she was walking through a dream; unfocused eyes, meandering steps. Overall, she looked about as approachable as a rabid sewer rat.

Spencer was so out of it that she didn't even see Signe. She walked right past her and up to the counter.

"Hi," she said dazedly.

"What do you want?" asked Glen as she approached. He eyed her suspiciously, taking in the blood-splattered clothes. His mech arm slid under the counter, reaching for the place where Signe knew there was a spare pistol, loaded with lethals. If Glen got jumpy and shot this girl, all the knowledge Torrin needed about the security systems guarding half the Core was gone.

"I'm a friend of Tor—" Spencer started.

Signe cut her off, pushing herself up straight in her chair and shouting, "Spencer, over here." She shot Glen a look and waved him off. He pulled his hand back above the counter, holding it up as though to say, *Sorry, I didn't realize you were friends with this horror-vid-looking bitch.*

"So, what brings you back to—" Signe started. But Spencer cut her off.

"I'm ready."

"You're ready," Signe repeated, not daring to trust the traitorous bubble of hope swelling in her chest. "Ready for what?"

"Ready to take down all this killswitch bullshit. Those fuckers who are in charge of it. The whole thing," Spencer spat, her voice losing its dazed quality and taking on a fiery fury. "I'm ready to burn this goddamn place to the ground."

Signe wouldn't have thought the Upper Lucaran woman capable of slinging cusswords like that, but then again, she wouldn't have expected her to turn back up down here, either. She looked Spencer over, eyes lingering on the reddish-brown stains covering her arms, her knees, and the front of her shirt.

"Are you sure?" Signe asked. As badly as they needed this woman, she didn't look like she was in the mind state to be making major life decisions right now. She needed to give her at least one chance to back out, even if it was just for the sake of her own conscience.

"I have nothing left," Spencer answered. Her voice broke. She pulled it back together. "And I know exactly who's to blame for that."

Signe studied the woman for a few long seconds. The expression she saw in Liv Spencer's eyes was one she knew well. It was the same one that had brought her to Torrin's crew almost a decade ago. Shock and grief with a healthy dose of pissed-the-fuck-off. She was ready, all right. Finally, Signe nodded.

"Follow me."

"Where?"

"The Penthouse."

THE NAME OF Torrin's hideout was a bit of a joke. Far from the fancy penthouses in the Core, Torrin's Penthouse was the sprawling top floor of an old, ostensibly abandoned manufacturing plant. Torrin had found the place and fixed it up, bringing in engineers and mechanics in the earliest days of his revolution, before Signe had left her cushy Core job. The bootleg mech enhancements those crew members made funded most of the crew's efforts.

Spencer hovered half a pace behind Signe as they entered the machine shop on the main floor.

"Brina, Perry," she said, waving at a few of Torrin's engineers. "You're working late."

"Better than being up there," Brina said, jerking her chin toward the ceiling.

"Trust me, I'd love to be snuggled up in bed right about now," Perry agreed, tapping his temple to activate his eyeshields as he reached for his soldering iron. They were avoiding Torrin's towering rage, then. Not that Signe blamed them—it was precisely what she'd been doing at that tea shop.

"Well, you're both in luck. I'm about to make Torrin's whole year."

"You planning to finally fuck the man?" Perry asked.

Signe wrinkled her nose. "What? No. You're disgusting. I'm bringing him..." She gestured toward Spencer, who was staring at the walls of the workshop in a mix of fascination and horror. The collection of illicit artwork Emerson had purchased on the veilrinth tended to have that effect on people. As did the massive graffiti tag Brina had added to the wall that read, ASCENT IS MURDER.

"And... he wants to see this... woman...?" Perry asked, looking Spencer up and down, focusing on the blood and her upper-district clothes in equal measure.

"Trust me," Signe said with a wink.

She and Spencer crossed the shop, passing piles of mech-arms, armguns, and more, all stacked up on workbenches littered with tools and homeless machine parts. When they reached the freight elevator on the far wall, Spencer cleared her throat.

"I'm... I'm not going to have to fuck this man either, am I?"

Signe raised an eyebrow. "Not unless you want to."

She shook her head hurriedly.

Signe shrugged. "You might want to wait until you see him before you decide. Most people find him pretty damn good looking."

The pair of them stepped into the elevator as the doors hissed open. "Then why aren't you fucking him?"

"Not my type." Signe gave the other woman a wink. *Also, he's batshit crazy.* She didn't say that part out loud.

The doors slid open, revealing Torrin's infamous Penthouse. The first thing Signe noticed was the quiet. Normally, the gathering space beside the kitchen was bustling at this time of night. Tonight, it was quiet as a morgue. Brina and Perry weren't the only crew members steering clear of Torrin, it seemed.

Whoever designed this factory had obviously not intended

for people to live in it, but Torrin's team of engineers, mechanists, and other assorted nerd types had managed to bully the layout into something that worked well enough for a rag-tag group of no-good revolutionaries. The kitchen had a refrigeration unit, an industrial convection oven, and a microwave with a rehydrator mod, which was enough to cook up any food they managed to get their mitts on and keep the crew fed and happy.

Beyond the kitchen was a sprawling living space furnished with castoff sofas, tables, and chairs. The only thing in the entire room that didn't look like it was from the days before the Fall was Emerson's terminal: an eight-foot-tall behemoth of fans, wires, holo-screens, and Lucre only knew what else.

The hallways branching off to each side of the living space led to the bedrooms. The rooms were little more than cubbies, in truth, but there was room in each for a bed and a small trunk full of essentials.

Liv Spencer's dazed, dreamlike walk was back as she exited the elevator. "Is that…"

"Bathrooms are down the hall," Signe said.

"Bath—no." Spencer raised a hand, pointing to a small, dark shape curled up on the back of the sofa beside Emerson's terminal. "Is that a *cat?*"

If she'd been having trouble making sense of things before, Signe was sure the poor woman had no idea what to think now. In New Avarita, pets were as rare as gemstones. Rarer, since you didn't have to feed a gemstone once you purchased it. The permit alone to have a pet was upwards of twenty thousand coin. Then, of course, you had to be able to take care of the thing.

Signe wasn't sure where the cat had come from. He'd just always been there, sleeping in the sunbeams streaming in through the penthouse windows and killing any stray rats that made their way up from the shop below.

"Signe, is that you?" said a voice from behind the wall of screens. There was the rolling sound of a chair pushing back, then Emerson's ghostly pale face appeared around the side of the terminal, framed by overlong dark hair. "Liv, you made it!"

His tone made it sound like Liv was just late to an afterparty or something, not wading into the filthy underbelly of New Avarita to join a highly illegal rebellion. Then again, Emerson's tone was always way too casual for this setting. That, combined with the fact that he was a good five to ten years younger than anyone else on the crew made it feel like the kid had somehow wandered into this crew by mistake.

Of course, that was about as far from the truth as you could get, considering Emerson was the one who had convinced Torrin to form this group to begin with. Twelve years ago, when the kid was only fourteen years old. Signe still wondered where he'd found the balls.

Liv frowned as Emerson skirted around the edge of his massive monitors, stepping into full view. "You're RinthRat12?"

Signe understood her surprise. Emerson Quinn somehow looked simultaneously nothing like he seemed on the rinth, and *exactly* like how he seemed on the rinth. He was six feet of nothing but skin and bones. His whole frame had a delicate sort of look to it, like he might keel over dead if you breathed on him too hard.

"I see you've dressed for the occasion," Signe said slyly. It was a well-known joke in Torrin's crew: even though Emerson hadn't left the confines of the Penthouse in over a year at this point, he still dressed in a full suit and loafers every single day. No one really knew why.

"Wha—oh, yeah," Emerson said. He smoothed his jacket, straightening in a mockery of professionalism. "It's always nice to make a good first impression, you know." He stooped over, scooping the cat from his perch on the back of the sofa. The creature let out a little *prrbbt* of surprise. "I tried to get Black Hat to wear a bow tie, but you know how he can get."

"Black Hat?" Spencer repeated dimly, still staring at the cat like it was a unicorn.

"Well, I couldn't exactly call him White Hat, could I?" Emerson said. Then, he chuckled to himself.

It was the kind of joke the kid made often; a joke made purely for himself without really caring if anyone else understood it.

"Right..." Spencer repeated. She looked around, taking in the size of the place, Emerson's terminal, and Black Hat, now purring contentedly in Emerson's arms. "Looks like you have a pretty advanced operation, here. But if none of you are working a normal job how are you not... How have you managed not to..." she trailed off.

"Not to get brain-zapped by the assholes on the Board?" Signe asked, remembering half a heartbeat too late that Liv Spencer's husband had been switch'd only a few days ago.

Sure enough, the other woman winced. Signe cleared her throat, moving on as quickly as possible by clapping Emerson solidly on the shoulder. The kid stumbled forward half a pace and Black Hat gave Signe a soft hiss.

"It's all thanks to our little rinth rat."

Spencer looked dumbfounded. "You've already done it, then? You've found a way to disable the killswitch?"

She didn't ask the last question—*then why am I here?*—but Signe saw it written all over her pale, vaguely cherubic face.

"Not exactly," Emerson said, scratching behind one ear, then cracking his knuckles absently. "There's no way I've found so far that can disable the switch altogether. It's implanted directly into the skull, and it's wired to release the pulse when tampered with, so trying to remove it surgically is a no-go, too. What I've done is—"

"Who the fuck is making so much goddamn noise out here?" Torrin asked. He stormed in from the left-facing side hallway, where his own quarters lay. "I'm trying to—" When he saw Liv Spencer, he stopped mid-rant, his face turning from angry red to its regular color within the span of about three seconds. "Liv Spencer."

He said her name like he was worried he was seeing things. Like he thought if he said it too loudly, she'd vanish in a puff of smoke like one of the half-baked magic acts down on Fulton Street.

Liv cocked her head to one side, examining Torrin Calix from head to toe. Unlike Emerson Quinn, Torrin looked exactly how you'd expect a man in his position to look. He was still dressed in the clothes he'd worn on his and Signe's doomed trip into Romy's territory a few hours before: black synthetic denim pants and a fitted gray shirt that put both his tattoos and his mech-enhanced arm on full display.

Every detail, from his perfectly kept beard, to his gruff right hand, to the tattoos climbing up the side of his neck, to the telltale steely glint in his eye, screamed *"dockworker-turned-crimelord."*

Many of the women in Lower Baranthrum seemed to like the look—several of the men, too. Though Torrin liked to have his fun wherever he could find it, he wasn't the type to settle down. If he had a normal career, someone might say he was "married to the job." As it was, he just came across as a madman obsessed with revenge. But a handsome one, even if he wasn't Signe's cup of tea.

"Welcome to my Penthouse," he said, stretching his arms out. "What brings you to my little corner of this shithole of a city-state?"

Spencer took a step forward, looking down at her blood-smeared blouse and pants. "The same thing that brings most people here, I'd imagine."

Her voice was steady now. Far steadier than it had been back in the elevator. Something had fortified her resolve again, whether it was seeing Emerson, being reminded about her husband's abrupt demise, or the cat, Signe wasn't sure.

"You're ready to help me give our friends in the Medial Complex a middle finger they can't ignore?" Torrin asked, his eyes glinting even more sharply.

Liv Spencer was the final piece of the puzzle. She had the information they needed, information not even Emerson had been able to hack into the Berger Security files to get. With her on board, they could finally make new strides forward. Stop dicking around diverting shipments and making half-assed assassination attempts.

With Liv Spencer on their side, they'd finally be able to make a plan that would let them strike the Board where it hurt. And not just any old plan: a plan that actually had a snowball's chance of succeeding.

"No," Spencer said. For a second Signe felt frustration claw up her throat. Then the woman set her jaw and balled her hands into fists. This time they looked less like she was clinging to sanity and more like she was ready to break shit. "I'm ready to help you burn the Medial Complex and the Principal Chairman's entire Board to the ground."

Torrin's prematurely sun-wrinkled face split into a grin—the first big, toothy smile Signe had seen on that man's face in months. The expression was gone less than a second later. He turned from Liv to Emerson, inclining his head. "Have we already made it official?"

Emerson's hair flopped animatedly as he shook his head. "Not yet." He deposited Black Hat gently in his nook on the back of the sofa, then returned to his terminal. Lights and colors flashed against the wall behind the terminal as he scrolled through menus and tapped instructions into his unicomm, completing a sequence he'd done probably half a hundred times in the past twelve years.

Signe stepped in front of Liv, meeting her eye. "Once Emerson works his magic, your old life will be gone. You won't be able to talk to anyone you know ever again."

And you'll have to kill them if they're unlucky enough to run into you, Signe thought.

Liv Spencer looked at her with dead eyes. "My old life is already gone." She left Signe's side, walking over to stand next to Emerson at his terminal. "What do you need to do to make this official?"

Signe's stomach dropped, the weight in her lungs returning, making her feel tense and a little claustrophobic. She pushed the feeling away. This was a good thing—they needed Liv on their crew. Still, she couldn't help feeling a pang of sadness for the other woman. Revenge was enough to fuel a person, for a time, but it provided no nourishment. It could keep you alive, but left a person hollow.

Emerson's eyes never left his screens, his fingers still tapping away at his holo keyboard. A dizzying display of menus and code flashed over all six of his monitors. "I can't disable your killswitch. But what I can do..." he paused, tapping in another sequence with his long, nimble fingers, "is trick the killswitch database."

"Trick it? Trick it how?" Spencer asked, brow furrowing as she stared at the monitors.

Torrin stepped up, leaning against the wall behind Emerson and folding his arms across his chest. "Trick it into thinking you're already dead."

And there it was: the simple yet impossible loophole Emerson Quinn had found in the killswitch protocol when he was just fourteen years old.

If he removed a name from the database altogether, he would activate their killswitch. If he tried to remove a name anywhere else in the official records, he could end up restricting a person's access to their coin, or shorting out their chip altogether, which would also activate the killswitch. But if he made one tiny entry in the baseline coding of one piece of Lucre's Algorithm, he could fool the system into thinking that a killswitch had already been pulled without impacting the rest of the chip's functionality.

On a large scale, the solution would never hold up. Honestly, even the twenty-some times they'd tricked the system so far might be too much, down the line. All it would take would be one careful auditor noticing a handful of supposedly dead people accessing the rinth to bring Emerson's whole system crashing down around them all.

They'd been lucky so far. Hopefully, with Liv Spencer on board, they'd be able to finally bring the whole system down before their luck ran out.

Spencer was silent for a few seconds, processing. Signe was sure she was thinking through all the people she knew back in Upper Lucara. Any family or friends, coworkers or neighbors. People she would never be able to see again. People who would be celebrating her Ascent by this time tomorrow.

After a few seconds, she took a deep breath. "All right, let's kill me, then."

10
LIV

If there are two words that describe society before The Fall, they are 'idleness' and 'waste.' The people of the world that came before were unproductive, entitled, and wasteful with everything from time to resources. The Algorithm is here to keep us safe, secure, and striving toward a better future for every citizen, until their time for Ascent arrives.

—THE HANDBOOK OF LUCRE, *CHAPTER 3*

CAMERA R-7 COVERS this area, here?"

"Not exactly." Liv cocked her head to the side, studying the 3D model hovering over Emerson's terminal. She raised a hand to point. "The sight path of R-6 covers this hallway with a 75-degree viewing angle, all the way to the third door on the right." She nodded as Emerson tapped his keys, adjusting the model to match. "And then this camera here—W-22—is four inches to the left of where you have it here."

"How can you be sure?" Signe asked, sounding skeptical.

Liv rolled her eyes, making sure to face away from the scary, rifle-toting woman as she did. "I thought you guys stalked and secretly radicalized me for months because you knew I would be sure," she said, keeping her tone light and nonconfrontational as possible.

Bobbing his head along to the music playing through the Penthouse sound system—an old-world genre he said was called 'jazz'—Emerson adjusted the position of W-22 and the model of Huldra Industries hovering midair grew another step closer to the one inside Liv's mind. She remembered every inch of the schematic. *146 cameras. 58 motion sensors. 395 chip scanners—one for each entrance, office door, and elevator.*

Even without her unusually precise memory, Liv was pretty sure Huldra's records would have been seared into her brain. After all, the Huldra job was what had kept her working late and away from home during what ended up being Liam's final weeks. How many dinners and evening chats had she missed out on because of this job? She would have told Byrnie to go fuck himself for asking her to stay late if she'd known they would have been her last.

Initially, Liv had been confused when Torrin had asked for Huldra's security systems instead of the ones she'd helped install in the Medial Complex. Huldra was responsible for programming and constructing all the chips in New Avarita, but even Liv knew enough about the powers that controlled New Avarita to know that the killswitch database wouldn't be left in the hands of Reina Arthur alone.

But of course, things weren't going to be as simple as charging into the Medial Complex, crashing the killswitch protocol, and skipping off into the sunset. Emerson had done his share of poking around the rinth and the veilrinth for information on the chips, but there was one piece of information that was stubbornly unavailable.

A vital piece of information that they needed before this operation could go a single step further.

What happened if the entire killswitch program went offline?

From what Emerson said, removing someone's name from the database meant they got switch'd. Crashing the killswitch database wouldn't do Torrin's revolution much good if it just automatically switch'd everyone in New Avarita.

Signe Remy had the answer there. She'd been one of Reina Arthur's security guards—Liv could see the Huldra Industries logo embossed onto the overworn bolts on her mech-arm. She was far from a tech expert, but she knew that Huldra kept the secrets of the chip's inner programming locked down on-site. They were stored in an air-gapped device located in the heart of the Huldra headquarters.

Liv hadn't known what 'air-gapped' meant, so Emerson explained the concept. Simply, it was a terminal that wasn't connected to the rinth. Liv couldn't imagine the point of a terminal that couldn't access the rinth—what could you even *do* on a machine like that? But the point wasn't to *do* things with it, Emerson said. It was more or less a digital vault: a bank for highly classified data.

Since it wasn't connected to the rinth, there was no way to hack it from here. The only way to access whatever data was on that terminal was to walk up to it and tap the keys on it yourself. Which was inconvenient, as it was located in one of the most secure structures in all of New Avarita.

After another hour or two, Liv was certain she'd relayed everything she knew about the Huldra security upgrades to Emerson. His model was now chock full of blinking red dots and arcing lines meant to represent camera and sensor view angles and scanner radii. Liv sat back on the couch, closing her eyes as Signe, Emerson, and a few more crew members whose names she didn't know yet started talking about the group's plans to breach the building and access the chip plans.

She flinched as she felt something brush against the back of her hand. Black Hat recoiled, offended. His tail stood straight up in the air as he marched to the far side of the couch.

"Oh, I'm sorry Black Hat," she said.

"Not used to cozying up to a furball, I take it, Spencer?"

Torrin Calix eased himself into the wingback chair directly across from Liv's seat on the couch. Liv had considered telling him she'd prefer that he just call her 'Liv,' but it was too late now to do so without making things awkward.

Torrin leaned back and tapped a few fingers on his unicomm menu. Emerson's jazz music faded out, replaced by the dark, pulsing rhythms of synthbass. The moment Black Hat noticed Torrin's lap was available, he stretched, then hopped down onto the floor and back up to rest himself in the crook between the man's figure-four crossed legs.

"No," Liv said. "I've never actually met anyone who has a pet permit from the Principal Chairman, before."

In New Avarita, it was harder to get a pet permit than a childbearing permit. She'd never really thought about it before, but now she realized, cynically, that it was probably because a cat couldn't grow up and get a job that helped make money for the CEOs on the Principal Chairman's Board. A stab of grief shot through Liv at the thought of childbearing permits. She pushed it away.

"You still haven't," Torrin said, bringing her back to the conversation. He tried to nudge the cat off his lap and onto the floor, but Black Hat was having none of it. "The Principal Chairman isn't real, anyway."

Liv flushed. She should have realized Torrin hadn't paid for a pet permit. Just on her walk through the machine shop downstairs, Liv had seen evidence of at least fifteen crimes punishable by prem-death. Besides, the powers-that-be in New Avarita thought everyone in this building—herself now included—was dead. Torrin could hardly march to his nearest administration office and ask to download a permit application.

Then, the second part of the man's statement crystallized in her brain.

"What do you mean the Principal Chairman isn't real?"

She expected him to tell her that his power was an illusion, or that the revolutionaries in this place didn't accept his authority.

"He's a hologram," Torrin said calmly, like he wasn't saying one of the craziest things she'd ever heard in her life.

Liv was silent for a second. Then, "Surely someone would have noticed if..."

"When is the last time you saw the man outside of a screen? Or without a protective shield that distorts things *just* enough?"

It was insane. But as Liv racked her brain, she knew she had never seen the man in the flesh without enough protective measures to hide the tell-tale fuzzy edges of a hologram projection. All things considered, she supposed it wasn't the most world-shattering thing she had learned in the past few weeks.

"What do you expect, Em, I'm not a fucking hacker," Signe said, across the room.

"It's not that difficult," Emerson was saying, holding up two small pieces of wire. "You just wind it like this..."

"Well," Liv said, turning back to Torrin, changing the subject away from the Principal Chairman's supposed unreality. "You must have a fair amount of coin if you can afford to feed the little guy."

Torrin gave up on his attempts to get the cat off his lap, reluctantly scratching Black Hat under his chin with the tattooed fingers of his right hand. The cat craned his neck back like he was trying to absorb the attention into his furry little soul. "We do all right."

A thought suddenly struck Liv and she frowned.

"What's the problem?" Torrin asked.

"Lucre's Algorithm... the killswitch protocol..." she started. "I, um, I assume you're familiar with where it came from?"

"Do you mean the version you learned in your Genstra education, or the truth?" Torrin asked, twitching an eyebrow.

"Ah..." Liv started.

"That's a trick question, isn't it?" asked one of the crew members Liv hadn't properly met yet. She slouched into the chair next to Torrin, reaching over to scratch between Black Hat's ears. "This is one of the few cases where the story's basically the same." She turned to Liv and gave an upward nod. "Alura," she said, by way of introduction.

"Liv," Liv said back.

Alura gave her a look that said, *duh,* then turned back to Torrin.

The man scowled, running his mech-hand through his hair. Liv wondered how disorienting it must be to get used to a mech-enhancement like that—did it feel like someone else was scratching at his head, or did you start to feel phantom sensations in that metal limb over time? Some engineer in some Huldra lab had probably calculated the probability of each.

"Content-wise, sure. Though the tone of the GenstraCo version is decidedly still bullshit."

"Always is," Signe said, rejoining the conversation as well. She perched herself on the far side of the couch from Liv, leaning forward to unlace her heavy black boots.

"Don't you dare take those off in here," said the other crew member Liv didn't know.

"I'll do whatever I damn well please, Gaius," Signe said, tugging the last knot free.

"Well, someone please open a window, at the very least," the man—Gaius—said.

Signe threw her boot at him in response.

Liv turned back to Torrin. "Well, if the content I learned as a kid was right…"

She struggled to find the words. Back in the early 2200s, the nation that used to exist on this land had been basically destroyed by famine, disease, all kinds of horrors. Then, came a man named Arnaud Lucre. He was the genius behind Lucre's Algorithm; the program that helped stabilize and structure New Avaritan society as they all knew it, today. His team had written the *Handbook of Lucre,* the book that now lived in nearly every classroom, jail cell, and hotel nightstand in the city-state.

As angry as Liv was now, she had to admit that, without the Algorithm—without Ascent to control the population growth in New Avarita—there was a very real chance their society would have crumbled in the years since the Fall.

Regardless of how awful the killswitch protocol was, the fact remained that Lucre had created it to solve a very real problem.

Even if the Board could be convinced to set profit aside, the few scant grow domes and meat labs in New Avarita weren't enough to support an ever-expanding population.

Then, there was the problem of space.

Everyone knew that the world outside of New Avarita's borders was uninhabitable. The city-state's bubble-like electric shield protected them from the radiation in the nuclear fallout zones to the north and east. The land to the west was nothing but deserts—the same deserts that had inspired *Wasteland Warriors,* in fact. And the only thing south of New Avarita was the ocean.

In short, if the population of New Avarita grew too big to fit within the city-state's borders, they'd all be in serious trouble.

Liv cleared her throat, trying again. "If we bring down the killswitch database, New Avarita's population is going to skyrocket, isn't it?"

"That's kind of the whole idea," Signe said, stretching her legs out and resting her socked feet on the pitted coffee table. Gaius and Alura chuckled. Emerson had disappeared behind his terminal again. The only sign of him was the quiet *tap-tap-tapping* of his fingers on his holo keyboard.

"Right," Liv started, bravely soldiering on even though she was pretty sure she was making a fool of herself now. "But what will happen with food production, then? What if overcrowding becomes an issue?" Her mind started to race. "Or disease? What happens when the next hurricane comes through Lower Baranthrum and there isn't enough room in the safe zones for everyone in the district to safely shelter?"

"Is there a point you're ramping up to, Spencer?" Torrin asked. He finally managed to shoo Black Hat off his lap so he could lean forward, resting his elbows on his knees.

"My point is that the goal of turning off the killswitch is to save lives, right?" Her heart hammered, her stomach turning as anxiety threatened to take over. She forced herself to meet Torrin Calix's steely gaze. "What if by turning it off, we accidentally alter the structure and systems of New Avarita so much that even *more* people die?"

There was no laughing now. Even the gentle tapping of Emerson's fingers on his terminal had stopped. For a few seconds, the Penthouse was still, silent other than the music playing on in the background. Torrin didn't meet her gaze. He pulled a small tool from his pocket, adjusting the screws on the joints of his mechanical hand slowly and methodically.

This is it, Liv thought. *I've taken things too far.*

Why couldn't she just keep her thoughts to herself? She had been here all of three hours and was already challenging the head of this overtly criminal organization to his face? You didn't even have to be particularly street-smart to know that was a dumb move. Would they kick her out and let her get switch'd, or would they just prem-death her right here?

Then, Torrin Calix returned the tool to his pocket and looked up, meeting her gaze at last. "What do you know about volcanoes?"

Liv blinked. "Volcanoes?"

It took her a second to place the term. Giant mountains that spewed lava and ash, killing everyone in a certain radius every few hundred or thousand years. New Avarita didn't have any volcanoes—thankfully—so they hadn't been covered in much detail in her schooling.

"Yes, volcanoes." Torrin leaned back again, stretching out his newly recalibrated mech-hand as he talked. "I've always found the bastards fascinating. Do you know why?"

Liv didn't dare take a stab at that one. She just shook her head mutely.

"I read some accounts about volcanoes on the veilrinth. One that was written before the Fall," Torrin recalled. "In one account, the mountainside was struggling before the volcano blew. There wasn't much of anything surviving there. The plants were shitty, scrubby little things. The animals were starving to death. You get the idea."

Torrin rested his hand comfortably on his knee, evidently enjoying the sound of his own voice as he continued with this tale.

"Then, the volcano erupted. It flooded the whole mountainside with a river of lava. The lava destroyed everything—the plants, the trees, the whole fucking ecosystem." He snapped his mechanical fingers. "Gone in a few minutes' time. All that was left was a bare hillside of solid rock when the volcano's job was done. Do you know what happened next?"

Liv shook her head again, eyes narrowed, following Torrin's story closely. She wasn't the only one: Signe, Alura, and Gaius were all listening intently, no matter how hard Signe was trying to look like this whole conversation bored her half to death.

"New life grew," Torrin said. He cracked a smile. Some people looked younger when they smiled, but, wearing this grin, somehow Torrin looked older—weathered and world-weary, like the effort of wringing this smile from his cheeks might just suck the rest of his youth away from him for good. "Not just new life—stronger and more vibrant life than the mountainside had before the damn volcano blew in the first place."

"So, you're saying that freeing the people of New Avarita to live without the fear of their chips will… what, bring on a cultural renaissance capable of fixing the problems that have existed since the Fall?" Liv asked, trying to keep the skepticism from her voice.

"I'm not saying that at all," Torrin said. He folded his mismatched arms over his chest. Black Hat jumped back into his lap. He stared at the cat for a few seconds, then sighed, scratching him behind his ears. "I'm saying that sometimes, the mountainside needs a fresh start. It's not the volcano's job to grow the new life—it's the volcano's job to blow things up enough that there's room for something new to come in and take over."

The man shooed the cat off his lap again, then pushed himself to his feet. "It's getting late. I'm turning in." He gave Liv a cutting look. "Glad to have you on the team, Spencer. Signe, you'll get her settled?"

Liv got the impression the man wasn't all that sure how happy he was to have her on board. She was poking holes in things he didn't want holes in. His volcano answer might have satisfied the rest of his crew, who were now talking and joking again as Gaius raided the pantry for a snack and Signe took over cat-doting duties with far more enthusiasm than Torrin had.

But it hadn't satisfied Liv.

His convoluted metaphor had answered her question, albeit in a roundabout way. She'd wanted to know his plans to prevent famine or overcrowding in the wake of the killswitch protocol's destruction. The answer was: he had no plan. His plan was just to burn down the old system and hope to Lucre the next system wasn't even worse.

Liv buttoned her lip, giving Torrin a nod as he left the common area of the Penthouse. It was too late for her to turn back. So, she would accept his answer for now. She would have to tread lightly and plan her moves carefully, but as much as Liv wanted revenge on the people who had killed Liam, Ayla, and everyone else she cared about in this world, she wanted more than that.

She had promised Ayla that she would try to protect Kiran. Throwing this entire world to the wolves wouldn't protect baby Kiran. A phantom scent played in her nostrils: lavender and honeysuckle. She would keep her promise to Ayla, one way or another.

The killswitch database needed to be destroyed, but Liv had no intention of leaving the future of New Avarita up to fate or Lucre's Algorithm or whatever people should believe in these days. There was a way to destroy the things that needed destroying without damning a significant portion of the people in New Avarita to becoming collateral damage. There had to be.

And Liv was going to figure it out.

11

REINA

Individual success and opportunity are central to what makes New Avarita great. The Algorithm will support each individualin their endeavors and reward them for their individual achievements on their path to Ascent. The only limit to the amount of success and wealth a person can gain on this level of existence will be their own creativity, work ethic, and intelligence.

—THE HANDBOOK OF LUCRE, *CHAPTER 4*

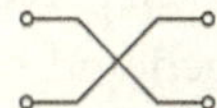

RESULTS: TEST 134—SUCCESS

Reina read the words hovering over her wrist, then reread them, then reread them again. As much as she wanted to believe them, she needed to be sure before she let herself dare to hope. She felt almost as though she was moving through a dream, her body drawn to the Dev Lab like metal to a magnet, as her shoes clacked against the pristine floors.

"Weston," she said as she entered, activating her eye shields. "I got the notification. I sincerely hope it is not a system glitch?"

The head engineer blinked, evidently surprised to be addressed by name. Reina couldn't fault him for the reaction—she didn't make a habit of learning the names of people who were so many wealth brackets beneath her. But the success of this experiment warranted the respect.

Assuming it truly *was* successful. If it turned out the notification she'd received was a glitch, she would forget the man's name again before lunchtime.

"It is no glitch, Madam Arthur," he said, recovering. He hurried to keep pace with her as she walked toward the testing cells at the back of the lab. "Twenty-six hours post-implementation. No signs of medical complications, internal bleeding, or discomfort."

Reina nodded smartly, concealing the way her heart had just skipped a beat and a half. "The body is accepting the implant, then. A good start. What are the figures on the enhancement itself?"

A pig snuffled around the central testing cell, separated from the engineers and scientists milling around the lab by a pale blue electrical shield. The animal looked completely healthy. She could see the surgical scar on its lower stomach, but otherwise, the beast sniffed and snorted, moving around his electrical enclosure like any normal pig. Hope started to swell in her chest, but she pushed the feeling down, keeping her gaze steely and her face flat.

Then, Weston said, "Fourteen percent."

Reina's calm mask dropped and she whirled to face the man. "Did you say 'fourteen,' or 'forty'?"

A smile tugged at the corners of Weston's lips. He suppressed it just in time, maintaining his professionalism. He hugged his holoboard to his chest, gazing at the pig almost lovingly. "Fourteen, Madam Arthur."

Fourteen percent.

The enhancement was working even better than projected. If Weston's readings were right, this pig could live on a mixture of substances containing only fourteen percent traditionally digestible foods. The remaining eighty-six percent of the creature's 'food' was synthetic fuel. More specifically, the synthetic fuel manufactured by Xirloc. It was currently the least profitable brand in Huldra's portfolio. With this enhancement, that was all going to change.

The hope bubble was back in Reina's chest, swelling a little larger with every breath. She was going to be wealthier than the rest of the advisory board combined once this hit the market.

"You've arrived just in time for our next test," Weston said. "We are trying a twelve percent mixture this time."

Twelve percent vitamins, protein, and other essentials. The rest pure fuel—and, eventually, revenue—courtesy of Xirloc.

Once they adapted this enhancement for a human stomach, a person could live indefinitely off concoctions like the one in the pig's dish. The people in the Core would resist, of course—Reina herself shuddered at the idea of giving up her meals at *The Chop* in favor of that grayish sludge. But there were citizens down in Lower Baranthrum and Old Altum who would gladly invest in an enhancement that made it easier and cheaper to feed their families.

She would just have to figure out how to market it. Or perhaps she could take it to the advisory board. They could require every person under a certain income level to get this enhancement. Or perhaps everyone would have one, but those with means could choose to turn off the effects, like the alcohol filters. She made a note on her unicomm to explore the possibility of adding such a feature to the product.

Coin and accolades flashed before Reina's eyes as she watched the pig snort down the new mixture. She would be lauded as a savior of New Avarita's poor, and rake in additional revenue for her trouble. If she played her cards right, here, Huldra Industries would see its most profitable quarter in decades when this hit the market.

And, perhaps, they could do away with the practice of Ascent.

The thought bubbled up in her mind without permission. She flinched from it, at first, but when she took a moment to examine it, she had to admit there was something there. Lucre had created his Algorithm to solve for the problem of mass starvation and overpopulation, after all. If the people of New Avarita could survive on easy to manufacture fuel instead of resource-intensive food… well, for the first time in centuries, maybe it would be possible to envision a future for New Avarita that didn't require regular culling of the population.

She'd have to find a way to ensure everyone still maintained the chip install procedures, though. Huldra and its subsidiaries would take an estimated seventy-three point hit if chip installations ever became optional.

Reina felt like she was floating on a cloud of invincibility for the rest of the morning. She worked furiously, preparing a presentation surrounding her latest success. Testing on the pig would carry on for months, she knew, to ensure there were no unforeseen long-term side effects. The enhancement wouldn't be ready for its first human candidates for another year or two, but now that she had solid data, she could present her findings to the other advisors on the Board.

If for no other reason than to shut Cora Calvin's trout-like mouth.

By the time Reina strode into the central tower of the Medial Complex that afternoon, the bubble of hope in her chest had swelled to at least the size of an orange, making her feel light and airy as fresh-whipped chocolate mousse.

"We call the Principal Chairman's Advisory Board to order on this, the—" Cora started.

"I'd like to request the floor," Reina interrupted. The Teras System executive shot her a look that could have soured even synthetic milk. Normally, the expression would have sent a jolt of anxiety coursing through Reina's veins. But not today. Nothing—not even Cora Calvin—could bring her down today.

"You have the floor, Madam Arthur," said Eliza Vinco.

As though that woman had the authority to grant or reject Reina's ability to speak. Laughable, even on Reina's worst day. But today was not a day for strife or mockery. Today was a day to take the highest of high roads.

Reina shot her a saccharine smile. "Thank you, Madam Vinco." She reached over the table, connecting her unicomm to the Board Room's system with a wave of her wrist. A holographic image floated over the center of the table, the projectors humming slightly as the image spun in the air.

"What are we looking at, Madam Arthur?" asked Jasper. He gave her a smile almost as fake as the one she'd just given Eliza. "Forgive me, we aren't all as technical as you."

"You're looking at the future, Master Koegen," Reina said. "This is a prototype of the Esoph-Enhancement I've been working on at InsertiaTech, Huldra's biggest mech-enhancement brand."

For the next twenty-three minutes, Reina ran through her presentation. She displayed video footage of their test subject, images of the prototype, and buckets of data in the form of graphs and charts and profits. She displayed estimates for Koegen Corp's profit margin on the nutrient paste needed by the Esoph-Enhancement, data on how population increases could boost profits at Lobos Transport, and increase the need for housing, which would give a boost to Teras Systems.

Her presentation was flawless. It outlined the benefits of this enhancement for every executive in the room. When she finished, she left the image of the enhancement itself spinning over the table and took her seat.

The room was silent for ten seconds. Then thirty.

They must all be struck speechless by the amount of coin flashing before their eyes.

Finally, Clement Rye cleared his throat. Rye was a quiet man—if even *he* was moved to speak by her presentation, surely they were all seconds away from agreeing to implement all the measures Reina had proposed. The metaphorical hope-bubble in her chest swelled even larger, like a frog's vocal sac stretching mid-croak.

"The product itself is intriguing," Clement began, "and I can see the profit potential. But I do have some concerns regarding the... implications of such a product. And some of the promotional measures you've suggested to boost adoption rates."

The tight smile on Reina's face threatened to falter. She kept it in place. "Such as?"

"Overriding the Algorithm to increase childbearing permit acceptance? More expendable income for the lower classes? After a time, the people of New Avarita will begin to get dangerous ideas regarding their individual sovereignty, I fear."

Winston Amos spoke next. "Yes, without the pressing threat of starvation, I wonder how long it will take for the people to begin questioning Ascent and the need for Lucre's Algorithm altogether."

The bubble started to waver and wilt. "Would that be such a bad thing?"

Silence met her words again.

It was broken, once again, by Clement Rye. "I... I wonder if you understand the greater purpose served by the Ascent program?"

"The purpose of Ascent is to prevent famine and overcrowding, Master Rye," Reina said tightly. It was more than insulting that he would insinuate she was one of the starry-eyed masses who still believed Ascent was the sign of a person fulfilling some greater calling. "With this enhancement, famine will be a fear of the past. As for overcrowding, Madam Calvin's corporations will no doubt be able to devise some creative housing solutions for—"

"Lucre's *original* purpose in devising the Algorithm and promoting Ascent was to prevent famine and overcrowding, that's true," chimed in a new voice. Louis Gideon of Medla House. Reina's stomach sank. The hope bubble wilted further, like a three-day-old balloon. Louis was almost always her ally in these meetings. But his tone here suggested she would not like what he was going to say next. "But in the past few generations, the system has come to have a secondary but even more vital role in New Avarita."

"Population control has become secondary to... population *control*,"

Cora Calvin said, her voice twisting in evident pride at her absolutely elementary word play. Reina fought to keep her face from souring at the expression on the woman's wrinkled face.

Of course, Reina knew they could use the Algorithm and the population's beliefs about Ascent to control the people. It allowed them to eliminate unproductive or problematic members of society. The crime rates in New Avarita were lower than anywhere else in the world, according to the last data she'd seen. But there were other ways of governing. Without Ascent, they would be free to trade with the rest of the world—the nations that had cut them off or placed unmanageable sanctions on them due to their hatred of Lucre's tactics.

Surely, the benefits outweighed the drawbacks.

But she should have known. The members of the Chairman's Advisory Board had one common goal. Not the goal of a prosperous New Avarita—not even the goal of personal profit, though that was surely a close second.

The common goal of every soul in this room was self-preservation. That goal made the idea of doing away with Ascent and returning to a world where death was not something that could be doled out remotely from this sterile Board Room more terrifying than the scariest Vinco horror vids.

She was starting to lose them, one by one. As soon as any Board Room argument began to sway one way, it was hard to stop it from gaining momentum. No one liked to be the odd one out. If you were the odd one out enough times, you might just find yourself on the wrong side of an Advisory Board vote of no confidence.

"It's difficult enough for the figure of the Principal Chairman to manage a population the size of New Avarita, Madam Arthur," Winston Amos started. "Can you imagine trying to keep an even larger population in line *without* our greatest tool for encouraging compliance?" The Grimme-Folson United exec shook his head slightly.

"But consider the profits—"

"Profits won't do us a bit of good if there's an uprising that challenges the Principal Chairman's power—*our* power—Madam Arthur,"

Audrey Lobos said. Reina's last hope for an ally in this argument. The hope bubble wilted further, shrinking to the size of a withered, rotten apple core.

Lobos lowered her tone, leaning toward her. "I'm sorry, I believe you might have gotten caught up in science for the sake of science here, Reina." Audrey raised her voice again. "I'd like to file a motion to request that InsertiaTech and Huldra Industries stop all production and experimentation on this esophageal enhancement. All in favor?"

As the ayes rolled in, the bubble in Reina's chest finally burst. Hope soured into defeat and anger... but also into fear. She had done damage to herself here today. But nothing was unsalvageable.

And so, when the vote came to her, she found her mouth forming the word *aye* right alongside the rest of them.

The people in this room had no interest in governing the people of New Avarita, or solving the problems from before the Fall, or advancing humanity or science in any way. They'd grown so used to their position; balancing precariously, keeping their feet firmly on the throats of the New Avaritan population, that they had forgotten what it would feel like to stand on sturdy ground again.

The facade of willful ignorance that had shielded Reina from the ugly truths about Lucre's Algorithm, the farce that was the holographic Principal Chairman, the Advisory Board, had been cracking for months now—maybe years. She tapped out a message to that head engineer, alerting him that a cease-and-desist order was incoming from the Principal Chairman's office, and they were to stop all work on the Esoph-Enhancement project. The moment she selected SEND, all her illusions finally shattered altogether, like a pane of glass dropped on solid pavement.

In that moment, Reina knew two things with complete clarity. First, that she was no longer sure she wanted to serve on the Advisory Board. Second, that she was powerless to leave, knowing she'd be selected for Ascent before her resignation letter uploaded to the server.

She kept her face a mask of curated disinterest as her mind went into free fall and the walls closed in around her.

12

LIV

The Algorithm will eliminate the stressors of unplanned births and missed opportunities by optimizing the procreation process. Instead of leaving things up to chance, New Avarita will build a better, purer future for all by approaching future generations strategically.

—THE HANDBOOK OF LUCRE, *CHAPTER 9*

LIV CHEWED HER lip, lost in thought as Signe led her down the right-side hall of Torrin's Penthouse. They stopped in the doorway to a room less than half the size of her dormitory at university—a place Liam had fondly called her "shoebox."

A pang shot through her chest at the memory.

"This is where you can keep all your shit," Signe said, tapping the top of a small dresser. It was the only piece of furniture in the room aside from the tiny, cot-like bed. "Whenever you get some shit, that is. Do you have any clothes that aren't covered in…" She gestured toward the stain on Liv's shirt.

Liv swallowed, struggling not to look down at it. She'd had the chance to wash her face and hands since arriving, but the stains on her clothes were more stubborn than the ones that had coated her skin. Every time she looked at them her stomach roiled with anger.

She was pissed at the Board, obviously, but she had to admit to herself that she was mad at Ayla, too. Why couldn't she have kept her mouth shut? Once the Correxion Group guards showed up, she had to have known the fight was lost.

Ninety-seven point three percent of all Correxion Group confrontations resulted in arrest or citation. One point eight percent resulted in prem-death for the perpetrator. The remaining point nine percent resulted in the prem-death of one or more Correxion officers and then the prem-death of the perpetrator.

Ayla hadn't had Liv's ridiculous memory, so she might not have known the *exact* statistics, but she had to have known the odds were worse than impossible. Why had she kept fighting?

Ayla was smarter than that. 'Lose the battle, win the war,' wasn't that the saying?

"Got any old shoes our new recruit can have? Or are you gonna make her run around Lower Baranthrum in these fancy-ass loafers like she's Emerson 2.0?"

"Why can't you give her some of your old boots?" Alura called back.

"Because she could fit both feet in one of my boots."

It was an exaggeration, but not by much—the ex-enforcer's feet were at least five sizes larger than Liv's.

Everyone in Liv's family had small feet.

Or, rather, they had back when they were alive.

The thought hit Liv like a gut punch. She was the only member of her family left. She was an only child. Her mom was selected for Ascent when Liv was only eight. Her dad had followed suit the year after Liv and Liam's wedding. And now Liam was gone, too. Even her chosen family was gone, with both Ayla and Kiran getting switch'd this year.

And now she was alone. Untethered. Set adrift in this world with nothing and no one to anchor her with any semblance of belonging.

"Here."

Liv looked up, rising from her thoughts like a drowning soul breaking the surface of the water at the very last moment. She flinched when she saw Signe standing less than a foot from her. She flushed with embarrassment at her reaction as she saw that the woman was holding out a small pile of neatly folded clothes topped with a pair of sneakers. The shoes looked old and beat up, but they looked about the right size—and Signe was right, they'd be far more convenient to run around in than her flapping penny loafers.

The intimidating mercenary woman left her alone in her cubby after that. Liv knew she should sleep, but even after she changed into a pair of borrowed sweatpants and an overlarge shirt and crawled into her new bed, her brain wouldn't stop spinning. It was hard to believe that just over a week ago, she had been laying in her own bed, Liam right beside her.

She could still feel it, if she closed her eyes: his arms around his waist, the slow, steady pulse of his breath tickling the hairs at the nape of her neck. Back then, her biggest worries had been about whether she'd finish the week's work assignments on time and whether their childbearing permit would get approved.

The memory already felt faded and blurry, like something glimpsed through a frosted window or an over-pixelated rinth-generated image.

She'd lost so much in such a short period of time. The rage burning in her belly told her revenge would heal all those wounds; that blowing the entire Medial Complex to hell would give her the sense of justice she craved. But at the end of the day, Liv Spencer wasn't an emotional creature. She was a logistics engineer: a person who had spent her entire adult life working out the details and minutiae to make sure things went as smoothly as possible, considering every possibility, every scenario, every downside, and accounting for it expertly.

Not even wrath could override those instincts.

After another hour of tossing and turning, Liv finally gave up. Her legs and mind were both too restless. The Penthouse had gone silent a long while ago. Even revolutionaries needed sleep, apparently. The clock on her unicomm blinked on her wrist. 04:23. Not quite five o'clock in the morning. Hugging Signe's shirt around her, Liv padded out of her tiny room in stockinged feet, heading back toward the common area of the Penthouse.

Just as she'd suspected, the common area was dark and silent, the only light came from Emerson's terminal monitors, humming quietly in the corner, and the neon signage visible outside the windows. Liv paced over to the window, resting a hand on the cool glass and looking out over the streets of Lower Baranthrum. They were unlike anything she'd grown up with, drenched in multicolored light and ringed with buildings made of brick instead of just metal and glass.

Instead of the modern curves and angles of the architecture in the Core or the prefab uniformity of Upper Lucara's structures, the buildings here looked... distinguished. There were arches and bonneted windows. Stone rain caps winked out in the distance, and a few of the roof peaks even had finials, though most of them looked broken and weathered.

Looking down, Liv saw a tangle of wires and haphazard scaffolding that led all the way to the street below. The smokestacks of the manufacturing plants to the north still belched black smoke up toward the smog filters, even at this hour.

It was beautiful in an odd sort of way. A playground of forgotten buildings from a forgotten age.

When Liv was a kid, she'd wanted to become an architect and design buildings like the massive skyscrapers in the Core—the ones that nearly brushed the top of the projected dome that protected New Avarita from the radiation poisoning outside. She'd ultimately chosen a way less exciting path. And it was a good thing he had, she realized dimly. Who knew what would have happened to her if she'd made a name for herself in architecture? She might have accidentally pissed off the wrong executive and gotten herself switch'd before she even reached the age of thirty.

Liv let out a huff of air through her nostrils, a sound halfway between a laugh and a sigh.

"What was that?"

Liv jumped halfway out of her borrowed sweats at the unexpected sound of a voice behind her. She whirled around to see Emerson's pale face peeking up over the edge of his terminal.

"Shit," she managed to vocalize when her heart rate slowed back down below 150 beats per minute. "You scared me. I didn't know you were there."

"I heard you come in," Emerson admitted in his unsettling yet refreshingly direct manner. He walked out from behind his terminal, still dressed in the same pressed suit he'd been wearing the night before. Black Hat purred, curled up in the crook of his left arm.

"Why didn't you say anything?"

Emerson shrugged, sinking onto the couch beside the window. "Thought maybe you didn't want to talk to anyone."

Liv lowered herself into the chair across from him. Emerson Quinn—RinthRat12—the man who had, until a few days ago, been one of her closest friends.

Or so she'd thought.

She picked at the sleeve of her borrowed shirt for a few seconds, then looked up. "Do you even like *Wasteland Warriors*?"

"Hmm?"

"I know you targeted me. Signe told me." She leaned forward, resting her elbows on her knees. "I'm assuming you found me in some Berger Security employee file and hunted me down on the rinth?"

He didn't deny it.

"So. *Wasteland Warriors*. Do you even like it?"

Emerson cracked a smile. "Do you really think anyone who *didn't* like the game could kick as much ass as I do at it?"

He really had been great at it. She still remembered raising an eyebrow at the stat chart on his profile when he'd first reached out to her:

RINTHRAT12:
LEVEL: *97*
CHARACTER XP: *650*
SPECIALTY: *STEALTH (28), CRAFTING (32)*

She hadn't even known a specialty level could go above 30 at the time. Or that a character could master more than one specialty—an option that unlocked at level 80, she later learned.

Emerson's smile faltered and he returned his attention to the cat on his lap. "Why do you care?"

Liv shrugged, bringing her feet up to sit cross-legged and leaning back in the chair. "Just trying to figure out how much of the person I thought I knew for the past year and a half is real."

Emerson considered her for a second. "The people who know me on the rinth know me better than the ones I know in real life."

"Bullshit," Liv said. "I didn't even know your real name."

"You still don't."

Liv blinked. She sensed that he wasn't done talking, so she kept quiet and waited.

"Signe's real last name isn't Remy," Emerson continued. "Torrin doesn't even know his proper last name, I don't think; his parents both got switch'd before he turned five. He grew up in one of the children's shelters down here after that. But who cares? Knowing a person's name doesn't tell you jack shit about them."

Liv's chest ached at the mention of Torrin's upbringing. What a rough thing to go through at such a young age. She'd heard horrible things about the children's shelters even over in Upper Lucara. She hated to think what the kids growing up in the facilities in a place like Lower Baranthrum had to go through.

Something in Emerson's tone when he mentioned the facility caught her attention and she paused, choosing her words carefully. "Is that where you met Torrin? That shelter?"

"Me? No," Emerson said looking up in surprise. He cracked a smile. "Do I look like I'm forty-some years old? Hell no." He looked around conspiratorially. "Can you keep a secret?"

Liv smiled despite herself. "I can, but I don't know about Black Hat..."

"Black Hat is my best secret-keeper," Emerson said. "Isn't that right, buddy?" He scratched the cat under his furry chin. A purr rumbled low in the animal's chest, permeating the rest of the room. After a long minute, Emerson looked back up at Liv. "I'm a spoiled little rich kid, just like you."

"I'm not a—" Liv started, protesting.

"Yeah, you are," Emerson interrupted. "It's all right, that's not your fault any more than it's Torrin's fault he ended up in that shelter. Or any more than it's Signe's fault she's a sour-faced jerk."

Liv gave him a wide-eyed look, then glanced over both shoulders. Signe didn't appear out of the shadows to punch him into next week for insulting her. "Okay, you're a 'spoiled little rich kid,'" she said, adding air quotes with her fingers for emphasis. "Where did you grow up?"

"Austrum."

She blinked. He really *was* a spoiled little rich kid, then. Besides the Core, Austrum was the nicest and most expensive part of New Avarita.

Average household income was over nine-hundred thousand coin per year. Population of less than eighty thousand people. Average home size was two thousand square feet—more than 2.5 times the size of Liv's townhome back in Upper Lucara.

Some of the most lucrative private install jobs she'd done for Berger had been for homes in Austrum.

"Who are your parents?" she asked. If they lived in Austrum, she'd probably recognize the surname, at least.

"Assholes who weren't shy about smacking around a little kid," Emerson said. Liv's stomach dropped. He was silent for a second, but when he looked back up at Liv, he was smiling again. "I came down to Lower Baranthrum as soon as I figured out how to trick the database into thinking I'd died. Picked a new name for myself and went straight to the docks."

Liv leaned forward on her knees, fascinated. "Why the docks?"

As a kid, she'd always been told the docks were a dangerous, dirty place. Not exactly the kind of place she'd expect a rich kid from Austrum would think to run away to.

"Do you know who Emerson Quinn is?"

"Is this a trick question?"

Emerson grinned at her. "He's the main character from a book published in the mid-2100's. It's called *Amid the Waves*."

"Published in the mid-2100's?" Liv asked. That was before the days of the first Principal Chairman. *Unless that Principal Chairman had been a hologram, too.* "But those books have all been purged from the rinth."

"Not the veilrinth," Emerson said. "I first cracked into the veilrinth when I was about ten years old. Read everything I could find on there. But *Amid the Waves* was one of my favorites." He cocked his head to one side, smiling to himself. "It's about this fisherman who sails across the Atlantic. Finds untainted land outside of New Avarita. Builds a new home."

"You were planning to try to get on a boat," Liv said. "It's a good thing you didn't—the guards down there would have shot you full of holes if you even set foot on the deck of one of those ships. If, by some miracle, you *did* make it on board, your chip would have circuited out as soon as it left port and you hit the edge of the barrier."

"Yeah. It's a good thing I ran into Torrin on the docks that day instead. He saw through me in a second. I wasn't as grimy then as I am now."

Liv snorted as Emerson smoothed his pristine white shirt.

"When he learned how I'd managed to trick the killswitch protocol, he convinced me to stay and try to save New Avarita instead of leaving." He gestured around the Penthouse. "Everything you see now, Torrin and I built that together. We were in lock-step in those early days."

The unsaid implication of that qualifier hung in the air like cigar smoke.

Liv picked at her cuticles, staring at her fingers. "What did you think about what he said tonight? About the volcano?"

Emerson said nothing. She looked up and he was staring out the window. After a long second, he turned, snapping his gaze to hers. "What did *you* think about it?"

Liv hesitated. She couldn't exactly say *I think it's a load of bullshit* to the guy's right-hand man. But she couldn't just say nothing, either. If she just aimlessly went along with this plan, she'd be breaking her promise to Ayla, creating a world that was ridiculously unsafe for Ayla's son, Kiran—for everyone.

She chose her words carefully, finally landing on, "I worry about what consequences that approach might have for New Avarita."

Emerson shrugged. "If we waste all our time thinking about consequences, we'll never do anything at all."

His tone was the same vaguely disinterested tone he'd been using all night, but Liv noticed that he wasn't meeting her eye either. Instead, he was staring determinedly at Black Hat, examining the cat's whiskers as he rubbed his face on Emerson's fingers. She got the impression that he wasn't any more comfortable with Torrin's *burn-it-all-down* mentality than she was. She just needed to coax that out of him.

"True," she allowed. "But who's to say we can't do both? Continue with Torrin's plan and try to make plans for what comes after?"

"Sounds like a lot of plans to keep track of."

"Well, it's a good thing I'm a professional plan-maker." Liv faltered. "Or, at least I was."

Emerson looked back up. "You still are." The words were so simple, spoken so carelessly, but they were exactly what Liv needed to hear. "What kind of plan are you thinking of? For after."

Liv rolled her bottom lip between her teeth, thinking. Whenever she started work on a new layout at Berger, she'd focused on one thing: the numbers. *What was the square footage? How many doorways? How many windows? What was the client's budget? How many rooms did they need secured?*

She couldn't make a plan for the future of New Avarita. Not yet. Not without hard data. "To really make a plan, we'll need to run calculations. Population growth projections, grow-dome capacities, housing need estimates, all kinds of math." She pulled up a map of New Avarita on her unicomm, letting it hover in the air between them. Her brain spun as she studied the floating image, and a realization struck her between the eyes. "But before any of those numbers matter, we'll need one thing."

"What's that?"

"More space." Liv outlined the city-state's limits with one finger. "No one leaves New Avarita. The train lines end at the shield border. Do we know what's out there?"

"And you just accused me of not really knowing *Wasteland Warriors*," Emerson said wryly.

"Ha, ha," Liv said flatly. "I doubt there's roving bands of mercenaries out there, but honestly, who knows? To handle the population burst that will happen after the killswitch protocol is destroyed, we'll need more space. That means we need to find habitable land outside of New Avarita."

"What the hell am I walking in on, here? A pajama party?"

Liv jumped, collapsing her holo-display and spinning in her chair to see Signe Remy stalking into the room. Even unarmed and in her nightclothes, the woman was intimidating. There was just something dangerous about the way she held herself. She radiated a confidence that non-lethal people simply didn't have.

And that distinctly lethal woman had just overheard Liv plotting to go against her boss's plans. Her first eight hours in New Avarita's rebellion and Liv was already defying orders. Not a great start.

Emerson, on the other hand, seemed completely unfazed at her appearance. He cocked his head to one side. "If this is a pajama party, I think I'm overdressed."

"You're always overdressed," Signe snorted. She crossed the room, stopping right in front of Liv, then held out her hand. "Wrist."

Liv's stomach dropped, but she held out her wrist as ordered. Signe tapped on the edge of her forearm, just beside her wrist bone. The display sprang back to life, reloading the last image Liv had shared: the map of New Avarita with her markings circling the boundaries.

Signe studied the map in silence for a few seconds while Liv's heartrate continued to skyrocket.

Finally, Signe frowned. "So, do we think our best bet is west or north?"

Liv's brain short-circuited. "What?"

"To find new land that isn't fried to shit." Signe pointed at the northern edge of the city-state. "I think west's our best bet. Mostly because I think it'll be the easiest spot to sneak one of your little flying machine things past the barrier there."

"Drones," Emerson inserted.

"Yeah, whatever."

Liv shook her head, trying to clear it. "I'm sorry… you're not going to rat me out to Torrin?"

"Rat you out? For what? Trying to make a plan that doesn't end in fiery torment?" Signe said. She slouched onto the couch next to Emerson, leaning over to give Black Hat a cursory scratch. "Believe it or not, I have no interest in starving to death, and I'm pretty sure the rest of New Avarita would agree with me there." She shrugged. "I like Torrin and all, but the guy gets tunnel vision sometimes. The way I see it, we're just taking some extra initiative and solving a problem before it blows up in his fucking face. He'll thank us when the time comes."

"Right," Liv said. She nodded sharply, then repeated, "Right. Okay, Emerson you have drones? Can they take bio readings?"

"No idea," Emerson said. "Never done a bio reading before. But I'm sure someone on the veilrinth's got the right sensors."

"Great," Signe said. "You find those, I'll work on finding a place we can sneak a drone past the barrier after we wrap up the Huldra job tomorrow." She looked at Liv. "And you're going to get some sleep. Because you look like absolute shit."

When Liv got back to her cubby, her legs weren't antsy anymore. She crawled into her lumpy, uncomfortable bed, rolling to face the wall away from the door. Her thoughts drifted to little Kiran Junior. Where was he now? Locked up in some Medla House nursery until he was old enough for his chip install, no doubt. Alone.

Hopefully, wherever he was, he was at least warm and safe for now. She wouldn't be able to save him from getting chipped... but there was still a chance she could save him from the killswitch protocol.

"I'm going to save him, Ayla," she whispered into the darkness. "I promise."

When Liv's eyes finally fluttered shut, she thought she smelled a phantom scent of honeysuckle and lavender playing in her nostrils. She slept more soundly than she had since Liam died.

13

SIGNE

The dichotomy of safety and sovereignty is a false one. There cannot be one without the other. The Algorithm seeks to take the mental load of nonessential decisions off the people of New Avarita, protecting their most important freedoms while giving them the space to strive toward their ultimate goal.

—THE HANDBOOK OF LUCRE, *CHAPTER 13*

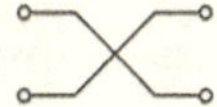

SIGNE HADN'T SET foot in the Core in years. The last time Torrin had risked sending her, she'd almost been made three times within an hour: twice by facial sensors and once by an old enforcer colleague. But now, here she was, sitting on a sleek train filled with smartly dressed people immersed in their unicomms as they traveled toward that glistening hub of greed and gilded bullshit.

At least she was less likely to be recognized this time because, as Emerson had so kindly pointed out, she'd gotten *"old as shit."*

She couldn't say the kid was wrong, though. Her face was lined with wrinkles and scars she hadn't had back when she worked for Reina Arthur. Her hair was long instead of cropped close to her skull, and it was streaked with gray. The only thing that remained the same was her boots. They weren't the same pair, obviously, but the same exact type. She always sprang for the real thing instead of relying on black market knockoffs.

As much as she hated giving one of the Teras brands a single coin, she hated sore feet and blisters more.

Aside from the boots, Signe wore a dark blue jumpsuit—the same exact color and style as the ones Alura and Gaius were wearing, sitting on the train beside her. The logo stitched into the collar of each suit marked them as employees of Electro-View: a subsidiary of Propagn Advanced Systems that handled electrical maintenance in the Core.

Much like Signe's aged face, the disguise wouldn't hold up under close scrutiny, but most of the people in the Core thought too highly of themselves to look twice at anyone who actually worked with their hands. That disdain would help them slip past the human eyes while Emerson and Liv's map kept them clear of the electrical eyes altogether.

"What are the chances Wonder Girl actually got everything right?" Alura asked, mind clearly in the same place.

Signe shot her a look and raised an eyebrow. "You'd better hope she did. Otherwise, this ugly-ass jumpsuit is the last thing we're ever going to wear."

There was a lot riding on Liv Spencer's supposedly miraculous memory at the moment. But Emerson hadn't spent over a year trying to recruit the woman on a whim. Clearly, he thought she knew what she was talking about.

Right on cue, Emerson's voice sounded in Signe's ear. "She got everything right." A group channel, from the look on Alura and

Gaius's faces, broadcasting into all three of their ear enhancements at the same time. "You three will be in and out and back at the Penthouse in time for dinner."

"Depending on who's cooking, we might not want that," Gaius said.

Signe snorted. "Like you've ever turned down free food in your life."

"Was that a fat joke? C'mon, Signe, I thought you were better'n that."

"Not a fat joke. A moocher joke, if anything."

"Oh, well, that's alright, then."

"Quit flirting and get your heads in the game," Emerson said.

"Is that how you flirt, Em?" Alura asked, leaning back and peering out the window to gauge their progress. They were speeding toward the needle-like Huldra headquarters now. The train car was loud, full of so many morning commuters that no one outside of their unicomm channel could hear their quiet conversation. "No wonder you've never brought anyone back to the Penthouse."

"I mean, for him to bring someone *back* to the Penthouse he'd first have to *leave* the Penthouse," Signe said.

Alura snorted.

"All right, all right, very funny," Emerson said drily. "Now, if you're ready to get to work…"

Gaius, Alura, and Signe all flinched in unison as Emerson broke into their eye enhancements. Signe's field of vision suddenly included a mass of hovering holographic pointers, and when she looked at the central Huldra building out the window she could see splashes of red and yellow—active camera views and sensor zones per Liv's recollection of the security systems she'd helped install the month before.

How fortunate for their organization that she'd finished up that job right before the series of events that pushed her over the edge and out of her cushy Upper Lucaran life. Signe's stomach twisted. She had no idea how Torrin would have pulled off something like that, but she had a sneaking suspicion there may have been more than luck involved in the process.

"It would be great if you literally ever gave us a heads up you were about to do that, Em," Gaius said, rubbing his eyes.

"And miss out on the chance to shut you three up for a few seconds?" Emerson said in their ears. "Never."

"You're such an asshole," Signe chuckled.

"Maybe," Emerson allowed. "But you have to admit I'm *just* good enough at my job to get away with exactly how much of an asshole I am. It's a delicate balance I've spent years curating."

Gaius snorted. "Careful, that's some Board-sounding shit right there."

"'To know your enemy, you must become your enemy.'"

"Didn't know you were a philosopher," Signe said as the train glided to a stop. Here in the Core, there was no squealing of brakes or halting, jerking motions like the transports back in Lower Baranthrum. Just a smooth transition from rocketing down a track at close to a hundred miles per hour to sitting at a standstill.

"It's Sun Tzu." When no one reacted, Emerson sighed audibly. "From *Art of War*, you heathens."

"Sorry, we haven't all read the entirety of the veilrinth," Signe muttered, pushing herself to stand.

The commuters all around them closed out their VR interfaces and rose, lining up like cattle in a Koegen Corp facility, filing one by one toward the slaughterhouse. Signe, Alura, and Gaius lined up right alongside them, following the flow of primly-dressed bodies out of the transport and onto the streets of the inner Core. Signe blinked as her eyes adjusted to the sunlit streets.

The sunlight was the same here as it was in Lower Baranthrum, obviously. The same sun filtering through the dome-like, electronic barrier that stretched over all of New Avarita like a soap bubble. Yet here, the light seemed brighter, somehow, like even the sun didn't want to be associated with the streets and docks to the south.

It was probably the reflections off all the buildings and transports. Not a speck of rust in sight, just gleaming, glittering behemoths of steel and glass. She remembered the first time she'd ever arrived in the Core—when she'd come to enlist in enforcer training at the ripe old age of seventeen. She'd been just as dazed by the sight of the district then, but more 'wonderstruck' and less 'fucking irritated.'

Her eyes flicked back up to the electronic barrier overhead as her hand drifted to the left hip pocket of her jumpsuit. Emerson's drone lay there, pressing against her hip bone. After this job, she'd need to find a gap in that barrier to slip the drone through, sending it out into the nuclear wasteland beyond to search for a speck of habitable land. But that was a problem for later.

The problem now was right in front of them. Huldra Industries. The building rose like a periscoping cobra, tall, narrow, and intimidating. Signe's heart beat a steady path up-up-up her throat. *Was Reina inside at this very moment?* She envisioned her old boss standing at her office window high above them, peering down, arms folded behind her back. The thought made Signe's skin crawl.

This job was worse than risky. She could see the security plans in her eye enhancements still. So much fucking gadgetry. Electronic eyes and ears, watching, waiting, ready to strike at any moment. They needed to be as careful as possible if they were going to survive this.

"Going mute," Signe said over the group channel.

"Sir, yes sir," Emerson said. He was always mocking her background in security work. To be fair, she made it easy for him when she used lingo like that.

Still, she rolled her eyes, then nodded to Gaius and Alura and the three of them took off around the edge of the Huldra building at a quick-but-not-too-quick pace.

There was only one official entrance to the headquarters—a splotch of red on Signe's display dark enough to make it look like the building was bleeding out. The entrance was so tangled with cameras, facial sensors, and chip scanners that it was impossible to even pretend to walk through those doors without getting caught. In short, if any of Torrin's supposedly dead crew members tried to enter Huldra Industries that way, they'd be swarmed by Correxion officers or security mechs in half a heartbeat, then switch'd half a heartbeat after that—unless Reina decided to keep them alive for questioning. Even in that case, they'd be switch'd before dinner.

Thankfully, Liv's memorized schematics and Emerson's tech

wizardry gave Signe and the others another option—a back door.

Well, it wasn't really a door. Technically, it was a part of the HVAC system. In early spring, the weather was pretty pleasant, hovering around the mid-70s Fahrenheit. But New Avarita got hotter than a grow-dome at high sun during the summer months. Quality air temperature control was a must for any building—especially the ones positioned in the Core and the districts farther north, away from the breezes off the Atlantic.

Huldra's headquarters wasn't just any old building, though. It was the second-largest building in the Core, aside from the Medial Complex itself. A building that massive had to have an HVAC system to match. If the schematics Liv had helped Emerson create were accurate, once they got inside, the air vents would be large enough to crawl through until they reached the second floor.

The entry point, on the other hand, would be a bit of a squeeze.

Signe stood at one edge of the building, pretending to lace up her boot while really keeping a lookout for any nosy passersby. Gaius did the same on the other corner, fiddling with his unicomm settings as though struggling to recalibrate something. As they kept watch, Alura positioned herself under the angled mouth of the duct system.

Her mech-arm didn't have a gun. Instead, it was equipped with all kinds of other useful tools. Out of the corner of her eye, Signe could see her flipping through settings. *Take your fucking time, by all means.*

Finally, the woman set to work at the vent. There was a slight *hum* of tiny machinery as Alura's laser-cutter sliced through the grate. The jangle of metal on stone came next as Alura pulled out a section of the vent's mouth and stowed it gingerly behind the utility box a few feet away.

Signe looked back to the corner she was guarding. Still no one approaching. Instead, everyone flocked to the main entrance, immersed in VR games, work, or unicomm calls while they waited in the long line at security. Signe remembered pitying the poor bastards who had to wait in line to go to work every day. She had always simply walked past them and cut straight to the front: a privilege of walking a half-step behind the woman who owned the building.

When Signe looked back to the vent, Alura was nowhere to be found. Gaius went next, leaving her to watch both corners as he grunted and groaned, struggling to squeeze his broad frame through the grate.

"Security mech incoming," Emerson said, breaking the radio silence.

Shit.

The second Gaius's kicking legs disappeared up into the vent, Signe darted out of the alley. She leaned her back against the front of the SocieCorp bank near the back of the line of workers waiting to get into Huldra's headquarters. She pulled up a strategy game on her unicomm, mimicking the rest of the bored commuters in line. A split second later, the security mech whizzed by. Signe averted her face, avoiding its facial scanners as it beeped and whirred through the line, making a beeline toward the main doors.

"Close one," Emerson breathed as the mech zipped on out of sight.

"No kidding," Signe muttered. She pretended to answer a call on her unicomm, giving herself a reason to back out of line again without suspicion. She stalked back into the alley and examined the vent. "This is why you need to start coming on these jobs, Em. Your scrawny ass would have had no trouble fitting through this opening."

"You know the boss man won't risk that," Emerson said. "He loves me too much."

Signe snorted. Torrin Calix loved one thing and one thing alone: revenge. She shot one look over each shoulder, then made a beeline for the vent. Emerson might have access to the security mech database, but he didn't have access to Huldra's cameras just yet. That meant that there would be no eyes on the alley while Signe tried to muscle her way up into the vent.

Please, let me have an easier time at this than Gaius did.

Signe pulled Sally from its hiding place, tucked along the back waistband of her jumpsuit. She'd collapsed the gun into its smallest form—something not much larger than a pistol—but still, the weapon wasn't exactly designed for stealth. She gave it a loving pat, then boosted it up into the vent opening.

"Catch," she said to the group channel. She held her breath, then tossed the gun inside, cringing as she waited for the deafening metallic *clang*. But it never came. Gaius or Alura had managed to catch it, thank Lucre.

The vent was definitely a tight squeeze. Her journey through it wasn't as smooth and easy as Alura's, but it wasn't as much of a struggle as it had been for Gaius, either. She was thin enough to make it through the mouth easily, but her lanky height made the curve at the top a bit of a challenge.

A few less-than-graceful moments later, she landed, crouched beside Alura. She held a hand out to Gaius, taking Sally back and threading the weapon back into its makeshift holster. Then, the three of them knelt in silence for a few seconds, waiting.

No alarms sounded. No footsteps came running. Emerson didn't pipe into their ears warning them of impending doom. Nothing.

Signe cracked a smile and slipped out of her heavy boots. She tied the laces together and looped them over one shoulder, then signaled for them to move forward, silent and prowling through the vents of Huldra headquarters.

Emerson's beacons led them through the twisting steel tunnels. None of them dared speak, sliding their sock feet over the bottom of the vent to avoid making any sound as they crept forward. Signe could hear the sounds of movement beneath them, above, them, all around them. This was the least dangerous part of this job by far, but the sensation of floating just above the heads of her enemies, unseen and unheard, was unsettling. She almost couldn't wait to be out of the vent and in the thick of it, disguised by her coverall and the fact that everyone here was too damn busy to take much notice of a few low-level workers.

"Just one more curve and you'll be in the maintenance room," Emerson's voice intoned, as if he could read her thoughts.

The beacon blinked up ahead, pulsing on the surface of a grate that came halfway up Signe's torso. She peered through the metal slats. No sign of life, but that made sense—according to the map, this grate led into a maintenance closet. That closet was their destination for two reasons.

First, it was unlikely that anyone would be there, sitting in the darkness, to witness three grown-ass people emerging from the vents like pesky rats. Second, every maintenance room in Huldra's headquarters was equipped with an access panel. That access panel was the only thing that would prevent them from getting scanned or spotted by facial sensors as they made their way through the rest of headquarters and up to that air-gapped terminal.

Alura's mech-arm worked its magic on the vent again. This time, she used a magnetic attachment to unscrew the screws from the inside, enabling them to put the vent back into place when they left the maintenance room. In the dark closet, Signe slipped her boots back on, then addressed Emerson through her unicomm again.

"All right, Em. Where's this access panel?"

"Should be down by the floorboards, on the opposite wall from the vent," Emerson said. The area lit up in her VR-enhanced vision.

Gaius dropped to his knees in front of the spot. Sure enough, Signe saw a small, raised panel there. Gaius hovered his forearm over the baseboard, pausing as Emerson used his unicomm to make a proximity-based connection. After several long seconds of Gaius crouching in the dark, arm outstretched at an awkward angle, the access panel sent a shimmer of green light hovering over its surface.

"Connection is a go," Emerson said. "Gaius, you'll need to stay here so I can maintain the link. Alura and Signe, give me one second..." A few moments of silence, then, "All right, the cameras outside this door are running on a new scan pattern. You'll have a window... *Now.*"

Signe and Alura gave Gaius a nod, then slipped out the maintenance room door and into the hallway beyond without another word. Signe could see the orangish arcs of light that represented the camera's viewfinders arcing away from them. Before the cameras had the chance to arc back, she and Alura slipped down the hallway and out of range.

Hopefully no one would enter the maintenance room at all, but if they did, an Electro-View worker using an access panel probably wouldn't raise too many red flags. Gaius would be all right. With Emerson now knee-deep in Huldra's internal systems, hopefully she and Alura would be just fine, too.

Signe and Alura moved through the halls, Signe taking the lead, Alura falling in a half-step behind. It had been a long time since Signe had been inside one of Reina's buildings. It was still just as pretentious as she remembered: a strange mix of shining chrome fixtures, bleeding-edge tech, and classic art. She wondered dimly if that creepy, abstract statue was still up on the fifteenth floor—the one that had always reminded her of a nightmare she'd had as a child. But there would be no time for sight-seeing today.

It was a risk for her to be here at all, but she was the only member of Torrin's crew who knew her way around the place. Even with all Emerson's gadgets and a floorplan born of Liv Spencer's flawless memory, there was no substitute for the easy posture of a person who actually knew where they were going.

Emerson intoned instructions in their ears, warning them to veer off course into one hallway or another whenever he saw Huldra security officers on the cameras approaching them, or worse, whenever a security mech came wheeling their way. The security officers could cause trouble if they sensed something about them was suspicious and thought to stop them, but if they ran into a security mech, they were fucked on-sight.

Security mechs would automatically scan the chips of anyone roaming these hallways to confirm they had the clearance to be where they were. If either Signe or Alura were scanned it would raise red flags, not only because they weren't supposed to be here, but because they weren't supposed to be alive.

In short, if they ran into a single mech on their path between here and the server room on the fourth floor, it was game over, not just for today's mission, but for Torrin's entire revolution.

No pressure.

Their path through Huldra's hallways was less direct than a shitty Lower Baranthrum transport line, but after a quarter of an hour, she and Alura managed to make it to the fourth floor without stepping face-first into the reddish-orange beams of a single camera or running into a single security officer, mech, or scanpoint. If anyone reviewed the footage carefully, they'd notice two Electro-View workers meandering around in a few camera angles, but if the rest of the day went to plan, there would never be any reason for anyone to review that footage.

Today, they weren't stealing anything except for information.

"There's the door," Alura muttered as the pair of them came to a stop halfway down the hall. It was a bit unnecessary, seeing as Emerson's display projected so many beacons on the door it looked like a damned fireworks display. Signe decided to give the other woman a pass, though—it had been a stressful morning.

They both pulled up random electrical schematics on their unicomms, pretending to study them intently for the benefit of the engineers and other businesspeople rushing by with their eyes glued to their own holo-displays.

"Yeah, and there's a scanner right there," Signe said, pointing her gaze up to study the bright red bar hovering over the door with distaste. "Can you override it, Em?"

"Yes," Emerson said. "I mean, am I sure, no. But I think so." There was a pause. "Ah, shit."

"What?" Signe intoned, looking over her shoulder. No mechs came wheeling into view.

"The scanner system for this door is on a continuous loop."

"Meaning?" Alura asked, scrolling to another random electrical schematic pulled from the rinth and pretending to puzzle over it.

"Meaning I can block the signal, but if I block it for too long it'll sound off a tampering alarm."

"Define 'too long,'" Signe murmured.

"One second, maybe less."

Signe nodded. Too short a window for both her and Alura to get through the door. Maybe too short for even one of them to get through, if Emerson's estimates were off. The already insane risk of going through that door had just spiked by about a thousand percent.

Signe hesitated for a fraction of a breath, then said, "Alura will stay out here. I'll make the link solo."

"Solo?" Emerson asked.

"I'll make the link with a little ferret named Emerson in my ear," she amended.

"Much better," Emerson said. "On my go." There was a few seconds' pause. Signe inched closer to the door, still apparently lost in the nonsensical schematics hovering on her holo-display. She was an inch from the door when Emerson hissed, "Go."

The red light on the scanner bar over the door flickered off. At the same moment, the locking mechanism winked green. Signe grabbed the handle, twisting and pushing the door open. She slipped inside and closed the door behind her as quickly as possible.

Again, she waited for a few seconds, eyes squeezed shut as she steeled herself for the sound of alarms or the whirring of security mech's wheels on the smooth tile floor of the hallways. But there was nothing. Nothing but the soft beeping and humming of a dozen terminals running at once. Signe opened her eyes, letting out all her anxiety in a single breath as she took in her surroundings.

She had never been in any of the server rooms at Huldra before. She wondered dimly if her security clearance as an enforcer would have let her access this room if she'd wanted to. Probably, but she'd never had much use for technology beyond her unicomm and enhancements. She'd never even thought twice about trying to walk through the boring, slate-gray door now locked tightly behind her—honestly, she'd never even noticed the door before at all. A thought suddenly pulsed through Signe and she gripped Sally's stock, tucked beneath the folds of her jumpsuit.

"You'll be able to get me back out, right?"

"No, I thought you wanted to move here. Damn, I've already forwarded your mail and everything," Emerson said.

Signe snorted. *Forwarded her mail.* Trust Emerson to make a joke that hadn't been relevant since the mid-2100s.

"As long as everything goes smoothly and you're able to move as fast as you did last time, yes, I can get you back out," Emerson said. "Now, let's get what we came here for."

Signe nodded, even though Emerson couldn't see her. She walked through the sea of terminals, making her way toward the back left corner of the room where Emerson's beacon glinted merrily. Even without the beacon, Signe thought she could have figured out this was the place she needed to go. This terminal was older than the other ones in the room—almost archaic.

Strike that: it *was* archaic. So archaic, in fact, that a prox-link wouldn't work. But they had planned for this. Signe pulled out the series of wires Emerson had given to her back at the Penthouse. She twisted them together, then connected one end to the port in the wrist of her mech-arm, then fed the other under the surface of the terminal. She grunted slightly as she struggled to reach, fumbling in the darkness for a few seconds before she was finally able to insert the cable into the appropriate port.

When the cable clicked into place, Signe took a step back, shooting a glance over her shoulder toward the door as Emerson took control of the terminal. She didn't hear any signs of a disturbance or alarm outside. If there were any signs of trouble, she knew Alura would tell her, but there was always the off-chance that Alura wouldn't be *able* to tell her—if she was scanned by a security mech and carted off to the nearest Correxion station for questioning, for instance.

"Fuck."

Emerson's curse wasn't panicked—just the calm, disappointed curse of a man who'd discovered something irritating. The word snapped Signe's mind away from thoughts of swarming security officers and back to the task at hand. There were no fewer than thirty windows open on the terminal now, all hovering in front of the monitors at various depths as Emerson leafed through them. Schematics and spreadsheets and patents shuffled around so quickly there was no way Emerson could actually read all of it.

Obviously he was reading it, somehow. He kept highlighting passages and then flipping back to schematics, then flipping right back again.

"What's wrong?" Signe asked. "Does bringing down the system activate all the switches?"

"No," Emerson said. His tone was grim.

"Isn't that good news?" Signe raised an eyebrow. "Unless you *wanted* to kill everyone? I always knew you were a sociopath."

"The killswitch functionality is the parent function of the entire chip's coding," Emerson said, not even acknowledging Signe's jibe. Signe wasn't sure what the words he'd just said meant, but Emerson never missed the opportunity to shoot her a well-crafted comeback. Whatever this was, it had to be bad.

"What does that mean?"

There was a pause. Some more windows shuffled around on the screen. In her mind's eye, she could almost see the tiny furrow in Emerson's brow as he hunted through the documents, hoping to find something that would prove his original statement wrong. Apparently, he came up empty, because her unicomm picked up a wave of static that she recognized as a heavy sigh.

"It means we can disable the killswitch protocol without killing everyone… but we can't disable the killswitch protocol without disabling the chips altogether."

"So what? Just—" Signe paused as the implications of what Emerson had said crashed over her like a wave.

She looked down at her mech-arm. It was powered and controlled through her chip. So was her unicomm. And her eye-enhancements. Her ability to read without the words jumbling together like popcorn in the microwave. All of that and more was processed through the tiny, Huldra Industries chip implanted in the back of her skull.

The people of New Avarita managed their coin, their entertainment, their work, their fucking home door locks all using their chips. If the chips went offline without warning, all of New Avaritan society would collapse into chaos. No one would be able to access their coin, the transports wouldn't let anyone enter, so people would just be stuck wherever it was they'd last gotten off when the system went down, or they'd have to walk. If they had to walk, they'd better hope they didn't have mech-legs, because those would be offline, too.

Before the Fall, people had lived without chips just fine. But nowadays? If the chip system went offline tomorrow, the streets of New Avarita would look like a scene out of *Wasteland Warriors* by Tuesday.

She swallowed. "So… what do we do? There has to be a way around it…"

"I would have to recode the entire base script that controls the chips," Emerson said. "And to do that, we'd have to bring the chips offline, anyway. Although maybe we could do it in waves… Take the chips offline a few at a time, just long enough to run the new code… but we'd have to be wired into this terminal the whole time."

"How long would that take?" Signe asked. "Alura still hasn't sounded the alarm, we might be able to—"

She cut off as Emerson laughed bitterly. "Signe. I'm good. But I'm not that good. Even if I had the new code written and tested right now—which I don't—it would take days to update every chip in New Avarita. Longer—weeks."

"Fuck," Signe said. "So, what does this mean? Back to the drawing board?"

She didn't even know what *back to the drawing board* meant for them now, though. If taking the killswitches offline wasn't possible, then what was the plan? Emerson couldn't dupe the system into thinking Torrin's crew was dead without actually killing them for much longer. Every day they flirted with disaster just by walking outside the Penthouse. All it would take is for one crew member to get caught and scanned and the whole operation would crumble.

Her unicomm went silent for a few seconds. When it clicked back on, it wasn't Emerson's voice in her ear, but Torrin Calix himself.

"Sit tight, Signe," he said. His voice was completely level, no signs of panic. Maybe in those few seconds of dead air on her end, they'd cooked up a plan on theirs. "Emerson is pulling out a bunch of schematics and coding shit. We can look into it all when you're back."

Signe stared blankly at the terminal in front of her until the windows began to wink out of sight, one by one. Eventually, the monitors were blank again, the terminal humming softly in the otherwise silent room.

"That's it, Emerson has what he needs. You can sever the connection and get out of there. We'll discuss the details once you're back at the Penthouse."

"All right." Signe groped under the terminal, pulling the cable free. She detached it from her mech-arm next, winding it up and tucking it into the pocket of her coveralls. She didn't know what there was left to talk about, but judging from the tightness in Torrin's tone, she wasn't sure she'd like how that conversation went.

SIGNE ARRIVED BACK at Torrin's Penthouse just after nightfall. The first thing she saw when the elevator doors *dinged* open was Emerson Quinn's face, peering out from behind his terminal. He looked even paler than usual, which was saying something. Not that Signe was surprised: patience had never been Torrin's strong suit. Being told he needed to go back to the drawing board this late in the game would almost certainly have sent the man into a towering temper.

But as she stepped out of the elevator and caught sight of Torrin Calix, he wasn't running his hands through his hair, breaking shit with his mech arm, or otherwise raging around the Penthouse. Instead, he was sitting in his armchair, elbows resting comfortably on his knees as he leaned forward, examining a hologram of the Medial Complex with Liv Spencer at his side. Liv looked like she was on the verge of throwing up.

Gaius and Alura were already there. She'd purposely gotten herself separated from them back in Old Altum, pretending to need to take a piss while really heading toward the barrier to slip one of Emerson's tiny drones out of her pocket.

"So, we have a plan, then?" Signe guessed, kicking off her boots as she strode into the living area. She didn't address her lateness. Drawing attention to it with excuses would only be more suspicious.

"Of course we have a plan. We always had a plan," Torrin said.

Liv shot her a look around Torrin's back—a look that said *what the fuck do I say?* Signe's stomach dropped. "Whoa, whoa, whoa. Tor, we *had* a plan, but you heard what Emerson said. If we take the killswitches offline, it will—"

"Signe. We broke into Huldra today to answer one question," Torrin interrupted. "We wanted to see if bringing down the database would kill everyone in New Avarita." He smiled, looking up from the hologram. "And it won't. So, onward."

"Right, but Torrin," Signe said, shooting a look at Emerson, then one at Alura, who was shrugging out of the Electro-View jumpsuit by the door. "Without the chips…"

"Getting rid of the killswitch protocol is more important than keeping the chips."

Signe heard the steel in the man's tone. He was calm on the outside, but she knew firsthand what that steel meant. It was the calm that came before the rage. Arguing with him would only result in a few new holes punched in the walls of the Penthouse. She had to try, anyway. "You have a mech-arm, for fuck's sake, Torrin. What are you going to do if—"

"Live with one arm."

"And you'll live without access to your coin? Without being able to open your own front door? Without your unicomm or access to the rinth?"

Emerson shook his head silently behind his terminal. He must have already tried to take this tack.

"People did it for thousands of years before the Fall. They can do it again."

"Not overnight, Torrin," Signe said. "You're not stupid, you know this is going to cause a panic. People are going to die, Torrin, and not a clean, painless death like the killswitch, either."

"It's not our job to fix all the problems of the world. It's our job to create enough disruption to make space for people to make a better world after."

Signe ground her teeth together. She couldn't believe what she was hearing. Torrin had always been a reckless son-of-a-bitch, but this was a new level of stupidity. Signe wouldn't stand for it. "And if the rest of us refuse to help you burn this world to the ground? What then?"

Torrin's eye took on a dangerous glint. He turned off the hologram and pushed himself to his feet, cocking his head to one side, looking for all the world like a bird of prey ready to rip out her entrails. "Is that what you're going to do? Refuse to help me?" He huffed out a laugh. "You're a talented soldier, Signe, but that's all you are: a soldier. I have plenty of those." He nodded at Gaius and Alura. "If you won't help, there's plenty of others who'll take your place."

Signe shot Emerson a meaningful look. The boy took the hint. He swallowed. "And if some… *non*-soldiers on the team aren't… fully comfortable with this plan? What then?"

Torrin's eyebrow shot up. He looked at Emerson, then at Liv, neither of whom were meeting his eye. "Is this a mutiny, then?" he huffed out a mirthless laugh, then twitched the fingers of his left hand. His mech-arm buzzed and whirred and in the blink of an eye his armgun barrel was out, a lethal round primed and ready.

"I created this group for the purpose of bringing down the Board. I thought every single one of you knew that when you decided to join it," he continued. "Anyone not interested in bringing down the Board shouldn't be here. If you'd rather be truly dead, I can fucking arrange that."

He rotated around the room, first pointing the barrel at Signe, then Emerson, then Liv. When the barrel reached Gaius, he threw his hands up. "Hey, boss, I never said anything about a mutiny." He looked to Alura, then shot Signe a warning glare. "Give Signe and Em a second to process the change of pace here, eh? No one here is a Board bootlicker. I'll burn this whole damn city-state down if I can see them fall."

"Yeah," Alura agreed. She looked uncertain, glancing down at her own mech-arm, no doubt imagining it hanging, heavy and useless at her side without the power it got from her chip. But it was clear she wasn't about to argue with a man waving around a loaded and primed armgun. "I'll live with one arm if it means the killswitch protocol goes down in flames."

Signe shared a look with Emerson, then Liv. Their silent consensus was clear: there was no point in fighting with Torrin like this. They couldn't stop him unless they wanted to die. Signe was no coward, but she was also no idiot. There was no use in wasting her life on this fight. Not yet.

She put up her hands and shook her head slowly. "Sorry, Tor. It's just not the news I was hoping we'd get today."

Torrin stared at her down the barrel of his armgun for a long moment, evaluating. Then, he disarmed the weapon and lowered his arm with a tight smile. "Could have been better news, yes. But the plan goes forward as designed." He paused. "Oh, and Signe?"

"Yeah?"

"If you ever refer to a killswitch death as '*clean*' again, I'll show you just how messy death can be."

"Understood, boss," Signe said.

The tension in the room faded as Alura raided the kitchen cabinets for a snack and Emerson resumed his usual *tap-tap-tapping* on his holo-keyboard. But this wasn't over. Signe knew they couldn't just ignore what they'd learned today, and judging from the looks Liv was shooting her, she wasn't alone in that thought.

Pulling the chips might bring an end to the killswitches and the Board but it would also bring New Avarita to its fucking knees. Bringing down the killswitch database to save New Avarita was like shooting a man in the head to save him from drowning. There had to be a better path forward. And if there was, Signe planned to take it—whether or not Torrin Calix agreed.

14

LIV

The Algorithm is infallible, but humans are not. As we prepare ourselves to rise to the next plane of existence, we must be prepared to handle crime, disease, and other human faults. The Office of the Principal Chairman is in charge of keeping society running smoothly so every citizen can pursue their ultimate goal.

—THE HANDBOOK OF LUCRE, *CHAPTER* 34

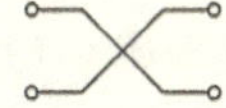

IN THE PAST week, Liv had lived a dozen lives. She'd been a wife, a widow, a law-abiding citizen, a rebel. Now, it was time to add one more title to the list of increasingly concerning monikers:

Traitor.

She looked up at the buzzing neon sign for FISHERMAN'S WHARF, a pub just off the docks. A seedy looking place for a seedy meeting. Fitting.

An overwhelming cacophony assaulted Liv's eardrums as she pulled the door open. The inside of the pub was twice as sketchy as it had looked from outside, if that was at all possible, and far too crowded for a Monday. Steel tables dotted the room, seemingly at random, and shadowed booths lined all four walls. The bar rail in the center was manned by a tired-looking woman with two mech-arms, both bootleg from the looks of them. Holo-ads floated between the tables, projected from the lights on the ceiling, advertising everything from the latest flavored vodka to pornographic VR games.

Liv kept her head down, cutting quickly across the crowded bar to find Signe sitting in the back corner booth. It had been three days since Signe returned from the Huldra mission. Three days since she'd managed to shake Alura and Gaius long enough to slip Emerson's drone through a small gap in the nodes projecting the southwestern edge of New Avarita's protective barrier.

Now, it was time to see if the drone had brought them any hope.

She frowned as she slid onto the bench across from Signe. "Tea?" she asked, eying Signe's steaming cup.

"No, it's beer. The refrigeration system here just sucks ass," Signe said sarcastically. "Yes, it's tea."

"Hmm," Liv said.

Ninety-nine-point-seven percent of all bar patrons in Lower Baranthrum drank alcohol. Eighty-four percent drank hard liquor. Of that eighty-four percent, sixty-three percent preferred dark rum. Liv hadn't bothered to research the percentage of Lower Baranthrum drinkers who preferred tea. That data had not seemed relevant in her efforts to blend in at this bar. Clearly, Signe didn't care about things like that.

"What, did you want me to get hammered while waiting for you guys?"

"You know, they make enhancements to filter out the effects of alc—"

Signe waved a hand. "Yeah, yeah, I've heard it a thousand times. You know what's even easier than priming some enhancement with alcohol-filtering enzymes every few weeks?"

"Not drinking the alcohol in the first place?" Liv guessed.

Signe winked and pointed at her. "Bingo."

"You do that, then," Liv said. "I'm going to try to actually fit in in this place."

"Good luck with that," Signe snorted.

Liv ordered a rum and cola from the bar. She regretted it the instant she took a sip. The flavor transported her back through the years to all the university parties where she and Liam had turned off their alcohol filters and dumped cheap, synthetic rum right into their half-full cola bottles. Would there ever be anything that *didn't* remind her of her husband? Of what she had lost?

But the pain she felt now was better than the idea of forgetting any small part of the life she and Liam had had. Of the life they'd wanted. So she took an overlarge gulp of her drink and relished her grief.

She and Signe sat in silence for a few minutes, sipping their drinks as they waited for the last member of their little group of defectors to arrive. They couldn't meet at the Penthouse—not if they wanted to keep Torrin in the dark. The Penthouse was outfitted with nearly as many cameras as Huldra Industries, and Lucre only knew how many bugs. Organic and electronic.

If they wanted to have a truly private conversation, they needed to meet somewhere outside Torrin's earshot. Liv craned her neck, looking around the dingy pub's interior. One camera at the doorway. Another swiveling around the bar. Neither camera captured their corner booth, Liv noticed. Of course, Signe would have taken that extra precaution.

The cameras weren't Berger products. They were GenTech from the looks of the—one of the half-dozen competitors that were all actually owned by Huldra, in the end. That meant they wouldn't even have sound isolation capability. With how loud this place was, they could have one of those cameras pointed at their booth all night with Torrin hacked in and watching them live and he'd have no idea what they were saying.

Signe had chosen their spot well.

Of course, there was still one concern: Torrin Calix showing up in person. Liv didn't know what he did when he left the Penthouse, but she couldn't imagine a man like that was a stranger to the bars of Lower Baranthrum.

"Are you sure Torrin doesn't know about this place?"

"Oh, he definitely knows about it," Signe said. She took a sip of her tea, thinking. "Actually, I think this is where he first met Emerson."

"What?" Liv felt the color drain from her face. She looked around again, expecting to see Torrin's bearded face at one of the neighboring tables, sipping a whisky and waiting patiently for their betrayal to start so he could mow the three of them down with his armgun.

"Relax. He never comes here. He won't go anywhere near the docks these days."

Liv still wasn't so sure. She adjusted herself in her seat, suddenly unable to get comfortable. "Maybe we should have tried to meet in one of the other districts, just to make sure."

Signe ran a finger around the rim of her cup. "You don't know Torrin like I do. He won't come here." She raised her steel-gray eyes to meet Liv's. "Honestly, I think that man would rather walk down the main street of the Core wearing his real face than come here."

"I doubt that."

Signe studied Liv for a few seconds. Then, she nodded her head toward the western wall of the bar. "Did you see the foster shelter across the street from here on the way in?"

Liv nodded. She'd seen it. Run by GenstraCo in the same way this bar was run by Koegen Corp, no doubt—in name only. The building had been run-down and grubby-looking, the bars on the windows and industrial door locks making the place look more like a prison than a home for kids.

"Torrin grew up there," Signe said. "With his younger brother."

Based on what Emerson had told her a few nights before, Liv wasn't exactly surprised. Then again, after actually seeing the shelter, she could understand why the man might genuinely avoid coming within spitting distance of these docks now that he didn't have to.

Signe paused, taking a sip of tea, then amended. "Well, Torrin grew up. His brother didn't get the chance."

Liv leaned forward in her seat, horrified. "He didn't get switch'd?"

It was rare for a child to get selected for Ascent in New Avarita, but not unheard of. But Signe shook her head. "Prem-death. Either died of some sort of virus or got shot with a lethal while trying to hustle for Romy the Wolf. Stories vary. And I'm not stupid enough to ask Torrin himself what happened." The ex-enforcer shook her head. "Either way, it happened before Torrin was done with his Genstra-mandated education."

Liv's chest felt hollow at the thought. *Sixteen.* Torrin Calix had lost everyone he'd ever loved before the age of sixteen. Now she could see why the man wouldn't want to come anywhere near this place. She could also see why he was so hell-bent on destroying the Board and the killswitch protocol. If his parents hadn't gotten switch'd, he might never have needed to go to that care facility. His brother might still be alive.

Feeling bad for Torrin Calix didn't change their plans tonight, though. Liv had plenty of hate for the Board herself—they all did. But she didn't want to get revenge if it meant destroying the entire city-state of New Avarita. Revenge wasn't worth it if it meant ruining baby Kiran Voland's chance of growing up healthy and happy, if it meant breaking her promise to her dying friend. The system was pretty screwed up, but people still depended on it to live. While there was a chance that blowing it up overnight might make things better in the long run, doing so would sure as hell make things worse in the immediate.

Signe had just gone to the bar to get another cup of tea when the third member of their party walked through the doorway. Emerson Quinn. He'd opted out of his usual suit and loafers, instead wearing a pair of plain pants and a hooded jacket made of synthetic leather. Even with the wardrobe change, Torrin's top hacker looked like a time-traveler still getting used to his new surroundings.

He craned his long, thin neck, finally catching Liv's eye as she waved him over to their table. Unlike Signe, Emerson seemed to have no issue tucking into alcohol. He ordered two shots of the cheapest synth-whisky, draining them both within seconds of sitting down.

"Is our company really so terrible?" Liv asked slyly.

"Signe's is," Emerson said, wiping the corner of his mouth.

"You're just sour because I made you leave the Penthouse," Signe said, leaning back in her chair and blowing on her fresh cup of tea to cool it. "When was the last time, three years ago?"

"Let's be clear, you can't *make* me do anything," Emerson said. "And it's been barely a year since the last time." He looked around, eyebrow raised. "I feel like I haven't missed much."

Liv opened her mouth to ask why Emerson had stayed locked up in the Penthouse for a whole year, but she didn't get the chance before Signe clapped her hands together.

"All right, enough bullshitting," the ex-enforcer said. "Your little contraption has been outside the bubble for a few days. I assume you have news for us, since you're the one who said we should meet."

Emerson tapped on his wrist dialing up some data that was completely indecipherable to Liv. "I absolutely have news for you." Keeping his unicomm-equipped wrist flat on the table, holo-display hovering a few inches above it, he waved his other hand at a passing serving mech, tapping in an order for another two shots of synth-whisky.

"Are you... are you sure that's the best idea?" Liv asked, concerned.

"Don't you worry about me." Emerson shot her a grin. "With the hundreds of enhancements I've upgraded my body with, did you really think I don't have an alcohol filter?" He leaned forward, pointing at a few lines of text on his holo-display. "So, to the southwest, the bio-readings are clear as far as radiation goes, but the soil samples I took were basically just sand. Trying to grow anything out there will be a tough putt. By which I mean it'll basically be impossible."

"All right, well, that's not good news."

"Right," Emerson said. He reached out to collect two more tiny cups of foul-smelling whisky from the rusted tray attached to the serving mech. Then, Emerson cocked his head to one side.

"Fortunately, there's better news when we head more northwest."

Signe leaned forward, resting her elbows on the table and studying Emerson's holo-display closely, though Liv was pretty sure the other woman didn't understand the strings of numbers and letters any better than she did. "There wasn't too much radiation there?"

"Not in the areas I scoped out," Emerson said.

"You found a spot with low enough radiation to support a few grow domes?" Liv asked.

"Better," Emerson said. He scrolled to a new section of completely nonsensical code, pointing out another few lines of text. "I found a huge stretch of land with no measurable radiation at all."

"What?" Liv said, nearly spitting out the sip of rum and cola she'd just taken.

"Yep," Emerson said. "At least, that's what it looks like." He pointed to another portion of the readings, then pulled up a vid file. It was grainy and jumpy, but Liv could still make out the basics. When she caught sight of a large, dark area on the holo-display, her breath stuck in her throat.

"Is that..."

Emerson nodded. "That's a lake, my friend." He scrolled through more lines of code. "Water readings are nontoxic."

"What's the soil like?" Signe asked.

"Dry," Emerson said. He drained another whisky, then scrolled over to a new section of readings on his holo-display. "But along the western edge of the lake there's a lot of good land."

Up until the Huldra job, this news would have been game-changing. The best news possible. After all, the original plan had just been to find tenable land for the purposes of expanding New Avarita's borders. Now, that wasn't going to be enough to save them.

They were stuck between two sides of a vice grip: with the killswitch protocol still in place, the Board would still have the power to stop them from expanding the borders. Without the killswitch protocol in place, they'd have no chips and much bigger problems than overcrowding.

In short, the news of habitable land outside of New Avarita's bubble was good but alone, it wasn't enough. Now, it was just one piece of a larger puzzle they were trying to assemble. A puzzle that would give a giant middle finger to the Board, save the people of New Avarita from the killswitch, and keep Torrin happy. And, critically, a puzzle that would somehow do all of that without destroying the chip system.

For the next hour, the three of them debated their options. First, Emerson suggested breaking into the Medial Complex, pulling the switch on all the Board members, then taking over control of New Avarita from there. The killswitch protocol would still be active, but maybe they could change the algorithm's parameters so that no one would ever meet them, effectively sidestepping the program.

It was a solid option, assuming Emerson could change the parameters without inadvertently activating the protocol in the process. It was also an option that meant murdering nine people in cold blood, which made Liv's stomach churn.

At what point did their actions make them just as bad as the Board?

Next, Signe suggested Emerson just leak his bio-readings on the veilrinth. If enough of the population knew the land outside of New Avarita was safe, surely there would be an uprising, a revolution a thousand times the size of Torrin's little crew. But with the killswitch protocol active, the Board could easily pull the plug on a revolution of any size. Any dissenter could be switch'd immediately. Then, they'd redouble their sensors around the borders—maybe even add chip scanners or security mechs—preventing anyone else from sneaking drones or cameras outside the city-state without their knowledge, and switching anyone who tried to leave the Board's domain.

"Anyone with a chip in their skull is completely powerless, then, as long as the killswitch protocol is in place," Emerson said, running his hands through his hair until it stood up at odd angles.

"Maybe Torrin's right," Signe said. She had bags under her eyes now, from hopelessness or exhaustion, Liv wasn't sure. Maybe a combination. "Maybe just killing the chips altogether is the best path forward."

At that moment, a thought slammed into Liv's brain like a sledgehammer. *Anyone with a chip in their skull.* Of course, that was everyone in New Avarita... or rather, *almost* everyone in New Avarita.

Liv's mind drifted to her neighbor Ayla, to little baby Kiran. If Ayla, a Medla House surgeon, had come to the conclusion during pregnancy that she didn't want her baby implanted with a chip, that she wanted to give birth at home and try to help her baby escape the system she'd helped to uphold for the past fifteen years or longer, then surely there were other parents like her. Other babies born outside of Medla House facilities. Other parents who would go to any length necessary to keep their baby from getting chipped.

They couldn't destroy the chip system in New Avarita without creating chaos. What they *could* do was create a society outside of New Avarita where the chip system was completely irrelevant. But only if they could get to those babies before the GenstraCo officers did. She breathed in, smelling honeysuckle and lavender instead of the smoky bar air, just for one instant.

"What's wrong with you?" Signe asked.

Liv jerked back to the present, realizing she had been staring off into space for the better part of a minute.

"Is your one drink going to your head already?" Emerson chortled, shooting his fourth whisky down in a single gulp.

"How long does it take for Medla to chip a newborn?" Liv asked.

"What?" Emerson asked, taken aback. "I don't know, they have to be like a month old, right? But who knows—they stay in the facility where they're born that whole time."

"Only if they're born in a facility," Signe said.

"Every baby is born in a facility," Emerson pointed out.

"No, they aren't," Signe and Liv said in unison. The two women shared a bemused look. Then Signe said, "They're supposed to be, but you'd be surprised at the lengths some people will go to in order to avoid going to a facility to give birth."

"What do you know about that?" Liv asked. She realized she had no idea where Signe had come from. Was it possible her parents had done the same thing Ayla had done? Was Signe just like baby Kiran? Another child forced to grow up without parents when theirs were switch'd for not playing by the Board's rules?

"A lot," Signe said bitterly. She took a sip of her now lukewarm tea. "My father was one of the officers in charge of tracking those parents down." She blinked, as though just realizing something. "Or is, I guess. He's still alive. As far as I know."

"He's still alive?" Emerson asked. "Holy shit, he must be, what, ninety-five years old?"

"*Ninety-five*? How the fuck old do you think I am, Em?" Signe asked.

"Oh, wait, I know this one. You're like, fifty, right?"

"Fifty?" Signe raised an eyebrow. "Fuck you, I'm nowhere near fifty."

Emerson shrugged. "You're the one ordering tea at a damn bar. I'm just reading the cues, here."

"So, there is an entire Correxion Group department keeping tabs on expecting mothers? Watching for potential defectors?" Liv asked, steering the conversation back on course. She had the seed of an idea now. A plan radically different from Torrin's—a plan nowhere near as satisfying and fast-moving—but a plan that might just make a difference in the long run. And, perhaps most importantly, a plan that could save Kiran *now*.

Signe nodded, swirling the dregs of the tea in her cup. "There is. As soon as a person gets their hormone blockers out, their chip information is farmed out to a Correxion officer assigned to the case. They can track hormones, vitals, and location from that point until the baby comes. And if you don't turn up at a facility when the readings show you've gone into labor then..."

"I know what happens then." Liv winced. She could see Ayla in her mind's eye, slumped over, her forehead still shining with the sweat of giving birth, eyes blank and lifeless, hands outstretched, reaching for her son.

Signe gave her a curious look but didn't ask her to elaborate. "Right. Well, after that happens, the guards transport the kids to a Medla facility with space for them. After they're chipped, they try to find adoptive parents, or they send them to a foster facility if they can't find someone to take the kid in."

Liv stirred the melting ice chips in her cup with her straw, thinking. "What if we could get to those parents before the guards did? Mark them as dead in the killswitch database. Sneak them out of New Avarita." She looked up, picturing Ayla again, this time before she'd given birth. When she'd been pleading with Liv not to take her to a Medla House facility. Pleading with her to help her keep her baby away from the surgeons and their chips and scalpels. "They'd go with us. I know they would."

Emerson nodded slowly. He opened his mouth to speak, but Liv was on a roll, now. She knew what the new plan was. What it had to be.

"We can make a new city outside the border of New Avarita. Instead of crashing the chip system and watching everything burn, we'll create something from scratch that doesn't depend on chips at all."

And then, once the colony outside the barrier was big enough, they could find a way to reach the people inside New Avarita; show them the new way of life that was possible. And *then* Torrin—or more likely, whatever revolutionary came after him—could bring the chip system down. Or leave it up to the people to decide whether they would rather live without chips or live with Ascent. Give people a choice rather than making a slapdash decision that would change the fate of every New Avaritan citizen without their consent.

It was a long game: one they'd be playing to win decades in the future instead of weeks or months. But Liv would rather die building a better world than live to see whatever chaos Torrin Calix wanted to bring raining down upon them all.

"With what supplies?" Signe asked, eyebrow raised.

"We'll... we'll steal supplies. Smuggle them out through the barrier."

"Just how much heavy equipment and rations do you think you can carry on that skinny back of yours?" Signe asked. "Even if we managed to pilfer everything we needed, we'd have a damn hard time getting a whole city's worth of shit through the barrier in one go. I think the guards would spot a transport filled with building supplies slipping out into the waste."

After another round of drinks and a lot more back-and-forth, they finally had the bones of a halfway decent plan.

Liv and Signe would fake their deaths to Torrin and leave the city through the barrier and establish their new colony. It would be backbreaking work, but Emerson had the tougher job—it was his job to get Torrin to see reason or, at the very least, stall him from destroying the chip system until the colony was up and running.

From within the borders of New Avarita, Emerson would also be able to keep an eye on the killswitch system, find citizens willing to take a chance and leave New Avarita to build a new life outside the borders, and coordinate regular supply drops to Liv and Signe at the barrier. In short, it was a plan that fell somewhere between 'optimistic' and 'stupid,' but it was the best they had.

But Liv still had one piece of unfinished business. She hadn't promised Ayla that she would build a better life away from Kiran. She'd promised her old friend that she would save her son by building a better life for him.

The dock workers a few tables down broke into song. Emerson waved the server back over, and the three of them sat in silence, thinking. Another round of drinks appeared on their table, then disappeared down their throats.

"There's one more thing," she said, interrupting the quiet that had fallen at their table. "I need something before I can leave New Avarita."

"What's that?" Emerson asked.

"I need a baby."

Signe chuckled and clapped Emerson on the back. "Well, I can't help you out with that, but maybe Em here can get you sorted."

Emerson almost spit out his latest shot of whisky.

Liv flushed but pressed on. "No, not like that. Not a new baby. I need a specific baby." She clenched her fists on the surface of the table. "I won't leave New Avarita without him."

"I didn't know you had a kid," Signe said, sobering.

"I don't." Liv took a deep breath, then told them both the whole story. The tale of her last day in Upper Lucara. Her account of the thing that had finally pushed her over the edge and made her want to burn New Avarita and everything it stood for to the ground.

"I promised Ayla that I'd protect him," she finished.

Silence hung over the table, then Emerson asked, "Do you know where he is?"

Liv shook her head. "I don't. It'll be one of the Medla facilities in the upper districts, though."

Emerson turned to Liv. "You done any security work on those facilities?"

She had, in fact, done security work on those facilities. Berger had overhauled all of Medla's systems just under two years ago. The job had taken a year by itself. She nodded. "I can get us in and out without being caught. I'm sure of it."

She was far from sure of it, in reality. Medla House had some of the most intense security she'd ever implemented. But she had built this entire plan around Kiran. She needed to rescue him, and showing doubt in front of Signe and Emerson wouldn't get her there.

"And our reward would be... planning our escape with a squalling baby?" Signe asked.

"There'll be plenty of squalling babies out there eventually, if things go right," Liv said. Her voice was on the verge of begging. Usually, that would embarrass her. But not now. Not today. This was too important. There was no room for pride at this table.

"She has a point," Emerson said. "The parents of New Avarita might be hesitant to take their little bundles of joy outside the barrier." He cocked his head to one side. "But if we can show that even you two bozos can raise a kid out there.... Well, that might just improve our chances at recruiting more people to join our little commune."

Hope sparked in her chest. Then Emerson's gaze flickered and that hope sputtered out like a spent candle.

"But you said you don't know what facility he's in, right?"

Liv shook her head hopelessly. There were a dozen Medla facilities between Upper Lucara and the Core. He could be in any of them. It was hopeless.

"What if we had a way to find out where this kid is?" Signe asked.

Liv and Emerson turned toward her in unison. The candle of Liv's hope flickered to life again in her chest.

"I told you, my father is still alive. He's still in Lower Baranthrum." She took a breath. "What if I paid him a visit? If I could get access to his unicomm, we could get his entry credentials for the Medla House infant database. We could search by the mother's name and find where this baby of yours is being kept."

"Doesn't..." Liv paused, trying and failing to think of a more delicate way to phrase her question. "Doesn't your dad think you're, um, dead?"

Signe shrugged by way of answer.

Emerson narrowed his eyes, studying her carefully. "Can we trust him?"

"I don't know," Signe admitted. "He's been on the side of the Board for a long time."

Liv considered Signe. "You used to be on the side of the Board. So did I. So did..." She broke off before she could say Ayla's name. Then she shook her head. "If a member of Reina Arthur's private security can change her mind... why not a Correxion officer?"

Emerson chewed his lip. "This is a terrible plan."

"Maybe," Signe said. She drained her last few sips of tea like she was shooting straight liquor. Then, she met Liv's eye with an expression that made her heart soar with hope. An expression of determination and solidarity. An expression that said they wouldn't be leaving New Avarita without fulfilling Liv's oath. They wouldn't be leaving without Kiran. At the very least, they wouldn't be leaving without doing their damnedest to save him. "But it's the only plan we've got."

15

SIGNE

New Avarita is rich in possibility and opportunity, but the disaster of the Fall has left us poor in terms of space. The Algorithm will determine the proper distribution of space among residential, commercial, industrial, and agricultural needs, giving every citizen the resources they need to focus on achieving their ultimate goal.

—**THE HANDBOOK OF LUCRE, *CHAPTER 28***

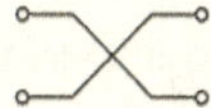

AT THIS POINT, Signe was pretty sure she had completely lost her mind. Sure, Torrin's plan was a little reckless. She didn't like the idea of living without her mech-arm any more than anyone else in the city-state would. But was the best alternative really just starting over outside the barrier with nothing?

Assuming they could grow their own food and get enough supplies to build some semblance of a little society out there, who was to say anyone would even come join them? Or, worse, what if a lot of people came to join them—enough that someone caught Emerson's workaround—and their little shanty town was discovered? There was a chance the Board couldn't trigger the killswitch on a chip that was out of range, sure. But that wouldn't stop them from just bombing the fuck out of whatever little society they managed to scrape together.

It had seemed like the best option at the time, sitting in that dark and dusty bar. Now, Signe was actually pretty sure they just had no good options left at all.

But it wasn't too late. She could still change her mind. Right up until the last second, honestly. Because Liv was still working with Torrin to build a blueprint of the Medial Complex. They were still going through their plan of attack, pretending all was normal, all while she, Liv, and Emerson planned to sabotage the job at the last minute. Not spectacularly enough to get them all caught, of course. Just a subtle sabotage that would cause the job to fail.

A sabotage Signe could still back out of, should she decide Torrin's plan was actually the lesser of the evils, in the end.

Or if her guilt at the idea of betraying the man finally overrode everything else.

When she'd first come to Torrin, she was young, alone, and scared. She'd had nowhere to go. Torrin Calix had given her a roof, a job, and something to live for. He might be a reckless, rageful son-of-a-bitch, but he'd given her a way to channel her own rage into something that felt useful. Something bigger than herself.

Sure, he was short-sighted and kind of an asshole, but that was how the man got things done. He'd started as an orphan, made his way up to earning a living on the docks, then abandoned it all the second he met Emerson, adapting to a whole new way of life as soon as a new path was presented.

Maybe that was why he expected his current plan to work. If Torrin succeeded, if every chip simultaneously went offline, he expected the people of New Avarita to adapt and step into a new life just as easily as he'd done so many times in his own forty-some years. But most people weren't like Torrin Calix. Most people were fucking cowards, terrified of change.

Most of the people of New Avarita would cling to the familiar system they had even if they knew the truth about Ascent, about the Principal Chairman, about everything.

Hopefully, when this was all said and done, he would see that. Then, he could come join the new colony they'd form outside the barrier. He could help them create the world he'd wanted for New Avarita.

But that wouldn't happen. No, a man as stubborn as Torrin wouldn't let something as minor as repeated failure get in the way of his plans. Which meant, eventually, Torrin Calix was going to get himself killed for this. And when he did, if she went through with this betrayal, at least a small bit of that blood would be on her hands.

And if she didn't go through with it, the blood of everyone who died when they essentially recreated the Fall would be. She couldn't stand that. Which is why she was about to travel to the one place she thought she'd never go back to.

Signe pushed the thoughts away, but that only revealed the buzzing, frantic energy underneath. It crackled over her skin, turning her stomach and making her feel itchy, like there were tiny little bugs crawling all over her. *Relax*, she chided herself. She regularly charged into firefights and smugglers' dens and worse.

Surely she could handle a simple conversation with her father.

It was raining when Signe pushed open the main doors of the factory, stepping out onto the streets of Lower Baranthrum. She pulled up the hood of her jacket, then turned on the old-school holo-projectors sewn into the lining. New features projected over her face; a slightly broader nose, brown eyes instead of grey, a wider-set jaw. They didn't use these often, since anyone who looked too closely would be able to tell it was just a projection. It would never fool security systems like the ones in the Core, but it should be enough to fool the shitty, outdated cameras down here in Lower Baranthrum.

Listening to the constant *pat-pat-pat* of drops hitting the plasticky surface of her hood, Signe crossed the street, heading north.

Switch'r's Alley was directly north of the street that held Torrin's Penthouse. Half the people Signe passed would be packing illegal arms, the other half would be zoned out of their brains on Romy's fabbed drugs. All of them would be desperate—they didn't call it Switch'r's Alley for nothing. This was a part of town where people only lived if they had nowhere else to go, a place for people whose lives were already over—Lucre's Algorithm just hadn't caught them yet.

Technically, it was the place Signe herself probably belonged.

Signe flipped Sally's safety off, not bothering to cover the ugly red glow of the trigger. The more people who knew she was primed and ready to shoot, the fewer people would try to fuck with her. Still, some of the people here were desperate enough to try something even with a three-foot-long gun in their face. She caught two hustlers trying to wire coin off her unicomm with hacked prox-readers. A third came at her, illegal arm-gun raised, demanding the codes to her accounts. Signe sidestepped the hustlers and stunned Mister Arm-Gun with a nonlethal round.

The people here seemed to get more reckless every time Signe dared to cross through. *Would they still be this desperate if it weren't for the killswitch?*

Signe chewed her lip, glaring down another hustler as she walked, holding eye contact until the other woman backed away, off to find an easier mark, most likely. The constant threat of instant death was no joke—Signe should know, she lived with that fear every day. The fear that, one day, the Board would find Emerson's hack, and it would be lights out for all of them. Still, she doubted it was the killswitch alone causing the shitshow that was Switch'r's Alley.

More likely it all came down to coin.

The Board had a lot of it. The further you got from the Core, the less of it people had. If Torrin's plan succeeded, there wouldn't be any more coin—not for anyone. Coin wasn't a tangible thing like it had been before the Fall. These days, coin was just bits of code that lived inside a person's unicomm. Once the chips went down, New Avarita's coin would too.

Would that make people more or less desperate?

Without coin, it wasn't like everyone was suddenly going to magically link arms and start singing around campfires. The people of New Avarita had been born and bred believing that coin was their god. If it suddenly vanished, it wouldn't mean their god was dead—it would mean they would find a substitute to squabble over instead. It could be food stores, pockets of land, who the fuck knew.

New Avarita was a powder keg. The last thing it needed was a shock to the system. As much as walking through Switch'r's Alley made Signe want to burn the Medial Complex to the ground and launch the ashes into the Atlantic Ocean, she understood that New Avarita wasn't ready for outright revolution. Not the kind Torrin had planned, at least.

Not yet.

But if she played her cards right today, she could lay the first building blocks of a future where New Avarita would be ready. Then the Board wouldn't stand a chance.

Theoretically.

Past Switch'r's Alley, Signe moved through a factory district, then into a part of town positioned along the edge of Old Altum. This neighborhood was where Lower Baranthrum's rich (if they could really be called that) lived. Factory managers, newscasters for off-hours broadcasts, advertising directors for smaller subsidiaries, all of them lived and raised their families in neighborhoods like the one Signe had grown up in.

The transports here were still rusted and creaky, the signs still aggressively neon, the restaurants skewing more toward "dive bar" and less toward "drinks lounge," but the streetlights actually worked.

Instead of towering apartment buildings stacked over factories that choked the air with smog, Signe's childhood neighborhood was a maze of neat—if rundown—brick townhomes. The shingles were made of discarded iron, making the whole street sound like it was full of discontented windchimes on rainy days like today. Signe knew the sound well. It was the soundtrack to her entire childhood.

Her boots clomped through the murky puddles as she snaked through the winding rows of nearly identical townhouses. Once she passed the Northeast Transport Station, the scene became so familiar Signe thought she might vomit right there on the sidewalk. She'd walked this route a thousand times or more as a kid, coming home from school to see her father and wait for her mother to get home from her nursing shifts at the nearest Medla facility.

Signe had been close with her father then. He'd been the one to quiz her on her schoolwork as she sat, perched on the kitchen counter while he stirred pre-packaged synthetic slop into a pan. Now? Well, now the man thought she'd been dead for almost ten years.

Coming here might be a colossal mistake. After all, she hadn't avoided this place since joining Torrin's crew just for fun. Her father was loyal to the Algorithm and the Principal Chairman. Did he actually love Signe? Probably… But still, if it came between ratting out his own daughter and betraying his city-state, Signe didn't have a whole lot of confidence that he'd choose the latter.

She marched up the rain-slick stone steps of unit 4783, pausing at the familiar, now-faded paint reading POULSON. She still remembered the day her mother had painted the moniker on the stoop, the weekend after they had moved in. Her dad had just gotten promoted to the infancy monitoring force. The pay raise hadn't been high enough to get them out of Lower Baranthrum altogether, but they'd gotten damn close.

Signe hesitated for a moment, standing a few feet from the door. Then, she heard a voice behind her.

"Can I help you?"

Signe turned, breath catching in her throat as she caught sight of the man standing there, a magna-umbrella projecting from his unicomm, repelling any raindrops before they could strike his perfectly pressed Correxion Group uniform. He was balding, Signe noticed, his grayish-black hair thin on his forehead and near the crown of his head, revealing pale brown skin.

"Yes, Mister Poulson," Signe said, recovering as quickly as possible. "I'm here to—"

"I'm not expecting visitors today, ma'am," her father said. He bustled up the steps, then went to reach for the doorknob.

"Wait—" Signe said. She thrust a hand out, nudging his hand out of the way. In the process, her own hand came to rest on the knob.

Signe's stomach contracted as the lock clicked. He'd never removed her chip from the home's internal security system.

"What the hell is going on here?" her father burst. He reached for his wrist, no doubt preparing to call up his standard-issue armgun. "Who are you?"

Signe raised both hands. "Wait." She tapped the side of her hood, removing the projections obscuring her features and looking at her father through the droplets of driving rain. "Hi, Dad."

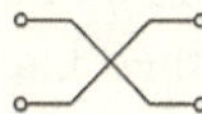

AKSEL POULSON RECOVERED from his shock surprisingly quickly. He ushered her out of the rain, leading her into a foyer that was both hauntingly familiar and painfully alien.

She pulled off her dripping coat, hanging it up beside the door as she kicked the boot dryer built into the baseboards. Hot air rushed out, leaving her boots warm and bone-dry in just a few seconds. When she looked back up, pushing aside the rain-damp curls that had escaped from her ponytail, she saw her father was still staring at her.

He opened his mouth, closed it again, then opened it one more time. "Do you want a cup of tea?"

Signe snorted. "Tea? Don't you want to know where I've been the past ten years?"

"You bet your ass I do," her father said. He bustled past her into the townhome's kitchen. Signe heard a series of beeping and clattering noises. When she followed, she found him wrestling with the settings on a Teras Bruumaster. "But this conversation feels like one that requires a drink. I stopped drinking, though. Tea's the best

I've got these days—I hope that's all right."

Stopped drinking?

Signe's eyes widened a bit before she caught herself, reeling the expression back under control. An Aksel Poulson without a cheap-ass version of an expensive, imported spirit in one hand was an Aksel Poulson Signe didn't recognize. Maybe this wasn't as big a mistake as she'd thought it would be.

"Tea's great," she said, edging around the table to take the seat that had once been hers. The table and chairs were new, but the view out the window was still the same: a clear-shot view to the grow-dome along the south edge of Old Altum. "Is that the lettuce crop I see growing in over there?"

"Kale," her father said, twisting to make a face as he poured steaming water into two waiting mugs.

"Urgh," Signe agreed. "Mom would have been pleased, though."

"That health nut," her father agreed. He crossed the kitchen, setting one mug in front of Signe and cupping the other between his calloused right hand and his metallic left one.

For all the good it did her, in the end.

"So. What do you need?"

"What makes you think I need something?" Signe asked.

"You didn't come back from the dead to sit in some shitty Lower Baranthrum townhouse and drink second-rate tea with me, Signe," he said.

"You don't know that," Signe said, taking a sip. Admittedly, the tea *was* second-rate. Still, it was hot and it gave her something to do with her hands.

"Yeah, I do," her father said. "You hardly ever came back to visit even when you were alive." He shook his head. "How the hell are you still kickin'? You were gone. I saw the data. I got the Ascent report from Reina Arthur herself."

Signe hesitated for a heartbeat, the truth hovering on the tip of her tongue. Her father might have stopped drinking, but he was still wearing a Correxion Group uniform. Coming here was at least a six out of ten on the "stupidly dangerous" scale. Coming clean about where she'd been the past ten years just because being home felt *nostalgic* would be like, an eleven.

"I'm sorry, dad. I wanted to tell you I was alive. But the Silver Guard has some strict-ass rules," she said, telling the lie she'd concocted with Liv and Emerson instead.

"The Silver Guard?" her father frowned. "There's no such—"

"That's what you're supposed to think," Signe said apologetically. She pointed a mech-finger at him. "And you'd better pretend you still think that, for the record. I could get in deep shit for telling you about all this."

She wove an elaborate story about how she had spent the last decade rising up through the ranks of the Principal Chairman's secret enforcer squad, discovering and neutralizing threats, even helping to coordinate defense outside the borders of New Avarita. It was all bullshit, but with the help of several fiction books written before the Fall that Emerson had read on the veilrinth, Signe thought she made the tale at least eighty percent believable.

Maybe seventy.

Her father seemed to accept her story, but with Aksel Poulson, appearances could be deceiving. His years in service to Correxion Group had made him nearly impossible to read. Signe was a little jealous of the skill, honestly.

Finally, he leaned back in his seat, the steel chair legs thudding against the floor at the shift in weight. "So, you've established how you're still alive," he said slowly. "But you still haven't told me why you're here." He looked around the modest kitchen with a rueful expression, then rested his hands on the table. "I assume it's not because the Principal Chairman has grand plans that need an aging Infant Monitoring Agent from the worst district in New Avarita."

Signe paused. This was it. The riskiest part of this entire mission. She tapped a complex rhythm with the fingers of her right hand. A holo-menu appeared, one only she could see, projected directly into her eye enhancements rather than into the air. Signe hid her hesitance behind a sip of tea, being careful not to shatter the mug with the strength of her mech-arm's grip.

Then, she reached out, gently grabbing hold of her father's right wrist with her own right hand. "It's not," she said.

Her wrist hummed softly as Emerson's code rushed through the link she'd just made between her unicomm and her father's. A soft, orange light pulsed beneath her skin as the code ran, reflecting against the surface of the table.

Her father's eyes started to drift to the place their hands met and Signe's stomach leapt into her throat. He wasn't the most technical of people, but even he knew what a prox-link was. If he saw that pulsing light, he would know something was wrong. He'd know she'd come here to take something from him. Her whole story might just come crashing down. She had to do something—now.

"I'm here to talk about Mom," she blurted out.

Her father's deep grey eyes—eyes the exact same shape and color as Signe's own—flicked up to stare at her curiously.

About Mom? She chided herself. What the fuck would she need to talk to her father about mom for? Her mother had been dead almost twenty years, now. Switch'd just after missing out on a promotion to a higher-end Medla facility in Old Altum.

The orange light on Signe's wrist was growing stronger now, flickering softly as Emerson's hack struggled to break through the encryption protecting the infancy data records on her father's unicomm, hunting for the child of one Ayla Voland. She had to say something. Something interesting enough to hold her father's attention. Something that would warrant a visit—a return from the dead, ostensibly—to discuss. Something that couldn't be discussed over unicomm.

Then it hit her.

Signe swallowed. "Do you remember how we celebrated the day of Mom's Ascent?"

Her father's brow furrowed, and he nodded, looking perplexed. "Of course, I do. What does this—"

"That day," Signe pushed forward, holding her father's gaze forcefully. "What did we do?"

"We played all her favorite music and danced until our feet hurt," her dad said, smiling softly at the memory. "And we cooked her favorite meal—fried snapper and synthetic rice."

"And at the ceremony, I read a passage from her favorite poem, remember?" Signe pressed.

That had been horrific. It was before she'd gotten her ReadRight enhancement. She'd completely mangled the reading, but everyone had been so happy to celebrate the Ascent that no one really minded.

"Signe, I don't underst—"

Signe leaned forward, unicomm hack half-forgotten as she immersed herself in a different memory: the day she'd begun to lose faith in the Board. The day Marxus had died right in front of her for no damned reason, just because Reina Arthur was through using his services. The memory of the first time she'd begun to ask questions like "*Why is Ascent a good thing?*" and "*Who decides when someone's life's purpose is fulfilled?*"

"Mom was selected for Ascent because she'd fulfilled her purpose for Medla House—for all of New Avarita. She wasn't moving any higher. She was getting older. Remember how bad her knees were getting? She had trouble staying on her feet all day. She'd helped all the patients she could. A new crop of younger, freshly trained nurses was on their way in to take her place. Right?"

"Right..."

"But Mom was more than just an employee of Medla House. Mom loved haikus. Mom knew every damned word of every damned Light Brigade song ever written." Signe chuckled at a memory. "Mom was a horrible but eager cook." She sobered, eyes boring into her father's. "So, I start to wonder. Did she really fulfill her purpose here in this world? Or did she just stop being useful?"

Her father was silent for a long moment. Then he cleared his throat. "Those are some horrible questions you're asking, Signe." He nodded at the rivets on her mech-arm, embossed with the symbols of

Huldra Industries. "Questions that could get you kicked out of your fancy new security gig."

"No," Signe said bitterly. "They're questions that will get me killed. You know that as well as I do."

"So why are you asking them?"

"Someone has to," Signe replied. Her unicomm's light winked off. She coughed, pulling her hand away and pretending to use it to muffle the sound.

"Signe," said Emerson's voice, barely more than a whisper in her ear. "I've got the data. You need to get out of there. There's a security mech patrol heading your way. Less than three minutes out."

Signe rose suddenly. Security mechs patrolled the nicer parts of the city all the time. If she didn't get out of here before they arrived, she'd be stuck here for hours while they swept the streets, scanning the chips of anyone and everyone that crossed their sensors.

"I'm—I'm sorry," she said, stammering as though she was just realizing the severity of what she'd just said. As though she hadn't said those exact words a hundred times before. "I shouldn't have come here. I shouldn't—"

Signe's father looked at her sadly, uncertainly, worry clouding his eyes. "You should stay. You're clearly going through something. Maybe I can—"

"T-minus two minutes," said Emerson's voice in her ear.

"Don't worry about it," Signe said, pulling another step away from her father's outstretched hand. "Forget you ever saw me."

She retrieved her coat from its spot beside the door and pulled her hood back up, activating her holographic disguise again, then strode to the back door of the townhome. The mechs weren't here yet, but there was no point in risking greeting them head-on on her father's front stoop.

"Am I… Am I ever going to see you again?" her father asked.

"I don't think so." Signe looked over her shoulder and cocked her head to one side. "Remember? I'm already dead."

Emotion tugged at her unexpectedly. She'd spent the past decade resenting this man for his loyalty to the system. Now, here he was, willing to risk getting switch'd just to see her again. Maybe he wasn't such a lackey after all. Maybe he was just an aging, lonely man who'd lost everything. The exact type of person best-suited for the second phase of the new plan. The type of person who might be willing to leave New Avarita and start a new life outside the borders of the city-state, living without using their chips and raising a new generation of kids who'd never know what it felt like to cheer for someone's death as long as it came at the hands of the Algorithm.

Then, her father said, "Do whatever you can to kick those traitorous thoughts out of your head, Signe. If you don't, you'll actually be dead before long."

All her hopes of converting her father and stealing him away to start a new life outside the city dissipated like smog in a breeze. Nothing had changed. Not really. Aksel Poulson was still the same man he'd always been, just with less hair and a mug of tea instead of a cup of whisky.

Signe forced a nod. "I'll do that."

She could tell from her father's expression that he didn't believe a damned word of it.

"T-minus one minute. You're really flirting with fucking disaster here, Signe."

It was raining even harder now. Signe pulled her hood down more securely. She left her father standing in his kitchen. She didn't know if he watched her go, because she didn't look back.

16
REINA

The Algorithm prioritizes skills that help keep our society thriving and pure. Citizens pursuing careers that serve the core functions of society and produce value for those responsible for keeping New Avarita healthy will be rewarded.

—**THE HANDBOOK OF LUCRE, *CHAPTER 31***

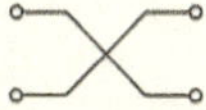

THE ARTHUR PENTHOUSE was quiet. The children were, of course, not home, and Braxton had gone to bed hours ago, leaving Reina alone in the sprawling quiet. For several hours now, the only sound had been the gentle bubbling of the saltwater fish tank behind her and the whisper of her brush dragging across the canvas.

Reina had spent the past thirty-odd years building a career as an engineer and executive, but she'd never lost her love for the visual arts.

Every time she had the chance to turn off all the screens and holograms, savoring the tactile feeling of the brush in her hand, she took a moment to imagine a life where she had never caved to her father's wishes. A life where she had studied art rather than engineering at university.

She wouldn't be living in a penthouse in the central Core, that was for certain. No, Reina imagined instead a small townhome in Old Altum. An old building made of crumbling bricks, surrounded by grow-domes, far from the central tram lines and the Core and everything else.

If she had lived that life, she would never have met Braxton. Her children would never have been born. And, in all likelihood, she would have been chosen for Ascent long before the age she was now. Painting wasn't the most profitable of careers. It wasn't even one of the arts that could easily be packaged for mass consumption, like holovid production or music. Her father had been right to steer her away from it all those years ago.

Still, she pretended she was there, in that small, sunlit townhome, as she daubed and dragged the colorful pigments over the canvas stretched over her easel. The scene taking form on the canvas was one Reina had painted half a dozen variations of already. It was the view off the back porch of her childhood home.

Reina's father had been an executive with KoegenCorp and had taken the corporation up on an initiative that built homes inside a handful of the grow-domes in Old Altum. The idea had been long-abandoned, those homes bulldozed to make way for more structured rows of corn or cabbage. It was one of the reasons she hated Jasper Koegen so much, if she was honest with herself. She still lamented the fact that her own children had never known what it was like to wake up to the smell of new plant growth and peaty soil every day.

In Reina's painting, the world inside the grow-dome was exactly as she remembered it: perfect. The perfect temperature, the perfect humidity. Solar lights inside the dome replicated the perfect level of sunshine for the plants inside, no matter the time of year. Outside the grow-dome, however, she painted angry, gray skies. Lightning split the clouds like eggs cracked into a pan. The dichotomy of the world she and her fellow Board members projected to the people of New Avarita... and the world as it truly was.

Was beauty truly beautiful if it was nothing but an illusion? Or was that all beauty had ever really been?

She sighed, leaning back to study her work. The commentary was subtle... but nowhere near subtle enough. She would never be able to sell this piece. She couldn't even show it to anyone. Anyone who saw this piece would be able to see her doubt in Lucre, in the Principal Chairman's Office, in New Avarita as a whole, bleeding from the canvas. She'd find herself on the wrong end of a Board termination vote in a heartbeat.

Still, it felt good to get the emotions out of her body. Fear. Anger. Guilt. Frustration. And above all of it the intolerable, itching feeling of claustrophobia.

As far as Reina could see it, she had two choices. She could continue to serve on the Board; continue working with the people who insisted she stifle her own innovation and flush potential profits down the drain. Or she could die. And, without the Esoph-Enhancement, she might end up dying, anyway, what with Jaya Ravenna circling her like a shark circled a bleeding swimmer.

It wasn't a choice at all, in truth. After all, Reina Arthur was many things: executive, inventor, artist... coward. When she did reach Ascent someday, the people speaking at her ceremony would no doubt talk about how strong she was. But ambition was not the same thing as strength. She would stay inside her perfectly sculpted grow-dome forever if it meant she could continue to ignore the storm raging outside.

Her role in the Medial Complex had given her this sprawling penthouse. She had enough coin to eat fresh meat and drink real, imported wine every day for the rest of her life. As much as she liked to daydream about a life as a simple painter, scraping by and living a life of quiet anonymity, Reina wasn't sure she could give up everything she had, even if it wouldn't be a death sentence.

Not just a coward, then. But a selfish coward. Well, so be it. There was some relief in admitting it. Besides, what use was taking a stand if there was no chance at success? Was there really any difference between martyrdom and suicide? The intangible vise around her squeezed even tighter.

At that moment, a light blinked to life on her unicomm. It was a call from her offices at Huldra. She glanced at the time reading, raising an eyebrow. It was four thirty-seven in the morning.

Curiosity won out and she accepted the call. But there wasn't another human on the other end of the line. It was a file from the automated call-screening system in her offices. The call's timestamp showed it had come into her office almost twelve hours ago but had just been verified as authentic and cleared through the security system.

Frowning, Reina played the message. A holographic figure sprang up over her wrist, rotating slowly in midair. It was a man. He looked vaguely familiar, tall and thin, a Correxion Group sigil on the left shoulder of his jacket. Reina squinted, studying him carefully, trying to place him.

"Madam Arthur," the man said, his voice sounding vaguely tinny over the recording. He must have an older model of unicomm installed—before she'd fixed that microphone bug. "I'm sorry to disturb you, but I've just been made aware of a potential threat to the Principal Chairman and the rest of your Board."

Reina cocked her head to one side, setting down her paintbrush and holding up her wrist to study the man more closely. She knew she had seen him before. The location stamp of the call indicated that it had come from a neighborhood in Lower Baranthrum. Not one of the tower's security personnel, then. Or someone she would have known growing up in Old Altum. Who was this man?

"Someone inside the Medial Complex is thinking some dangerous thoughts."

Reina's blood ran cold. *Did he know?* How could he know the storm raging inside her skull when she barely understood it herself? What did he want? A payout to keep quiet? She narrowed her eyes, studying the hologram more closely. What kind of person would have the guts to blackmail a member of the damned Board?

The man in the recording hesitated, licking his lips and looking around before saying, "A member of your top-secret Silver Guard. She has compromised her position, revealing herself to me and asking questions no self-respecting New Avaritan should be asking."

Silver Guard? Reina frowned, heart rate starting to slow as curiosity replaced panic once again. What the fuck was a Silver Guard?

At that moment, Reina recognized the man in the hologram. Her blood ran cold all over again. Somehow, she knew what he would say next an instant before he said it.

"I know Signe Poulson is alive," said the man; Signe's father. She had spoken to him only once before—the day she saw her old security lead's name on the Ascent log for the day. "She is alive and expressing dangerous thoughts about Ascent, Lucre's Algorithm, and the Board. With how close she is to the Principal Chairman…" he shook his head. "I worry that she might—"

Signe Poulson is alive. Reina closed out of the message, cutting off the woman's traitorous father as he started listing the threat his daughter posed and the things he wanted in return for reporting her. Signe couldn't be alive. Reina had seen her name on the Algorithm's Ascent report herself. That was almost ten years ago. She had been so confused as to why Signe had been selected. But Lucre's Algorithm often worked in mysterious ways, so she hadn't bothered thinking on it all that long.

Reina had seen the logs, the timestamp. She'd signed off on orders to dispose of Signe's remains via incineration when located. Had she ever actually followed up to ensure those remains had been found and incinerated? Likely not. And if Signe had not had enough close family or friends to throw a celebration for her Ascent, perhaps no one else had bothered to follow up, either.

But no. She was being ridiculous. Aksel Poulson was either lying or he was mistaken. There was no other option.

Still, the thought needled at her, refusing to let go. Even if Signe had somehow managed to fake her death, she still wouldn't have been able to leave New Avarita—the borders of the city-state were guarded by scanners, facial sensors, security mechs, and more. It was impossible to navigate New Avarita unnoticed and unseen—the Board had purposely designed it that way.

But Aksel Poulson's call had come in from Lower Baranthrum.

If there was anywhere in New Avarita where a person might just be able to slip through the cracks unseen and unnoticed, it was Lower Baranthrum. Most of the scanners and sensors in that district were outdated or broken, and as long as someone avoided the northern neighborhoods and the docks, they could go without seeing a security mech or a Correxion Group uniform for weeks, maybe longer.

But even if Signe had managed to avoid having her chip scanned for the past ten years, she couldn't avoid using her chip altogether. Reina frowned, then tapped her temples, logging into Huldra's database. She wouldn't be able to access all of her records from here, but she'd be able to see the ones she needed. The records that would either confirm Aksel Poulson's story or prove the man to be a liar.

First, she accessed the personnel files, pulling Signe's chip identification data from the archives. Next, she used her administrative access to log into the enhancement user database. As a member of her personal security team, Signe Poulson had had dozens of mandatory enhancements. But there was at least one enhancement that Reina could almost guarantee the woman would still be using, if she was in fact still alive.

Her Huldra-issued mech-arm.

For the next quarter of an hour, Reina pored over the lines of coding scrolling through her vision, hunting for Signe's chip identification data in the mess. Finally, on the sixteenth page of results, Reina found what she was looking for: Signe Poulson's chip had last been used to power her mech-arm enhancement at around 03:00 on April third. Reina's eyes flicked to the current time and date readings projected into her VR environment by her unicomm, even though she already knew what she was going to see.

05:12, APRIL 3

Reina tapped her temples again, leaving the sprawling void of Huldra Industries' usage data behind and returning to her penthouse living room. She leaned back in her chair, forgoing perfect posture for once and sitting in a position that could only be described as a slump.

Signe Poulson was alive. She had last used her mech-arm only two hours ago. She had somehow managed to fake her own death and had been living in secret for nearly a decade. It shouldn't be possible.

How many other people had slipped through the cracks this way? How many people had found whatever loophole Signe seemed to have found in the system. The Signe Poulson Reina remembered had been good at many things: marksmanship, interrogation, leadership, rinth poker. But her technical skills had always been on the "poor" side of "mediocre." If Signe had managed to find this loophole, there was no telling how many illicit characters were running around Lower Baranthrum, living on borrowed time.

Unless her old security lead wasn't working alone.

Reina would have to report this to the rest of the Board. She opened a comm link to the other advisors and began tapping out a message. Her team could find whatever gaps existed in Lucre's Algorithm. Once they closed those gaps, the protocol would activate on any chip listed as deceased in the database.

Once they closed those gaps, Signe Poulson would be dead for real.

Reina sat in the relative silence for a few long moments, listening to the steady humming of her fish tank and the growing bustle of early-morning traffic on the streets far below her penthouse window. Signe had evaded capture for almost a decade. And then she had turned up to her father's house—the house of a Correxion officer. Why?

It was a foolish decision at best. And the Signe Poulson she knew had been no fool. Reina deleted her half-drafted alert to the rest of the Board, bringing up her VR link to the Huldra Industries database instead.

"What are you up to, Signe?" she muttered quietly to herself. For the first time in days, the claustrophobia started to lift. Reina felt like maybe, just maybe, there was room in this world to breathe after all. She needed to find out what Signe Poulson had been looking for when she visited her father. And there was only one place that might have the answers she sought.

Brow furrowing, Reina ran a sequence she hadn't run since her GenstraU days, sinking into the lawless wasteland that was the veilrinth.

17

SIGNE

Thanks to generous donations from several community leaders, New Avarita's governing body will reside in a central structurebuilt for the sole purpose of keeping our society strong. This structure will be named the Medial Complex and will be located in the beating heart of our great city-state. The Medial Complex will serve as a location where the Principal Chairman and his advisory board can meet, work, and coordinate their efforts to keep New Avarita's citizens safe, healthy, and thriving.*

—THE HANDBOOK OF LUCRE, *CHAPTER* 48

**Full list of donors in Appendix L*

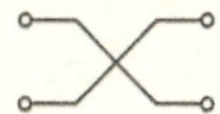

SIGNE THOUGHT SHE'D lost her ability to get pre-mission jitters. Apparently not. Even her mech-arm seemed to know something was up. Its fingers twitched, drumming against her kneecap, translating the anxious signals firing off inside her brain into a series of complicated rhythms.

She sat shoulder-to-shoulder with Alura and Gaius in a shiny Lobos Transport car, speeding toward the Core. So far, the mechanics of the mission weren't all that different from the Huldra job the week before. The main difference was that this time, Torrin Calix was with them.

And, most importantly, this time, Signe was rooting for the job to fail.

To be fair, she was actually rooting for Torrin to abandon the job before they reached the finish line. But he wouldn't. Which meant she knew full well the day would end in disappointment and defeat, probably with the lot of them looking for the bottom of a bottle of whisky back at the Penthouse while they regrouped.

"All right, you've got about three stops until you're at the tower," Emerson's disembodied voice said, echoing in all four of their unicomms at once.

"Wow, it's a good thing you're here, Em. I don't think we would have figured that out," Signe intoned drily. She could see the central tower of the Medial Complex out the transport window already, its tall glass windows glittering, crystalline, in the light of the setting sun.

They arrived at the central transport station just after 19:00. The timing of their arrival was crucial. By 19:00, a large portion of the people working in the complex would have already gone home for the evening, but the restaurants and shops on the ground floors would still be bustling. Instead of trying to slip past the sensors and mechs guarding the main entrances, their team would split up and slip in through the back doors of four different businesses.

Signe's assigned restaurant was the most expensive one in the Medial Complex—probably the most expensive restaurant in all of New Avarita. It was called *The Chop,* and it served exclusively natural foods—no synthetic plant substitutes or lab-grown meats here. Signe had never actually eaten the food there, but she had stood guard in the shadows a hundred times or more, keeping an eye on Reina Arthur as she ate her 2,000-coin steaks and drank wine imported from the countries across the sea.

Signe smoothed her white synth-cotton shirt, pulling the left sleeve down to more firmly cover the metallic glint of her mech-arm. She strapped a beat-up chip jammer onto her right forearm, covering her unicomm. It wasn't a particularly sophisticated piece of technology and wouldn't fool any but the most basic of scanners. However, according to Liv's schematics, Berger Security had been specifically instructed not to update the security systems on many of the shop and restaurant back doors.

These doors needed to be propped open for lengthy periods of time to receive deliveries, and the staff was constantly shifting and changing. These factors would make it more trouble than it was worth to manage advanced security on those doors.

And so, naturally, those doors were the perfect target.

Signe pulled a cigarette from her pants pocket, lighting it discreetly with a zap from her mechanical left thumb. She then sidled over to stand next to the loading dock door, taking long draws and huffing out the smoke. She didn't take the smoke into her lungs—if she did, she was bound to cough and ruin the whole illusion.

It wasn't too long before the door creaked open, revealing a heavyset man pushing a hovercart full of overflowing garbage bins toward the recycling tube in the alley. Back alleys all over New Avarita had tubes like these. They sucked up the trash, sorted it, and then repurposed the materials into everything from compost for the grow-domes to synthetic materials that made everything from plastic transport seats to the threads that made up Signe's shirt.

"Hey, what the fuck are you doing out here?" the man asked, spotting Signe as he turned around.

For a heartbeat, Signe thought she'd been made. Then, she noticed that the man's eyes were jumping between the cigarette and her fraudulent THE CHOP logo, printed onto her shirt by a program on Emerson's terminal.

"We're dyin' in there. Packed with rich assholes, floor to rafters. Get your ass back inside."

Signe did her best to look guilty-but-not-too-guilty. She dropped her cigarette, squishing it underfoot and dropping her head low.

"Sorry, sorry, I'm coming," she said. Keeping her mechanical left hand hidden in her sleeve, she slipped through the doorway and into the bustling kitchen of *The Chop*. Signe held her breath for a few seconds after crossing over the threshold, but no alarms buzzed out. The chip jammer had worked on the outdated security scanner.

The heavyset man shooed her out of the kitchen and Signe put on a grim face, walking out onto the floor of the restaurant.

He hadn't been lying. The place was absolutely bursting with people. Mostly unfamiliar faces—newly rich blood, evidently—but Signe recognized a few people. Audrey Lobos, heir to Lobos Transport, was there, seated with a group of people dressed in business attire sporting the StarBuilt logo. StarBuilt was an architecture firm under Teras System's umbrella. They must be doing some deal for new transport line construction or something.

Signe also caught sight of a famous holovid actress and her latest beau, and a few other lower-level executives she vaguely recognized. Some idiot had brought their screaming children with them, by the sound of the wails coming from the back corner of the place. Imagine, wasting thousands of coin on food for a toddler to chuck on the floor.

"Signe, Gaius, Alura, are you in?" said Torrin's voice in her ear.

"In," came Gaius's deep voice. Alura muttered the same a second later.

"In," Signe intoned next.

"And Emerson, do you have visual?" Torrin asked.

"Sure do, boss."

Unlike the system at Huldra, the Medial Complex's camera feeds were accessible through the rinth. Apparently, a few of the more paranoid Board members had insisted on being able to access the security visuals through their unicomms, so Berger Security had set up encrypted connections, making the camera feeds accessible from anywhere in the city, if you had the right permissions.

Or if you were Emerson Quinn.

"All right, ready for phase two. Emerson?" Torrin said.

"Heard," Emerson said. There was a moment of silence, then, "The door to the fire safety stairs on the western edge of the building will be unlocked until the next scan cycle in… three minutes and forty-seven seconds."

Signe grabbed a stack of empty plates from a nearby table, hurrying to the dish station to deposit them in the sink. Then, she strode past the kitchen, grabbing the first plate of hot food she saw and slipping out of the pass-out section of the restaurant before anyone else noticed what she had done.

Her uniform and the plate of food in her hand made her invisible to customers and staff alike as she bustled through the restaurant floor, hurrying toward the doors that opened into the atrium of the complex. Signe deposited the plate onto a random table, then hurried away, slipping out the frosted glass doors.

Emerson accessed her eye enhancements a few seconds later. After the sharp buzz and shock of the hack subsided, Signe's vision was cluttered with the same cues she'd seen during the Huldra Industries break-in the week before. She could see yellow streams of light arcing from dark corners, showing the angles of the cameras hidden in the shadows. Red bars indicated scanners and facial sensors.

Signe ducked into a corner that was protected from the camera angles on either side of it. She quickly shrugged out of her white shirt emblazoned with THE CHOP logo, leaving only the plain black shirt beneath. Paired with the black pants she was already wearing and her usual black boots, it was an utterly forgettable outfit. She ditched the white shirt by tossing it into the waste receptacle on a passing maintenance mech, then made her way quickly-but-not-too-quickly toward the fire stairs Emerson had mentioned a few seconds ago.

By the time she skirted the final set of yellow arcing camera paths and slipped through the doorway, Gaius, Alura, and Torrin were all already gathered in the stairwell.

"Cutting it a little close, don't you think?" Alura asked.

She had shed her imitation *Lucre's Grille* uniform in favor of a gray shirt and black pants. Torrin and Gaius were dressed equally forgettably; Torrin in a gray jumpsuit that covered all of his tattoos, and Gaius in a black shirt that could have been pulled off the rack at any general supply store in New Avarita.

"How much time did I have left, Em?" Signe asked.

"Fourteen seconds."

Signe shrugged at Alura, shooting her a grin. "See? Plenty of time left."

Her grin faded from her face as she turned to look at Torrin. The man was usually focused, but right now, he was… absorbed. Possessed. His face could be an image result for a rinth search for the term "tunnel vision" as he stared up the darkened staircase, lit only by emergency lighting.

The emergency staircase took them as far as the eighth floor. The ninth floor and above—the most secure sections of the central tower—had outdoor emergency stairs leading to slide-like chutes that carried someone down the final two floors. This setup had the double benefit of being a quick, uninterrupted path to the ground for the most important people in the tower and maintaining increased security. The stairs were clearly visible from the streets of the Core. The chute was hard to climb, and its mouth was equipped with a scanner to track all the parties who escaped in the event of an actual emergency.

In short, emergency stairs would only be able to carry them so far on this journey. Their destination—the Board Room itself—would take some additional skill and risk to get to. But the Board Room was the only place from which a person could access Lucre's Algorithm. Back in the days when the Principal Chairman had been a real person and not a figment of the Board's imagination, the Algorithm had been accessible only from his office, but by the time Reina Arthur took her seat and brought Signe to stand guard behind her, things had changed.

Getting into the complex itself undetected had been risky. But breaking into the Board Room? That was something that had never been done or even attempted in all of New Avarita's history, as far as Signe knew. Once they left the emergency stairs and started trying to walk the halls of the tower itself, their chances of being made and killed went up by about a thousand percent. So, as they reached the top of the emergency staircase, Signe made her final attempt to reason with Torrin.

One last attempt to make the man see reason before they had to rely on the tough love of experience and failure to snap him out of his obsession.

"Are you sure we're ready for this?"

Alura snorted softly. "It's a little late for that now, don't you think?"

"A little," Signe allowed, not taking her eyes off Torrin. He wasn't looking at her. His eyes glowed with greed as he studied the thick steel door at the top of the stairs. Not a good sign. Signe charged on anyways. "But not entirely. This is where everything could *really* go to shit. If we need to back out and regroup. If we need to try another day or try another tactic, now is the time to do it."

She could feel Emerson stalling. There was no way he hadn't cued up the cameras on this floor by now. But he would be on Signe's side here. He, Liv, and Signe had made a game plan for what happened if Torrin Calix could not be swayed from his mission. If she couldn't convince him to turn back, then she'd have to betray him today. Betray the man who had given her a home and a purpose for almost a decade.

It would be for his own good—and the good of everyone in New Avarita, honestly—but still, Signe couldn't deny it would be a real dick move.

"Back out?" Torrin hissed. "I'm not backing out. This is our chance to stab the Board in its fucking throat." He turned toward Signe and reached out, resting a calloused, tattooed hand on her mech-arm's shoulder. "Don't get cold feet on me again now, Signe. This is our chance. The one we've waited for all this time." His eye sparked with that batshit crazy fire again and Signe knew the conversation was over.

Torrin would need to learn this lesson the hard way.

She twitched her fingers, sending the *negative* response to Emerson through her unicomm. The kid's voice chimed over the shared channel a second later. "All clear."

Emerson disengaged the locks and Gaius eased the door open. He peered around the corner, even though he'd already gotten the all-clear from Emerson, who had access to every camera in the damned building. It was just human nature to check with your own eyes. Gaius then waved the rest of them forward and they slipped silently into the stillness of the eighth-floor corridor.

It was nearly 18:00 at this point, but still almost half the offices were lit, their occupants hunched over their terminals, studying lines of code or poring over rows of data or communication logs. Everyone in New Avarita had to work to avoid getting switch'd, but the people who worked this high in the Principal Chairman's offices had something else driving them forward. Signe could almost smell the ambition rolling off them—the hunger for power and prestige. It was a scent that had gagged her every day when she worked in this tower.

She couldn't say she missed it.

Signe led their crew forward, moving purposely through the halls. None of the workers took any notice of them, but they did have to duck into abandoned offices hastily unlocked by Emerson twice to avoid security mechs as they swept through the corridors, scanners beeping and wheels whirring. When they arrived at the main elevators, Signe positioned herself on the edge of one corridor, just out of the golden glow of the camera's reach. Torrin took the other side of the hall while Alura and Gaius remained right in front of the elevator.

With the help of Alura's mech-arm attachments, the pair of them slid a steel panel off the wall beside the elevator's call sensor. They were careful not to trigger the sensor itself—it was equipped with a scanner that, if tripped, would run their chips to determine what floors they were allowed to access. Obviously, they weren't allowed to access any floors at all. So, in other words, if activated, it would sound an alarm that would shatter everyone's fucking eardrums.

Signe kept her eyes on the adjoining corridor, listening for footsteps or the whirring of security mech wheels. Normally, Emerson would keep an eye on the cameras for them, but right now he was immersed in something way more important. There were no indoor stairwells leading to the tenth floor. The elevator was their only option. Emerson needed to take control of the elevator's programming. Then, he'd need to trick it into thinking it had already scanned an approved chip in order for it to take them up to the tenth floor.

He'd also have to access the camera files for the elevator, wiping their footage from it before the Correxion officers and private security on guard caught sight of them.

Signe's ears pricked as she caught the telltale *thud thud thud* of assertive steps on expensive carpet. Someone was coming.

Just as she was about to sound the alarm, Torrin did the same. "Security mech approaching from the north," he intoned, communicating through their shared unicomm channel so she didn't have to shout.

"Fuck," Signe intoned. "We've got company coming southside, too. Where are we at with that hack, Em?"

For once, the kid didn't have a smartass retort. He really must be focusing.

Signe started to sweat. It was ironic in a way; they'd planned for this mission to fail from the beginning, but there was a difference between it failing in the controlled way she, Liv, and Emerson had planned and it failing now.

If it failed the way they'd planned, the four of them would scurry back to the Penthouse tonight with their tails tucked between their legs. If it failed now, they were all going to die. She met Gaius's eyes as she glanced back toward the elevator. Fear glinted there, brighter than a mega-watt flashlight.

But at that moment, Emerson's voice sounded in their channel.

"All right, elevator is clear, but it won't be for long."

"How long?" Torrin asked.

"One minute. The security protocol will catch this gap if I don't remove it in the next forty-eight seconds."

A timer appeared in the corner of Signe's vision, counting down. 47... 46...

The team didn't need Emerson to tell them twice. Signe and Alura ran as soft-footed as possible, skidding into the elevator just as Torrin replaced the panel and slipped past the temporarily deactivated scanner. Normally, they'd select their destination on their unicomms, but since they hadn't been scanned, no floor menu appeared. Emerson must have taken care of that on the back end as well, though, because the elevator zipped into life immediately, rocketing upward so quickly that Signe's knees almost buckled.

Emerson's timer ticked down steadily. 14... 13... 12...

They arrived at the top floor of the central tower—floor twenty-four—just as the timer ticked into single digits. All four of them spilled out of the elevator, crashing into a passing man. The man reared back, affronted as Gaius collided with his shoulder.

The fingers on Torrin's mech-arm flicked side to side and Signe could tell he was scrolling through his armgun's ammo options, searching for a silent round. But there was no need for anyone to die today.

Signe gripped Torrin's forearm, shooting him a look that said, *trust me.*

Torrin shook her free, metallic fingers continuing to scroll through his armgun's settings, ignoring her entirely.

The passing man looked up from his holo-display, taking in the sight as the rest of them exited the elevator. Signe held the stranger's gaze for a second, then gave him a brief nod. Her heart hammered a path up her throat as she willed the man to walk by, willed Torrin Calix not to do anything stupid, willed this moment to pass uneventfully. All it would take would be for this man to feel a shred of suspicion and they'd be swarmed by security mechs in seconds.

Then, the man returned her nod, looking back down at his holo-display and moving on down the opposite hallway.

The gang released a breath in unison once he was out of sight, following the directions fed to them by their eye-enhancements toward the Board Room. Not that Signe needed the directions; she had walked these halls a thousand times or more. The carpeting was new, and the artwork on the walls had changed, but the path was the same. She felt almost like she'd traveled back in time as she moved through the broad, lush halls.

"How did you know he would do that?" Torrin asked, shooting Signe a look.

"I spent a decade in this tower, Torrin," Signe said. "No one questions someone coming out of the elevator—people assume the scanner there will stop anyone from getting somewhere they don't belong."

"Too bad they didn't account for Emerson Quinn," Emerson said in their ears. The words were accompanied by the sharp cracking sound as the hacker popped his knuckles.

"Don't get too cocky yet," Signe intoned darkly. "The hardest part of your job is still to come, my friend."

Her words held two meanings, but only she and Emerson knew that.

The Board's trust in their elevator system turned out to be a somewhat fatal flaw. Even with the recent Berger Security upgrades, the security on the twenty-fourth floor of the Medial Complex was way laxer than it had been back in Huldra's headquarters. The cameras were easily thwarted by sticking to blind spots or bowing your head to pass when there was no blind spot, hiding their faces from any facial sensors embedded into the cameras. According to Emerson's access to the security mech system, there was only one mech patrolling the entire floor at this hour, and it was currently on the far side of the building.

The door locks of the Board Room were more of a challenge. The access ran on a completely insular system, like the one they'd encountered at Huldra. Emerson couldn't disable the locks through the rinth alone. He needed a proximity link to get into the system.

Torrin whipped out his mech-arm's multi-tool, opening an access panel near the baseboards in the hall beside the Board Room. This time, Alura volunteered to maintain the link. She crouched down by the baseboard, holding her unicomm interface a few inches from the panel. After a beat of silence, Emerson spoke again.

"I can disable the scanner on the server room door for up to twenty-nine seconds. After that, you'll have..." Another pause, then, "nine minutes before that security mech comes around and catches Alura out here in the hallway."

Nine minutes.

In less than nine minutes this would all be over. Then, she could stop nursing the guilty feeling in the pit of her stomach—the one that sprang up every time she thought about how they planned to betray Torrin.

Within nine minutes, the plan would have failed. They would be sneaking back through these hallways, heading back to the Penthouse. Torrin would be in a foul mood for a few days. He would rage and storm and hole himself up in his room. But when he emerged, he'd finally be ready to see reason. To make a plan that didn't require blowing up the entire infrastructure of New Avarita.

Unless he discovered that she and Emerson had betrayed him, of course.

Then he'd most likely kill them both.

Nine minutes.

Would that be long enough to show Torrin that the hack didn't work? Long enough for him to be ready to give up and regroup? Or would he stay at that terminal, stubbornly requesting Emerson to try again and again while the clock ticked down and Alura was discovered?

Signe hesitated, looking down at Alura. "You sure you're alright out here? I can keep the link if you want."

"You sure about that, Signe?" Emerson's voice cut in sharply.

It was a shit time to make a change to their plans. She knew that. But still.

"It's all right, Signe," Alura said. She slapped one thigh, tense in her crouched position by the door frame. "I missed leg day yesterday anyway."

Signe snorted. She nodded, then paused for another second. Before she had the chance to second-guess herself, she pulled Sally from the place where the gun lay, tucked behind her left shoulder. She snapped her wrist, flicking the gun out to full length, then handed it to Alura.

"Watch our asses, would you?"

Alura raised an eyebrow, looking from Signe to the gun and back again. Signe didn't blame her—she was infamous for her borderline unhealthy attachment to the weapon. "You sure?"

Signe nodded toward the doorway. "What am I gonna shoot in there? A terminal?"

"You never know," Alura said, reaching out to accept the gun. "You might come across a real-life Rinth Rat in there."

Signe chuckled and Emerson's voice sounded in her ear, "Ha-ha, very funny," he said to the group's channel.

Half a second later, Emerson spoke again. This time, the tone was sharper. Signe could tell he was talking to her on a private channel instead of broadcasting to the entire group. "I can disable the scanner again if I have to, Signe. She'll be able to get in and escape with the rest of you."

"Right," Signe said under her breath. "Right."

An instant later, Emerson cut the scanner on the Board Room door, then overrode the locks. Torrin grabbed the long, stainless-steel handle the instant the lock winked green, swinging open the door and striding inside like he was a long-standing member of the Board arriving for another meeting. He looked cool and collected, but Signe had known the man for years. She knew that underneath his black shirt, Torrin Calix was nothing but a sentient pool of sweat and adrenaline right now.

The Board Room was almost identical to what Signe remembered. The carpeting was fresh and the table had been refinished with a darker stain than she remembered it having last time she was here, but otherwise the room was unchanged. The stained-glass windows spread cool moonlight out in a dim, glowing kaleidoscope pattern on the surface of the table, over the floors, over the faces of Gaius and Torrin beside her.

And there, in the center of the room, was the terminal. The digital central nervous system of all of New Avarita. Torrin's muted footsteps thumped along the carpet as he paced forward, staring at the room and the terminal in near disbelief.

Here they were. After a decade of building their crew and fighting to stay alive, Liv Spencer had provided the final piece of the puzzle to get them here. Ironic that Liv Spencer had also started poking the holes that would ultimately sink Torrin's plans to the bottom of the metaphorical ocean.

"This is it?" Gaius asked, examining the interface built into the Board Room table. It was simple, just a standard hologram projector and a few input ports. "This is the terminal that controls… everything?" His nose wrinkled. "It doesn't even look as fancy as Emerson's janky terminal."

"Hey, don't talk shit about my girlfriend," Emerson said.

The comment was normal enough, but Signe could hear the strain in the kid's voice. Not that she blamed him. As hard of a time as she was having betraying Torrin, Emerson would be having at least twice as much trouble.

He'd been in Torrin's crew almost his entire life. He'd helped Torrin form the crew in the first place. The life in the Penthouse in Lower Baranthrum was pretty much the only life he'd ever known. It was a life he was hoping to keep after today, too. While she and Liv ran off into the wastes outside the city-state, Emerson was hoping to stay put, coordinating from within.

In other words, if just one thing went wrong today, Emerson would lose everything.

Signe's anxiety ratcheted up another notch.

Torrin reached out, activating the terminal by tapping on the table. A holographic display popped up, prompting him to submit to a chip scan. Torrin followed Emerson's instructions, overriding the chip scanner and opting for a manual login entry instead. A new menu popped up and the chip scanner whirred as it powered down.

The next steps went by quickly. Torrin had memorized Emerson's credentials years ago, as a safeguard in case the kid got caught up in something and died. After a few dozen keystrokes, the terminal whirred threateningly, then the menu vanished, replaced by a display that held nothing but a series of long strings of numbers and text.

She, Gaius, and Torrin stood there for a moment, awestruck. This was it. The messy, convoluted innards of the killswitch database. Lucre's Algorithm, written a hundred and some years ago by a mad scientist with a dream. The system that controlled every aspect of life in New Avarita.

For a second, Signe was tempted to say "fuck it" to her plan with Liv and Emerson. These sinister lines of nonsensical-looking code had murdered her mother and Marxus. Not only that, but they were responsible for making sure no one outside the Board had an ounce of meaningful control over their own lives. This Algorithm, scrolling by on this archaic screen, was the reason why the people of New Avarita were forced to work for the Board's profits or die. The reason why the people not only put up with that shit but thanked the Board for it and celebrated when someone died at their hands.

She could live without her chip for the sake of destroying that system, couldn't she? She'd just remove her mech-arm and live with one arm instead of two, go back to reading without the help of her ReadRight enhancement. Things wouldn't be so bad.

But there was more at stake here than reading enhancements and mechanical limbs. Liv was right. If every chip in New Avarita went offline at once, "chaos" would be a fucking understatement.

"Everything all right in there?"

Alura's voice, transmitted from the hallway outside through their unicomms, jolted them all out of their stupor at once.

"Yes, Alura, we're in," Gaius said.

"This is almost over," Torrin said, running his fingers softly over the glowing keyboard projected onto the table in front of him. "Emerson, what's the sequence?"

Emerson paused, just for half an instant—just long enough for Signe to try one last-ditch attempt to change Torrin Calix's notoriously stubborn mind.

"Are you sure you want to do this, Tor?" she asked. His eyes flicked to hers, and she clenched her jaw, holding his gaze. "There's no turning back once you pull this trigger."

But she could tell already that trying to convince him at this point was a lost cause. He cocked his head to one side, almost playfully. "That's the whole point, isn't it?" He turned his attention back to the terminal. "Emerson. The code."

"Quickly, if you don't mind," Alura said. "I'm a little exposed out here."

Anxiety shot through Signe again and her decision ping-ponged backwards again. Forget the threat of chaos. They should call off the plan. Let Torrin kill the chips. But it was too late. Emerson was already reading off the code.

Not the real code—the one that would implode the killswitch system once and for all. Instead, the code Emerson was giving Torrin was a locking code. Once Torrin input the string of letters and numbers Emerson was feeding him, it would lock them out of the Board Room terminal indefinitely. It would probably take Reina Arthur's top engineers to get anyone back into the terminal after this.

Hopefully, Torrin would believe that the locking mechanism was an unforeseen defense rather than sabotage. They could abandon the useless, locked terminal and flee the complex to regroup. Torrin would be frustrated, but if everything went to plan, he would never be any the wiser.

Torrin finished keying in the code, then stared at it for a long moment. For a heartbeat, Signe thought he might be on the verge of changing his mind. Then, he submitted the program. At first, nothing happened. She, Torrin, and Gaius stood in the silent dark for a full breath, bathed in the dim light streaming in through the stained-glass windows and shining with sweat.

"Is that… it?" Gaius said.

At that moment, all hell broke loose.

Screeching alarms sounded outside in the hallways, and blinking beacons winked to life in Signe's enhanced vision, indicating that every single one of the security systems had activated simultaneously.

Fuck, fuck, fuck.

This wasn't supposed to happen.

"Guys… Guys what the fuck is happening?" Alura's voice said over the unicomm. Signe winced as she heard the sound of fists banging on the Board Room door—Alura trying to get in—barely audible over the din of the alarms.

"Yeah, Emerson, what the fuck is happening?" Torrin shouted.

"I don't know," Emerson said, sounding harried. "There must have been a trigger I didn't notice in the database. A failsafe."

"Can you override it?" Gaius asked. His eyes were on the door to the room like he was expecting armed guards to bust in any second.

Not an unreasonable expectation, at the moment.

The fingers of his mech-arm twitched, activating his armgun. Lethal ammo, Signe noted. Of course, if they didn't get out of here before the security guards came, they'd be on the receiving end of lethal rounds, too, so she guessed it was only fair. Her brain whirred, thinking fast. There had to be a way out of this. There was always a way out, she just had to be smart enough to find it. She began combing through Liv's schematics on her unicomm.

"No, I can't override—" Emerson started.

Signe cut him off. "Can you override the door to get Alura in here with us?"

"Get Alura in here? Are you crazy?" Gaius asked. "We'll be cornered if we stay in here."

"No we won't, trust me," Signe said. She tapped on her forearm, annoyed to see that it was shaking. Her holo-display activated, projecting the blueprint Liv and Emerson had built of the tower's security system. She zoomed in on the Board Room, pointing out a small, vertical shaft leading away from the room. "We should be able to get out through the air filtration system if we move quickly."

Gaius looked to the wall where the vent was, then back to the holo-display. "That looks like a long drop."

"It's about two floors down, but there's a fan grate halfway that we could use to slow our fall."

"Oh, good. You want us to jump fifteen feet into a moving fan blade?"

Signe chewed her lip. "Emerson can override the fan." She heard the sound of Alura's fists, still banging on the door outside. "And how are we coming on disabling the door locks and scanner for Alura?"

"Not good, Signe," Emerson's reply came, flat and emotionless.

"What is going on?" Alura asked.

"What do you mean not good, Emerson?" Signe asked, blood draining from her face. There had to be a way out of this. There was always a way out.

"I mean not fucking good," he said, snapping and suddenly sounding closer to panicked than Signe had ever heard him. She could imagine his hands running through his too-long hair, his gaunt face lit by the displays hovering over his terminal. "There's a lockdown protocol that triggered when I locked the terminal."

"What do you mean *when you locked the terminal?*" Torrin asked slowly, speaking for the first time since the alarms went off.

"I-I meant unlocked," Emerson lied hastily.

It wasn't convincing. It was the first time Signe had ever heard the kid stutter.

The muffled sound of shots sounded from the far side of the door. Lethals, Signe could tell from the reverb.

"Alura?" Gaius said through the unicomm. "Alura, what's going on out there?"

"Guards!" Alura said.

More shots fired. This time, Signe recognized the sound intimately. Sally. Alura was firing, using the gun Signe had left with her. The shots were followed by the metallic ping of rounds striking steel.

"And security mechs," Alura finished. "Don't worry, I won't let any of the bastards scan me. Not as long as I'm still standing."

Gaius was at the door now, pounding, like that would somehow override the lockdown protocol keeping Emerson from springing the Board Room doors open. Emotion clawed up Signe's throat. Alura and Gaius had come into Torrin's crew just a few weeks apart. They were closer than siblings now. If they didn't manage to get Alura out of here, Gaius would never be the same.

Of course, if they didn't manage to get Alura out of here, the security mechs would eventually scan her chip and discover Emerson's back-door workaround. Then, they'd all be found out and switch'd.

More shots fired on the far side of the door.

What had she done?

"Alura!" Gaius shouted again.

He primed his armgun, firing a round at the iron door first, then the wall beside it, trying to bust his way out by force. But Signe knew there was no point. Every wall, door, and window in the Medial Complex was reinforced against lethal rounds. You'd have to set off a bomb in here to make more than superficial dents in the surface.

"You guys need to get out of there," Emerson's voice came over the unicomm again. He projected a view through their eye enhancements—security cam footage that lay superimposed over their vision.

A dozen guards flocked toward the room from every direction. Security mechs streamed behind them, scanners primed.

Fear shot through Signe. This wasn't how any of this was supposed to go. No one was supposed to get hurt.

"We're not going anywhere until you break this fucking door open, Emerson," Gaius shouted. He slapped the door with the heel of his hand.

"No, he's right." Alura's voice was steady as it came through the unicomm channel. She sounded certain, strong, and unflinching. "If you guys have a way out, you need to take it. I'm fucked. But don't worry. I'll go out keeping our most important secret."

Through her eye enhancements, Signe could see the camera view for the hall right outside the doorway. Alura looked right at the camera and Signe felt like the woman was looking her right in the eye.

Alura saluted and shouted, "Fuck the Board!" Then, she lifted Signe's firearm, pointing the weapon toward the back of her skull. Signe could tell she was trying to position it right over the chip.

"Alura! No!" Gaius shouted.

At that same moment, Alura activated the trigger, sending a lethal round through her own skull.

The next several moments were a blur of color and sound. The guards advanced down the hallway, pausing briefly at Alura's lifeless form before moving toward the door to the Board Room. Signe was vaguely aware of Torrin using the tools on his mech-arm to open the grate on the northern wall of the room. He forced a still-screaming Gaius in first, then went in himself, leaving Signe to bring up the rear. Signe pulled the grate back into place behind her, then leapt down the vent, using her mech-arm to slow her fall by digging her metallic fingers into the air duct wall.

By the time she reached the fan—which Emerson had managed to stop—the guards had made their way into the room above. She could hear their heavy boots stomping around above her head. By the grace of some deity or another, she, Gaius, and Torrin managed to crawl through the vents, spilling out onto the streets of the Core before the enforcers caught up. But as they ran farther and farther from the tower, from the failed job, from Alura's cooling body, Signe's heart rate didn't slow.

The danger wasn't over.

She imagined a timer in the corner of her vision, like the one Emerson displayed when they were racing against a clock for a job. Alura was dead. It was Signe's fault. But that wasn't bad enough.

Torrin wouldn't meet her eye. He had caught Emerson's slip-up back in the Board Room. He hadn't bought Emerson's lie. And, no doubt, he remembered how Signe and Emerson had challenged his plan after the Huldra break-in. How they had threatened not to work with him.

He knew what Emerson had done—that he had locked Torrin out of the killswitch system instead of helping him override and destroy it. Signe could tell from the way he avoided looking at her that he knew she was in on it.

And it was only a matter of time before he decided to pay them back in kind.

18

LIV

Advancements in body modifications have resulted in exciting opportunities for the citizens of our new world. Employers must obtain the appropriate permits and approvals from the Principal Chairman's office if they would like to require a specific modification. Each request must include:

i. The essential job functions that will be enhanced or enabled by the modification.

ii. The duration of employer-funded support for the management and upkeep of the modification.

iii. Plans to uninstall controlled modifications (i.e., weaponry) in the event of the end of the employment relationship.

It is through this care, consideration, and governance that we keep our society healthy and pure.

—**THE HANDBOOK OF LUCRE,** ***CHAPTER*** **27**

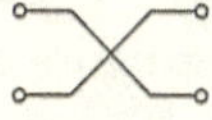

SOMETHING WAS WRONG.

Liv didn't know what, but she could feel it the second she walked into the main room of the Penthouse. Signe and the others weren't back from the Core yet, but she didn't need them to return to know something was wrong. The signs were right in front of her.

Sign number one: Emerson Quinn was not at his terminal.

Instead, he sat on one of the ratty old couches, staring off into space. Black Hat seemed to know something was wrong, too. The cat sat curled up right against Emerson's chest, laying at a precarious angle as he struggled to be as close to the man's face as possible. Emerson was turning something over in his hands. Over and over again.

Sign number two: the thing he was turning over in his hands was a pistol.

Liv cleared her throat. Emerson didn't even look up. "Did… did he destroy everything?"

That got Emerson's attention. He looked up at her and Liv's blood ran cold. His eyes were dead. Red and puffy, too, like he had been crying. Liv had never been great at dealing with someone in the throes of an emotional breakdown. Curse her perfect memory, she still recalled in crystal-clear detail every time she'd failed to comfort a friend in the past. Like the time Ayla had broken up with her secondary school boyfriend and Liv had comforted her by letting her know that less than two percent of all people end up marrying their school-age partners, anyway.

"Check your enhancements," Emerson said dully, calling Liv fully back to the present.

Liv pulled up her unicomm. Clicked through a few menus. Opened access to the rinth. "So, Torrin didn't manage to burn it all down," Liv said slowly, taking a tentative seat on the couch across from Emerson. "That's… that's a good thing, isn't it?"

Maybe things had gone fine, and Emerson was just having a change of heart. Overcome by the guilt of betraying a man who had been a mentor and father figure to him. The young man just stared at Black Hat, running his left-hand fingers through the cat's fur.

His right hand still gripped the pistol so tightly Liv was worried he might set it off by accident.

Finally, he looked up at her and said, "No one was supposed to die."

The room spun as Liv took in the word. *Die.*

She slid off the couch, sinking to her knees in front of Emerson. "What happened? You have to tell me. You have to—"

At that moment, the elevator doors sprang open, and Liv's eardrums were met with a roar of sound.

"What do you mean *when you locked the terminal*?" Torrin Calix shouted. He thundered into the Penthouse, armgun primed and raised, pointed directly at Black Hat, still curled up against Emerson's chest.

Torrin raised his other arm, projecting something through his unicomm. A string of code. The code Emerson had said would bring down the killswitch system. "I should never have trusted you after what you said after the Huldra job. I should have known you'd try to pull some bullshit like this. Did you even try to write something that would kill the database, or did you know you planned to fuck me over from the start?"

Emerson hurriedly shooed the cat away from the barrel of Torrin's armgun, pushing himself to his feet and raising his hands. He dropped his own gun and it fell to the floor just beside Liv.

"Torrin, I can explain."

Liv slid sideways, out from between the two men, before rising to her feet. She craned her neck toward the elevator, catching sight of Gaius first, then breathing a tiny sigh of relief as she saw Signe half a pace behind him. Then, she realized who was missing and her stomach sank. Her eyes immediately flicked to her shoes. *Alura's* shoes. The ones the woman had given her without a question the first damn night they'd met.

Now that woman was dead.

And it was all Liv's fault.

"Yes, please, explain," Torrin said. Liv's attention jolted back to the center of the room, where the crew leader was poking Emerson in his sternum with his mech-arm fingers, his thumb drifting perilously close to the trigger of his armgun. "I'm dying to hear this."

"I didn't account for the—"

"You didn't account for a fucking lot of things," Torrin interrupted. Apparently, he wasn't dying to hear what the younger man had to say at all. "Just like I didn't account for my most trusted crew member to turn on me the moment we were on the edge of the victory we've been clawing our way towards for the past twelve years."

"The victory you were gunning for tonight is *not* the victory I had in mind when I dragged you off those docks," Emerson said. His voice was lower and raspier than Liv had ever heard it. Behind him, Black Hat yowled, stretching his paws up Emerson's back, trying to climb back onto him. Emerson gently pushed the cat back down onto the couch, taking a step away from the sofa and toward Torrin.

"What the fuck are you talking about, Emerson?" Gaius said, moving forward to join the fray. His eyes were bloodshot, his cheeks stained with freshly dried tears. Liv's stomach churned again. She was pretty sure this was the first time she'd ever seen Gaius without Alura,. The pair were attached at the damn hip.

Or at least they had been.

"Alura sacrificed herself to help the rest of us get out of that death trap back there—are you saying that you set that trap?"

Liv glanced at Signe. The woman met her eyes from across the room and Liv saw her own anxiety pulsing back toward her. Torrin wasn't supposed to find out they'd planned this. He was supposed to think it was an honest miscalculation. The algorithm was supposed to be just more impenetrable than they had thought. No one was supposed to die. This was supposed to be a clean strike-out. Now... Now it was all ruined.

Signe looked at Emerson, then stepped forward, opening her mouth.

Emerson talked over her, cutting her off and drowning her out. "I did. But it wasn't meant to be a trap. It was supposed to just lock you out of the system. It wasn't supposed to set off any alarms. No one was—" His voice cracked and he cleared his throat, trying again. "No one was supposed to die."

"Oh, people are going to die, all right. And I don't just mean Alura," Torrin said. He prodded Emerson's chest again, his thumb quivering, like he was desperate to empty his armgun's clip into the skinny hacker.

Liv's stomach churned. Her plan had not only gotten Alura killed. It was going to get Emerson killed, too. And Signe. Probably herself.

"Torrin, calm down," Signe started, moving forward.

Torrin charged on like she hadn't even spoken. "Do you know why I've kept you around for the past twelve years?"

Emerson gritted his teeth. "I'd assume at least a portion of it is because you've come to like and respect me—"

"No," Torrin said coldly. "I've kept you around for two reasons." He counted them out on the fingers of his right hand, keeping his mech-arm pointed directly at Emerson's chest. "Initially, I kept you on because you were the only one who knew the hack that made this whole operation possible. Once you taught me that hack, I let you stay because I thought could trust you." Torrin shrugged. "But that's not true anymore, is it? That makes you useless to me."

Emerson flinched visibly. Liv could see why. After whatever Emerson had gone through in his younger years, he'd found not only a revolutionary leader in Torrin, but also something of a father figure. Seeing their twelve-year relationship boiled down to a transactional analysis of his usefulness had to hurt.

"Well, Torrin, I stuck around for two reasons," Emerson said. "First, because I thought you were fighting for something I thought was worth fighting for." He swallowed. "But then you got tunnel vision. Shutting off the chips and turning New Avarita into a lawless wasteland isn't exactly something I'm willing to fight for. So I gave you the wrong code. I didn't want to set off any alarms, I just wanted to lock down the system and make you take a second to think about—"

"You're not in control of me, Emerson Quinn," Torrin roared. His outburst had drawn the attention of the other crew members currently in the Penthouse. People emerged from the corridors on either side of the living room, lurking and listening. Liv them peering out around the corner, feet planted in the hall like they were afraid to enter the living quarters. She didn't blame them.

"*You're* not even in control of you, Torrin," Emerson said back. He hadn't raised his voice, but Liv could feel the hurt and rage emanating off of him all the same.

Torrin gestured toward the gathering crew members with his free hand. "These people joined me because they—"

"Joined *us,* Torrin."

Torrin stared at Emerson for a second, then continued as if he hadn't spoken. "They joined me because they knew I'd do whatever it took to win. To crush the Board. To take down their fucked-up system of power and—"

"And destroy life as we know it in the process?" Emerson asked. "Torrin, do you hear yourself? You don't even sound like the man I met on those docks all those years ago." He shook his head sadly. "I never wanted to betray you. You're like a fa—"

Emerson's words were cut off by the blast of an armgun.

Liv didn't need to know much about firearms to know that had been a lethal round. The entire Penthouse shook with the force of it. Liv screamed and dropped to the ground. When she looked back up, she saw Torrin standing there, his mech-arm splattered with bright crimson droplets, his armgun barrel smoking as it protruded from his silver wrist.

Emerson Quinn had slumped backward onto the couch. Blood poured from a gaping wound in his chest and his eyes were wide and staring, pointed toward the ceiling. Already they were beginning to film over. *Just like Liam's had, slumped on that dining table, hands still outstretched, fingers curled where they'd met Liv's just a moment before.*

Black Hat nosed at the boy's hand, chirping as he tried to worm his furry head under Emerson's fingers. But the fingers didn't even twitch. Emerson was gone already. Emotion surged up Liv's throat so violently she thought she might vomit. First Alura. Now Emerson. How many people would have to die horribly because of this stupid fucking plan of hers?

"If you never wanted to betray me, you shouldn't have," Torrin said softly, looking down at Emerson's corpse. Then, he raised his voice to address the rest of them again. "I know Quinn didn't act alone. I plan to root out every last traitor in this organization. And I know just where to start."

He whirled around, turning toward the elevator doors where Signe still stood, thunderstruck by what she'd just witnessed.

"Signe Remy. Or should I switch back to your old name, Poulson?" Torrin said. He stalked toward her. Signe reached for her shoulder, then stopped. Liv's gut sank another inch as she realized Signe didn't have her rifle. For the first time since Liv had met the woman, Signe was unarmed. "It seems that, after a decade in bed with the Board, you still have some soft spots for them, don't you?"

Liv's eyes flicked to the floor at Emerson's feet. To the pistol he'd been turning over and over again in his hands when she'd walked in. Was it loaded? She reached for it.

"Fuck you," Signe said. "I don't have a soft spot for the Board. I just have—"

"Save it for whatever god you believe in, Signe," Torrin said. He raised his armgun, priming his next round.

Signe was unarmed.

Signe was helpless.

But Liv wasn't.

"Torrin, wait," she said. Her knees shook as she forced herself to stand tall, taking a step forward, one shaking arm held behind her back. The pistol she held there whined softly as it primed a shot. Was the round lethal? Nonlethal? Liv didn't know how to tell. She'd never shot a gun before. She'd never even held one before.

For once in her life, Liv Spencer was utterly unprepared.

"This was all my fault. I sabotaged the job. Not Signe."

Torrin turned on her. "You think I didn't know that already, Spencer?" he said. "Bringing you into this crew was a mistake. All the time and effort I wasted getting your husband switch'd. I should have known an Upper Lucaran brat would never have the stomach to do what needs to be done." Flecks of spit flew from his lips as he spoke.

Liv felt lightheaded. "Getting my husband switch'd?" she repeated.

What was he talking about?

But Torrin didn't have any intention of making himself any clearer. "I'm going to clean all the little Rinth Rats out of my organization tonight," he said. "If you want to die next, I can make that happen."

He swiveled his stance, aiming the barrel of his armgun directly between Liv's eyes. She felt herself go almost cross-eyed as she stared at the shiny metal barrel. Her body seemed to move of its own accord as she whipped the pistol out from behind her back.

Liv squeezed her eyes shut. If she shot Torrin, he would shoot her, too. This was it.

All the time and effort I wasted getting your husband switch'd, he'd said.

She set her jaw, opening her eyes again and staring Torrin Calix right in the eye. If she was going to die today, she was going to take this asshole with her.

"Signe, run," she said, her voice calmer than she'd ever heard it before. "Keep to the plan."

Liam, I'm coming home.

Then she pulled the trigger.

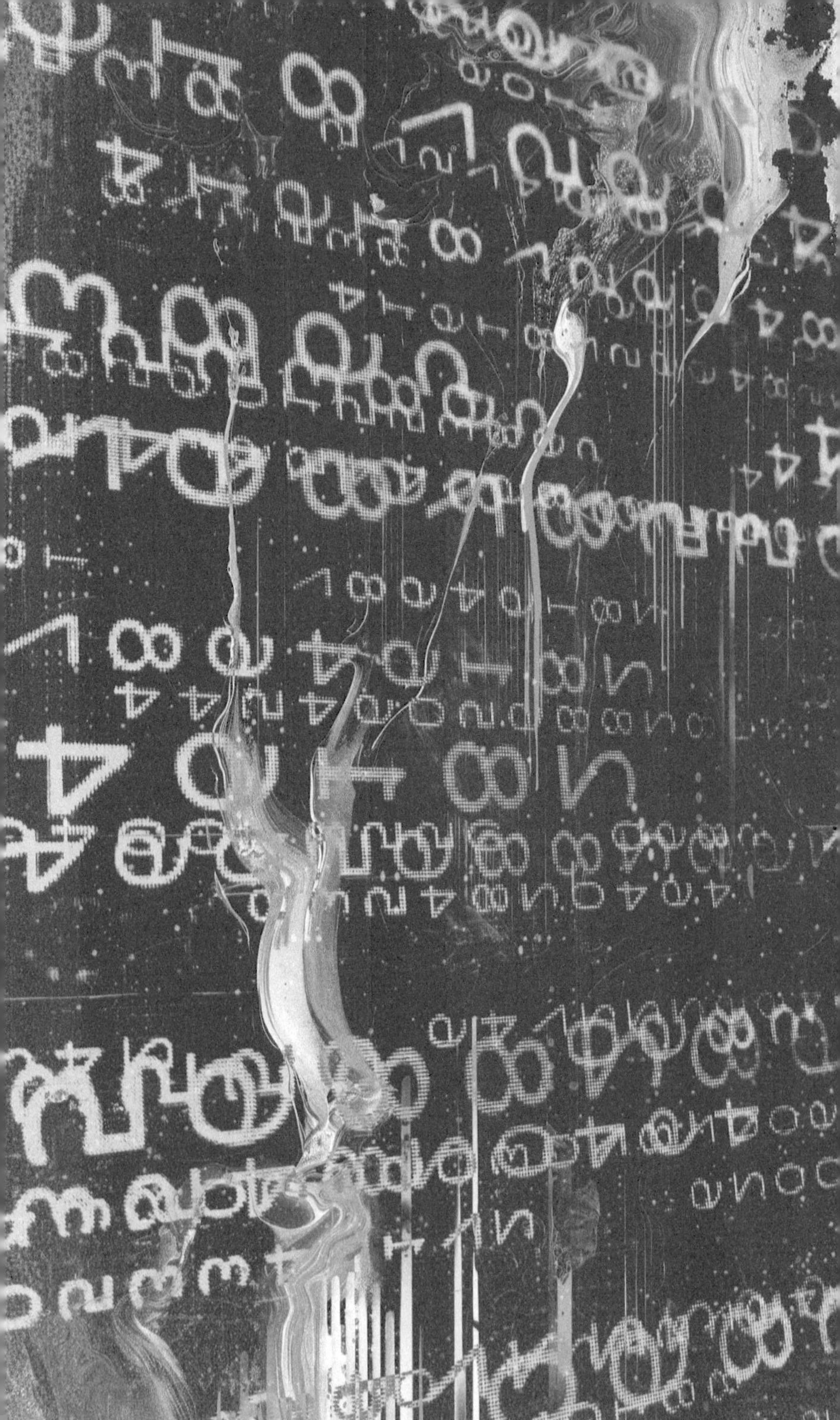

19

SIGNE

New Avarita consists of five districts, but it is paramount that these districts never elect their own leaders or governance. All of New Avarita must be united under the Principal Chairman or all hope of building a people who will be better, stronger, and more worthy of Ascent than the failed society before the Fall will be lost.

—THE HANDBOOK OF LUCRE, *CHAPTER 12*

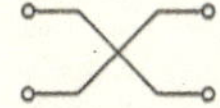

WHEN ALURA SHOT out her chip, Signe's reality got all blurry. Smudged, like a camera lens someone smeared with Vaseline. But when Liv Spencer raised that pistol—where the fuck had she even gotten a pistol?—everything snapped back into crystal-clear focus.

"Signe, run," Liv said. Her voice was flat. Dead. "Keep to the plan."

As the woman's finger twitched, Signe did run. But she didn't run for the elevator, the windows, or any other escape route like Liv had probably intended. Instead, she ran directly toward Liv.

The pistol kicked as it released its round. In that same instant, Signe jammed her right shoulder into Liv's, knocking the woman to the floor and falling to crouch protectively over her. Torrin's armgun fired at almost the same time as Liv's pistol. The round flashed past, so close that it ripped through a chunk of Signe's hair.

Liv's round found a lot more than hair, hitting Torrin square in the chest.

The man wheezed and stumbled back, staring down at the blood soaking through his shirt in disbelief. Gaius ran forward to catch him. He slung Torrin's right arm over his shoulder, struggling to keep the man upright. Torrin's armgun whirred, priming another shot. He coughed. Blood dotted the floor.

Signe rolled off Liv, crawling arm-over-arm into the meager cover of the ratty sofa across from Emerson's terminal. Liv snapped out of her post-tackle daze and rolled the other way, sliding behind Torrin's armchair. Signe braced herself, waiting for the shot to fire, but it never did. After a few seconds, she peeked out from behind the couch to see Torrin's head slumped downward. His limbs hung heavy as Gaius struggled under his weight.

Liv's round must have taken the man right through the heart. He was unconscious now, but he'd be dead within minutes.

"What the fuck?" Gaius shouted. He fell to his knees, laying Torrin down on the floor and pressing his hands to the man's chest, trying to staunch the bleeding.

More members of the crew were gathering now. Emerging from the halls on either side of the living area. Some mouths were slack with shock, others tight with rage.

Signe rose to her feet, glancing around warily. Gaius's eyes snapped to hers, his face a mix of horror and wrath. Signe recognized the expression. Ironically, it was the same one she had worn the day she watched Marxus get switch'd all those years ago. The moment she had lost faith in the Board and everything they stood for.

Now, those emotions were all directed at her.

"You set us up," Gaius said softly. "You sabotaged the job." His eyes flicked between her and Liv, then finally jumped to Emerson's lifeless form, slumped backward on the couch, his blood soaking into the cushions. "Why?"

"He didn't give us a choice," Liv started. She was still holding the pistol as she rose, shaking, from her hiding place behind the armchair.

"Do you realize what would happen if he'd succeeded, Gaius?" Signe started. "If the whole chip system actually went down? Then—"

"I'd rather live without my chip than without Alura," Gaius interrupted. He gestured toward Torrin with his chin. "I think he'd rather have lived without his chip than not at all." He gestured toward the people lurking, thunderstruck, in the hallways on either side of them. "Maybe the rest of the people here—the rest of the people in all of New fucking Avarita— would feel the same. But you thought you knew better." He shook his head, looking at Signe. "You always do."

Signe's eyes flicked around the Penthouse. If she and Liv wanted to survive long enough to try to fix this, to salvage whatever they could of their plans, they needed to get out of here. Now.

Acting on instinct, Signe leapt forward, tackling Liv to the floor again. They crashed to the carpet at Emerson's limp feet just in time. Gaius's armgun flashed, and a lethal round buried itself in the wall right where Liv's head had been a moment before. Signe looked down at herself, then Liv. No blood. That was a good sign.

But she and Liv had just betrayed and murdered the leader of this revolution, and Gaius wasn't the only jackass in here with a bootleg armgun.

She could hear others priming now, lethal rounds clicking into place as the barrels extended from metallic forearms. They were on the opposite side of the living room from the elevator now, and even if they somehow managed to get across a room full of pissed-off members of Torrin Calix's trusted crew, the elevator doors would never shut before someone got a few shots off. If they were going to get out of here, they had only one option.

"Window," Signe said to Liv.

"What?"

"Now—go, go!"

They barely made it to their feet before they had to collapse to the ground again, narrowly missing having their innards splashed all over the wall by Jerome's armgun. The round made a full fucking crater in Penthouse floor where it hit. He must have jacked up the power settings on the gun. *Fantastic.*

Signe pulled herself up, reaching for Liv again, but the other woman pulled back.

"Wait," she said. She dove to avoid another shot, then rolled under the grasping arms of Lena Martin, a newer member of the crew. Everyone was getting in on the action, now.

"The fuck are you doing?"

"We can't just leave him here," Liv said.

For a second, Signe thought Liv was talking about Emerson. They would never be able to drag his body out of this Penthouse. Then, the woman did the second craziest thing she could have possibly tried to do at that moment—she reached for Black Hat.

The cat hissed and spat, clawing out of her arms twice, running back to tuck himself under Emerson's limp left arm.

"He doesn't want to go, Liv," Signe said. She had made it to the window, army crawling on her forearms for the last few feet.

"Emerson would want—"

"For fuck's sake," Signe said under her breath. Gaius had stopped messing around. He was coordinating the gathered crew now. They'd corner her and Liv in seconds—the Penthouse wasn't that fucking big.

Black Hat wriggled out of Liv's arms, leaving thick scratches down the woman's forearms. Before she could reach for the cat again, Signe grabbed her by the waist. Then, she dove for the window, her mech-arm extended, metallic fingers balled into a fist. The plate of glass shattered on impact, and the pair of them tumbled out into the night.

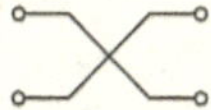

THE PENTHOUSE WAS six stories off the ground, but Signe wasn't dumb enough to jump out a window without at least something of a plan. They crashed through a rusted scaffolding and landed on the roof of the abandoned textile factory next door. The fall was far enough that it knocked the wind out of them but didn't cause any major damage.

Signe took the lead, half-dragging Liv behind her as they pelted through the dark alleys of Lower Baranthrum.

"Where are we going?" Liv asked, sounding slightly out of breath, whether that was from the running or just general panic, Signe wasn't sure.

"Somewhere safe," Signe said back.

"Does that even exist anymore?"

Signe shot Liv a pitying look. "Did it ever?" She held out an arm, stopping Liv from moving forward as a transport zipped along the rail line in front of them. Once it had passed, she pulled Liv forward again, heading north and east.

If it ever had, it certainly didn't now. A kernel of doubt settled deep within her core. Had they done the right thing, or had they just made a colossal mistake? Could Torrin's plan have been better for New Avarita? Maybe Gaius was right: maybe the people would have celebrated the death of their chips.

But at her core, she knew that was ridiculous. Sure, some people in the city-state would have embraced their new freedom… but a hell of a lot of the people living here liked their digital shackles. If everyone suddenly lost access to their coin, their unicomms, their fucking mechanical limbs without warning, all of New Avarita would spiral into a dystopian hellscape.

Maybe someday, someone would be able to take down the killswitch protocol some way they had never thought of. Tonight, however, she and Liv had one goal, and it was a tall order: survive.

Signe had never been afraid of the streets of Lower Baranthrum before, but without Sally slung over her shoulder, she felt naked enough to waste the time skirting Switch'r's Alley entirely instead of cutting through. The route took them closer to Romy's territory than she would normally have risked at this time of night, but honestly, at this point, Romy the Wolf was the least of her fucking problems.

After over half an hour of cutting through the darkened streets, avoiding the pitiful handful of tubheads patrolling down here, and ducking into side alleys whenever they heard the telltale whirring of a security mech's wheels, the familiar streets of Signe's childhood neighborhood came into view.

Signe's stomach surged as she thought about the last time she'd been here. It had only been a few days ago. In that time, everything had changed for her. How did these streets still look exactly the same when the world had just crumbled?

Liv didn't say a word as Signe led her further east. She seemed to have gone numb. When they were right on the border between Lower Baranthrum and Old Altum, Signe cut back south for half a block.

It was still there.

In school, Signe and her friends had called this place *the least popular Lobos Transport Station in all of New Avarita*. It looked like that title still fit.

Where most of the train lines spanned all of New Avarita, connecting at major hubs that let a passenger wind through all the districts without ever leaving Lobos-owned land, this line was a relic of a failed experiment. The Lower-Alt line only ran between Old Altum and Lower Baranthrum. It stopped at specific homes and businesses, operating more as a short-distance transport than the rapid transports Lobos invested their coin in these days.

People in Old Altum rarely had any need—or want—to come to Lower Baranthrum, so really the only people who used this line were the few people who lived in the townhomes in this part of town and worked up in Old Altum. Which meant there weren't many people using this station. Especially not at this time of night.

Signe saw only three shadows on the platform, waiting for the next train. None of them wore the telltale helmet of a Correxion officer. She led Liv around the back of the station, leading her through the gap in the crumbling stone and into a small, cave-like space that held the electrical relays for the transport line. It was just as warm as Signe remembered, the humming of the generators drowning out most of the outside world.

It was dark enough that Signe couldn't see much of Liv's face, but a sliver of streetlight filtered in from outside, catching the edge of the other woman's cheek as she peered around.

"I used to come here when I was a teenager," Signe said, sliding a pair of crates from the shadows and sitting down on one, resting her elbows on her knees. She peered down at the ground between her boots, picking up a small hypodermic needle with her mech-hand and holding it up. "Looks like other teenagers are still coming here. For the same reason my friends and I did."

Liv still didn't say anything; just stared around with those too-wide eyes.

Signe had spent so much time hidden away in this little cave, fucked up on Romy's latest concoctions that she barely remembered her last year of her GenstraCo-mandated education. She'd started exploring the drugs when her mom got switch'd—she was supposed to be celebrating, but she had still felt sad and didn't know why. The drugs had helped a little… And hurt a lot.

The time she'd spent in this little area, holed up with Gregor and Dezria, laughing about stupid shit and slowly destroying their bodies and minds had almost set her down a path that would have had her prem-dead before she reached the age of twenty. It had been Dezria's overdose—the day after graduation—that had pushed Signe to try to clean her shit up. She wasn't ready to die then, and she wasn't ready to die now.

As much as she hated Reina Arthur, the Board, and the time she'd spent supporting their bullshit, she had to admit that the strict no-drugs-or-alcohol rules she'd had to follow working private security were probably the reason she was still alive today.

Well, that and the work of Emerson Quinn.

At the thought of Emerson, bile clawed its way up Signe's throat. She'd given the kid a lot of shit over the past nine years, but he was the closest friend she'd had since Marxus got switch'd. He'd been a pain in the ass sometimes, but he was funny and brilliant and dedicated to making New Avarita better than the mess it was now.

Now, he was dead. Thrown out like a sack of garbage on a waste transport the second he stopped being useful. After all these years, all this time, all his posturing and grandstanding and bullshit, Torrin Calix was no better than the Board.

"It's all my fault," Liv said, breaking her silence for the first time since the Penthouse.

"I mean, you did what you had to do. Saved my ass, for starters," Signe said.

"What? No." Liv looked genuinely confused. "Liam. All my fault."

"It wasn't your—"

"Yes, it was," Liv cut her off. "You heard Torrin back there. He switch'd Liam to get to me. To push me over the edge. To get me to join his little… his little… cult."

Signe sucked her teeth. "Liv, Torrin didn't have the power to switch anyone. The Board—"

"You're going to tell me with a straight face that there's no chance Torrin Calix found a way to bribe the right people inside Vinco to get Liam fired." Liv shook her head. "Before he died, Liam was consumed by a story he'd been researching. Something big. What if Torrin was his source? Leaked information Liam should never have known? Got him twisted up in something way too big for him to handle. Got him put on the Board's radar in the first place."

Signe didn't have an answer to that. She sat in silence for a long second, listening to the building creaking and groaning in the wind around them.

"Torrin got Liam switch'd. And he did it to get to me. It's all my fault."

The woman's voice was shaking now. And that set off something inside of Signe. She reached over and shook Liv Spencer by her frail little shoulders.

"Pull it together. You can't fall apart now. Then everything that happened back in the tower would be for nothing." Signe let out a shaking breath. "It can't have all been for nothing."

For a second, Liv was silent. Then, the woman took a deep breath. It was like she became someone else, in that moment. She straightened her spine, her eyebrows lost that pinched, verge-of-tears look, leaving behind a face that looked like it was forged out of iron.

"What did happen?" she asked. "Back in the tower?"

Signe shook her head, not wanting to relive it. But if Liv fucking Spencer could pull it together, she could, too. She dove into the horrible story, describing what had happened in as clinical a way as she could. The end of the recollection was met with a long, loaded silence. Then, Liv asked the question Signe had been asking herself since the moment their group separated, leaving Alura alone in the hallway outside the server room.

"Did we make a mistake?"

Signe found the other woman's eyes in the dim light sneaking in through the cracked walls. "Maybe."

Another pause. Then, "How many of you would have died in that tower if Torrin actually got what he wanted?"

Signe leaned back, raising an eyebrow as she thought it through. If Torrin had succeeded in shutting down Lucre's Algorithm, there was a very real chance that all four of them would have ended up trapped in that tower. The chips wouldn't have been operational, but still, there were an awful lot of bodies in the Medial Complex. They might have been swarmed by guards or security mechs before they made it out.

Even if they *did* make it out, they could have been massacred on the street by panicked people wondering where the hell all their coin had gone. In reality, Torrin's plan had been just as reckless as their own. Not that that did anything to combat the guilt spreading through Signe's entire body like a disease.

"I can't believe Emerson is gone," Liv said softly. She looked up at Signe. "I know I didn't know him as long as you did, but even when I didn't know who he was, he was one of my best friends."

Signe nodded. "How long were you guys playing that stupid Western game together before you decided to drag your ass down to Lower Baranthrum?"

The purposeful avoidance of mentioning the trigger for what had made her drag her ass down to Lower Baranthrum in the first place hung heavy in the air between them for a long second.

Then, Liv shook her head. "Over a year." She chewed her lip. "Long enough that he was the first person I wanted to talk to when Liam died."

If Signe had a single nurturing bone in her body, she probably would have reached out to comfort the other woman. Instead, she just folded her arms and said, "It's fucked up that Torrin did that."

"Was he always so…"

"Stupid?" Signe finished. She sighed. "No, no he wasn't. Or maybe I just used to be a lot stupider myself, who knows." Signe shot Liv a rueful smile. "He was always passionate. When I first joined, it was all about siphoning profits away from the Board by making bootleg products. But he got more and more tunnel vision as his attempts to stick it to the Board got more intense."

"In his defense, the Board deserves to have it stuck to them pretty fucking intensely," Liv said.

Signe snorted. A few weeks ago, when she first met Liv in that tea shop, she would have never guessed this little memory whiz from Upper Lucara would last more than a day in Torrin's crew. Now… Well, it was safe to say she'd underestimated Liv. She might barely know the stock of a gun from its barrel, but she was tough in other ways. Resilient and stubborn and just a little crazy.

"So, what's the plan?" Signe asked. "We can't stay in Lower Baranthrum—Gaius and the others will have put a thousand-coin bounty on each of our heads by now."

"We can't exactly go back into the other districts, either," Liv mused. "Not unless we want to risk getting scanned and switch'd."

Signe swallowed, her vision flashing back to the security cam footage of Alura in that hallway. The image of her raising Sally's barrel to the back of her head and pulling the trigger. Alura had done that to protect the rest of the crew—to prevent herself from getting scanned and prevent the Board from finding Emerson's hack. It'd be a pretty shitty way to say "thanks" for that sacrifice if they got themselves scanned and got the whole crew killed anyway.

"You know what we have to do, Liv."

The little cavern fell silent for a few seconds. Then Liv said, "Leave."

"Leave," Signe agreed. She leaned back, drumming her fingertips on her kneecap, thinking. "As long as the sensors in that section of the western barrier are still on the fritz we should be able to sneak out through there. We can gather some supplies before we leave, head toward that lake Emerson found."

"And then what?" Liv asked. "How do you suggest we get more supplies from New Avarita? Or coordinate the rescues we planned in the future?" She dropped her head between her knees. "Without Emerson, there's no way we can do all that, Signe."

"I wasn't suggesting we do all that," Signe said. "I was suggesting we get our asses outside the barrier."

"And what, just leave everyone else here?" Liv asked, aghast.

"Liv," Signe snapped. "Most of the people here *like* being here. Most of the people here believe in the Board. They don't want to be rescued."

"You know that's not true." Liv paused, leaning forward until her face was bathed in streetlight, showing the contempt in her expression. "You're just running away. Being a coward."

"There's a difference between being a coward and being practical," she snapped. "We can come back someday. Get word to someone on the inside, see if we can set up a contact. But if we don't get out of New Avarita soon, we won't live long enough to do any of that."

Liv's face sagged, making her suddenly look about ten years older than she was. "I know. I know."

Signe nodded tightly. The conversation was closed, then. They'd be leaving New Avarita, just like they'd planned. She pulled up her unicomm menu, tapping out a supplies list. "We'll need water—

enough for a few days at least, just in case we get turned around trying to find that damn lake. Then we'll need some basic building materials." She flexed the fingers of her mech-arm. "Thankfully, this will be able to do a lot of that work for us. Then there's the problem of food. We can probably lift some nutrient supplements or something, but we'll have to learn how to grow some shit eventually."

She trailed off as she realized that Liv was chewing on her lip, clearly holding something back.

"What is it?"

"You can, um. You can get a head start."

Signe raised an eyebrow. "A head start."

"Yeah. Just a day or so."

Signe sighed. "Liv, you can't just hide out here forever. Eventually the fuckers who still use this place to shoot up will find you, for starters, and even if they don't—"

"I'm not staying here."

"Okay, then where are you planning on going?"

A long pause. "Do you still have the data?"

"What data?"

"The lunch specials for the bar down on Lefter Street," Liv said drily. "You know what data I mean."

Signe wasn't used to hearing sarcasm come out of the woman's mouth, but that was only the second strangest thing about that sentence. She did know what data Liv meant. The data Signe had stolen from her father's unicomm. The location of Kiran Voland Jr.—the still-unchipped baby Liv was hell-bent on rescuing.

"Liv, there is no way you can pull that job off alone."

"Probably not."

"—and without Emerson, you won't even have eyes on the camera system inside the facility."

"Nope."

Signe shook her head. "I can't let you do this, Liv. You're going to die or get scanned. Then we're all fucked, and—"

"I'm not leaving without him," Liv shouted. She paused for a second, then lowered her voice. "Look, I'm not expecting you to go on this mission with me. But I made a promise that I would protect him. I've gotten enough people killed already. I can't sacrifice him, too. And don't worry. If I'm going to get caught..." She held up the pistol. "I know what I need to do to keep everyone else safe. So, I'm going to ask you one more time: do you have the data?"

Signe studied her in the dim light, then shook her head with a mirthless laugh.

"You're not going to change my mind," Liv said, misreading the reaction. "Not in a million years."

"All right," Signe said. She pulled up the data she'd taken from her father. The information about the facility, room, and bed the child of Ayla Voland was being kept.

Liv held out her wrist, preparing a prox-link for the file transfer, but Signe pulled her own wrist back.

"If you're going on this suicide mission, you're not going on it alone," Signe said. "I'd rather die giving the Board one last middle finger than starve to death out in the wasteland anyway."

Liv's eyes glinted in the near-darkness. She lifted her pointed, narrow chin and gave a single nod, her tangled brown hair falling in front of her face.

"Get your middle fingers ready, then. And let's get to work."

20

REINA

Communication chips have been a convenience since the mid-2100s. Thanks to the generosity of the Algorithm, every citizen will receive a chip between six weeks and six months of age. At this age, the skull has not yet hardened, making the installation process safer and the healing process easier, giving each citizen the optimal chances of success in their pursuit of their ultimate goal.

—THE HANDBOOK OF LUCRE, *CHAPTER 11*

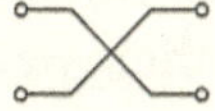

REINA ARRIVED AT the Medial Complex just under two hours after the break-in. Everything was still in absolute shambles. Correxion officers lined the walkway leading up to the main entrance, scanning each chip manually with an old-fashioned hand scanner as people arrived on the scene. Three of Reina's private security guards waited on the sidewalk out front. They surrounded her in a protective V-formation as she walked from her transport to the tower doors.

"How many offenders were present?" Reina asked the guard to her right.

"Unconfirmed, Madam Arthur," the man said. "One is neutralized in the corridor outside the Board Room. The others are still at large."

Still at large. How was that even possible?

It shouldn't even have been possible for them to enter the complex unscanned to begin with. Even more impossible was the fact that they had managed to get so high in the central tower. Unless maybe they had an insider? Someone within the tower who had gotten them in? But everyone who worked in the complex knew that breaking into the Board Room would be grounds for arrest. Who would risk it? And why?

"We aren't sure how they got in, yet," the guard said, echoing her thoughts. "Which isn't helped by the fact that we can't identify the neutralized actor."

"Can't identify them?" Reina asked, incredulous. "What do you mean you can't identify them?"

The guard looked around, then lowered his voice. "Blew out her chip. Before our squad could scan it." He mimed holding a gun to his head and firing it.

Reina winced. "Did anyone recognize her? Could you get a facial scan? Is she from the Principal Chairman's office?"

"Negative to all of the above," the guard said. "She wasn't captured on camera at all before the incident. And her face is less than intact now." He looked around as the Correxion officer at the door waved them through. "This is something better discussed behind closed doors, Madam."

Reina nodded. *Could it be Signe Poulson?* But why would she spend almost a decade in hiding only to break into the Medial Complex and shoot out her own chip?

The inside of the complex was just as hurried and unsettled as the sidewalk outside, but there was no damage Reina could see. In fact, aside from the general air of unease in the building, Reina saw no visual sign that this was anything other than a normal Thursday night anywhere from the main entrance to the elevator. The Board Room was sealed off, so they had no recourse but to meet in the twelfth-floor conference room instead, which took some of the grandeur out of things.

In the Board Room, with its stained-glass windows, mahogany table, and arcing views of the Core, it was easy to feel like a god.

Here in this small room with one simple window, a stainless-steel table, and slightly worn carpeting, Reina felt acutely human.

Once all nine members of the Board arrived, the doors to the conference room were sealed tight, blocking out the security guards, assistants, and other staff outside. When all was quiet, Reina cleared her throat.

"What do we know so far?"

"I think we should be directing those questions toward Cora," Eliza Vinco said, shooting the Teras Systems executive a look.

"Me? Why me?" Cora snorted.

"Look around you, Cora. We are meeting in this substandard hovel because there has been a break-in of our headquarters," Eliza said. "Wasn't it your subsidiary that did the security for this building?"

"Berger Industries," Clement piped up from across the table. He drummed his stubby fingers on the tabletop. "They've done most of the security work in the Core."

Reina frowned. That included her own headquarters, if she wasn't mistaken. She'd have to pay for an entirely new upgrade now, if Berger's work was proven to be shoddy. That's what she got for allowing her team to hire one of Cora's companies to begin with.

"The breach is only the beginning of our problems," said Winston Amos. "Thankfully, we did manage to apprehend one of the infiltrators."

"Was it your officers or one of our private security who subdued them?" asked Audrey Lobos.

"Neither," the Grimme-Folson United executive said. He pushed himself to his feet, pulling something from beneath the desk. "She shot herself. Aimed directly for her chip. This was the weapon we found with her."

He set the object on the desk and every bit of air evaporated from Reina's lungs. It was the same type of rifle she armed her private security force with. Not a current one: the model they'd issued around a decade ago. From the exact time Signe Poulson had worked for her.

Reina didn't want to believe the dead woman still laying in the corridor outside the Board Room was Signe Poulson. Still, she had a gut feeling. Even at the best of times, Reina hated gut feelings; she'd been trained her whole life to trust data over instinct. But she couldn't deny this one.

Signe Poulson had been inside the Medial Complex last night. Whatever these invaders were after, that was the reason Signe had gone off the grid. She was wrapped up in their mission, whatever it was.

Reina fought to keep her face still. "Yes, the guards who fetched me briefed me on the matter so far," she said. "How severely has the chip been blown out? Is any of the data salvageable?"

"That's what I was hoping you'd be able to answer for us, Madam Arthur," Winston said. He pulled something from the pocket of his fitted, genuine-cotton jumpsuit and set it on the table.

A chip.

Or rather, the remains of what had once been a chip.

It was completely shattered. Bits of steel were sprinkled on the tabletop like little snowflakes. Thankfully Winston's men had cleaned the blood and brain matter off the pieces, but still, it made Reina shudder, knowing that this device had been inside a person's head—*Signe Poulson's head?*—just a few hours before.

She reached out, scooping up the pieces and examining them in her palm. "Is this all of the parts?"

"All we were able to recover," Winston said. "Do you think you'll be able to pull any residual data from it?"

"Maybe," Reina said, doubtfully. "What about other identifiers?

Did the intruder have a mech-enhancement of any kind?"

Winston nodded. "Mech-arm." The air whooshed from Reina's lungs. *A mech-arm. Just like Signe had.* "But it was bootleg. No identifying licensure or anything."

Bootleg. Not like Signe's.

"This is precisely why we need to crack down on bootleg mech-enhancements in the southern districts," Cora said primly. "Correxion officers need to be trained in—"

"Don't try to turn this around on me, Cora," Winston said dangerously.

Reina held out a hand. This was becoming ridiculous. The Board's infighting was infuriating at the best of times. Now? Here? In this tiny, inauspicious room while Reina's mind was already spinning like a top? It was unbearable. "I'll do what I can with the chip. Maybe I can pull something from it if I'm able to reengineer it."

Much of the chip was still intact. There was a good chance she'd be able to strip at least a serial number from it, which she'd be able to reference against Huldra's records and pull the identity of this chip's user. However, if she succeeded in that endeavor, she had no intention of telling the rest of the Board. Not yet.

The identity of the infiltrator would remain a mystery. At least until she figured out what on earth Signe was up to, and how she'd managed to stay hidden for so long. And once she sorted out exactly why she was so invested in her old security guard's return from the dead.

"Excellent," said Winston.

"Have we identified the origin of the breach?" asked Jasper Koegen.

Winston turned to face him. "It's funny you should ask that, Master Koegen. The breach is believed to be your restaurants down on level one."

"My restaurants?" Jasper said frowning. "But how—"

"The doors, they weren't upgraded with the rest of the security patch last year," Cora said, almost salivating at the chance to pin the blame for this on someone else. Despicable. And unsurprising. "At your request, if I remember correctly, Master Koegen."

"All right, well, let's get those doors upgraded now, then," Jasper said, irritated.

"In the meantime, I think we should station security mechs by those doors at all times," Clement piped up.

"Already done," said Winston.

"Excellent," Reina said. "So, there is no immediate danger from this group of infiltrators now, then. At least not to the Board."

"I don't know if I'd say—" Winston started.

Reina waved a hand as though unconcerned. "This isn't the disaster I thought it was. We can prevent this issue from spiraling or recurring with two simple measures."

"I think I should handle the security of—"

"First, I'll dedicate some staff to reconstructing this chip, see if we can't put a face to this mysterious infiltrator," Reina continued, speaking over Winston as though he hadn't interrupted in the first place. "And second, we avoid using one of Cora's companies for security ever again."

After another brief argument between Cora and Jasper over whose fault the security breach ultimately was, the meeting ended. Reina made her way back down to her transport and programmed in the Huldra Industries headquarters. Ostensibly, she was returning to her headquarters to handpick a team of trusted Huldra employees who could help her put the fragmented chip in her palm back together. Truthfully, Reina had no intention of doing any such thing.

She and she alone would confirm the identity associated with this chip.

She walked through the doors of Huldra's headquarters, heading for her private office. She'd almost reached the blessedly soundproof door when she heard the clicking of Jaya Ravenna's radically uncomfortable-looking shoes approaching from the dark side of the hallway.

"Madam Arthur, I heard what happened over at the Medial Complex."

"Yes, I'm pretty sure the whole Core has heard about it," Reina said drily. "I've just come from a Board meeting and the matter has been handled."

Jaya blinked—her usual expression of condescending surprise. "So soon? Well, that is comforting." She inclined her head to one side. "A few of us here were starting to worry if you might be losing your touch for leadership."

"Were you?" Reina asked. She didn't have the time or the energy for this waste of breath and space today. She drew herself to full height, looking down the bridge of her nose at the woman standing in front of her. How had she been afraid of this chirping cricket of a woman for so long? "Go find something useful to do before I find someone more capable to head up engineering for Huldra."

"There is no one more capable than—"

"Did I say 'more capable'?" Reina said. "Perhaps I simply meant 'less irritating.'"

With that, she strode through her office door, then waved her wrist behind her to seal the entrance shut before Jaya could try to follow. She couldn't truly fire Jaya simply for being irritating—if she could, she would have done that years ago—but if she threatened it enough times, maybe the woman would learn to shut her mouth and stop her efforts to undermine Reina's authority.

Of course, there was always the off chance that the Algorithm would deem Jaya ready for Ascent on its own and Reina could be rid of her once and for all. She doubted she would be so lucky.

Alone in her office, Reina activated every security protocol she had at her disposal—including several that had not been installed by Berger. Next, she slid out her retractable workbench, activating her magnifying eye enhancements and pulling out her most delicate set of specialty tools. It had been a long time since she had constructed a chip directly, but she still remembered the patterns of the tiny wires and circuits better than she knew the layout of her own penthouse. After over an hour of sweating and squinting, Reina managed to construct the chip enough to pull the serial number out using a prox-link with her own unicomm.

She checked the records in Huldra's database, then breathed a sigh of relief. This chip was not Signe's. It belonged to a woman named

Alura Byron. A woman who had been dead for nearly six years.

The list of walking ghosts in New Avarita had just doubled, if Aksel Poulson's report about his daughter had been true. This confirmed something she'd believed since she heard Aksel's account: if Signe had found a way around Lucre's Algorithm, she wasn't working alone. How many others were there out there, living off the grid down in Lower Baranthrum? And, more importantly, what were they up to?

She leaned back in her chair, drumming her fingers on her kneecaps for a few long moments. It was never safe to access the veilrinth—if the rest of the Board flagged what she was doing, she'd be facing an uncomfortable inquiry at best. But her firewalls and security measures here were stronger than the ones back in her penthouse. And the answers she was searching for would never be listed on the Board-approved rinth. Besides, if it was discovered she had accessed the veilrinth from Huldra's headquarters, she could make the argument that she had only done so in an effort to track down the Board tower infiltrators.

Which was true, in a sense.

Still, it was a risk. She stared at her office wall for several long moments, considering. One of her oldest paintings hung on that wall: an image of her mother in profile, standing on their front porch, the vivid greenery of the grow-dome's plants reflected in her eyes. She'd painted it when she was still in mandated education. Back when she still thought she might go to university for art. Back when her life had been full of colorful daubs of paint instead of bland, steel symmetry.

There is no art without bravery.

It had been her favorite quote at the time. The words of Lillian Smith, a famous painter from the mid-2260's.

Reina may have continued painting in all the years since. But when was the last time she had been brave enough to create something that could truly be called "art?"

She gritted her teeth, stiffening her resolve, then sank into her VR environment, plunging headfirst into the sea of banned materials, black market dealings, and anonymity that was the veilrinth. She pulled up all the identifiers that linked back to Signe's chip, then combed through illicit messaging boards, lists of viewer profiles for banned holofilms and books, bootleg enhancement listings, and more, searching for matches: the footprints only the most experienced of hackers would know they needed to worry about leaving behind.

Every time she found a link, a puppet account that tied back to Signe's chip, a comment posted from the unicomm serial number registered to that chip, she felt like she had found another morsel on the breadcrumb trail that would ultimately lead her to Signe Poulson.

When Reina emerged, the sky outside her window was dark again, and she had nearly the whole story.

A story of how a disillusioned enforcer had met someone called RinthRat12 on a messaging board about an old, banned holofilm from the 2100s. A story of how that disillusioned security guard had then been fed a steady diet of anti-Board materials and long-banned books until she finally agreed to set an in-person meeting.

After that, the trail went cold, but from the materials this mysterious RinthRat12 had sent, the goals of the group Signe had joined were clear. The materials included essays from the days of the first Principal Chairman about the ethics of Lucre's Algorithm, films centered around the tragedy of mothers and brothers and partners whose loved ones were selected for Ascent, leaving them behind, books about life in the world outside of New Avarita—in countries where Lucre's Algorithm had never been adopted.

This group meant to destroy the killswitch protocol.

Reina felt her heartbeat pulsing through every inch of her body from her eardrums to the tips of her toes. The way the chips were programmed, it wouldn't be possible to escape Ascent without destroying the entire fabric of New Avaritan life. It would take years—maybe even decades—of slow, subtle changes to the chips' programming to separate the two functions and pave the way for the destruction of the most destructive part of Lucre's Algorithm. Signe had infiltrated the Board Room—the place that housed—among other things—the central database. They had come to crash the system and send New Avarita into chaos.

As much as Reina had come to hate and fear the killswitch system, she still had to admit it was a good thing they had failed. Imagine how the value of Huldra would have plummeted if every chip in New Avarita went offline. She shivered just thinking about it. She would have gone from wealthy and powerful to utterly destitute overnight.

Of course, everyone would have, she reasoned. Physical currency had died out completely in the mid-twenty-second century. Without the chips, no one in New Avarita would be able to access their coin.

All of it made sense… all of it but one critical piece. The piece that had alerted Reina that Signe Poulson was still alive after all. Aksel Poulson's message. Signe had gone through the trouble of taking herself off the map entirely. She had risked everything to leave Reina's protection, fake her own Ascent, disappear into the most disgusting parts of Lower Baranthrum.

And then, inexplicably, almost a decade later she had met with her father out of the blue. A Correxion officer, a man she had to know might report her and destroy the cover she'd spent nine years maintaining. Why? What could she possibly have stood to gain from a conversation with a man like that?

Reina hesitated for a moment, then dove back into her research. Huldra, Medla Systems, and a few other corporations guarded their secrets fiercely, keeping the important things in airgapped terminals locked behind scanners and doors and security mechs. Eliza Vinco wasn't anywhere near as cautious. All of Vinco Telecom's records were on the rinth—behind firewalls and ransomware protection protocols and more, but still accessible if you knew the right keystrokes.

The halls outside Reina's office grew quieter and quieter as Reina worked. The clock on her unicomm was blinking 05:00 by the time she cracked the rest of the code. She felt like the puzzle pieces were sliding together in front of her eyes as she examined Aksel Poulson's unicomm records from the day his message had come through Huldra's communication system.

The breach was well-hidden, but it was there. Signe had extracted a data file from her father's chip that day.

A file containing the names, locations, and birth dates of newborns being held in Medla House facilities. Not just any newborns: orphaned newborns. Unchipped newborns.

She tapped her temples, closing out of her VR enhancement and for a long moment she sat in her office, staring out the window at the brightening sky. She had been awake more than twenty-four straight hours now, chasing down the answer to this puzzle. Now that she had the answer, she was left with a choice.

Did Signe plan to kidnap New Avaritan children and steal them away? It wouldn't help Signe herself escape the killswitch protocol, but she could prevent whatever infants she took from being subjected to a life where an algorithm decided whether they lived or died. Signe would have to target a Medla House facility to steal the children from. Then, she likely meant to slip past the barrier that surrounded New Avarita and seek a new life outside the city-state's walls.

That was her plan. It had to be. And now that Reina knew it, she had two options. She could report her findings to the Board… or she could try to help Signe Poulson succeed.

She chewed her lip, considering. This plan was far from brilliant. If Signe was caught, the Board would vote to override the Lucre's Algorithm and trigger Ascent for anyone caught helping or supporting her. And that was a best-case scenario. More likely, they would be sentenced to a painful prem-death.

She studied the painting on the opposite wall again.

After a few more moments of deliberation, she pulled up her unicomm and made a video call. After a few seconds, a disheveled Louis Gideon appeared, hovering over her right wrist.

"Madam Arthur?" he said groggily. "It is five o'clock in the morning."

"Yes," Reina said curtly. "Louis, I wanted to talk to you about the security system at your central Medla House facility. It was another Berger installation, was it not?" She paused.

"It was," Louis said bitterly.

"I thought so." Reina paused again. "I think your security might be in need of an upgrade. What's say I meet you at your headquarters later this morning? See what Huldra can do to keep your interests safe."

21

LIV

The Algorithm collects and analyzes health markers from all citizens, but does not act upon these things. All decisions related to how, when, and whether to receive treatment for any and all ailments (and the cost of such treatments) rest with each individual and their healing entity. Such individual agency is paramount to each citizen's ability to earn Ascent.*

—**THE HANDBOOK OF LUCRE, *CHAPTER 9***

**A full list of exceptions, including childbearing, unauthorized enhancements, etc. in Appendix G*

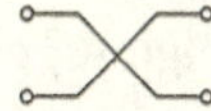

JUST OVER TWENTY-FOUR hours after the disastrous events in the Medial Complex, Liv awoke in a filthy gap in the walls of a desolate Lobos Transport station. The air was moist, hot, and stuffy, but it was better to be uncomfortable than to be dead, and those were Liv's only options at the moment.

Signe returned a few minutes after Liv awoke. She had a backpack stuffed full of food, washcloths, and other essentials. Liv blinked, clearing the sleep from her eyes. Signe also had a new mech-arm—bootleg, and with an armgun attached to the forearm. Liv didn't ask where it had come from. She could guess.

People died in Switch'r's Alley every day.

What would Liam think if he could see me now?

The thought of Liam sent her spiraling down like droplets of blood washed down a drain. He'd been gone nearly a month now. She'd worked hard not to sit still long enough in the past few weeks to let herself feel anything. But the loss hit her unexpectedly at times like this, when her thoughts drifted to her husband, or their home, or the life they'd shared.

The life that was gone forever, now. Replaced with a life of crouching in musty walls and stealing armguns from corpses. She knew she didn't want to go back to being as ignorant as she'd been back in that Upper Lucaran townhome. But sometimes, in her weaker moments, she thought that if someone gave her the chance, if someone handed her a button that would reverse time if she pressed it, sending everyone and everything back a month, she'd press it.

Honestly, she'd press that button even if she couldn't change anything. She'd press it just to spend another day with Liam. To spend one last day in the life they'd shared together.

"All right," Signe said, dragging her from her thoughts an instant before she broke down completely. From the looks of it, Liv wasn't the only one on the verge of a breakdown. The older woman looked almost as ill as Liv felt. "Tomorrow's the day." Signe patted her knapsack. "We've got enough supplies here to feed us for a few weeks."

She left the last part unsaid, but Liv heard it anyway: *If we survive that long*. If they died tomorrow, they wouldn't need the supplies in that knapsack.

Oddly, Liv felt nothing at the prospect of dying. Not that she *wanted* to die. But she was tired. Tired of fighting, tired of running, tired of losing everyone and everything she cared about, over and over again.

One way or another, all of that would end tomorrow.

"Have you got the code ready?" Signe asked.

Liv nodded, pulling it up on her unicomm. It was, as far as she knew, the last thing Emerson Quinn had ever written. He'd tapped out these strings of code on his terminal the night of the Board Room break-in. Before it had all gone wrong. When Liv had sat there, watching him write it out that night, she'd had the sense that she was witnessing the beginning of a new era—an era where their plan came together and a new generation of New Avaritans could rise up and, someday, fight back.

Now, it felt less like a beginning and more like an ending. A parting gift from Emerson. A way for him to help them close out this terrible adventure from the far side of the veil.

The code would give them access to a small, private transport tram in the Core. One of the "Executive Fleet," the only trams in all of New Avarita that weren't planted with tracking devices.

There were 60 transport trams like it. 10 were reserved for the Principal Chairman and his Board members at all times. Only 9 of those were ever actually used, of course. 3 were out of commission, according to the Lobos logs. Between 30 and 40 were generally in use for top-ranking executives in the Core. Over the past month, less than 4% of the time were all 57 operational trams in use at the same time.

If their plan went off without a hitch, they would be able to get baby Kiran out of that Medla facility and into the tram. Then, there was a chance they could make it to the barrier untracked and unseen. Theoretically speaking.

The plan felt thin, but it was all they had. By the end of tomorrow, either she would have fulfilled her promise to Ayla, or she wouldn't have. Either she would be out of New Avarita, or she would be dead. And if she was dead, either she'd discover there was a rich afterlife where she could reunite with Liam at last, or she would discover there was nothing but darkness. Either way, it would all be over. Finally.

"You all right there, Spencer?"

Liv blinked, looking back up at Signe. She'd been spaced out for the better part of a minute.

Signe reached out, patting her arm. She used her mech-arm, Liv noticed. Signe Remy was many things, but touchy-feely was definitely not one of them. "It'll be all right. We'll make it in and out just fine. Unless my good ol' dad reported my visit and they've figured out what we're up to. Or if Em's code doesn't work like we planned. Or—"

Liv gave her a look. "You're not the best at being comforting, did you know that?"

She gave a lopsided grin. "I have heard that before, yes."

Liv checked the time on her unicomm. Glowing red text read 02:30. "We've got four hours until we need to catch the tram into the Core," she said. "What do we do until then?"

Signe pulled her jacket off the jagged bit of stone she'd been using as a coat hook, then balled the garment up and lay down on the dusty floor. "Get some sleep. We've got a big day ahead of us."

LIV DIDN'T SLEEP a single second that night. Instead, she just laid in the near-darkness, staring up at the dripping ceiling of their little cave, waiting for the grayish light of dawn to creep in through the cracks in the walls. Dread and relief coursed through her in equal measures when her alarm finally sounded.

Was this the last time she'd hear that alarm?

They donned hooded coats and left their hidey-hole, making their way to the transport station in northwest Lower Baranthrum: the same transport station Liv had arrived in the first night she met Signe at that tea shop. Signe processed their train payments through a series of burner unicomm settings to disguise their trail if Gaius and the others were still looking for them. Another gift from Emerson, those burner unicomm links.

She hadn't even known him all that long outside of the rinth. Still, he'd been the only constant between her old life—the one where Liam and Ayla were alive and well—and the new, hellish life she'd been living ever since they died. He was a good friend and a good man, and he hadn't deserved to die the way he did. Thoughts of Emerson turned her mind to his beloved cat. She wondered dimly if Black Hat was still in the Penthouse. Would anyone remember to feed the creature now that his best friend was gone from this world?

"Spencer, where's your head at?" Signe said, snapping Liv out of her spiraling thoughts about dead friends and grieving cats.

Liv blinked herself back to the present, glancing around the transport as it bumped along the crappy old rails that led from Lower Baranthrum through the district of Old Altum. Everyone around them was immersed in their unicomms, reading the day's Vinco Telecom news alerts or catching up on holovid shows that had released the night before. Still, there was no way to know who was listening.

"Nothing. Nowhere. Here." She shook her head. "I'm fine."

"Yeah, you definitely sound fine," Signe said. But she didn't press the issue.

Realistically, Signe was probably just as lost in her thoughts as Liv was. She might play the tough guy pretty well, but the woman wasn't made of stone. She'd known Emerson a hell of a lot longer than Liv had. And Alura. And Torrin.

Liv had lost three loved ones over the course of a few weeks. Signe had lost as many in the span of a few hours. She had to be as close to the end of her rope as Liv was. She was just doing a better job of hiding it.

They didn't risk using their burner unicomm channels again at the next transport station. The trams that ran into the Core were always top-of-the-line. A bit of code might not flag at a transport station down in Lower Baranthrum, but there was no guarantee the same thing would work here. Usually, Emerson would do a manual override when someone was taking a Core train. Thankfully, it was only a mile and a half on foot to the yard where the private transport trams were kept.

"Are you sure the baby crap will be there?" Signe asked as they walked, keeping her voice low and speaking through Liv's ear enhancement, even though there was no one within earshot.

"Baby crap," Liv repeated. "You'll have to be a bit more specific."

"You know, the food." Signe gestured at her chest. "I don't think we have time to get the enhancements we'd need to make that food ourselves."

Liv snorted. It was true, there were enhancements available to help adoptive parents or biological fathers breastfeed their children, but it was also true that, even if they pulled off every part of today's plan without a hitch, they'd have *minutes* to spare when they made it outside the barrier, not the hours they'd need to get an enhancement like that installed.

But they wouldn't need the enhancements. The Medla facility they were heading toward had a huge supply of infant nutrient supplements on hand. It was illegal to access or transport those nutrient supplements without the proper approvals, of course. But, considering they were also planning on transporting a stolen infant today, Liv figured the supplements would be the least of their worries.

"Yes, I'm sure it will be there."

"How do you know?"

Liv chewed her lip. She knew because she never forgot anything. That rule wasn't exclusive to diagrams and security systems. Liv remembered every conversation she'd ever had. That included a conversation with Ayla a few months before Kiran Senior's death—before Ayla started to withdraw and change.

Ayla had looked harried. Her hair was a mess and her pale gray scrubs were covered in indeterminate stains. Her pregnant belly was barely visible, just the tiniest bump above her waistband. She rubbed at her lower back, scowling.

"I'd be doing better if it wasn't for all the damned stairs in that facility.

Did you know they keep the supplements two full floors below the surgical suite? And the elevators have been out since Tuesday. I swear to God, I'm going to strangle whoever organized this fucking facility if it's the last thing I do."

It had been a passing comment about an inconvenient part of her work environment, but it would be pivotal today. Unless the facility had moved the supplies between Ayla's complaint and today.

Just another thing that could go hopelessly wrong.

"Trust me," she finally said. "I know."

The streets of the Core were steeped in memories of Liv's past life. Places she had met Ayla for lunch on sunny Saturday afternoons. Corners where she and Liam had walked, hand-in-hand, from the transport station to the downtown clubs back in their university days.

She thought about the way Liam had always been able to calm her down when she was feeling anxious. The nights they'd spent enjoying synthetic wine with Ayla and the elder Kiran. The memories seemed like they belonged to a different person, now. A younger, more naïve person. A happier person, blissfully unaware of the fucked-up world she was living in. A blade stabbed into her stomach as she thought of little Kiran Jr, screaming as the Correxion officers took him away from Ayla's crumpled body.

Was stealing him away from a safe medical facility to bring him out into the unknown waste beyond the barrier really the right thing to do? Was she stealing him away from blissful ignorance and delivering him to a life of unnecessary hardship?

But between a soothing lie and a challenging truth, Liv knew the answer was obvious.

They reached the private transport station just after 08:00. Right on schedule.

Liv gestured to an empty bench across from the transport station. "Let's sit here so we don't look so suspicious."

"I think the hooded coats in eighty-degree weather will sail that ship for us," Signe said drily.

"Touché."

"Fuck, you sounded just like Emerson there."

Liv winced. "Sorry." It was true. Emerson was the only person Liv had ever heard use archaic words like that.

She and Signe sat side-by-side on the bench, watching the transport station for a few long minutes. There were no guards—no people at all, really. This wasn't a transport station like the giant mass-transit Lobos facilities. People important enough to use private transports wouldn't bother to travel to this station to hop into their own personal, self-driving tram. Instead, the cars were sent out when the rich and powerful of the Core called for them. Two zipped out on their tracks, heading toward the downtown portion of the Core in the few minutes they sat there watching.

There weren't any human guards there, but that didn't mean the coast was entirely clear. After a few minutes of watching and waiting, Liv caught sight of the silvery glint of a security mech's shell, flitting in between the parked trams on freshly greased wheels. It was too bright of a morning to see the light from the scanner whirring around the machine's base, but Liv knew it would be on.

"Security mechs," she said quietly.

Signe nodded. "And some cameras." She flicked her eyes upward and Liv saw them, perched like birds of prey, lenses angled down to search for any mice stupid enough to set foot inside the parameters of their viewfinders.

Liv's pulse quickened. She could guess their angles based on the cameras' make and positioning, but this security set-up wasn't a Berger Securities job. Or, at least, not one Liv's team had done while she worked there. Without the schematics to this transport station, she felt blind despite her eye enhancements and the bright morning sunlight.

"Relax, Spencer," Signe said, clearly noticing her anxiety.

"Relax?" Liv hissed back. "They're going to catch us on camera and then—"

"And then what? They'll know two people stole a private transport?" She let a huff of air out of her nostrils. "I'm pretty sure they'll figure that out when we steer the thing right up to the barrier and use it to sneak a stolen baby out of the city-state."

"You do realize that if we get switch'd once we're outside the barrier, Kiran's going to die, right?"

"We'll only get switch'd if we get identified." Signe pulled her hood more firmly around her face, then activated the holo-projectors sewn into the fabric. A new face flitted over Signe's features, altering them just enough to make her look like a different person without changing her features entirely. "Just don't let yourself get scanned."

Liv took a deep breath, then activated the holo-projectors in her own hood. For a few seconds, she was distracted by the fuzzy light now filtering her view of the world, but her eyes adjusted quickly. With their hoods up on a sunny, hot day, they would definitely look suspicious, especially since they were walking into an area that rarely saw foot traffic. But at least they wouldn't look entirely like themselves when they did it. Anyone who looked too closely would know they were using filters to hide their true faces. But it would buy them a few minutes.

They waited for the security mech to flit past again, then made their move. Two more trams had zipped out of the station in the time they'd spent waiting. Liv glanced at the time reading on her unicomm. 08:37. They'd waited long enough, gathered all the intel they could. It was time to get to work.

Liv pulled up Emerson's hack on her unicomm, getting her wrist close enough to the frontmost tram on the tracks to establish a prox-link. After a few seconds, the light above the handles winked green and she and Signe yanked the doors open, sliding into the bench seat inside the transport.

Unlike the mass transit trams Liv had ridden in all her life, the private transport car was quiet, dim, and temperature-controlled. An automated voice chimed out.

"LOCATION NOT FOUND," it said, sounding halfway between robotic and human in a way that made Liv's arm hairs stand at attention. *"LOCATION NOT FOUND. ALARM WILL SOUND IN TEN… NINE…"*

"You got this?" Signe asked.

"Working on it."

Despite the cool temperature inside the tram, sweat beaded on Liv's brow as her mind flashed through Emerson's instructions, step by step, beat by beat. Pain welled in her stomach as she realized she could almost hear his voice in her ears as she worked.

She scrolled through the tram's terminal options, bringing up the menu for "maintenance."

"SIX… FIVE…"

Liv then scrolled her own unicomm over to Emerson's code and furiously punched in an access override, then formed another prox-link, this time with the control function of the entire tram system.

"THREE… TWO… LOCATION FOUND."

Liv slumped back against the seat in relief and Signe clapped her once on the knee.

"Cutting it a little close there, Spencer," she breathed.

"I doubt it's the last time today, either, Remy," Liv said back. "So you might want to buckle up."

Signe let out a huff of laughter. "You know, it's a shame you didn't join the crew until right before we all got doomed, Spencer. I think you're starting to grow on me."

"Hey, I'm not throwing in the towel yet," Liv said. "We've still got a chance to make it through this day."

"We've got at least an equal chance of dying horrible, painful prem-deaths."

Liv shook her head as the tram rattled forward, following Emerson's instructions and leading them toward the Medla House facility in the center of the Core. "Always such a ray of sunshine."

"It's your job to bring the sunshine," Signe said. She lifted her new mech-arm, indicating the barrel of the arm-gun. "I'll bring the thunder."

"You sound like the hero in a shitty action holovid," Liv groaned.

"Let's hope I can act like the hero in a shitty action holovid," Signe said, looking out the window.

Liv's stomach dropped so low in her stomach she thought it might fall out onto the tram floor. They had arrived. She could see the Medla House logo glinting in the sunlight up ahead. A stream of people dressed in medical scrubs and office attire marched through the front doors, waiting patiently as the automated system scanned each one before granting them entry.

They obviously wouldn't be using the front doors of the facility to enter, but still, the sight of all those scanners flashing red in the shadows of the towering, glass structure made Liv's skin crawl. At least she knew where the scanners were inside. Unlike the transport station, she'd managed the last security upgrade in the Core's Medla House facilities back at Berger. Back in that dark bar on the docks of Lower Baranthrum, she had described the blueprints to Emerson in detail.

There hadn't been time to program those security blueprints into their eye enhancements the way Emerson had before the jobs on Huldra and the Medial Complex. They'd thought they'd had more time.

They should have had more time.

The private transport veered off the main track and onto the service line that ran behind the facility. When they reached the back door, Liv rolled out the lefthand door while Signe mirrored her to the right. The move looked a lot easier in the holovids, Liv thought bitterly as she rubbed a freshly-scuffed elbow, watching the transport trundle away down the line and out of sight.

"What are the chances that we never see that little car again?" Liv asked.

"Emerson coded it to come back," Signe said, staring after the transport. "It'll come back."

Liv just nodded in response. She was probably right. Besides, it didn't feel right to question Emerson's skills—not when he wasn't here to defend himself.

But whether the transport returned or not, they had a job to do now. And that job required getting through this back door without setting off every alarm in the facility. A job that, in the absence of Emerson's hacking abilities, fell to Liv.

Keeping her hood up and her holo-projectors on to at least partially conceal her facial features, Liv sidled up to the rear door of the facility. The door was just a tall slab of shining iron It was fitted with a scanner at about wrist-height and a camera that winked from just above the threshold, both of which Liv was careful to give a wide berth.

"Don't get scanned," Signe breathed as Liv inched closer and closer to the door.

"No kidding," Liv replied. Not a helpful reply, but in fairness, Signe's warning hadn't exactly been helpful either. Clearly she realized it, because she didn't fire back.

Liv pulled up her unicomm menu, scrolling around until she found the data stripping code Emerson had written for Signe's visit with her father. She inched close enough to the door to link with the terminal that controlled the scanner, then turned to Signe.

"Ready?"

Signe flicked the fingers of her new mech-arm. A tingle ran down Liv's spine as she heard the armgun prime. It was a sound she hadn't heard since the Penthouse. Since the armguns of Torrin Calix and the rest of his crew had been aimed for her head, primed with lethals, ready to shoot.

"Ready," Signe said.

Liv closed her eyes, then executed the code.

The code they had couldn't actually break through the door locking mechanism—that was too advanced for this simple, duct-tape solution. But that wasn't the goal. After all, Liv Spencer knew Berger's protocols inside and out. She knew where the cameras and scanners were, sure, but she also knew the system's weaknesses. The glitches. The stripped screws in the system's build.

One such weakness was what happened for 2.7 seconds after a minor security breach.

When Berger's system detected a minor security breach, it didn't send the system into lockdown or set off the alarms and send in the cavalry. Berger's security systems were designed to counter the majority of minor breaches—such as an unauthorized data request. However, for 2.7 seconds after each minor breach, the local terminal—the source of the breach—would go offline. In less than a second, the terminal would be scrubbed and returned to full functionality. But for those 2.7 seconds, the affected terminal—in this case, the rear door scanner of Medla House—was vulnerable.

As the red light on the scanner flickered, Signe pulled back on her mech-arm's pointer finger. The crack of a lethal round shot through the otherwise silent alleyway, blasting through the door's locking mechanism.

With the locks shot out and the scanner rebooting, Liv grabbed the door handle and yanked the back door open.

The back hall was quiet as they spilled through the doorway. But Liv had known it would be. Or at least, she had hoped it would. According to the data they'd stolen from Signe's father, no deliveries were scheduled at this Medla facility until half-past ten. Hopefully, no one would discover the blasted door lock until then.

Liv grabbed the back of Signe's hood, dragging her backward as the door hissed shut behind them. The other woman crashed into her, slamming her slight frame back into the polished surface of the door. Without saying a word, Liv raised one arm, pointing out the cameras to Signe. There were four surrounding the door: three pointed down each corridor leading away from the back entrance, and one positioned just above their heads, swiveled back and forth, covering everything past the doorway.

The cameras were XR-477 models. *The XR-477 had a 40-degree North/South radius.* If they stayed exactly where they were, it wouldn't be able to see them.

Of course, if they stayed exactly where they were, an actual human—or worse, a security mech—would stumble by and see them eventually.

Liv pulled up the holographic blueprint of the facility she and Emerson had made together, letting it spin gently over her right wrist. She tapped on a door that was highlighted in vivid green on the three-dimensional map, the first stop on their break-in. After that stop, they could stop worrying so much about cameras and focus their fears solely on the zillions of scanners filling these halls.

"Destination one is going to be down that hall," Liv whispered, pointing down the hallway to the left of the doorway.

"Can we get there in two seconds?" Signe breathed back.

"Two point-seven seconds," Liv corrected. "And no, I doubt it." She licked her lips anxiously, looking around. "But as long as we get away from the door in those two point-seven seconds, no one will know where we came from." She indicated the bright green doorway on the map again. "And once we get here, these faces should vanish from the cameras forever," she indicated her disguised, hooded face. "Hopefully we'll be long gone before someone even flags it on the footage."

This whole plan felt haphazard, like a school project thrown together with too much glue and not enough planning the night before it was due.

Signe had to know it, too, but kindly, she didn't say so. Instead, she just nodded and said. "All right. What the fuck are we waiting for?"

Liv swallowed, then reached up, stretching her arm toward the camera until she was able to make a link. She triggered the code again, and the instant the cameras started to reboot, she hissed *go.*

She and Signe took off down the lefthand hallway, walking as fast as they could without breaking into a run. The further they got from the abandoned back door, the more signs of life and movement Liv heard. Footsteps and muffled voices and the clicking of assistance mechs. But they still didn't see another soul as they slipped toward that doorway.

There were no patient-facing facilities in these back halls, only rooms dedicated to storage, deliveries, and laundry. The latter of those three functions was what they were looking for.

The laundry facility's door had no scanner. It had no handle, either, just a ridge on the floor that triggered the door to open automatically. Liv and Signe slipped inside and as the door hissed shut behind them, they found themselves surrounded by whirring machinery and buzzing mechs. Signe's fingers twitched, priming her armgun, but Liv stuck out a hand, pushing her mech-arm down.

"Maintenance mechs, not security," she said.

Arm-like appendages moved clothes and sheets from the chutes extending from the ceiling into the washers and dryers. On the far side of the room, other mechs folded the clean, dry clothes and shrink-wrapped them in plastic before shipping them out on conveyor belts that would deliver them throughout the facility.

Liv reached into the bin of soiled clothes beneath the nearest chute and pulled out a sickly green synthetic fabric top and equally sickly green pants. She handed them to Signe. "Med tech uniform."

Signe wrinkled her nose, nodding toward the stacks of shrink-wrapped clothing on the opposite side of the bustling laundry facility. "What if I want a disease-free set?"

Liv shook her head. "These mechs inventory all the cleaned stuff as they go. We take something from that pile we sound an alarm."

"And we take something from this pile and all we get is hepatitis?" Signe said. "Perfect."

Still, she shrugged out of her hooded jacket and pulled the green-colored garments on over her tank and stretchy pants. Liv fished in the sea of possibly disease-riddled clothing until she found a vivid red set in something resembling her size. The surgeon's attire would make her stand out like a neon club sign in these hallways, but unfortunately it was the only outfit likely to get her into the suite where the orphaned infants were kept without raising any eyebrows.

Once the bright red uniform was pulled on over the shirt and slightly-too-baggy pants she'd borrowed from Signe a few weeks before, she turned and raised her arms.

"What do you think? Surgeon material?"

"Sure," Signe grunted. She reached out, peeling something off of the shoulder of Liv's top. Liv wrinkled her nose as she saw what it was: a bit of Skin-Tape. *Gross.* "Let's just hope no one looks down."

Liv glanced down as Signe wiggled her feet. Signe's combat boots stuck out from the bottoms of her pant legs. Liv's own feet were still tucked snugly in Alura's old sneakers. Neither of the pairs of shoes were brightly colored or overly noticeable but they were obviously not medical-facility-ready shoes. She looked back at her partner. "You know where you're headed?"

Signe nodded. Then, "See you on the other side?"

"The other side of the facility, or the other side of the veil?" Liv asked, half-joking.

"Guess we'll find out in a few minutes, won't we?"

And with that, the pair of them slipped out of the laundry facility, following the trail of maintenance mechs toward the main floors of the facility. Liv took a deep breath as the pair of them parted ways, Signe headed toward the med supplies closet and Liv making her way toward the surgical suite.

The clock on her unicomm read 08:57. This was it.

"This is for you, Ayla," she whispered. Then, she triggered the automatic doors and strode into the bustling main floor of the facility.

22

SIGNE

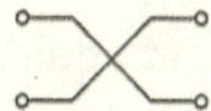

The borders of New Avarita are closed as a matter of safety and security. The barrier erected around New Avarita is the only thing protecting our citizens from hazardous conditions and impure societies. Any citizen who exits the barrier's protection will not be permitted to return for fear that they will contaminate our glorious society.

—**THE HANDBOOK OF LUCRE, *CHAPTER 31***

SIGNE HAD BEEN inside her fair share of medical facilities in her forty-some years. She'd gotten injured badly enough to need surgeries a few times and come on half a dozen occasions for enhancement installs. Then there was the time she'd almost died of a horrible infection and been trapped in a bed, hooked up to machines for the better part of a week.

No matter how many times she entered one of these facilities, the weird, ice-cold energy never failed to creep her out.

Probably because every person in the facility was either a medical worker or someone there for treatment. No visitors or guardians were permitted for safety and to prevent the spread of disease. Every patient, young or old, entered the facility alone, received their treatment alone, and was released alone. As a full-grown adult, Signe had just walked herself in and out. But the little kids were a lot eerier to see; led through the too-sterile hallways like bewildered, terrified puppies by assistant mechs.

For years, Signe had bought the story that it really was just a safety measure. But now, she knew better. It was just about control. Every tiny detail inside the facility was carefully curated and tracked, from the scanners at every entrance to the color-coded staff uniforms to the strict payment plans the patients had to agree to in order to get treatment. It had taken Signe the better part of five years to pay off the fees from that infection, even with her private security salary. Some people never found their way out from under the thumb of the agreements they signed inside these walls.

Signe slipped through the hallways of the facility, checking her map on her unicomm surreptitiously every few turns.

Why the fuck had she agreed to this harebrained mission, again? Liv had been convincing at the time, but now that she was in the thick of it, she couldn't imagine why she hadn't told the woman to forget this kid and just made a beeline for the barrier instead.

She nodded, tight-lipped, at a medical assistant dressed head-to-toe in yellow, continuing to walk at a quick, confident pace. The medical assistant gave her a second look but kept walking. Signe snagged a spare holo-board from a nearby terminal and pulled up a random screen, holding it out in front of her as she walked. Maybe if she looked busy enough, everyone else would just mind their damn business.

Mechs wheeled past, carrying shrink-wrapped bedding, blood samples, and medicines. Signe kept close to the walls, trying to look like she knew where she was going and being careful to keep her mech-arm tucked inside her filthy, hideous green sleeve. It wasn't illegal for a medical tech to have a mech-arm, to be fair, but it would be next to impossible for someone on a med-tech salary to afford one, so if anyone caught sight of it, that would raise some questions she didn't feel like inventing answers to.

And, of course, if anyone saw the armgun attachment, she wouldn't be able to invent an answer that would satisfy anyone with even half a brain.

The door to the storage closet Liv told her to find wasn't equipped with a scanner. Signe twisted the handle, ducking inside and closing the door behind her. Thank all the gods anyone had ever believed in: Liv was right. This room was stocked, floor-to-ceiling, with newborn-related shit. Signe took a quick circle, examining the diapers and sanitary wipes and blankets. She then slid an arm under her disgusting, borrowed uniform, pulling out a two-shoulder knapsack.

She set to work quickly, throwing diapers and nutrient supplement packs and more into the pack haphazardly, not taking the time to organize anything. She zipped the bag back up, tucking it under her uniform again, wearing it on her front beneath her sickly green top. She looked down, inspecting it. It was a bit lumpy, but if no one looked too closely, they might just assume she was pregnant.

"What are you doing in here?"

Signe spun around on her heel, coming face-to-face with a man dressed head-to-toe in black. A facility administrator.

"I was looking for…" Signe started. She glanced around wildly, then rested her hand on the top of a cleaner mech, propped up and forgotten in the corner. "This. We've got a really awful mess up on six," she said, naming the floor she remembered housed viral patients. She wrinkled her nose. "Vomit everywhere."

"Vomit…" the man repeated. He shook his head. "Damn, am I glad I'll never be stationed up on six."

Signe forced a smile. Her heart rate started to calm. "Yeah, consider yourself lucky." She tapped the button to activate the floor-cleaning mech and started to back her way out of the storage area, being careful to keep her left arm hidden inside her sleeve and angling herself away from the administrator altogether. "I'll bring it back as soon as I'm done."

"All right, thanks," the man said distractedly. Signe was three paces outside of the storage area when she heard him say, "Wait a second."

Her heart dropped.

"Gotta keep a record of all equipment check-outs," the man said.

When Signe turned, her stomach morphed into a churning pit of nausea and fear. He was holding a hand-held scanner out. A small, rudimentary model. Not one connected to any external databases, but one that would compare any chip scanned to the Medla House intake records.

Its red light flashed over her face before she could react.

BZZZZ.

The error message sounded on his reader first. The man frowned. Then, the alarms sounded in the rest of the facility.

"*UNAUTHORIZED PRESENCE DETECTED,*" said a cool robotic voice, echoing throughout the facility halls from every speaker in the damned building. "*LOCKDOWN INITIATED. PLEASE REMAIN CALM AND PREPARE FOR A CHIP SCAN. AT MEDLA HOUSE, YOUR HEALTH AND SAFETY IS OUR NUMBER ONE PRIORITY.*"

Fuck.

"Who are—" the administrator started.

The stealth mission had been nice while it lasted. Signe pulled back the left sleeve of her shirt, revealing her mech-arm. She flicked the metal fingers of her left hand, priming a nonlethal round. The barrel of her armgun protruded from her forearm, pointing toward the man's head.

"INTRUDER!" he shrieked. "ARMED INTRUDER!"

"I think the robot lady covered that," Signe said drily, nodding toward the speakers overhead, still blasting the warning about an unauthorized presence. Then, she flicked her fingers, launching the nonlethal round at the man. The armgun's firing mechanism was more sluggish than Sally's hair-sensitive trigger had been, but still, it did the job. The administrator dropped like a stone.

The halls filled with the sound of security mechs and Signe saw three separate cameras swivel to lock their electronic eyes on her as she moved through the halls. She launched a few rounds at the mechs, hitting one square in the scanner and popping the wheels off a second. That gave her a big enough gap to sprint through without getting zapped by the containment rods extending from their metal bodies. She shoved a few surprised med-techs and a yelling medical assistant aside as she ran down the hallway, back the way she'd come, looking for… she wasn't sure what. An escape route? Somewhere to hide?

She knew there wasn't going to be either of those things, though. Not for her, at least. She wasn't going to be getting out of here alive at this point. But that didn't mean the mission was a complete failure. She pulled up her unicomm.

"Liv," she said. "I've been made."

"I had a hunch," Liv said back.

Her voice was less than a whisper, clearly she was relying on her unicomm's sensors to transmit the words without making sound. Dread curled in Signe's stomach. She wheeled around, shooting two nonlethal rounds down the hall behind her. The medical staff were all ducking into side rooms, trying to stay away from her, but a pair of Correxion officers had joined the mob of security mechs on her tail now.

"Did you make it into the suite?" she asked, turning a corner at random. A few people screamed. "Oh, calm the fuck down," she yelled at them. "I didn't even do anything to you."

"I did," Liv said in the same quiet tone.

Another sound came over the channel, whistling breaths that didn't match Liv's breathing patterns.

"Did you get him?"

"I did," Liv breathed back. "I have him here with me. But I don't think I'm going to be able to get out with him." There was a pause, then, "I'm hiding in a storage cabinet. They're scanning everyone in the facility."

Shit.

"Is there any back way—" Signe started.

"Out of this cabinet?" Liv interrupted quietly, incredulous. "No, Signe. I'm afraid this isn't a magician's trick cabinet. It's just a regular old cabinet." There was more rustling, then a soft shushing noise. "This kid's going to wake up and start screaming, eventually," Liv said. "Even if he doesn't, they'll discover he's missing before long."

Signe turned another corner, almost ramming right into a security mech. She blasted its containment rod, watching it explode in a shower of steel and sparks, then spun around, sprinting the other way.

The counter on her stolen mech-arm listed fourteen rounds left in her armgun: nine lethal, five nonlethal. She couldn't keep up this cat-and-mouse game much longer. She leapt up onto a countertop, ignoring the screams of the staff positioned there, then swung up onto the railing above it, using the strength of her mech-arm to propel her over the railing and onto the next floor of the facility.

"I'm sorry, Liv," she said.

Her words were met with nothing but static and her stomach curdled again.

"Liv?"

Was she already gone? Had she been scanned? Or discovered and shot by a Correxion officer? What would happen to that kid now? This half-baked plan had been doomed from the start.

Then, a voice crackled through her unicomm. A voice that made her want to rip out her ear implants altogether.

"Signe Poulson."

She knew that voice almost as well as she knew her own. Reina Arthur.

They were well and truly fucked, now.

"Hey there, boss," Signe said. She fired a lethal round behind her, intentionally aiming high. The light fixture overhead shattered, showering the officers on her tail with bits of white-hot glass. "What is it? Wanted to say 'goodbye' before flipping my killswitch?" She grunted, pulling a countertop over to make a makeshift barricade in the hall behind her and ducking down behind it just as the Correxion officers unleashed a round of lethals at her. "That's sweet of you."

"I'm not going to switch you," Reina's voice said.

"Just like you wouldn't switch Marxus?" Signe shot back. The officers stopped firing and she launched herself forward, sprinting down the hall and ducking behind a corner as another round of shots rang out. "I assume you already got to Liv?"

"Liv Spencer, you mean? No. I have no intention of switching anyone today."

"Who is this?" Liv's voice crackled back through the channel.

She was still alive, then. For now. "Don't worry about it, Liv."

Then, something in Reina's phrasing hit her. *Switch.* That wasn't a term a law-abiding New Avaritan would use to describe Ascent. It definitely was not a term she'd ever heard Reina Arthur use before.

What the fuck was her game?

"My name is Reina Arthur."

A sharp intake of breath came through the channel from Liv's connection.

"You can kill us," Liv said. "But don't hurt Kiran, please."

"I'm not planning on killing any of you," Reina said, her voice tight. "I'm planning on helping you."

"Sure, you are," Signe said. "Helping us right into a cell."

Signe poked her head around the corner, firing a nonlethal directly into the neck of an approaching officer. He dropped, leaving her to face six officers with four nonlethal rounds left in her gun.

"With respect, Signe, I don't think you need my help to find the inside of a cell right now," Reina said.

It was a valid point.

There was a pause, then Reina continued. "I have administrative access to all the security systems for this facility."

"Bullshit," Signe said. "How stupid do you think I am? This isn't a Huldra building."

"No, but your little stunt in the Medial Complex scared Gideon enough that he handed the reins of his facilities over to me so I could make some improvements." She paused. "I should be thanking you—you've done more to discredit that onerous Cora Calvin in the span of a week than I've managed to accomplish in two decades."

"You're welcome, boss," Signe said drily. "Just doing my part."

She glanced up, noticing the ceilings here were low enough to reach if she jumped from the railing. Shooting a lethal into the ceiling above the officers for cover, she leapt from the floor to the railing, then used the railing as a springboard to crash through the ceiling tiles and into the space between the floors.

"Still doesn't explain why you'd want to help us," Signe grunted, grabbing hold of the support bar running between the now-demolished ceiling tiles and pulling herself up.

"My motivations are none of your concern."

"I have to disagree with you on that, boss."

Signe flattened, hugging her knapsack full of supplies to her belly. She winced as she heard shots fire below her. They peppered the ceiling tiles to her right, but none of them hit home. A sound of fussing and urgent shushing from Liv's connection told her their time trying to escape without the complication of a screaming infant was limited. Still. Reina Arthur's offer of help had to be a trick of some kind. What sort of trap was she trying to lead them into?

Then, Reina Arthur said the last thing Signe would have ever expected.

"Did you know I never wanted to be on the Board? I never even wanted to be an engineer." She sighed. "I wanted to be a painter."

"What?"

"But do you know where I would be if I had studied art? Tried to make my way in this world as a painter?" Reina continued, undeterred. "Dead. Oh, I'm sure they would say I had painted my magnum opus and fulfilled my life's mission, been selected for Ascent, moved on to the next plane as a reward, what a glorious thing." She sighed. "But in truth, I would have ceased to be a profitable enough investment for Lucre's Algorithm to approve. Or, perhaps I would have painted something that offended one of the members of the Board and I'd have the honor of being murdered by committee."

Signe crawled forward, forearm-over-forearm, barely avoiding the next batch of bullets as they punctured the ceiling tile she had just been flattened against.

"In short, Signe, my eyes are open, and my priorities have changed." Reina paused. "I am doing what needs to be done to save my own skin, in a way. You'll just have to trust me on that. Now, do you want my help or not?"

"Signe, I don't think we have a choice," Liv said, voice still so quiet she could barely hear it through her unicomm.

As usual, Liv Spencer was right. They were going to die or get caught if they didn't get help from somewhere. And they would die or get caught if Reina Arthur was leading them into a trap.

What was the risk?

"All right, fine, *Madam Arthur*," she said. "I don't trust you, but Liv's right, I don't really have a choice here. Can you get us out of this shitshow?"

"Sit tight," Reina said. There was nothing but silence for a few seconds over the channel, then a new alarm blared through the Medla House speakers.

"BREACH IN THE INFECTIOUS DISEASE LAB. BREACH IN THE INFECTIOUS DISEASE LAB. ALL STAFF AND PATIENTS RETRIEVE SECURE BREATHING APPARATUSES FROM THE BLINKING STATIONS ON THE WALL. BREACH IN THE INFECTIOUS DISEASE LAB…"

"All right, that should give you a few seconds," Reina said.

Signe's eye burned as the Huldra executive hacked into her eye enhancement the way Emerson had always done.

"Follow the path I've laid out here. That should get you to a—"

"Laundry chute," Liv finished.

It was a plan they'd considered early on in their strategy session with Emerson in the bar that night, but ultimately, they realized it wasn't possible to safely slide down a laundry chute with a three-week-old baby in hand.

Now, it looked like they didn't have any other option.

Signe swung down from her perch in the ceiling, following the blinking arrow filling her eyesight, projected through her eye enhancements by

Reina. She tore past half a dozen Correxion officers and a dozen more medical center staff, all preoccupied trying to affix facial coverings over their mouths and noses to filter out the toxic air that the false alarm Reina had set off was still squawking about.

At least, Signe hoped it was only a false alarm. If Reina had actually caused an infectious disease breach and Signe survived this chase to get hepatitis from these filthy clothes *and* catch some lab-grown disease, she was going to be *so* pissed off.

She let the blinking light of Reina's guide beacon fill her vision, drowning out the sounds of the security systems and clomping footsteps and buzzing security mech containment rods. The beacon led her down a broad hallway and through an atrium filled with buzzing alarms and flashing lights and nothing else. When she glanced toward the ceiling, Signe noticed that none of the scanners were blinking red, and all the cameras were dull, their lenses pointed uselessly at the floor beneath them instead of swiveling to take in the entire atrium.

"I don't understand why you're risking this," Signe muttered as she reached the far side of the Atrium. The door lock buzzed, then popped open as she approached, letting her pass. "If Louis gave you access to his security systems, won't he know you've helped us?"

Reina Arthur was silent for so long that Signe wasn't sure her message had gone through the channel at all. It wasn't until the laundry chute lock disabled and Signe had one foot inside that the Huldra exec answered.

"I believe in progress," she said.

"I'm sorry, did you say 'progress' or 'profits?'" Signe asked, She glanced behind her in time to see two tubheads round the corner. They shouted and she ducked into the chute. She heard their rounds hit the chute's cover just as she slid out of sight, falling two floors and landing in a pile of laundry.

"Both," Reina said. "The two are inextricably entwined. Something the other Board members seem to have forgotten."

Signe snorted. *Right.* It was awfully hard to profit off people if you kept killing them. It seemed like Reina Arthur might not have changed all that much after all. Strangely, that was comforting, in a way.

The laundry facility looked exactly the way it had when she and Liv had been here a few minutes (or was it hours? It fucking felt like hours) before. She could still hear the sounds of the alarms dimly through the ceiling, echoing through the walls, but the mechs here weren't part of the security protocol, obviously, so they continued their work as though nothing was wrong, flitting around, washing sheets and uniforms and shrink wrapping them, then zipping out to deliver them to empty workstations likely surrounded by armed guards.

For a second, Signe felt a flicker of guilt over the chaos they had wreaked on the patients of this facility. How many poor six-year-olds were cowering alone in their sickbeds right now, worried that they were going to face prem-death at the hands of the evil Medla House infiltrators?

No matter how much good Signe tried to do, she never seemed to be able to stop hurting people.

At that moment, the quietly bustling laundry facility was filled with a new sound—a sound Signe hadn't heard in a long time. The sound of an infant crying its tiny little heart out. Liv Spencer appeared a second later, arms wrapped around a screaming bundle, falling from another one of the half-dozen chutes extending from the ceiling of the laundry room.

"Liv, thank God," Signe said. She helped her clamber out of the bin one-handed, letting her keep the other arm wrapped around the squalling kid. "We need to get moving. A few officers saw me get in the chute on the third floor. They'll be coming here any second."

"Oh no," Liv said flatly. "Other than that, this job was going so smoothly."

Signe snorted.

"Rear door scanner is disabled," Reina's voice said, crackling through their unicomm channel. "And I've sealed the locks on all the stairwells and disabled the elevators." There was a pause, then, "No sign of life on any of the cameras on your level. You've got a clear shot out that back door."

"Odds the tram's there?" Liv asked, yelling over the sound of the screaming baby. Clearly, the kid didn't realize he was being rescued just yet. Hopefully he'd warm up to the idea of them sooner or later, because that high-pitched wailing was going to get old fast.

"One hundred percent," Signe said. She wasn't usually an optimist, but the private transport hack was Emerson's work. He'd always been a cocky son-of-a-bitch, but he was cocky for a reason. And that reason was that he knew his shit, he covered his bases, and he was almost always right.

Sure enough, when they exploded out the side door, stepping out into the morning sunlight, the private transport was sitting on its tracks, humming softly as it waited for them. Signe ripped one door open, ushering Liv and baby Kiran inside and slamming the door shut to muffle the sound of his piercing cries. She sprinted around the transport, pulling the opposite side door open. The sound of sirens filled the air. More Correxion officers arriving on the scene. No doubt some of Gideon's private security guards would be in those transports, too.

"You'll want to hurry, Signe," Reina said in her ear. "I don't have access to the security settings for the rest of New Avarita."

"Right," Signe said tightly. She slipped into the transport and let the door hiss shut behind her. As soon as they were tucked inside, the transport started bustling along its track, weaving through the streets toward Old Altum.

Signe ducked low as a Correxion Group transport whizzed by on the opposite track, heading toward the medical facility. The windows of private transports were blacked out, but still, she felt like the officers would be able to peer in and see right into her soul if she didn't avert her eyes as they passed.

"They're still combing the facility for you two," Reina said. "Still no bulletin about the infant. I'm guessing they haven't noticed they're missing one yet."

"Great, thanks for the help but, ah—" Liv said. She started tapping on her unicomm, trying to figure out how to sever the connection.

But Reina kept on talking.

"What is it you plan to do now, Signe?"

"Why would I tell you that? So you can hunt us down later and play hero for your friends on the Board?"

"I just helped you *evade* capture, if you recall," Reina said flatly. "You might want to consider, however difficult it is to believe, that I am actually on your side, here."

Staging an elaborate escape just to gain clout from tracking down the perpetrators and bringing them to justice seemed more like the kind of thing Cora Calvin would do, honestly. Still, Signe wouldn't put anything past Reina. Only the most cunning and ruthless of people managed to claw their way onto the Board.

"I assume you're heading for the barrier?" Reina said.

"The barrier?" Signe said, pretending to sound confused as she stripped off her sickly green med-tech uniform, then repositioned the knapsack on her back. "But isn't everything out there just dead, dry earth?"

"Don't patronize me, Signe, you know I can't stand that," Reina said.

"What happens when the rest of the Board finds out what you've done?" Liv asked, passing a still-screaming Kiran to Signe as she peeled off her own disguise.

"They won't," Reina said.

"How can you be certain?"

"I haven't survived this long by chance, Miss Spencer." Signe could hear the smug look on Reina's face in the executive's voice. "I think I can outsmart those idiots one more time."

The private transport whizzed west, weaving along the lines in the street, heading toward the edge of the Core. Kiran cried himself out, falling back into a fitful sleep in Liv's arms. The hacked unicomm channel was quiet for so long that Signe thought Reina had cut the connection. Then, she heard the executive's voice in her ear again.

"I have troubling news, Signe."

"More troubling than the idea of working with a woman cozied right up to the people we're trying our damnedest not to get switch'd by right now?"

"Yes." An image jumped into view in Signe's eye enhancements, footage from Reina's own eye enhancements. The view from the Arthur family penthouse. "I just received a unicomm alert from Louis. They know you have left the premises, and they know you've taken an unchipped child. They are setting up a blockade around the perimeter of the Core to trap you in."

"Shit," Liv breathed, clearly seeing the same thing Signe: a mass of Correxion Group transports whizzed past, clogging up every single transport lane.

"We'll have to go on foot," Signe said.

"Are you crazy?" Liv said.

At the same time, Reina said, "That would be unwise."

"I don't think we have another choice, Liv," Signe said, ignoring Reina's comment altogether. "They're going to stop every transport trying to leave the Core. That doesn't end well for us."

"We don't have our hoods and projector thingies anymore," Liv said miming over her face with one hand to indicate the facial disguises they'd left back in the Medla facility.

"Well, we'll have to make do without them somehow." She reached forward to override Emerson's coding on the transport, only to find out that an override was already in progress.

"You'll do no such thing," Reina's voice said. The transport flipped through route options, seemingly of its own accord, then settled on a winding path that ultimately led right along the border between Upper Lucara and Austrum, ending at the barrier on the northern edge of the city-state.

"What the fuck are you doing?" Signe said. She tugged on the door but the handles had been overridden, locked from afar by Reina Arthur, no doubt.

"I'm not bringing Kiran directly into a blockade," Liv said, hugging the infant closer to her chest.

"You won't hit the blockade," Reina said tightly. Signe's eye enhancements whirred again, bringing up a screen showing a series of maps and calculations. "Standard-issue Correxion Group vehicles only reach 95 miles per hour. Your private transport is currently moving at 110. Correxion Group's headquarters is on the southern edge of the Core. You'll make it past the Core's edge before they can set up their blockade there."

"But we don't have the scanner nodes disabled on the northern barrier," Liv said. She looked at Signe, eyes wide.

Unlike the miniature scanner that had caught Signe by surprise back at the facility, the scanner nodes on the barrier would definitely be connected to the central Core databases. If they got scanned at the barrier, it would set off a chain of events that would get every single member of Torrin's old crew switch'd within hours if not minutes.

"The tales of scanners being embedded into the barrier are… exaggerated."

"Exaggerated?" Signe pressed.

"False," Reina amended. When her statement was met by shocked silence, she said, "Do you have any idea how expensive it would be to equip the entire border of New Avarita with scanners?"

Signe stared out the window as the sights of the northern half of the Core flashed by, sparkling and glittering and clean in the mid-morning sunshine.

"So, is anything the Board says true, or is it all just bullshit?" Liv asked.

Signe could hear Reina's response before she gave it: *"It's for your own protection. It's for the good of the people of New Avarita. It's a necessary measure to keep our city-state safe."*

But Reina said none of those things. Instead, she said, "I'm coming to find that it may well all be bullshit."

Liv raised an eyebrow, giving Signe a look she had come to recognize from the woman: a look that said she was hatching a scheme. Signe could guess what that scheme was this time around. For their plan to succeed—for them to save more than just themselves and the baby Kiran—they needed a man on the inside. One with the ability to dupe the killswitch database and help them smuggle more people out of the city-state and into whatever society they managed to form outside the barrier.

Signe shook her head. Reina Arthur might have changed enough to help them today. But there was no way in hell she was going to risk her ass again and again to help them cut into her own profit margins. Liv didn't press the issue, but the way the woman held her lips—pursed together just a little too tightly—told Signe that this conversation wasn't over. Not forever, at least.

The private transport roared past the Core's district limits, speeding to the northern barrier within thirty minutes. Kiran was still out cold in Liv's arms, tucked up against the other woman's shoulder like a squishy, fragile rugby ball. They stepped out of the transport, looking up at the buzzing, bluish light of the barrier. It was fully intact here—no weak spot like they'd found on the western edge. There might not be any scanners here, but they still wouldn't be able to make it through without getting zapped with enough electricity to reanimate a corpse.

"Any chance you can disable the barrier, boss?" Signe asked.

"I cannot—but you can," Reina said. "One round straight to the central node of this piece here should take this section offline." She indicated the node through Signe's eye-enhancements.

"Here goes nothing," Signe said. She primed her armgun, aiming one of her dwindling nonlethal rounds directly into the central node. It flickered and sparked. The bluish light on the panel to either side of the node faded, revealing the world outside. All she could see from here was a hill of scrubby looking grass.

"Walk due north for a day. Maybe two," Reina said. "You'll find it."

"Find what?" Liv asked.

But Reina didn't respond.

Liv took a deep breath, looking back the way they'd come as the private transport zipped away on its track, heading back to the station they'd stolen it from. "Ready?" she asked.

Signe nodded, then gestured for Liv and Kiran to go first. The other woman cradled the infant's delicate little head, then ducked through the hole in the barrier. Signe hesitated, looking back at the tangle of streets, shining buildings, and sleek transports bustling back and forth.

"Take care of them, would you?" she said into the unicomm, thinking of all the people they were leaving behind. The people they may never get the chance to save. The people who were still stuck inside the fucked-up boundaries of New Avarita.

She didn't wait to hear Reina's response. Instead, she cut her unicomm connection altogether, then slipped past the barrier, following Liv into the unknown.

23

REINA

REINA ARTHUR WAS alone in her office when the summons came. Another emergency Board meeting. This made four in the past week—all due to security-related issues. Cora Calvin had to be sweating bullets by now.

As she should be, considering Reina had every intention of throwing her to the wolves.

Of course, there was always the chance that Louis would try to pin the Medla House disaster on her instead. The old Reina—the one that had lived inside her skull just a few days ago—would have been concerned about that. The Reina she was now had burst past a blockade of fear and niceties that had held her in a box for over fifty years.

The petty squabbles of the Board didn't scare her any longer. Either they would discover what she'd done and vote to oust her from the Board, or they wouldn't. There wasn't much use worrying about it in the interim.

Besides, she had covered her tracks well enough. The comm she'd used to hack Signe's channel was a prototype that she hadn't even shown her engineering team yet. She had destroyed the prototype immediately after breaking contact with Signe at the barrier.

She'd have to start over on that enhancement from scratch, but a unicomm upgrade could wait: it wasn't something the market was clamoring for, anyway.

It was just past noon when Reina arrived in the Board Room. She took in the faces surrounding the mahogany table. No one looked happy, which wasn't unusual. No one ever looked happy in this room. But, notably, no one even looked smug. Instead, the faces ranged from "grim" to "livid."

"Let's get this over with," Eliza Vinco said brusquely, entering the room behind Reina. "What's the problem this time?"

"I'm guessing it has something to do with the parade of Correxion Group sirens that have been blaring throughout the central Core all morning?" Reina said tightly, feigning ignorance.

"Indeed," Lobos said. "There has been another security breach."

"A breach? Where?" Reina asked.

If she was in a room full of smarter people, Reina might worry that she was overselling it. But she wasn't afraid of these fools anymore. They were blind as bats, each trying to steer New Avarita in their own direction. With that approach, they would succeed in steering the city-state precisely nowhere. There was a reason that living organisms didn't have multiple heads.

For New Avarita to move forward, the Board needed to be destroyed. And a new, true Principal Chairman needed to be installed. A role Reina felt uniquely suited to fill.

It wasn't something she could do overnight, but all great art required patience. Reina could bide her time.

"The central Medla House facility," Louis Gideon gritted out. He glared at Cora Calvin from across the table. "Another Berger Security installation."

"Seems you may have a rat in your organization, Cora," said Jasper Koegen.

She didn't. At least, not anymore.

Reina knew the truth, of course. Liv Spencer, Signe's accomplice, was another supposedly dead soul, walking the earth anew. She'd looked into the woman in the hours since the Medla House break-in. Former Berger Security logistics engineer. Seemingly passed by Ascent less than a week after the Board voted for an early termination of her husband, Liam Spencer. Cited in a Correxion report the day of her supposed Ascent for witnessing the extraction of a newborn from its legally unfit mother.

The same newborn that had gone missing this very morning, unless Reina was very much mistaken.

There was no question as to whose idea it was to undertake that harebrained scheme at the Medla House facility.

"—conduct interviews with all your staff members to suss out your traitor, Cora," Soren Otis was saying.

If even *Soren* was getting involved in this conversation, things were going more smoothly than Reina could have ever hoped. Usually, the man spoke so little that, for her first two years on the Board, Reina had been utterly convinced Soren Otis's mouth was glued shut.

"Master Amos could lend some officers to stand by. Perhaps Madam Arthur would consent to install advanced vital monitoring enhancements on key employees to sense signs of duress during questioning?" suggested Clement Rye—another traditionally quiet Board member. "For a fee, of course," Rye allowed, gesturing toward Reina. The air in the room felt thick, like honey. They were all getting nervous.

As well they should be.

"I would perhaps consent to do so free of charge," Reina said, drumming her fingers on the tabletop. "The measure would be for the security of the Board—myself included—after all." She paused, not because she was thinking, but to give her next statement more gravitas. "But I think that brings us to a rather larger question."

The only question the Board of New Avarita had ever cared about.

"Yes," Audrey said, picking up on Reina's meaning immediately.

"The question of profit loss. How much has this Berger Security debacle cost us all so far?" She looked around the table, then pulled up several screens of scrolling data on her unicomm. "Lobos Transport lost eighty-six thousand coin this morning alone when the trains stopped running through the Core during peak transit hours to make way for the barricade." She nodded toward Winston. "Master Amos offset some of those losses with the use of the officers' transports, but who's to say it won't be the transport lines these maniacs target next? Several of our stations recently had security installations done by Berger."

"The lockdowns at the central facility this morning have spooked our elective and plastic surgery client bases. We have already seen forty-nine canceled appointments for some of our most profitable procedures," Louis Gideon chimed in. He glared at Cora across the table. "What's more, several of our critical surgeries scheduled for this morning were delayed due to the incident. The delay will result in prem-death for some of those urgent patients, which means my company will have to compensate the families for the surgical fees or I'll have an uprising on my hands. I'll be out several million coin by the time this issue is settled."

Several other Board members chipped in with their estimated losses due to the break-ins at the tower and the Medla House facility. The conversation turned from true coin value to speculation as Eliza Vinco nettled over the losses she could experience if this mysterious terrorist group managed to take control of a holovid broadcast channel. From there, the conversion spiraled further as the other Board members realized the return on investment their ad runs would lose if Vinco Telecomm went down.

Normally, Reina would have tried to steer the conversation back in a more productive direction long before this point, but productivity wasn't the point of this meeting. The spiraling, the chaos, the fear... that was what she needed.

"Madam Arthur, how close are you to extracting any sort of identifiable data from the chip discovered at the break-in?" asked Cora.

Her voice was even more high-pitched than usual. She was right on the edge of cracking.

Reina took a moment to savor her fear. It was exquisite.

"I have a team working on it around the clock, Madam Calvin," Reina lied smoothly. "But this isn't about the terrorists. After all, without the opportunity to strike, these rats would be of no concern to us, would they?" She looked around the table at the rest of the Board. "We have a very serious security problem on our hands. A problem that stems from a single seat at this table."

Reina forced back a smile as every eye at the table drifted to Cora Calvin.

"Cora, you have allowed a terrorist group to fester right underneath your nose. You have allowed them to infiltrate your security company—the security company that we have trusted with our headquarters, the Medial Complex, even some of our homes." Reina looked around the table again. "I certainly think interrogations of all Berger Security officials are in order. We should surely take a vote on the early termination of several Berger officials, as well. But we cannot ignore the Berger Security official in this very room."

"You think I am involved in this… this bullshit?" Cora asked, losing her temper.

"I don't believe you are involved, Cora," said Reina. "But—"

"But your incompetence has led us here," finished Winston Amos. "Perhaps it would be best for the Board—for all of New Avarita—if Teras Systems found itself under new leadership."

Reina could feel her heart beating in her ears. *Victory*. After all these years of squabbling with Cora Calvin, letting that woman fill her with terror with a single flick of her over-penciled eyebrows, she would finally be rid of her. All it had taken was Signe Poulson returning from the dead and several acts of outright treason on Reina's part.

Amazing, the things a person could accomplish without fear. Or decorum.

The Board took a vote, and it was nearly unanimous, with only Cora Calvin and Jasper Koegen voting *nay*. Jasper Koegen was the next

Board member she needed to bring down, then. If she was patient and bided her time, she was certain he would give her an opportunity.

It would be weeks before Cora Calvin's switch was triggered. They needed to find a suitable replacement. Someone moldable. Someone malleable. Someone Reina could help boost into the role from a lower seat. Someone who would ultimately owe her their allegiance.

Signe Poulson and the rest of the dissenters who had infiltrated the Medial Complex could do as they pleased in the meantime. Reina had plenty of other things to keep her busy. It might take her a decade, perhaps longer. But before her children were gray, there would be new leadership in New Avarita. Leadership that didn't stunt her progress. Leadership that would not stifle creativity, invention, or profits out of something as base as fear. Perhaps it would take time to get there, but Reina didn't mind.

So long as her chip kept humming along in her skull, so long as she remained powerful enough to avoid being ousted from the Board, so long as she kept finding ways to escape her own Ascent, she had all the time in the world.

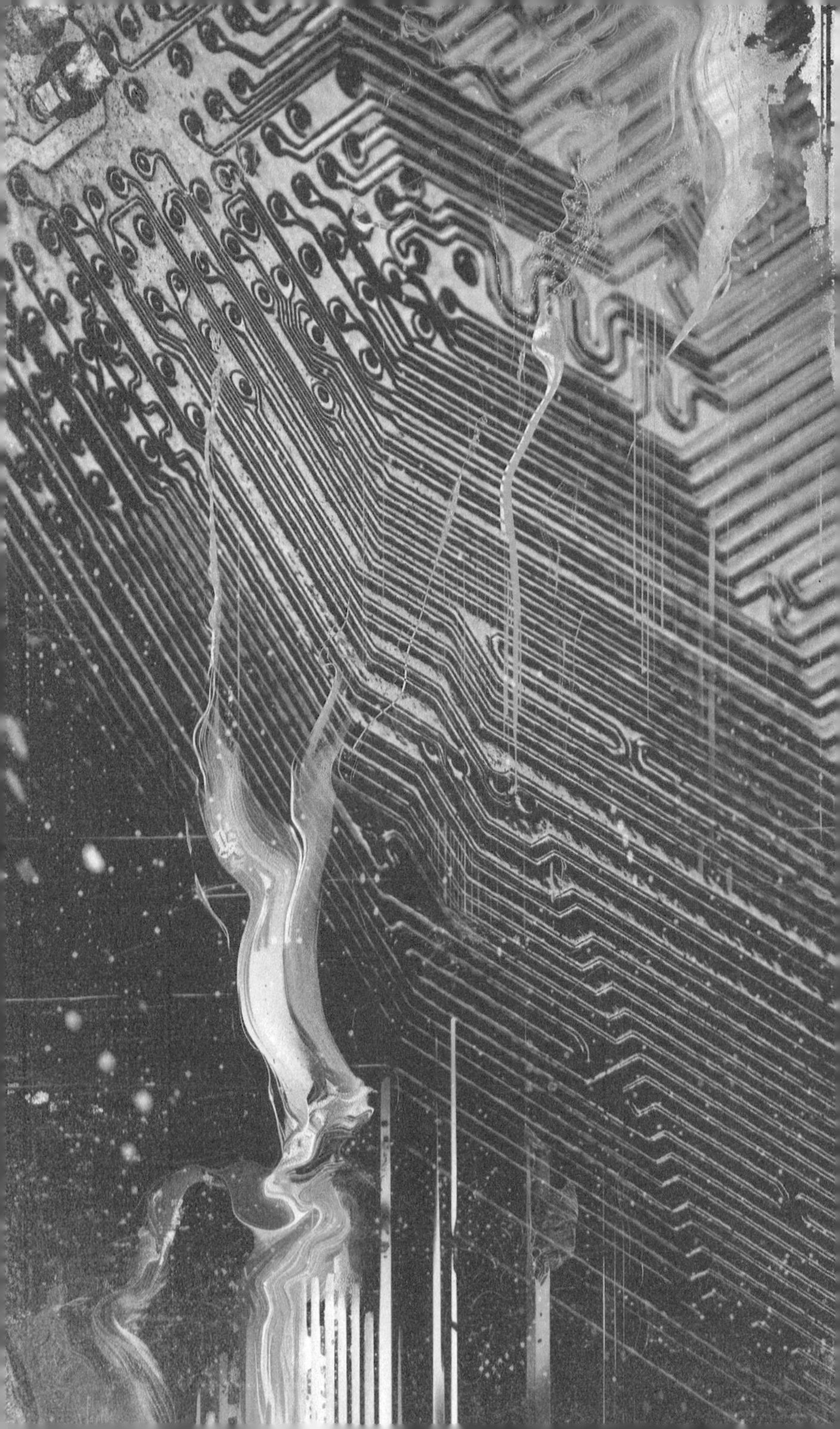

24
LIV

THE LAND OUTSIDE the barrier of New Avarita might not be radioactive, but it was just as barren and desolate as the graphics of *Wasteland Warriors* had promised it would be.

The air was drier, the heat more stifling, even the sun was brighter than it had been inside the city-state. Liv could feel it searing her skin to the point that she was almost sorry she had left her hooded jacket back in Medla's laundry facility.

At least she still had the red shirt from her stolen surgeon's uniform. She kept it draped over the infant in her arms, shielding him from the sun. *Infants could get sunburn in as little as fifteen to thirty minutes.* She remembered that—all the baby books she'd ever read on the rinth warned parents to keep their little ones away from the sun as much as possible. And so, Liv was going to try. Even if it meant shielding him with a dirty surgeon's uniform.

The baby was asleep, for now, tucked gently against her shoulder.

He was still so tiny; so fragile. In the panic of the escape from the Medla facility, Liv hadn't had much time to consider it. Now that things were quieter, she felt like she needed to handle him like he was made of glass.

"We did it," she whispered to him, leaning down to plant a kiss on the wispy curls poking out from the makeshift sunshield. "Your mom would be so happy."

Signe was half a pace ahead of her. She adjusted the pack on her shoulder with a grunt. "I think I lifted too much supplement."

Liv shrugged, adjusting the pack on her own shoulder—the pack holding the supplies meant to feed her and Signe until they could set up camp somewhere to start growing food of their own. "Better too much than too little, right?"

"Right, well, let's hope this one is hungry enough to lighten this pack up soon," Signe said, glancing back at the little bundle. "How much do kids this size eat, anyways?"

"Every two hours or so," Liv said, adjusting her grip on the sleeping bundle to pull Kiran's warm skin away from her sweat-soaked arm, just for a second. *20 milliliters of supplement every two to three hours, to be precise.* She'd always planned to breastfeed, but she'd done the research on supplements anyways. Just to be prepared.

"Right," Signe said. She looked at the bundle nervously. "Is it alright that he's sleeping this much? Or is he sick or something?"

Liv chuckled. "He's fine. Newborns sleep seventeen hours a day."

Signe lifted her hands in mock-surrender. "All right, all right. I don't know how any of this shit works—do I look like a doting mom?"

"No," Liv said. She cocked her head. "You look more like the overbearing, overprotective mom. But that's all right, I can be the one to dote on this little bundle."

Liv's stomach curled despite herself. Here she was, holding a baby she had every intention of raising. It was what she had wanted so acutely for so long. The thing she had stressed and sweated over as she and Liam submitted their childbearing permit request. Back then, never getting the chance to raise a child had been her greatest fear.

She'd gotten her one wish... but only after she'd lost everything else.

"Sounds fine to me," Signe said, distracted. She wiped sweat from her forehead, glaring up at the sun. "Is there no such thing as cloud cover out here? For fuck's sake."

Liv chewed her lip, pulling back the red shirt to look down at Kiran's sleeping face. "Do you think he needs a middle name?"

"A middle name?" Signe asked. "What is he, a rich prick from Austrum?"

Signe's words pulled another memory into Liv's skull. The memory of her first night in Torrin's Penthouse. The night of a conversation with Emerson Quinn, telling her all about his upbringing as a spoiled little rich kid in Austrum. Of course, 'Emerson' hadn't been his real name. And he hadn't truly been spoiled at all. He'd been taken advantage of and used by every person he'd ever met—including Liv, to an extent.

Her chest ached at the thought of everyone and everything she had lost, but of all of it, strangely, Emerson was the loss she felt most acutely at that moment. Their third team member. He should have been here. They would never have made it this far without him.

"What if we give him the middle name of Quinn?'" she asked. "After—"

"After Emerson," Signe finished. She was quiet for a second, then looked back, pulling back the shirt and brushing the newborn's cheek with one finger. Then she cleared her throat, pulling back. "If he's gonna be a tech whiz, let's hope he comes by it naturally, because he sure as shit isn't going to learn it from me."

The ground started to slope upwards, the sun cresting in the sky above as sweat pooled in the waistbands of their pants. Kiran woke up three times during the day, but even his shrillest screams seemed dimmer out here past the barrier. There was nothing for them to echo off—just gently sloping earth, frazzled-looking grasses, and the sun itself.

They went on like that for days. Trudging through the wasteland, stopping only to feed Kiran, feed themselves, or make a hasty camp for the night, sleeping a few hours at a time on the hard, dry earth, trying to get as far from New Avarita as possible, to find a likely spot to set up a permanent encampment, to make a new home for themselves, for Kiran, and, hopefully for anyone else they could rescue from New Avarita someday. Besides, she couldn't shake what Reina Arthur had said from her skull: *walk for a day, maybe two, then you'll find it.*

What was "it?"

Whatever it was, they didn't find it on the first day, or the second. Either their pace was slower than Reina had anticipated or the Huldra exec was as much of a liar as Signe had told her she was.

But when the sun sank low toward the horizon on the third day, Signe stopped suddenly. She broke the exhausted silence that had fallen a few hours before. "What the fuck?"

"What is it?" Liv asked, walking up beside her. It felt good to stop walking for a second. Her legs were burning and she had at least half a dozen blisters forming inside Alura's shoes.

When she drew even with Signe, she saw what the other woman was looking at. Her unicomm. Both of their unicomms had gone dark a few miles outside the barrier. Now, a faint light pulsed on Signe's forearm. A holo appeared above her wrist:

SEEKING... SEEKING... SEEKING... CONNECTED.

"Connected?" Liv asked, furrowing her sunburnt brow. "Connected to *what*?"

They had been walking for days. Liv had counted the steps. *231,539 steps total. Liv's stride was 2.1 feet. They had traveled 92.1 miles.*

Liv turned back, looking off to the horizon to the south. There was nothing there. Nothing but dirt and dust and scrub brush—they had lost sight of New Avarita on the first day. Her unicomm beeped and she looked down, seeing the same message appear over her own wrist. She peered closer at the holo. The connection symbol wasn't the one she was used to seeing, the mazelike graphic that indicated rinth connection strength. Instead, there was a small message in the corner that read, **NET STRENGTH: MINIMAL.**

"What the fuck is a net?" Signe asked, peering at her own identical message.

The pair of them looked at each other, then looked up the slope in front of them. Liv's exhaustion melted away, charged out of her veins by adrenaline as she hiked as fast as her sore, sunburned legs would carry her, being careful not to jostle Kiran too much as she went. She and Signe crested the hill in the last few moments of sunlight.

"No way," Signe said quietly.

Liv just stared on dumbly, unable to say anything at all.

There, in the distance, silhouetted by the light of the setting sun, was something the likes of which Liv had never seen. Was it a city? It was more spread out than any district in New Avarita had been. Buildings stretched broad and flat along the ground instead of reaching up, ever higher, into the sky. Pathways wound between the structures, and Liv could see unfamiliar-looking transports flitting this way and that, seemingly not attached to any sort of track like the transports in New Avarita were.

No bubble-like barrier of electronic shields surrounded the structures. In fact, several of the paths seemed to snake *away* from this knot of buildings, stretching into the distance, suggesting that this small, strange settlement wasn't the only one out here in this part of the wasteland.

Though it wasn't a wasteland: not truly. There was greenery down there, too—greenery *outside* of a grow dome. Rows and rows of tall, green stalks swayed in the wind to the northeast, nurtured by an apparatus flying overhead, raining water down onto the plants in neat arcs. Small white structures dotted the perimeter of the green fields, not unlike townhomes or apartments, but standing alone instead of crushed tightly together.

They stared in silence for a few seconds. Then, Signe broke down laughing. She laughed so hard that she had to set down the pack of Kiran's supplies and sit down on the hard earth at the top of the hill they'd just climbed.

"After all these years," Signe finally said when she was able to speak again. "I thought New Avarita was alone on this whole fucking continent. But no. There's another whole society less than a hundred miles past New Avarita's doorstep?"

"And they've done nothing to help us," Liv said quietly.

Signe sobered immediately. "Maybe they've got their own shit to deal with."

Liv adjusted her position, moving Kiran to her left shoulder and sitting down on the ground next to Signe. *Their own shit to deal with.* If that was true, could it mean that things here weren't any better than they had been back in New Avarita?

"What are we walking into, here?" she asked. She looked down at the baby, sleeping again, dead to the world against her shoulder. What kind of life were they leading Kiran into?

"I'm not sure." The other woman rested her elbows on her knees, peering out at the settlement.

Lights winked on, one by one as the sun fell lower and lower toward the horizon to their left. They weren't the vibrant neon lights of New Avarita. Instead, the light looked warm and buttery, filling the structures surrounding the swaying fields with a cozy glow. It reminded Liv wildly of the tea shop back in Lower Baranthrum—the place she had first met Signe. Like this settlement was a spot of calm in this chaotic world.

But there was no way they could know for sure if that was the truth or if the calm she felt was just an illusion.

The air took on a chill as the sun vanished altogether, leaving them perched alone on the hilltop, stranded between two worlds: the world they'd known, and the unfamiliar world on the horizon before them. Liv held Kiran close, snuggling the infant's head into the crook between her neck and her shoulder. She turned her head to give the top of his head a gentle kiss. As she did, she breathed in, and she swore she smelled the sweet scents of honeysuckle and lavender.

She pushed herself to her feet, then extended a hand down toward Signe.

Signe looked at her outstretched hand, then back up at her face. "You just want to charge in there blind?"

Liv cocked her head to one side. "I didn't take you for a coward."

There was a pause, then Signe grinned, grabbing Liv's hand and jumping to her feet. Her mech-arm creaked as she picked up their satchel of supplies again, slinging it back over her shoulder. Without another word, she, Signe, and Kiran Quinn Voland made their way down the hill, heading toward the winking lights of the unfamiliar settlement.

Might they be walking toward a fate worse than the one they had just left behind? Yes. But there was a chance they were walking toward something better.

Their futures awaited them.

For Liam's sake, and Emerson's, Alura's, Ayla's… for the sake of her mother and her father, and everyone else who had lived and died in the twisted world built by Lucre's Algorithm… if there was a better life out there, they had to find out.

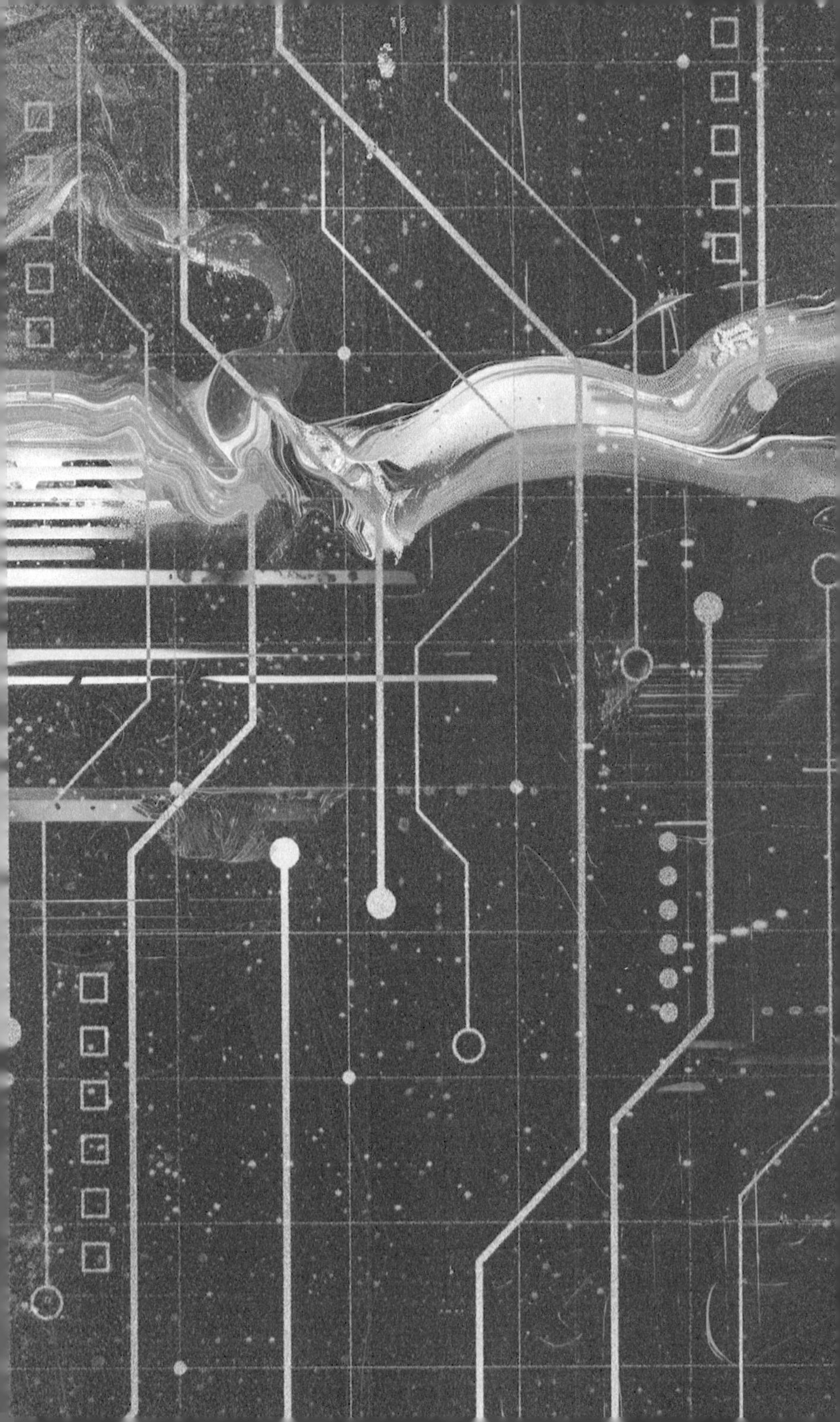

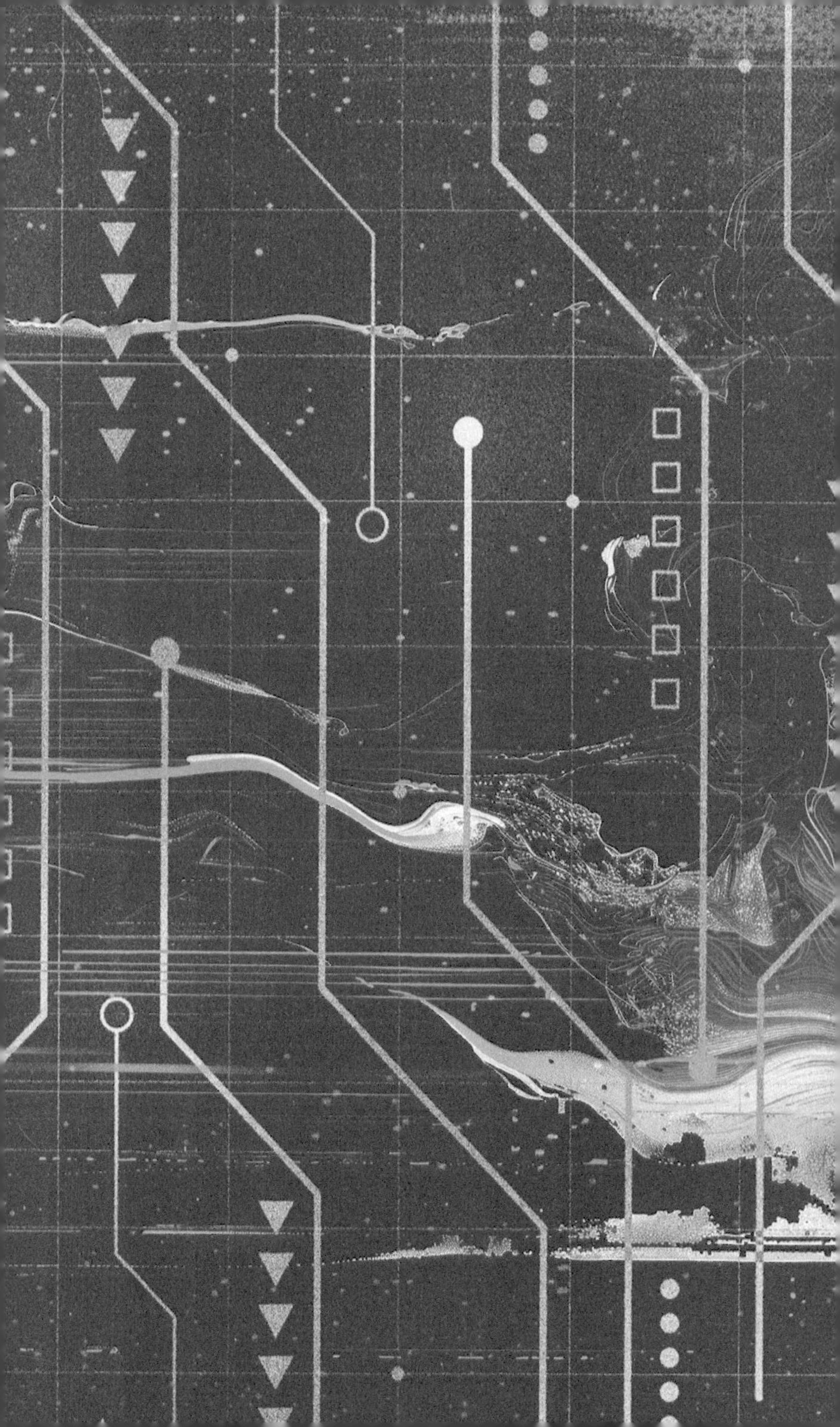

ACKNOWLEDGMENTS

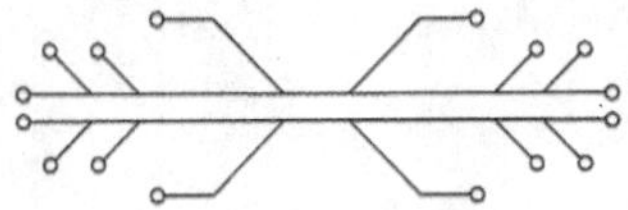

FIRST AND FOREMOST, I need to thank my bookish friends. Without the incredible support and inspiration I've gotten from the book community, I would never have had the knowledge and guts to release this book. Special shout-outs to Adrian, Greta, Frasier, Michael, Krystle, Andy, Ryan, Stephen, Dana, Nicholas, David, and so many others. I'm forever grateful for this community.

I also want to thank my incredibly talented cover artist, Katerina Belikova, and interior designer, Adrian M. Gibson (you get a bonus shout-out! lol), for creating a physical book that is more beautiful than I could have imagined.

To my editor, Kat Howard, for helping me make this manuscript as strong as possible. And to my audiobook team at Tantor Media, including my narrator, Laura Jennings, for giving my characters a literal voice.

To the lovely folks at Triada, specifically Brent Taylor and my wonderful agent, Laura Crockett. Thank you for taking this book-baby and working your magic to help bring it to life in formats I couldn't have achieved without you.

To my ever-supportive family, Haley, Mike, Mom, Dad, Kaylin, and Abby, for listening to me ramble about this project on and off for years during its drafting, editing, and publication process.

To my sweet kitties, Thorin Oakenshield and Evie, for... let's be honest, they're generally more of a hindrance than a help to my writing process, but I love them dearly, so they get a pass.

And finally, to every single person who has picked up this book: Thank you for taking a chance on a new author or a new story. I appreciate you more than you know!

—M. J. Kuhn, May 2026

ABOUT THE AUTHOR

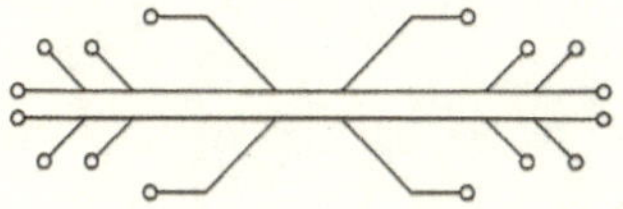

M. J. KUHN is a writer by night and a mild-mannered marketing employee by day. She is the internationally bestselling author of Among Thieves and Thick as Thieves, as well as a co-host of the SFF Addicts podcast and the FanFiAddict Book Club. She lives in the metro Detroit area with her very spoiled cats, Evie and Thorin Oakenshield.

STAY UP TO DATE

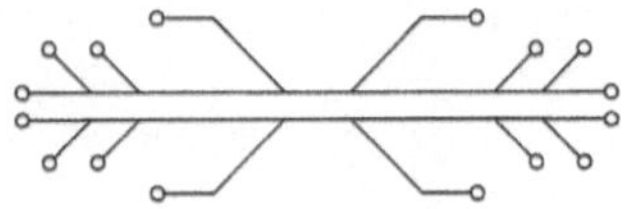

Scan the QR code below to visit M. J. Kuhn's website, sign up for her newsletter (including a free novelette), and stay up to date on upcoming projects, book releases, and much more.

FOLLOW M. J. KUHN ON:
TikTok: @mjkuhnbooks
Instagram: @mjkuhnbooks
Bluesky: @mjkuhnbooks
Website: www.mjkuhn.com

THANK YOU FOR READING

If you feel inclined to review *Killswitch Protocol,* then do not hesitate. Word-of-mouth is still king in this business, and your review is a way for authors to connect with new readers.

As a general principle, tell your friends, either in person or online, about the books you enjoy. Post reviews on social media and tag the author. Write a review and rate on Goodreads, Amazon, or whichever platform(s) you use.

And, if you'd like to read more books by M. J. Kuhn, check out the synopses for *Among Thieves, Thick as Thieves* and *The Ultimate SFF Story Bible* interactive journal in the following pages. Each book has a personalized QR code that you can scan to purchase it right away.

BUY IT HERE

AMONG THIEVES

— — —

A high-stakes heist novel set in a gritty world of magic and malice.

In just over a year's time, Ryia Cautella has already earned herself a reputation as the quickest, deadliest blade in the dockside city of Carrowwick—not to mention the sharpest tongue. But Ryia Cautella is not her real name.

For the past six years, a deadly secret has kept her in hiding, running from town to town, doing whatever it takes to stay one step ahead of the formidable Guildmaster—the sovereign ruler of the five kingdoms of Thamorr. No matter how far or fast she travels, his servants never fail to track her down...but even the most powerful men can be defeated.

Ryia's path now leads directly into the heart of the Guildmaster's stronghold, and against every instinct she has, it's not a path she can walk alone. Forced to team up with a crew of assorted miscreants, smugglers, and thieves, Ryia must plan her next moves very carefully. If she succeeds, her freedom is won once and for all. . . but unfortunately for Ryia, her new allies are nearly as selfish as she is, and they all have plans of their own.

BUY IT HERE

THICK AS THIEVES

— — —

Return to the gritty world of heists, magic, and deception in this high-stakes fantasy follow-up to *Among Thieves*.

Ryia Cautella, a.k.a. the Butcher of Carrowwick, and her motley crew have succeeded in the ultimate heist...with the most dire possible consequences. A terrifyingly powerful tool has fallen into the hands of Callum Clem, the criminal leader of the Saints, who was already one of the most dangerous men alive. With the newfound ability to force magic-wielding Adepts to his will, he is unstoppable.

With their group scattered throughout the five kingdoms of Thamorr—and not all on the same side of the fight—things seem hopeless. But can Ryia get the gang back together for one last job? Or will chess-worthy power plays and shifting loyalties change Thamorr as they know it?

LISTEN TO SFF ADDICTS

A WEEKLY PODCAST FEATURING INTERVIEWS AND WRITING MASTERCLASSES WITH YOUR FAVORITE SCI-FI AND FANTASY AUTHORS, HOSTED BY ADRIAN M. GIBSON, M. J. KUHN & GRETA KELLY. NEW EPISODES RELEASE EVERY TUESDAY IN AUDIO AND VIDEO.

JOIN THE FANFIADDICT BOOK CLUB

A WEEKLY BOOK CLUB PODCAST HOSTED BY M. J. KUHN AND FRASIER ARMITAGE THAT DELVES INTO THE BEST OF SFF. EACH EPISODE, THEY DISCUSS AND DISSECT A BOOK FROM THEIR TBR PILE, GEEKING OUT TOGETHER AND PROVIDING STORYTELLING INSIGHTS.

DON'T FORGET TO JOIN THE FANFIADDICT DISCORD!

SCAN TO LISTEN TO SFF ADDICTS

SCAN TO WATCH FFA BOOK CLUB

BOOK DESIGN

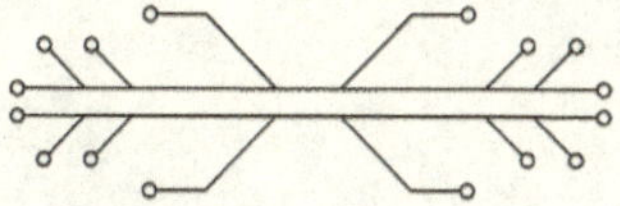

THIS BOOK—its cover and interior—was designed with love and passion by author and designer Adrian M. Gibson.

If you are in need of book design services, you can hire Adrian to bring your book to life at affordable prices. Scan the QR code below to see his portfolio and learn more.

SERVICES THAT ADRIAN OFFERS INCLUDE: Book interior layout, design, and typesetting (eBooks, paperbacks, and hardcovers), cover design and typography (cover artwork must be provided by client), chapter header and scene break graphics, adding artwork to interiors (original artwork must be provided by client).

IMPORTANT NOTE: Art that uses artificial intelligence will not be acccepted, and artificial intelligence was not used in *any* aspect of this book's design.

www.ingramcontent.com/pod-product-compliance
Lightning Source LLC
LaVergne TN
LVHW091140150826
845672LV00005B/992

9798993662008